COLLECTOR'S EDITION

COLLECTOR'S EDITION

A NEW HOPE

THE EMPIRE STRIKES BACK

RETURN OF THE JEDI

SCHOLASTIC INC.

New York   Toronto   London   Auckland   Sydney
Mexico City   New Delhi   Hong Kong   Buenos Aires

A New Hope, ISBN 0-439-68123-5, Copyright © 2004 by Lucasfilm Ltd. & ™.
The Empire Strikes Back, ISBN 0-439-68124-3, Copyright © 2004 by Lucasfilm Ltd. & ™.
Return of the Jedi, ISBN 0-439-68126-X, Copyright © 2004 by Lucasfilm Ltd. & ™.

12 11 10 9 8 7 6 5 4 3   7 8 9/0

Printed in the U.S.A.   23

ISBN 0-439-78402-6

First compilation printing, May 2005

Contents

EPISODE IV

A NEW HOPE

Ryder Windham
Based on the story and screenplay by George Lucas

A *long time ago, in a galaxy far, far away. . . .*

The Clone Wars were over, leaving entire civilizations in ruin. The Jedi Knights were all but extinct. And the Old Republic — the democratic galactic government that had prevailed for almost 25,000 years — had been replaced by the Galactic Empire.

Yet the Empire's supreme ruler, the evil Emperor Palpatine, remained hungry for even more power. To expand his rule and crush all remnants of the Old Republic, Palpatine had approved the construction of a secret weapon: the Death Star, an immense armored space station that could destroy an entire planet.

The Empire was not without opposition. The Alliance to Restore the Republic — commonly known as the Rebel Alliance — led the fight to overturn the Empire and bring justice and freedom back to the galaxy.

After Rebel spies learned of the Death Star project, they managed to intercept an Imperial transmission of the space station's technical data. The Rebels hoped the data would reveal a way to destroy the Death Star. The Empire was determined to recover the stolen plans . . . now in the possession of a young Senator from the planet Alderaan, Princess Leia Organa. . . .

Bursts of laserfire streaked after the consular starship *Tantive IV*, which was racing for the planet Tatooine. The ship was fleeing from the *Devastator*, an immense Imperial Star Destroyer that was firing nearly all its turbolasers at the elusive ship. Both vessels had just entered Tatooine's orbit when the *Devastator*'s lasers scored a direct hit on the *Tantive IV*'s primary sensor array. The array exploded, and the blast overloaded the starboard shield projector — which caused another explosion, damaging the power generator system and triggering a chain reaction throughout the ship. With no starboard shield and no power to its engines, the *Tantive IV* was effectively crippled.

Inside the battered *Tantive IV*, the crew raced to extinguish fires as more blasts rocked the ship. Struggling to remain on their feet, Rebel crewmen and troops ran through a narrow white-walled passageway, taking little notice of the two robots that stumbled along with them. The droids were C-3PO, a gold-plated humanoid protocol droid, and his counterpart R2-D2, an astromech with a domed head and cylindrical body who moved on three legs.

"Did you hear that?" C-3PO said to R2-D2 as the *Tantive IV*'s engines powered down. "They've shut down the main reactor. We'll be destroyed for sure. This is madness!"

More Rebel troops ran into the main corridor. The two droids stepped aside into a shallow alcove to avoid being trampled. The Rebels took up defensive positions and aimed their weapons at a sealed hatch at the end of the corridor.

C-3PO said, "We're doomed!"

R2-D2 replied with a series of beeps and whistles.

"There'll be no escape for the princess this time," C-3PO said just loud enough for R2-D2 to hear. Mere minutes before the Star Destroyer attacked, the *Tantive IV*'s commanding officer, Captain Antilles, had issued command/control instructions to the droids, ordering them to restrict and protect all references to Leia Organa's identity and presence onboard the *Tantive IV.*

The corridor was suddenly filled with the echoing sounds of metallic latches, clanking and moving around the ship's outer hull. Hearing the noise, C-3PO asked, "What's that?"

R2-D2 beeped nervously. The astromech suspected

that the Star Destroyer had used a tractor beam to draw the *Tantive IV* into the Destroyer's main hangar, and the clanking sounds were produced by a magnetic paralyzing pincer lock as it secured the captured ship. Indeed, that was exactly what had happened: The *Tantive IV* was now nestled in the Star Destroyer's underside hangar. Although the hangar remained exposed to space, the *Tantive IV* was trapped like a small fish in a sando aqua monster's belly.

Inside the *Tantive IV*'s corridor, the droids braced themselves against the alcove wall as the Rebel troops kept their eyes on the sealed hatch. Suddenly, sparks blazed at the hatch's frame as it was cut from the other side. Then the hatch exploded. Before the smoke cleared, a white-armored Imperial stormtrooper stepped through the shattered hatch and fired his blaster rifle at the Rebels. The stormtrooper was immediately cut down by a hail of return fire from the Rebels, but another stormtrooper appeared from behind him, firing as he stepped over his fallen predecessor. The second stormtrooper also fell to the Rebels, but there were more where he came from, and they kept on coming.

The stormtroopers were identical. Each wore a head-concealing white helmet that resembled a robotic face, with black polarized lenses for eyes and a grimacing vocoder for the mouth. Below the vocoder, jutting out from the helmet's chin, a grilled breathing filter was set between two artificial air-supply nozzles.

More stormtroopers poured into the main corridor. From their alcove, the droids watched helplessly as several Rebel soldiers were shot down. The Rebels fought back, and the corridor was filled with deadly, crisscrossing projectiles. When a laserbolt slammed into the wall near the droids, R2-D2 responded with a loud electronic shriek, then rolled forward on his treads. Not wanting to be left behind, C-3PO stepped after his companion. Laserbolts whizzed past their forms as the droids crossed the narrow corridor to a hatch that faced the alcove. Incredibly, neither droid was hit during their quick but harrowing exit.

Overwhelmed by the stormtroopers, the surviving Rebels retreated hastily to other parts of the *Tantive IV*. A squad of stormtroopers secured the corridor, then instinctively moved away from the hatch as a tall, caped figure entered. He was clad entirely in black, giving him the appearance of a menacing shadow amidst the white-armored stormtroopers in the white-walled passageway. His head was concealed by a helmet with a fierce-looking faceplate, distinguished by two recessed black oval visual sensors positioned above a triangular respirator. A life-support system control panel was affixed to his chest plate, and he carried with him the sound of his mechanical, labored breathing. Everything in his outward appearance suggested that the black-armored suit only barely contained the evil lurking within.

He was Darth Vader, the Sith Lord.

Darth Vader ignored the two dead stormtroopers near the exploded hatch and surveyed the fallen Rebels on the corridor floor. He felt neither pity nor remorse for the lives that had been extinguished.

These men brought this upon themselves. They sealed their fate the day they chose to oppose the Empire.

Stepping over the corpses, Darth Vader proceeded into the *Tantive IV*.

R2-D2 stood in a dimly illuminated subhallway that linked the *Tantive IV*'s port airlock to the escape pod access tunnel. He had lost sight of C-3PO almost immediately after they'd made their hasty exit from the main corridor, and assumed the golden droid had either gotten lost or found a good hiding place. The only reason R2-D2 had not yet attempted to find C-3PO was because he was busy making a holographic recording of Princess Leia Organa.

R2-D2 had run into the young woman as she hid in the subhallway. She had fair skin, dark brown hair, and wore a loose-fitting white gown and travel boots. She sounded distressed as she spoke, which was understandable, given the circumstances. The droid was still recording when she glanced at a hatch behind her, then turned back and bent to insert a data card into the slot beneath R2-D2's radar eye. The droid stopped recording.

From nearby, C-3PO cried, "Artoo, where are you?"

While Leia crept off to hide against the nearby wall, R2-D2 extended his retractable third leg to the floor and moved in the direction of C-3PO's voice.

"At last!" C-3PO said when he saw R2-D2. "Where have you been? They're heading in this direction. What are we going to do? We'll be sent to the spice mines of Kessel or smashed into who knows what!"

R2-D2 rolled away from C-3PO, heading for the escape pod access tunnel.

"Wait a minute," C-3PO said. "Where are you going?"

Princess Leia peeked out from her hiding place and watched the droids exit. She thought, *Unless that R2 unit delivers my message, all will be lost!*

As stormtroopers and captured Rebel troops marched by, Darth Vader stood in the consular ship's operations forum and wrapped his black-gloved fingers around the neck of the ship's commanding officer, Captain Antilles. Vader was about to proceed with his interrogation when an Imperial officer rushed up and announced, "The Death Star plans are not in the main computer."

Vader turned his visor to gaze at Captain Antilles. "Where are those transmissions you intercepted?" the Sith Lord asked as he lifted Antilles off the floor. "What have you done with those plans?"

Antilles gasped, "We intercepted no transmissions. Aaah . . . this is a consular ship. We're on a diplomatic mission."

Tightening his grip, Vader asked, "If this is a consular ship . . . where is the ambassador?"

When no answer came from Antilles, Vader decided the interrogation was over. There was a horrid snapping sound from Antilles' neck, then his body went limp. Vader tossed the dead soldier against the wall, then turned to a stormtrooper.

"Commander," Vader ordered, "tear this ship apart until you've found those plans and bring me the passengers. I want them alive!"

The stormtroopers marched off to search the ship.

Soon, a squad arrived at the adumbral port subhallway and moved quietly down its length. It didn't take long for a stormtrooper to spot Princess Leia's white gown against the dark-walled chamber.

"There's one!" the stormtrooper shouted as he raised his blaster rifle. "Set for stun!"

Leia stepped out from her hiding place, raised her laser pistol, and fired at the nearest stormtrooper. Her blaster was not set on stun, and the fired projectile punched through her target's armor, dropping him instantly. Leia turned to run but another stormtrooper fired a paralyzing ray at her back.

The princess was hit and went sprawling to the floor.

The stormtrooper squad stepped over to inspect Leia's inert body. "She'll be all right," said the squad's leader. "Inform Lord Vader we have a prisoner."

The sound of blasterfire from the subhallway reached C-3PO as he followed R2-D2 through the adjoining escape pod access tunnel. C-3PO had thought R2-D2 was heading for the next chamber, so he was surprised when he saw the astromech stop, turn, and open the hatch to an escape pod.

"Hey, you're not permitted in there," C-3PO said. "It's restricted. You'll be deactivated for sure."

R2-D2 moved into the pod and beeped back at the golden droid.

"Don't you call me a mindless philosopher, you overweight glob of grease!" C-3PO retorted. "Now come out before somebody sees you."

R2-D2 remained in the pod and whistled at C-3PO.

"Secret mission?" C-3PO asked, baffled. "What

plans? What are you talking about? I'm not getting in there!"

Yet another explosion rocked the ship, violently rattling C-3PO's metal joints. Without further hesitation, the golden droid stumbled through the open hatch and into the pod. He said, "I'm going to regret this."

The hatch snapped shut behind the droids. Then there was a muffled explosion as the pod's latches blew away and the pod ejected from the *Tantive IV.* The pod's rocket engines propelled it out of the Star Destroyer's open hangar and into space.

The ejected pod did not go unnoticed by the Imperials. On board the *Devastator,* the chief pilot saw the pod's image streak across his main viewscreen. The chief pilot said, "There goes another one."

But the *Devastator*'s captain had already checked his sensor scopes and ordered, "Hold your fire. There's no life-forms. It must have short-circuited."

The escape pod continued to plummet away from the Star Destroyer. Inside the pod, C-3PO peered through the small circular window that was the vessel's single viewport. Gazing back at the rapidly receding view of the *Tantive IV* within the Star Destroyer's main hangar, he commented, "That's funny, the damage doesn't look as bad from out here."

R2-D2 beeped an assuring response.

"Are you sure this thing is safe?" C-3PO said, unconvinced.

Soon, even the Star Destroyer was just a distant speck from the droids' perspective. And the escape pod kept falling, all the way to the harsh surface of the planet below.

After the stormtroopers revived Princess Leia, they placed binders on her wrists and escorted her through the *Tantive IV*. Leia could not help but notice that the white-walled corridors were now scorched and the air was heavy with the scent of blaster fumes.

Darth Vader and a black-uniformed Imperial officer stepped out through an open hatch and entered the corridor in front of the stormtroopers and Leia. The stormtroopers stopped walking, and Leia faced the Sith Lord.

"Darth Vader," Leia said. "Only you could be so bold. The Imperial Senate will not sit still for this. When they hear you've attacked a diplomatic —"

"Don't act so surprised, Your Highness," Vader interrupted. "You weren't on any mercy mission this time. Several transmissions were beamed to this ship by Rebel spies. I want to know what happened to the plans they sent you."

"I don't know what you're talking about," Leia said, feigning innocence. "I'm a member of the Imperial Senate on a diplomatic mission to Alderaan. . . ."

"You are a part of the Rebel Alliance . . . and a traitor," Vader snarled. "Take her away!"

As the stormtroopers led Leia out of the consular ship to the Star Destroyer, Vader and the black-uniformed officer turned to continue their inspection of the Rebel ship. The officer said, "Holding her is dangerous. If word of this gets out, it could generate sympathy for the Rebellion in the Senate."

"I have traced the Rebel spies to her," Vader said. "Now she is my only link to finding their secret base."

Walking faster to keep up with Vader's long strides, the officer added, "She'll die before she'll tell you anything."

"Leave that to me," Vader said. "Send a distress signal and then inform the Senate that all aboard were killed!"

As Vader arrived at a corridor intersection, Imperial Commander Praji stopped him and said, "Lord Vader, the battle station plans are not aboard this ship! And no transmissions were made. An escape pod was jettisoned during the fighting, but no life-forms were aboard."

Vader seethed. He said, "She must have hidden the plans in the escape pod. Send a detachment down to retrieve them. See to it personally, Commander. There'll be no one to stop us this time."

"Yes, sir," said Commander Praji.

Vader stepped to a viewport and gazed down at the sand planet. From space, it looked just as inhospitable as he knew it was on the surface.

To think I lived there once . . . that it was my home before the Jedi came and took me away. My mother breathed her last on this world, and for years I felt such . . . agonizing loss.

Now I feel nothing. This world means as much to me as a speck of dust, and all its inhabitants might as well be dust, too.

"How did we get into this mess?" C-3PO said. "I really don't know how." He and R2-D2 were trudging down a steep dune, and the sand was already getting into his gears. C-3PO sighed. "We seem to be made to suffer. It's our lot in life."

The droid glanced behind them. His footprints and R2-D2's treadmarks extended all the way back to the landed escape pod, which was still in sight where they'd left it. Had there been a less sandy spot to land on Tatooine, R2-D2 might have steered for it, but since Tatooine was a desert world, R2-D2 had only two choices: sandy desert or treacherous rock formations. R2-D2 wisely opted for sand, and beeped at C-3PO to remind him of this, but the golden droid wasn't listening.

"I've got to rest before I fall apart," C-3PO said, trying to remember the last time he'd had an oil bath. "My joints are almost frozen."

R2-D2 beeped, encouraging C-3PO to keep moving. C-3PO ignored him again and stopped to look around. There was a rock mesa to his right and sand everywhere else. "What a desolate place this is," he observed.

Tired of being ignored, R2-D2 whistled, made a sharp right turn, then started off in the direction of the rock mesa.

"Where do you think you're going?" C-3PO asked.

R2-D2 answered with a stream of electronic noise.

"Well, I'm not going that way," C-3PO said. "It's much too rocky. This way is much easier."

R2-D2 justified his change of direction with another round of beeps.

"What makes you think there are settlements over there?" C-3PO said.

R2-D2 beeped a very detailed explanation.

"Don't get technical with me," C-3PO chided with annoyance.

The astromech decided it was time to inform C-3PO about his mission, and uttered more beeps and whistles.

"What mission?" C-3PO said, dumbfounded. "What are you talking about? I've just about had enough of you! Go that way! You'll be malfunctioning within a day, you nearsighted scrap pile!" Thoroughly flustered, C-3PO gave a swift kick to R2-D2's right leg, then turned and headed off for the dunes. As he stormed off, he said in a scolding tone, "And don't let me catch you following me begging for help, because you won't get it."

R2-D2 rotated his domed head to see C-3PO walking away from him. He beeped again, trying to convince C-3PO to come with him.

"No more adventures," C-3PO shouted back as he continued walking. "I'm not going that way."

R2-D2 rotated his head to look away from C-3PO's departing figure, then rotated for another look at C-3PO's back. The astromech let out a forlorn, whimpering beep, then waited a moment longer. But when he realized C-3PO was determined to go his own way, R2-D2 turned his dome in the other direction and moved off, heading for the rock mesa.

"That malfunctioning little twerp," C-3PO muttered to himself several hours after parting ways with R2-D2. "This is all his fault! He tricked me into going this way, but he'll do no better."

Tatooine's skies had turned cloudy, but C-3PO could still feel the heat from the planet's two suns. He walked past the skeletal remains of a large, long-necked creature, and trembled at the thought that the deceased might have any living relatives nearby.

C-3PO noticed a metal O-ring was missing from his left knee joint, and realized it must have jarred loose. He knew there was no chance he'd ever find the disc-shaped piece of metal again. With each step, his sand-clogged gears made horrid grinding sounds. He was ready to give up.

Then he saw something on the horizon.

"Wait, what's that?" he said. It was an angular shape with a winking light. Despite the distance, the droid could tell he was looking at a large vehicle. "A transport! I'm saved!" In his loudest voice, he shouted, "Over here! Hey! Hey!" He continued shouting and waving his arms. "Help! Please, help!"

At first, he felt relief when he saw the transport turn and move in his direction. But after it arrived and C-3PO met the transport's drivers, he wished he'd gone with R2-D2 after all.

As Tatooine's two suns set, the temperature dropped. And from every shadowy hole and crevice that lined the canyon walls, nocturnal animals chirped and croaked and hissed in appreciation of the cool air that came with darkness.

R2-D2 had never been so spooked in his life.

He had already evaded sandpits, traversed circuit-jarring terrain, and boldly descended a high cliff to arrive at the canyon floor. However, these accomplishments had been merely challenges to overcome, and they did not bolster R2-D2's sense of courage. In his experience, dealing with nature was one thing, and dealing with organic creatures was something entirely different, especially when one was a stranger in their territory. Even though his primary photoreceptor was equipped with radar and allowed him to see in the dark, it didn't change the fact that nightfall was — for some large predators — the preferred time for scavenging.

Despite his wariness, R2-D2 kept moving. He was on a mission, and no one could ever call R2-D2 disloyal. And so he rolled forward on his treads, proceeding cautiously through the rock canyon.

A pair of lights flickered between two boulders, then winked off. R2-D2 paused. Using his sensors, the astromech detected a number of life-forms in this area. As he wondered if the lights on his own domed head might have attracted the life-forms, he heard some rocks fall. They were just small rocks, pebbles mostly, but R2-D2 knew that rocks usually didn't fall on their own.

Then he saw a small, dark form dart behind a boulder. R2-D2 couldn't help but emit a whimpering beep. He started moving forward again, hoping that the life-forms would stay where they were and allow him to pass.

Suddenly, a squat, hooded figure with glowing eyes jumped out from the shadows, shouted in an alien language, and fired an ionization blaster at R2-D2. The astromech shrieked as rippling charges of electricity traveled over and through his body. He didn't stop screaming until the charges crackled and died. Then his dome lights dimmed, and he pitched forward and crashed against the hard ground.

The shooter lowered his blaster. He called out to the surrounding shadows, and seven more hooded figures scurried out from their hiding places. All were short, most no taller than R2-D2 when standing. Like the shooter, they were completely shrouded in dark brown robes made of heavy cloth. Their only visible facial features were their glowing eyes: two bright yellow lights staring out from the darkness of their cloaked heads.

They chittered at one another with delight as they stepped up to examine the fallen droid. The shooter holstered his blaster, then directed his fellows to lift the R2 unit. They picked him up and carried him off to their waiting transport.

The transport was an enormous rust-covered vehicle with a high, sharply angled prow that appeared to cut into the night sky. The transport rested on four massive treads that elevated the hull from the ground. The hooded figures carried the deactivated R2 unit under the transport and set him on his feet, positioning him under an extensible repulsorlift tube. As the tube was lowered a short distance above the droid's head, one hooded figure quickly welded a restraining bolt to a panel on the front of the droid's cylindrical body. After the restraining bolt was secured, the repulsor switched on, and R2-D2 was sucked up into the transport. Having made their catch, the hooded figures entered the transport via a landing ramp.

R2-D2 reactivated to find himself in a scrap heap in a cramped, low-ceilinged chamber. Durasteel shavings had come to rest upon his head, but they fell away as he leaned away from a metal wall. Pushing various bits of scrap aside, he moved out of the heap, then rotated his dome to study his cluttered surroundings. He was surprised to see an old RA-7 servant droid nearby, seated with his back against a metal wall. The RA-7 gave R2-D2 a dismissive glance.

R2-D2 heard an electronic voice, and turned to face a red R5 astromech against another wall; the R5 rotated its characteristic head — shaped like an inverted cup — in greeting. Then R2-D2 spotted a binocular-eyed Treadwell droid and a box-shaped GNK power droid.

Curious, R2-D2 moved up a narrow aisle to explore the chamber. As he passed an ancient CZ secretary droid that was swaying back and forth amidst a pile of scrap, he heard a familiar voice call out, "Artoo?"

It was C-3PO. The golden droid had been hunched down against a wall, but seeing his friend, he struggled to his feet. "Artoo! It is you!" he cried happily. "It is you!"

R2-D2 beeped in salutation at C-3PO, who also had a restraining bolt secured to his chest. Both droids nearly stumbled when the transport suddenly lurched forward. Under the star-filled sky, the transport chugged off and headed out of the canyon.

The next morning, a squad of Imperial stormtroopers found the abandoned escape pod half buried in the sand. A *Sentinel*-class landing craft had delivered the stormtroopers to Tatooine, where they'd appropriated dewbacks — large four-legged reptiles — from the local authorities. The landing craft lifted away from the escape pod's impact site, leaving the stormtroopers and their dewbacks to search for any sign of the pod's passengers.

In addition to their standard armor and survival gear, the stormtroopers wore pauldrons — protective shoulder armor — over their right shoulders. All the pauldrons were black except for the orange one worn by the squad leader, Captain Mod Terrik.

Through the lenses of his stormtrooper helmet, Terrik looked from the open pod to the surrounding sand, searching for any signs of passengers. Because of winds and shifting sand, footprints didn't last long on Tatooine, so he considered himself lucky when he spotted the tracks.

"Someone was in the pod," Terrik announced to the other stormtroopers. He raised a pair of macrobinoculars to his helmet's lenses and scanned the desert, then added, "The tracks go off in this direction."

Near Captain Terrik, stormtrooper Davin Felth bent down to lift a shiny metal disk from the sand. Holding it up for Terrik's inspection, the stormtrooper said, "Look, sir — droids."

"Wake up! Wake up!" C-3PO said to R2-D2 as the transport came to a stop. R2-D2 had switched himself off, but — at C-3PO's urging — his dome's lights activated and he was immediately alert. Other droids were beeping and whirring nervously. Behind the protocol droid, a wide hatch opened and filled the cramped chamber with blinding bright light.

"We're doomed," C-3PO said.

After their reunion, C-3PO had told R2-D2 everything he'd learned about their short, hooded captors since they'd picked him up in the desert. They were Jawas, natives of Tatooine. They scavenged the desert for machinery, which they repaired, utilized, and sometimes sold to moisture farmers or other inhabitants. Even their transport — called a sandcrawler — was a scavenged item, a relic from the era of Tatooine's mining boom. The sandcrawler was large enough to serve as a mobile home for an entire clan of Jawas. It also was an autonomous mineral processing facility, equipped with ore crushers, a superheated smelter, and metal compactors. Being trapped in a vehicle with all these features was more than C-3PO could stand.

Jawas appeared at the open hatch, and a power droid tried to retreat into the chamber. C-3PO glanced at the Jawas, then back at R2-D2 and said, "Do you think they'll melt us down?"

R2-D2 beeped as a Jawa stepped up behind C-3PO.

"Don't shoot! Don't shoot!" the droid yelped. To R2-D2, he whimpered, "Will this never end?"

The Jawas herded C-3PO, R2-D2, and several other selected droids down the sandcrawler's main ramp. They had arrived at a salt flat, on which stood a domed structure and an evenly spaced series of five-meter-tall spires. The spires were vaporators, used to extract moisture from Tatooine's arid atmosphere. The place was a moisture farm.

Both R2-D2 and C-3PO had spent time on this same moisture farm before, a long time ago. From the astromech's perspective, the place hadn't changed much, but he refused to let old memories distract him from his current mission. As for the protocol droid, his memory was not what it had once been.

A Jawa nudged C-3PO, guiding him to take his place in line with the other droids beside the sandcrawler. A hulking R1 reactor drone stood to C-3PO's right, and a multiarmed Treadwell to his left. R2-D2 stood between the Treadwell and the red R2-5 astromech. Beyond the R2-5, a dome-bodied armored LIN mining droid hugged the ground at the end of the line.

R2-D2 and the R2-5 unit rotated their heads and glanced at each other. Besides their respective colors and head shapes, the two astromechs differed in cost and utility: R2-5 was substantially cheaper but R2-D2 could store more sets of hyperspace coordinates in active memory. Starpilots commonly referred to R2-5 units as R2s, but neither astromech took it personally.

Two human males — one old, one young — stepped out of one of the domed structures and approached the sandcrawler. The elder had grizzled hair and haggard features, and wore a sand-dusted robe over his farm tunic. The young man beside him had blond hair and wore a white tunic with a dark leather utility belt.

At the sight of the humans, most of the Jawas became so anxious that they ran off and hid behind the sandcrawler's treads. The Jawas' leader didn't run, but instead walked directly to the haggard-faced man and gibbered an enthusiastic sales pitch.

"Yeah, all right, fine," the older man said to the Jawa. "Let's go."

They'd only taken a few steps forward when a woman's voice called out, "Luke! Luke!"

The young man, Luke Skywalker, turned and trotted past some fusion generator supply tanks to arrive at the edge of a huge, deep hole. The hole was an open courtyard with arched doors and rounded windows set into its high mud-packed walls. Owned by the Lars family for two generations, the compound had been Luke's home for as long as he could remember. Luke leaned over the hole's edge and looked down. Two domestic vaporators extended up from the courtyard floor, and near them stood Luke's aunt Beru.

"Luke," Beru called up to him, "tell Uncle, if he gets a translator, be sure it speaks Bocce."

"Doesn't look like we have much of a choice,"

Luke said, "but I'll remind him." He turned and trotted back after the old man, his uncle Owen. Owen was looking at the red R2-5 unit in the droid lineup. The Jawa leader gibbered at Owen, who answered, "Yeah, I'll take that red one."

The Jawa leader yapped a sharp command and the other Jawas scurried out from behind the sandcrawler's treads to dust off the R2-5. Then, catching Owen's eye, the Jawa leader made encouraging gestures at the blue-domed R2 unit.

"No, not that one," Owen said, rejecting R2-D2. While Luke inspected the R2-5, Owen stepped past the Treadwell, then stopped to face the golden protocol droid. An almost identical droid had served on the Lars family farm a few decades back, so Owen recognized the model as a protocol droid. If Owen had had a curious nature or dwelled on the past, he might have wondered if he were looking at the same droid, but on this day, which followed many hard days, his only interest in droids was whether they would be useful to him on the farm. Giving the golden droid a quick study, he said, "You — I suppose you're programmed for etiquette and protocol?"

"Protocol?" C-3PO said. "Why it's my primary function, sir. I am well versed in all the customs —"

"I have no need for a protocol droid," Owen said, looking away. The golden droid's voice was vaguely familiar, but in Owen's limited experience, he figured all protocol droids sounded alike.

Thinking fast, C-3PO said, "Of course you haven't, sir — not in an environment such as this — that's why I have been programmed —"

Owen interrupted, "What I really need is a droid who understands the binary language of moisture vaporators."

"Vaporators!" C-3PO said as if it were the most wonderful word in the galaxy. "Sir — my first job was programming binary load lifters . . . very similar to your vaporators in most respects. . . ."

"Can you speak Bocce?" Owen asked.

"Of course I can, sir," C-3PO answered with pride. "It's like a second language to me . . . I'm as fluent in —"

"All right; shut up!" Owen indicated the protocol droid to the Jawa and said, "I'll take this one."

"Shutting up, sir," C-3PO muttered.

"Luke!" Owen shouted. Luke ran over. Owen gestured at the protocol droid and the R2-5 unit, then said, "Take these two over to the garage, will you? I want them cleaned up before dinner."

"But I was going into Toshe Station to pick up some power converters . . ." Luke whined.

"You can waste time with your friends when your chores are done," Owen said. "Now, come on, get to it!"

"All right, come on," Luke said to the protocol droid.

C-3PO glanced at R2-D2. The astromech emitted a whimpering whistle.

Luke glanced at the R2-5, who was getting a final dusting from some Jawas. Luke said, "And the red one, come on."

The R2-5 hesitated and stayed beside R2-D2, who let out a pathetic beep and began trembling.

"Well, come on, Red," Luke said. "Let's go."

The R2-5 rolled after Luke and C-3PO. R2-D2 started shaking so hard that he attracted the attention of a Jawa technician, who turned and zapped the droid with a control box. R2-D2 went suddenly silent and stood still.

The R2-5 was still rolling along when its top suddenly exploded, launching small parts all over the ground. As smoke poured upward from the R2-5's ruptured head, Luke called out, "Uncle Owen . . ."

"Yeah?" Owen answered, turning from his financial transaction with the Jawa leader.

"This Artoo unit has a bad motivator," Luke said, gesturing at the smoldering R2-5. "Look!"

Owen spun on the Jawa and bellowed, "Hey, what're you trying to push on us?"

C-3PO noticed the Jawa technician had reactivated R2-D2, and that R2-D2 was now practically jumping up and down, trying to attract attention so he wouldn't be left behind. C-3PO tapped Luke's shoulder, then pointed to R2-D2 and said, "Excuse me, sir, but that Artoo unit is in prime condition. A real bargain."

Luke said, "Uncle Owen . . ."

Owen looked away from the Jawa. "Yeah?"

Luke pointed at R2-D2. "What about that one?"

Turning back to the Jawa, Owen said, "What about that blue one? We'll take that one."

A few shy Jawas trudged up to the R2-5 unit, then glanced at Luke, waiting for his permission before they hauled off the droid. Luke waved his hand to fan away the smoke that was still coming out of the R2-5's head, then said, "Yeah, take this away."

C-3PO beamed at R2-D2, then turned to Luke and said, "I'm quite sure you'll be very pleased with that one, sir. He really is in first-class condition. I've worked with him before. Here he comes."

R2-D2 scooted away from the sandcrawler and headed for C-3PO and Luke. Luke said, "Okay, let's go." He turned and walked toward the domed structure, the main entrance to the Lars family homestead.

C-3PO moved close to R2-D2 and said in a low voice, "Now, don't you forget this! Why I should stick my neck out for you is quite beyond my capacity!"

The droids followed Luke into the entrance dome — their new home.

"Thank the maker!" C-3PO exclaimed with delight as he descended into a large tub. "This oil bath is going to feel so good. I've got such a bad case of dust contamination, I can barely move!"

C-3PO was with Luke and R2-D2 in the homestead's cluttered garage, which doubled as Luke's workshop. R2-D2 rested on a large battery. Luke sat on a bench, lost in thought as he played with a scale model of a T-16 skyhopper. He owned a real T-16, but he'd ripped its stabilizer while racing with friends through Beggar's Canyon, an ancient riverbed that had once been part of the Mos Espa Podrace circuit. Owen had been so angry with Luke that he'd grounded him for the season.

Another lost season.

"It just isn't fair," Luke said in frustration, tossing the model T-16 onto a table. "Oh, Biggs is right. I'm never gonna get out of here!"

C-3PO had never heard of Biggs, and didn't know why Luke was so upset, but he said, "Is there anything I might do to help?"

Luke looked at C-3PO, and the sight of the wide-eyed droid made a bit of his anger drain. He said, "Well, not unless you can alter time, speed up the harvest, or teleport me off this rock!"

"I don't think so, sir," C-3PO said. "I'm only a droid and not very knowledgeable about such things. Not on this planet, anyway. As a matter of fact, I'm not even sure which planet I'm on."

"Well, if there's a bright center to the universe, you're on the planet that it's farthest from."

"I see, sir," C-3PO said, sounding disappointed.

"Uh, you can call me Luke."

"I see, Sir Luke."

Luke grinned. "Just Luke." He knelt beside R2-D2 and began cleaning him.

"Oh!" C-3PO said, realizing the time had come for introductions. As he rose from the oil bath, he said, "And I am See-Threepio, Human Cyborg Relations, and this is my counterpart, Artoo-Detoo."

"Hello," Luke said to R2-D2.

R2-D2 beeped.

Luke was using a chrome pick to scrape several connectors on R2-D2's head. Examining it more closely, Luke said, "You got a lot of carbon scorching here. It looks like you boys have seen a lot of action."

Stepping out of the tub, C-3PO said, "With all we've been through, sometimes I'm amazed we're in as good condition as we are, what with the Rebellion and all."

At the mention of the Rebellion, Luke jumped up and whirled at C-3PO. "You know of the Rebellion against the Empire?"

"That's how we came to be in your service, if you take my meaning, sir."

Luke thought, *This is incredible!* He said, "Have you been in many battles?"

"Several, I think," C-3PO said. "Actually, there's not much to tell. I'm not much more than an interpreter, and not very good at telling stories. Well, not at making them interesting, anyway."

Luke's shoulders sagged. *Even if this droid were a good storyteller, I'm sick and tired of hearing stories about far-off worlds . . . stories that just make me want to leave Tatooine that much sooner.*

Luke hunkered down and went back to work on R2-D2. He felt a small metal fragment stuck in the upper corner of the data slot below the droid's head rotation ring, so he reached for a larger pick. "Well, my little friend," Luke said as he dug into R2-D2's data slot, "you've got something jammed in here real good. Were you on a star-cruiser or —"

The fragment broke loose with a snap, causing Luke to fall back to the garage floor. He sat up to see a flickering three-dimensional hologram of a young woman being projected from a lens on R2-D2's dome. Speaking via R2-D2's loudspeaker, the hologram said, "Help me, Obi-Wan Kenobi. You're my only hope."

Luke said, "What's this?"

R2-D2 beeped quizzically.

"What is what?!?" C-3PO translated with annoyance. "He asked you a question . . . What is *that*?"

The hologram repeated itself. The woman was dressed in white. She held her arms out, pleading, and said, "Help me, Obi-Wan Kenobi. You're my only hope." She glanced back over her right shoulder, then returned her gaze forward and bent her knees, extending her right arm like she was touching something. Luke thought, *Maybe she's switching off the holorecorder?* Then the hologram looped back to where it started: "Help me, Obi-Wan Kenobi. You're my only hope."

R2-D2 whistled in surprise.

"Oh, he says it's nothing, sir," C-3PO informed Luke. "Merely a malfunction. Old data. Pay it no mind."

"Who is she?" Luke said in awe. "She's beautiful."

C-3PO said, "I'm afraid I'm not quite sure, sir." In fact, both C-3PO and R2-D2 did recognize the hologram as Princess Leia Organa. But because Captain Antilles had commanded them to protect her identity and presence onboard the *Tantive IV,* the protocol droid could not reveal her name.

Luke couldn't take his eyes off the flickering image of the woman. The loop continued: "Help me, Obi-Wan Kenobi. You're my only hope . . ."

"I think she was a passenger on our last voyage," C-3PO allowed. "A person of some importance, sir — I believe. Our captain was attached to —"

"Is there more to this recording?" Luke interrupted.

R2-D2 let out several squeaks.

"Behave yourself, Artoo," C-3PO scolded. "You're going to get us into trouble. It's all right, you can trust him. He's our new master."

R2-D2 whistled and beeped a long message to C-3PO.

C-3PO looked at Luke. "He says that he's the property of Obi-Wan Kenobi, a resident of these parts. And it's a private message for him. Quite frankly, sir, I don't know what he's talking about. Our last master was Captain Antilles, but with all we've been through, this little Artoo unit has become a bit eccentric."

"Obi-Wan Kenobi?" Luke mused. "I wonder if he means old Ben Kenobi?"

"I beg your pardon, sir, but do you know what he's talking about?"

"Well, I don't know anyone named Obi-Wan, but old Ben lives out beyond the Dune Sea. He's kind of a strange old hermit."

Luke hadn't seen Ben in five seasons, since the time Luke and his friend Windy had ridden a dewback into the Jundland Wastes, a rocky region that consisted of a mesa and a canyon. The dewback had thrown them into a canyon and ran off. By nightfall, the boys were bruised and tired and lost. Then they'd heard a voice calling Luke's name. Incredibly, it had been Ben. He'd somehow found them, then guided them back to the Lars homestead. *I still don't know how he knew we were lost, or how he knew my name. But if Ben hadn't helped us . . .*

Luke gazed at the hologram again. "I wonder who she is. It sounds like she's in trouble. I'd better play back the whole thing."

R2-D2 beeped a short message to C-3PO.

"He says the restraining bolt has short-circuited his recording system," C-3PO translated. "He suggests that if you remove the bolt, he might be able to play back the entire recording."

"Hm?" Luke said, so captivated by the hologram that he wasn't entirely listening. *Remove the restraining bolt?* "Oh, yeah, well, I guess you're too small to run away on me if I take this off. Okay." He reached for a wedged tool and popped the restraining bolt off R2-D2's side. "There you go."

The hologram immediately disappeared.

"Hey, wait a minute," Luke said. "Where'd she go? Bring her back! Play back the entire message."

R2-D2 beeped innocently.

"'What message?'" C-3PO translated with disbelief. He raised a hand and whacked R2-D2's dome. "The one you've just been playing! The one you're carrying inside your rusty innards!"

Before Luke or C-3PO could further question R2-D2, Luke's aunt called from outside the garage. "Luke? Luke!"

Dinnertime already? "All right," Luke answered, "I'll be right there, Aunt Beru."

"I'm sorry, sir," C-3PO said, "but he appears to have picked up a slight flutter."

Luke handed the restraining bolt to C-3PO and said, "Here, see what you can do with him. I'll be right back."

As Luke headed out of the garage, C-3PO faced R2-D2 and snapped, "Just you reconsider playing that message for him."

R2-D2 beeped.

"No, I don't think he likes you at all," C-3PO answered, turning away.

R2-D2 beeped again.

"No, I don't like you either."

R2-D2 let out a sad, whimpering beep.

Luke left the garage and crossed the courtyard floor to the dining alcove, a cozy arched-ceiling excavation in the courtyard's wall. His aunt had just put some food in the bowl that was set before his uncle at the head of the table, and she seated herself as Luke walked in.

Luke sat down at the table and said, "You know, I think that Artoo unit we bought might have been stolen."

Owen glowered. "What makes you think that?"

"Well, I stumbled across a recording while I was cleaning him," Luke said, helping himself to the neatly prepared dinner. "He says he belongs to someone called Obi-Wan Kenobi."

Hearing this name, Owen and Beru exchanged a nervous glance, which went unseen by Luke. Chewing his food thoughtfully, he said, "I thought he might have meant old Ben." Looking to his uncle, he asked, "Do you know what he's talking about?"

"Nmm-mm," Owen mumbled, keeping his eyes on the food in his bowl.

"Well, I wonder if he's related to Ben."

"That wizard's just a crazy old man," Owen said. Luke knew his uncle didn't like Ben, but had no idea why. The night that Ben had found Luke and Windy in the Jundland Wastes and brought them back to the moisture farm, Owen had become furious. Not at Luke, but at Ben. Owen had told Ben to get off the farm and never come back. *I thought Uncle Owen would've been grateful to Ben for rescuing me. What does my uncle have against him?*

Owen continued, "Tomorrow I want you to take that Artoo unit into Anchorhead and have its memory erased. That'll be the end of it. It belongs to us now."

"But what if this Obi-Wan comes looking for him?"

"He won't," Owen said flatly. "I don't think he exists anymore. He died about the same time as your father."

Luke brightened. "He knew my father?"

"I told you to forget it," Owen snapped. "Your only concern is to prepare those two new droids for tomorrow. In the morning I want them up there on the south ridge working on those condensers."

"Yes, sir," Luke muttered. *Why is Uncle Owen so determined to keep me on the farm?* Knowing better than to argue with his uncle, Luke took a deep breath. "I think those new droids are going to work out fine," he said, doing his best to sound casual. Pushing the food around in his bowl, he continued, "In fact, I, uh, was also thinking about our agreement, about me staying on another season. And if these new droids do work out, I want to transmit my application to the Academy this year."

Owen's eyebrows raised, forming creases across his weather-worn forehead. "You mean the next semester before harvest?"

"Sure," Luke said. "There's more than enough droids."

"Harvest is when I need you the most," Owen said. "It's only one season more. This year we'll make enough on the harvest that I'll be able to hire some more hands. And then you can go to the Academy next year. You must understand I need you here, Luke."

"But it's a whole 'nother year."

"Look, it's only one more season."

"Yeah," Luke said, rising from the table, "that's what you said last year when Biggs and Tank left."

"Where are you going?" Beru asked, concerned.

"It looks like I'm going nowhere," Luke replied bitterly, stalking past his seated uncle and out of the alcove. "I have to go finish cleaning those droids."

As Luke headed out of the courtyard, Beru looked to her husband. "Owen, he can't stay here forever. Most of his friends have gone. It means so much to him."

"I'll make it up to him next year," Owen said. "I promise."

"Luke's just not a farmer, Owen," Beru said with a sad smile. "He has too much of his father in him."

Owen stared hard at Beru and said, "That's what I'm afraid of."

Luke stepped out of the homestead's entrance dome and kicked at the sand. *It's just not fair!*

He couldn't stop thinking about Biggs Darklighter, his best friend. He'd seen Biggs just the day before, at the Anchorhead settlement power station. Biggs had returned to Tatooine to tell Luke he'd graduated from the Academy and received an assignment as first mate on a space freighter. He'd also confided that he intended to jump ship and join the Rebel Alliance. That was yesterday, and Biggs was already gone.

I wish I could have left this morning with Biggs. What was it he called Tatooine? "A big hunk of nothing." Boy, was he ever right. And I'm stuck on it.

Luke stopped to watch Tatooine's giant twin suns set over a distant dune range. The hot wind tugged at his tunic.

There's no future here. Not for me. But something is out there. . . .

The suns sank and vanished beyond the horizon. Luke returned through the entrance dome and proceeded to the garage. It was dark inside and the droids were nowhere in sight. Luke took the droid caller from his utility belt and pressed a button that made a buzzing sound.

"Aah!" C-3PO cried in response to the caller's transmitted shock as he jumped out from his hiding place behind the Lars family landspeeder.

Luke grinned. "What are you doing hiding back there?"

"It wasn't my fault, sir," C-3PO said, his voice trembling. "Please don't deactivate me. I told him not to go, but he's faulty, malfunctioning, kept babbling on about his mission."

"Oh, no!" Luke said, his grin gone. He raced out of the garage.

The sky was already dark and filled with stars when Luke rushed out of the domed entrance. He took his macrobinoculars from his belt and raised them to his eyes, scanning the area for R2-D2.

C-3PO followed Luke onto the salt flat and said, "That Artoo unit has always been a problem. These astrodroids are getting quite out of hand. Even I can't understand their logic at times."

"How could I be so stupid?" Luke said, lowering the macrobinoculars. "He's nowhere in sight. Blast it!"

"Pardon me, sir, but couldn't we go after him?"

"It's too dangerous with all the Sand People around. We'll have to wait until morning."

Just then, Owen's voice called out, "Luke, I'm shutting the power down."

Luke turned and answered, "All right, I'll be there in a few minutes." He turned back for a final glance across the horizon, then muttered, "Boy, am I gonna get it!" Looking to C-3PO, he said, "You know, that little droid is going to cause me a lot of trouble."

Without hesitation, C-3PO replied, "Oh, he *excels* at that, sir."

Owen woke up early and went looking for Luke. After calling for him several times from the courtyard, Owen stepped into the kitchen, where Beru was preparing breakfast.

"Have you seen Luke this morning?" Owen asked gruffly.

"He said he had some things to do before he started today, so he left early."

"Uh?" Owen said, watching Beru insert food into a cooking unit. "Did he take those two new droids with him?"

"I think so," Beru said.

Owen looked out the doorway, then grumbled, "Well, he better have those units in the south range repaired by midday or there'll be hell to pay!"

Luke's sand-blasted landspeeder raced over the desert. In the vehicle's open cockpit, C-3PO was behind the controls and Luke sat to his left in the single passenger seat. The landspeeder traveled through the air a mere meter above ground level, and had a top speed of about 250 kilometers per hour. C-3PO didn't think they were traveling nearly that fast, but when he glanced at the speedometer, he wished he hadn't. He'd forgotten how much he disliked high speeds. The sight of low-flying bugs splattered against the speeder's duraplex windshield wasn't pleasant either.

But it hadn't been Luke's idea to put C-3PO in the driver's seat. Since piloting ground-effect vehicles was one of C-3PO's secondary programs, he had offered to take the controls so Luke would be free to scan for R2-D2's tracks. Luke had agreed.

After listening to C-3PO's account of R2-D2 heading for a rock mesa after landing the escape pod in the desert, Luke was fairly certain that the droids had landed in the Dune Sea, and that R2-D2 had been bound for the Jundland Wastes. Luke directed C-3PO to the Wastes, and when they failed to find R2-D2 anywhere on the rock mesa, they steered down into the canyon.

Luke checked the autoscan on the dashboard's scopes. "Look," he said, "there's a droid on the scanner. Dead ahead. Might be our little Artoo unit. Hit the accelerator."

C-3PO hit the accelerator, increasing thrust from

the landspeeder's three turbine engines. As expected, the landspeeder went even faster.

Unfortunately, the landspeeder's autoscan failed to detect the presence of Sand People.

Luke and C-3PO found R2-D2 trudging along on the floor of the massive canyon. C-3PO brought the landspeeder to a stop, then he and Luke left the vehicle and hurried over to R2-D2.

"Hey, whoa," Luke said, "just where do you think you're going?"

R2-D2 stopped and offered some feeble beeps.

"Master Luke is your rightful owner now," said C-3PO, angered by R2-D2's response. "We'll have no more of this Obi-Wan Kenobi gibberish . . . and don't talk to me of your mission either. You're fortunate he doesn't blast you into a million pieces right here."

"No, it's all right," Luke said. "But I think we better go."

Suddenly, R2-D2 emitted a flurry of frantic whistles and screams.

Luke looked to C-3PO and asked, "What's wrong with him now?"

C-3PO translated, "There are several creatures approaching from the southeast."

"Sand People!" Luke gasped. "Or worse!" He went to his landspeeder and fetched a laser rifle he'd brought along for the ride. "Come on, let's go have a look."

C-3PO could not remember ever hearing about Sand People. He would not have remembered the fierce nomads by their other name — Tusken Raiders — either. In any event, the golden droid was apprehensive.

Luke repeated, "Come on." The way he said it, he made it sound like there was nothing to worry about.

While R2-D2 remained near the landspeeder, C-3PO followed Luke to climb up behind some nearby boulders that were atop a ridge that overlooked the canyon. Luke propped his laser rifle against the boulder that he rested upon, then whipped out his macrobinoculars and peered through them to scan the canyon floor.

Almost immediately, he spotted two banthas: large, thick-furred quadrupeds, the beasts of burden to the Tusken Raiders.

"Well, there are two banthas down there," Luke told C-3PO, "but I don't see any . . . wait a second."

There was a slight movement near the legs of one bantha, then a humanoid figure came into view. The figure was clothed in a gauzy robe, and his head was masked by bandages, distinctive eye-protection lenses, and a metal-plated breath filter.

Luke said, "They're Sand People all right. I can see one of them now."

Suddenly, something clouded Luke's field of view, and he lowered his macrobinoculars in time to see that a Tusken Raider had quickly risen to loom directly in front of him. The Tusken Raider roared. C-3PO was so startled that he fell over backward.

The Tusken Raider clutched a gaderffii, a hand-fashioned double-edged axlike weapon, and held it high over his head. Luke snatched up his laser rifle, but the Tusken Raider swung his gaderffii and cleaved through the rifle's long barrel, knocking Luke to the rock ridge. The Tusken Raider swung at Luke's prone body, but Luke rolled aside to avoid being struck by the gaderffii. The Tusken Raider swung twice again, and Luke dodged those blows too. The fourth swing connected, and Luke was knocked unconscious.

Below Luke, R2-D2 huddled against the shadows under a rock ledge. The astromech trembled as three Tusken Raiders hauled Luke's unconscious body down to the canyon floor and dumped him unceremoniously beside some rocks near the parked landspeeder. Feeling helpless, R2-D2 watched the Tusken Raiders saunter over to the landspeeder. They began to strip the vehicle, tossing parts and supplies in all directions. Then they stopped.

A great howling moan echoed through the canyon. Hearing the sound, the three Tusken Raiders fled from the landspeeder. R2-D2 peeked out from the shadows to see the source of the sound: a shuffling humanoid in a dark brown robe with a head-concealing hood. R2-D2 couldn't imagine why the Tusken Raiders were afraid of the approaching lifeform, and wondered if perhaps they'd seen something he hadn't.

The hooded figure stopped beside Luke's unconscious form, then bent down and checked his pulse. R2-D2 beeped, and the figured paused. Then he raised a hand to pull back the hood, revealing a bearded old man with thinning white hair. The man turned to face the R2 unit, then smiled and said, "Hello there! Come here, my little friend. Don't be afraid."

Concerned for Luke, R2-D2 beeped.

"Oh, don't worry, he'll be all right," the man answered.

Luke stirred, then slowly opened his eyes to look up at the old man, who said, "Rest easy, son, you've had a busy day. You're fortunate to be all in one piece."

Luke's eyes widened. "Ben? Ben Kenobi?" It was the second time Ben had happened upon him when he needed aid. But Luke wasn't considering the odds against the repeated occurrence; he was just relieved. "Boy, am I glad to see you!"

Seeing that all was well, R2-D2 stepped out from under the rock ledge and approached Luke and Ben.

"The Jundland Wastes are not to be traveled lightly," Ben said cheerfully as he helped Luke sit up. "Tell me, young Luke, what brings you out this far?"

"Oh, this little droid!" Luke said, gesturing at R2-D2. "I think he's searching for his former master, but I've never seen such devotion in a droid before. . . ."

Ben smiled again at the blue astromech, who beeped at him. Then Ben returned his gaze to Luke, waiting for him to continue.

Luke said, "Ah, he claims to be the property of an Obi-Wan Kenobi. Is he a relative of yours? Do you know who he's talking about?"

Ben's smile was gone. His eyes were on Luke, but there was something in his expression that seemed simultaneously startled and alert, as if he'd just seen a ghost. Catching his breath, Ben eased himself back to rest against a boulder. "Obi-Wan Kenobi . . ." he said. "Obi-Wan? Now that's a name I've not heard in a long time . . . a long time."

"I think my uncle knows him," Luke said. "He said he was dead. . . ."

"Oh, he's not dead," Ben said, smiling as he glanced at the sky. "Not yet."

"You know him?"

"Well, of course I know him. He's me! I haven't gone by the name Obi-Wan since, oh, before you were born."

Luke said, "Well, then, the droid does belong to you."

"Don't seem to remember ever owning a droid," Ben said, eyeing the blue R2 unit more carefully. Although Luke had not mentioned the astromech's name, Ben did recognize R2-D2. They'd met decades before, on a starship that had been forced to make an emergency landing on Tatooine, of all places. Ben kept his recollections to himself, but muttered, "Very interesting . . ."

An inhuman barking sound echoed through the canyon. Ben looked up at the overhanging cliffs and said, "I think we better get indoors. The Sand People are easily startled, but they will soon be back. And in greater numbers."

As Ben helped Luke step toward the landspeeder, R2-D2 let out a pathetic beep, causing Luke to remember: "See-Threepio!"

Luke and Ben found the protocol droid sprawled on the rocks near where Luke had been attacked by the Tusken Raider. Wires dangled out from the open socket at C-3PO's left shoulder, and his left arm lay on the ground nearby. The two men lifted the droid to a seated position.

In a dazed voice, C-3PO asked, "Where am I? I must have taken a bad step. . . ."

"Well, can you stand?" Luke said. "We've got to get you out of here before the Sand People return."

"I don't think I can make it," C-3PO said. "You go on, Master Luke. There's no sense in you risking yourself on my account. I'm done for."

"No, you're not," Luke said sympathetically. "What kind of talk is that?"

Thinking of the Tusken Raiders, Ben said, "Quickly . . . they're on the move."

Ben and Luke helped C-3PO to his feet, gathered up his left arm, and returned to the landspeeder. Because the speeder had only two seats, the droids were placed atop the vehicle's rear section, on the panels that covered the repulsor field system generator: R2-D2's cylindrical body rested upon the panel behind the passenger seat; C-3PO sat behind the driver's seat and wedged his metal legs down into the open cockpit, between the seats. When the droids were secured, Ben climbed into the passenger seat and directed Luke to drive out of the canyon.

Ben's house was a dome-roofed hovel built upon an elevated ridge in the Jundland Wastes. The group had left the landspeeder parked outside, and were in the house's modest living area. The room was cool, clean, and minimally furnished, with only a few displayed possessions.

The damage to C-3PO's arm hadn't been serious, so Luke — despite a protest from R2-D2 — had decided to make the repairs himself. After giving Luke a toolbox, Ben had taken a chair beside a low round table. To Ben's right, Luke and C-3PO sat on the edge of Ben's bed, which was set in a concave alcove. R2-D2 stood near a storage chest on the floor and peered over the round table to watch Luke work on C-3PO's arm.

"Tell me, Luke," Ben said. "Do you know about your father's service in the Clone Wars?"

"No, my father didn't fight in the wars," Luke said as he reconnected a wire in C-3PO's arm. "He was a navigator on a spice freighter."

"That's what your uncle told you," Ben said. "He didn't hold with your father's ideals. Thought he should have stayed here and not gotten involved."

Luke turned to face Ben. "You fought in the Clone Wars?"

"Yes. I was once a Jedi Knight, the same as your father."

Luke looked away. "I wish I'd known him."

Ben said, "He was the best starpilot in the galaxy and a cunning warrior." He grinned at Luke and said, "I understand you've become quite a good pilot yourself." Then a faraway look came over his eyes. He added, "And he was a good friend. Which reminds me . . ."

Ben rose from his seat and walked past R2-D2 to raise the lid on the storage chest. "I have something here for you." He removed a shiny, cylindrical object. "Your father wanted you to have this when you were old enough, but your uncle wouldn't allow it. He feared you might follow old Obi-Wan on some damned-fool idealistic crusade like your father did."

Still seated on the bed, C-3PO turned to Luke and said, "Sir, if you'll not be needing me, I'll close down for a while."

"Sure, go ahead," Luke said.

C-3PO remained seated as he switched himself off. His eyes winked off and his head slumped forward.

Ben handed the shiny object to Luke, who stood and took it in his right hand. Luke asked, "What is it?"

"Your father's lightsaber," Ben said. "This is the weapon of a Jedi Knight. Not as clumsy or random as a blaster."

Luke's fingers found the activation plate, and the blade — a blue beam of pure energy — emitted instantly from an aperture at the end of the handgrip. The weapon made a humming sound. Fascinated, Luke tested the weapon, moving his arm to cut through the air with the glowing blade.

"An elegant weapon for a more civilized day," Ben commented as he returned to his chair. "For over a thousand generations the Jedi Knights were the guardians of peace and justice in the Old Republic. Before the dark times, before the Empire."

Luke deactivated the lightsaber and sat back down on the edge of the bed. Facing Ben, he asked, "How did my father die?"

Ben glanced away from Luke. Choosing his words carefully, he returned his gaze to Luke and said, "A young Jedi named Darth Vader, who was a pupil of mine until he turned to evil, helped the Empire hunt down and destroy the Jedi Knights. He betrayed and murdered your father."

Luke was stunned. *Why didn't Uncle Owen and Aunt Beru tell me this?*

"Now the Jedi are all but extinct," Ben continued. "Vader was seduced by the dark side of the Force."

"The Force?" Luke said.

"The Force is what gives the Jedi his power," Ben said. "It's an energy field created by all living things. It surrounds us and penetrates us. It binds the galaxy together."

R2-D2 beeped.

Rising again, Ben stepped over to R2-D2 and said, "Now, let's see if we can't figure out what you are, my little friend. And where you come from."

As Ben touched R2-D2's dome, Luke said, "I saw part of the message he was —"

R2-D2's hologram projector flicked on, and Ben said, "I seem to have found it."

Ben returned to his seat, and R2-D2 projected the

flickering hologram of the young woman so that she appeared to be standing upon the low round table.

"General Kenobi," said the woman's hologram, "years ago you served my father in the Clone Wars. Now he begs you to help him in his struggle against the Empire. I regret that I am unable to present my father's request to you in person, but my ship has fallen under attack, and I'm afraid my mission to bring you to Alderaan has failed. I have placed information vital to the survival of the Rebellion into the memory systems of this Artoo unit."

Ben glanced at R2-D2, then back at the hologram.

"My father will know how to retrieve it," the woman's hologram continued. "You must see this droid safely delivered to him on Alderaan. This is our most desperate hour. Help me, Obi-Wan Kenobi. You're my only hope."

The woman's hologram glanced over her right shoulder, then bent to adjust something, just as Luke had seen her do before. He now realized she must have turned in response to something or someone behind her, then turned back to manually switch off R2-D2's holorecorder. The hologram flickered off.

Ben sat back in his chair and tugged at his beard, thinking hard.

Luke said, "Who is she?"

Distractedly, Ben said, "She is Princess Leia Organa of the Royal House of Alderaan, an Imperial

Senator and, unbeknownst to the Empire, a leader of the Rebel Alliance. She's grown into a remarkable young woman."

R2-D2 rotated his dome to look at C-3PO, who was still shut down. R2-D2 would let C-3PO know that they could now speak freely about the princess in the presence of Luke and Ben.

Ben looked to Luke and said, "You must learn the ways of the Force if you're to come with me to Alderaan."

"Alderaan?" Luke said with disbelief. Rising away from Ben, he added, "I'm not going to Alderaan." He moved toward the door. "I've got to get home. It's late; I'm in for it as it is."

"I need your help, Luke," Ben said. "*She* needs your help. I'm getting too old for this sort of thing."

"I can't get involved!" Luke protested. "I've got work to do! It's not that I like the Empire — I hate it! But there's nothing I can do about it right now. It's such a long way from here."

"That's your uncle talking."

Luke sighed. "Oh, boy, my uncle. How am I ever going to explain this?"

"Learn about the Force, Luke."

Exasperated, Luke said, "Look, I can take you as far as Anchorhead. You can get a transport there to Mos Eisley or wherever you're going."

Ben looked away from Luke and said, "You must do what you feel is right, of course."

What I feel is right? How can he say that? I'd like to help Ben and . . . her, whoever she is. But is it right to run out on Uncle Owen and Aunt Beru? They're the only family I've got, and I'm not going to let anything happen to them. If that's not right, then maybe I'd rather be wrong!

While his squad of stormtroopers continued their search on Tatooine for the Death Star plans, Darth Vader traveled by Star Destroyer to deliver Princess Leia Organa to the Death Star.

The Death Star was, quite simply, the largest starship ever built. Shaped like an orb, it was 120 kilometers in diameter, the size of a Class IV moon. Its quadanium steel outer hull had two prominent features: an equatorial trench and — on its upper hemisphere — a concave superlaser focus lens. The trench contained ion engines, hyperdrives, and hangar bays; the superlaser had enough power to annihilate entire worlds.

In addition to its superlaser, the Death Star's weaponry included more than 10,000 turbolaser batteries, 2,500 laser cannons, and 2,500 ion cannons. Its hangars contained 7,000 TIE fighters and more than 20,000 military and transport vessels.

The crew, troops, and pilots made up a population of more than one million.

But despite all these staggering numbers, at least one person on the Death Star was concerned about the Rebellion.

"Until this battle station is fully operational we are vulnerable," said Commander Tagge. He was in a conference room, seated at a circular black table with six other high-ranking Imperial officials. Tagge was looking to his right at the seated figure of Admiral Motti, the senior Imperial commander in charge of operations on the Death Star. Tagge continued, "The Rebel Alliance is too well equipped. They're more dangerous than you realize."

Admiral Motti sneered, "Dangerous to your starfleet, Commander — not to this battle station!"

But Tagge wasn't finished. "The Rebellion will continue to gain support in the Imperial Senate as long as —"

"The Imperial Senate will no longer be of any concern to us," interrupted a gaunt older man with hollow cheeks who had just walked into the conference room. He was Grand Moff Tarkin, the Death Star's conceiver, and he entered with Darth Vader at his side. In the Imperial hierarchy, Tarkin reported only to the Emperor, and Vader served Tarkin as the Emperor's enforcer of evil.

Vader remained standing while Tarkin took his

seat between Admiral Motti and Commander Tagge. Tarkin continued, "I have just received word that the Emperor has dissolved the council permanently. The last remnants of the Old Republic have been swept away."

"That's impossible," Commander Tagge said. "How will the Emperor maintain control without the bureaucracy?"

Tarkin said, "The regional governors now have direct control over their territories. Fear will keep the local systems in line. Fear of this battle station."

"And what of the Rebellion?" asked Tagge. "If the Rebels have obtained a complete technical readout of this station, it is possible, however unlikely, that they might find a weakness and exploit it."

From beside Tarkin, Darth Vader said, "The plans you refer to will soon be back in our hands."

To Tagge, Admiral Motti promised, "Any attack made by the Rebels against this station would be a useless gesture, no matter what technical data they've obtained. This station is now the ultimate power in the universe. I suggest we use it."

Vader warned, "Don't be too proud of this technological terror you've constructed. The ability to destroy a planet is insignificant next to the power of the Force."

Motti sneered and said, "Don't try to frighten us with your sorcerer's ways, Lord Vader. Your sad devotion to that ancient religion has not helped you conjure up the stolen data tapes or given you clairvoyance enough to find the Rebels' hidden fort —"

Suddenly, Motti stopped speaking. Vader never actually touched Motti, but the Dark Lord made a pinching movement with his gloved hand and caused Motti to desperately reach to his own throat. The admiral was choking. His eyes remained fixed on Vader as his body spasmed.

Pinching the air with his fingers, Vader said, "I find your lack of faith disturbing."

Tarkin eyed Vader, then said, "Enough of this! Vader, release him!"

"As you wish," Vader said. He lowered his hand.

Air rushed into Motti's lungs and his head slumped forward. Breathing hard, he stared at the table, then looked up to boldly glare at Vader.

Tarkin said, "This bickering is pointless. Lord Vader will provide us with the location of the Rebel fortress by the time this station is operational. We will then crush the Rebellion with one swift stroke."

Luke, Ben, and the two droids were speeding through the Jundland Wastes, heading for the community of Anchorhead, when they came upon what was left of the Jawa sandcrawler. Smoke billowed from fires that still burned inside and around the bulky, rusted vehicle. Dozens of Jawas lay dead, their small forms scattered across the sand.

Luke stopped so he and Ben could examine the wreckage. The sandcrawler's hull was riddled with blaster damage, and it appeared the entire Jawa clan had been wiped out.

"It looks like the Sand People did this, all right," Luke said to Ben. "Look, there's gaffi sticks, bantha tracks. It's just . . . I never heard of them hitting anything this big before."

"They didn't," Ben said. "But we are meant to think they did." Gesturing at the bantha tracks, he continued, "These tracks are side by side. Sand People always ride single file to hide their numbers."

Luke said, "These are the same Jawas that sold us Artoo-Detoo and See-Threepio."

Ben pointed at the scorched dents in the sandcrawler's hull. "And these blast points, too accurate for Sand People. Only Imperial stormtroopers are so precise."

Baffled, Luke asked, "But why would Imperial troops want to slaughter Jawas?" Searching for his answer, he looked at R2-D2 and C-3PO, who stood next to the parked speeder.

The droids, Luke realized. *The stormtroopers want the information in R2-D2!*

Then a more awful realization hit Luke. He said, "If they traced the robots here, they may have learned who they sold them to, and that would lead them back . . . home!"

Luke bolted for the landspeeder.

"Wait, Luke!" Ben shouted. "It's too dangerous!"

Not heeding Ben's warning, Luke jumped into the landspeeder, punched the ignition, and sped away from the burning sandcrawler.

Luke saw the rising smoke from kilometers away.

The Lars homestead was consumed by a fiery blaze. Luke's landspeeder was still slowing to a stop when he jumped out. Dense black smoke poured out from the garage roof. He shouted, "Uncle Owen! Aunt Beru! Uncle Owen!"

No response.

Luke didn't know where to look first. Dazed and afraid, he stumbled past debris, hoping to find his uncle and aunt alive. *Maybe they weren't here when the stormtroopers came. Uncle Owen might have gone to check some vaporators . . . but what about Aunt Beru?* The hole that had contained the courtyard now resembled a small volcano, erupting large clouds of gray smoke.

Don't be dead! Luke's mind raced. *Don't be dead don't be dead don't be dead!* His eyes darted to the entrance dome. More fire, more smoke.

Then he saw them.

Two charred, smoldering skeletons, lying in the sand outside the entrance dome.

Luke choked and looked away. Then something inside him snapped, and he forced himself to look back at what the stormtroopers had done to his aunt and uncle.

I'm not afraid. The Empire has taken everything away from me, but I'm not afraid. Because now I don't have anything to lose.

He stood there, gazing deep into the flames, and felt his anger and determination build.

On the Death Star, two black-uniformed Imperial soldiers preceded Darth Vader down a dark, narrow corridor lined with recessed doorways. All the doors were closed, and behind each was a detention cell. The soldiers stopped in front of one door and it slid up into the ceiling. Darth Vader ducked through the doorway and the two soldiers followed. While the two soldiers stood at either side of the open doorway, Vader stepped to the center of the cramped cell and loomed over the lone prisoner who sat on a bare metal bed that projected from the wall.

Princess Leia.

Darth Vader said, "And now, Your Highness, we will discuss the location of your hidden Rebel base."

There was an electronic hum from behind Vader, then a spherical black droid hovered slowly into the cell. A ringed repulsorlift system wrapped around the droid's midsection in such a way that the sphere almost resembled a scale model of the Death Star with its equatorial trench. But unlike the Death Star, which appeared to have a smooth surface from a distance, the droid was festooned with bizarre devices that jutted out at asymmetrical angles. The devices included an electroshock assembly, sonic torture device, chemical syringe, and lie determinator.

It was an interrogator droid.

Leia's eyes went wide with fear. The droid extended its syringe and hovered toward her.

The cell door slid closed, and the interrogation began.

Luke drove his landspeeder back to the ruined sandcrawler. In his absence, Ben had prepared a pyre near the sandcrawler, and he returned to find C-3PO and R2-D2 placing the Jawa corpses onto the flames. The droids stopped what they were doing and watched Luke as he stepped away from his landspeeder and went to Ben.

Ben saw the torment in Luke's face and said, "There's nothing you could have done, Luke, had you been there. You'd have been killed too, and the droids would now be in the hands of the Empire."

Luke didn't have time for pity. He said, "I want to come with you to Alderaan. There's nothing for me here now. I want to learn the ways of the Force and become a Jedi like my father."

Ben nodded. When the last Jawa had been placed on the burning pyre, the two men loaded the droids onto the landspeeder and drove off.

En route to the group's destination, Luke had a hard time concentrating. He couldn't stop thinking about his aunt and uncle, and what the Empire had done. But after the third time he'd strayed off course, Ben suggested they park the landspeeder and take a moment's pause.

Luke parked on a high, craggy bluff that overlooked a canyon. The droids followed Luke and Ben to the edge of the bluff and gazed out over a wide, haphazard array of runways, landing pads, craterlike docking bays, and semidomed structures that sprawled across the stark canyon floor.

"Mos Eisley spaceport," Ben said. "You will never find a more wretched hive of scum and villainy." Glancing at Luke, he added, "We must be cautious."

Ben and Luke got the droids onto the back of the landspeeder, then the group resumed their journey. This time, Luke stayed on course.

Because Tatooine was in the Outer Rim of space, far from Republic and Imperial activity, Mos Eisley had long been a haven for thieves, smugglers, and pirates. Frequent travelers knew better than to stay in town too long. Curious tourists usually wound up wishing they'd stayed at home.

But by any standards, the drive into the city was quite an eyeful. Street traffic consisted of not only landspeeders and swoop bikes but large quadrupeds, including dewbacks and long-necked rontos. Some pedestrians were human, others mechanical, but most were aliens that Luke had never seen before. To resist gawking, he kept his eyes on the road in front of him and steered carefully through the busy streets.

Approaching a congested intersection, Luke slowed the landspeeder to allow some pedestrians to pass. Suddenly, five white-armored stormtroopers emerged from the sides of the road. All carried blaster rifles. One stormtrooper — the squad leader with an orange pauldron over his right shoulder — waved at Luke, signaling him to pull over. Luke had driven straight into a checkpoint.

The stormtroopers were looking at C-3PO and R2-D2, who were in plain view on the landspeeder's rear section.

Luke felt stupid for not trying to conceal the droids under blankets, then thought, *Could these be the same stormtroopers who killed Uncle Owen, Aunt Beru, and the Jawas?* He hadn't expected a confrontation with stormtroopers so soon, and he was unprepared. His heart raced. *One false move and they might open fire. What should I do?* He glanced at Ben, who responded with a reassuring smile. Luke kept both hands on the speeder's steering wheel and looked up at the squad leader.

The stormtrooper asked, "How long have you had these droids?"

"About three or four seasons," Luke lied.

Ben gazed pleasantly at the stormtrooper and said, "They're up for sale if you want them."

Behind Luke, C-3PO trembled. Luke thought, *For sale?! What's Ben talking about?*

The squad leader said, "Let me see your identification."

"You don't need to see his identification," Ben said in a calm, controlled tone.

Looking to his fellow stormtroopers, the squad leader said, "We don't need to see his identification."

Ben said, "These aren't the droids you're looking for. "

"These aren't the droids we're looking for," the squad leader repeated.

Luke gave another quick glance at Ben. *He's hypnotizing the stormtroopers. But how?*

Ben said to the squad leader, "He can go about his business."

Looking at Luke, the squad leader said, "You can go about your business."

"Move along," Ben said.

"Move along," echoed the squad leader, gesturing with his hand for Luke to proceed. "Move along."

Luke drove the landspeeder away from the stormtroopers. A few minutes later, Ben directed him to park in front of a rundown blockhouse cantina on the outskirts of the spaceport. The moment the speeder had stopped, a Jawa ran up to run his small hands over the vehicle's hood. As Luke shooed the Jawa away, C-3PO helped R2-D2 off the back of the speeder and muttered, "I can't abide those Jawas. Disgusting creatures."

"Go on, go on," Luke said, waiting for the Jawa to move off. Then he turned to Ben and said, "I can't understand how we got by those troops. I thought we were dead."

Ben said, "The Force can have a strong influence on the weak-minded."

Luke glanced at the cantina and said, "Do you really think we're going to find a pilot here that'll take us to Alderaan?"

"Well, most of the best freighter pilots can be found here," Ben said. "Only watch your step. This place can be a little rough."

"I'm ready for anything," Luke said as he followed Ben to the cantina's entrance.

C-3PO saw three Jawas loitering in front of the cantina near a large dewback. He turned to the astromech and said, "Come along, Artoo." The droids moved fast to catch up with Luke and Ben.

Luke followed Ben into the cantina's entry lobby. Like most buildings in Mos Eisley, the cantina was essentially a hole in the ground that was covered by a domed roof. Its interior was dark, and the air was filled with thick smoke and fast music. Beyond the entry lobby, a short flight of mud-packed steps descended into a crowded room. A U-shaped bar dominated the room's center, and the walls were lined by small booths that offered some slight possibility for private conversations. Most of the patrons were aliens, as were the Bith musicians who performed at the bandstand to the right of the bar.

Ben made his way to the bar and immediately struck up a conversation with a human spacer. Luke remained at the top of the steps in the lobby for a moment, overwhelmed by the sight of so many exotic creatures. C-3PO and R2-D2 walked up behind him, then Luke descended the steps. As C-3PO followed him down to the cantina floor, Luke heard a chime from a device in the lobby behind him.

A gruff voice shouted from behind the bar, "Hey, we don't serve their kind here!"

Luke caught sight of the bartender, a disheveled, middle-aged man with hardened features. The bartender was glaring at him. Confused, Luke said, "What?"

"Your droids," the bartender said. "They'll have to wait outside. We don't want them here."

Luke realized that the chime had sounded from a droid detector. He was also aware of the angry stares from several patrons. Turning to C-3PO, he said, "Listen, why don't you wait out by the speeder. We don't want any trouble."

"I heartily agree with you, sir," C-3PO said. He climbed the steps back to R2-D2, then both made their exit from the building.

Luke glanced at the bar. Ben was still with the spacer, who appeared to be making introductions with a Wookiee, a hulking, fur-covered alien with a simian muzzle and sharp teeth. An ammunition bandolier was wrapped around the Wookiee's shaggy torso, and a laser-firing bowcaster was slung over one arm. Luke guessed the Wookiee's height at around 2.25 meters, maybe more.

The spacer moved off, but Ben continued talking with the Wookiee at the bar. Luke stepped up to the bar so Ben and the Wookiee were to his right. Luke tried to look casual. *I'll just stand here and watch Ben's back.*

Luke reached across the bar to tug at the bartender's sleeve. The bartender turned his battered face to scowl at Luke. Luke ordered a small cup of water. The bartender gave it to him.

Luke took furtive glances at the various spacers and aliens: a pair of Duros leaning against a wall, a white-furred Talz with a small Chadra-Fan, an Ithorian sitting in a corner, and a couple of Tin-Tin Dwarfs. *I've never seen so many nonhumans in one place.*

Somebody on his left shoved him hard.

Luke whirled to face a tusked humanoid alien with bulbous black eyes. The alien spat out, "Negola dewaghi wooldugger?!?"

Luke looked away from the alien. *If I ignore him, maybe he'll just go away.*

Luke felt a blunt finger tapping his left shoulder. He turned, expecting to see the tusked alien, but instead he confronted a ghastly-looking man. The man's right eye was blinded and the flesh around it was severely scarred. His nose looked as if it had barely survived an unfortunate encounter with a meat shredder. Gesturing at the tusked alien beside him, the man leaned in close to Luke and said, "He doesn't like you."

The man's breath was foul. Not knowing how else to respond, Luke mumbled, "I'm sorry."

"I don't like you either," said the man with the hideous face. "You just watch yourself. We're wanted men. I have the death sentence on twelve systems."

Luke replied, "I'll be careful."

The man seized Luke's arm and snarled, "You'll be dead."

Luke was still being gripped tightly when Ben turned to face Luke's antagonists. Ben said calmly, "This little one's not worth the effort. Come, let me get you something." Behind Ben, the Wookiee just stood back and watched, waiting to see how the situation would play out.

The man with the disfigured face moved with alarming speed and strength, flinging Luke away from the bar. As Luke crashed into a nearby table, his attackers reached for their blaster pistols.

"No blasters! No blasters!" the bartender shouted too late as he dropped behind the bar.

Luke looked up from where he was sprawled on the floor and saw Ben's hand dart to his belt and draw a lightsaber. The blade flashed on and swept past the blaster-wielding criminals. The disfigured man fell back against the bar, a deep slash across his chest. The tusked alien screamed and his right arm — severed at the elbow — fell to the floor, still clutching the alien's blaster.

The entire fight had lasted only a matter of seconds. Luke hadn't noticed just when the band had stopped playing, but he was suddenly aware that everyone had gone silent, and the only sound in the cantina was the hum of Ben's lightsaber. Ben maintained his position, holding his lightsaber out from his body as he stared at his two defeated opponents. He glanced out across the room. If anyone else had been looking for a fight, the look in Ben's eyes was enough to discourage them.

Ben deactivated his lightsaber. Almost immediately, the band started playing again, and the patrons went back to their drinks and conversations. It was business as usual again in the Mos Eisley cantina.

The Wookiee followed Ben over to Luke. Ben reached down for Luke's hand to help him up from the floor. Luke said, "I'm all right."

Ben nodded at the Wookiee and said to Luke, "Chewbacca here is first mate on a ship that might suit us."

Luke tilted his head back to look up at the Wookiee. *He's definitely more than 2.25 meters.*

*   *   *

Outside the cantina, R2-D2 and C-3PO were standing near Luke's parked landspeeder when they saw the stormtrooper squad marching up the street. Then they saw a man walk quickly out of the cantina. The man stopped the stormtroopers and began talking to the squad leader. The man was very animated, and he kept pointing at the cantina as he described the fight he'd just seen.

C-3PO moved closer to R2-D2 and said, "I don't like the look of this."

Inside the cantina, Chewbacca had guided Ben and Luke to a booth that had a circular table with a cylindrical light at its center. The booth was against the wall opposite the band, so they would be able to converse without shouting. The booth also offered a clear view of the entry lobby. Chewbacca sat with his back to the wall so he could watch the entry. Ben and Luke sat with their backs to the bar and faced Chewbacca.

They were soon joined by a tall, lean man with dark hair who wore a white shirt with a black vest, pants, and boots. As he moved past the table, Luke noticed the man had a blaster pistol in a quick-draw holster against his right thigh.

The man sat down beside Chewbacca and introduced himself. "Han Solo. I'm captain of the *Millennium Falcon*. Chewie here tells me you're looking for passage to the Alderaan system."

"Yes, indeed," Ben said. "If it's a fast ship."

"Fast ship?" Han said, sounding a bit insulted. "You've never heard of the *Millennium Falcon*?"

Ben asked, "Should I have?"

Han bragged, "It's the ship that made the Kessel run in less than twelve parsecs!"

Ben was not impressed with what he heard as obvious misinformation, and gave Han a look that said so.

Han continued, "I've outrun Imperial starships, not the local bulk cruisers, mind you. I'm talking about the big Corellian ships now. She's fast enough for you, old man. What's the cargo?"

"Only passengers," Ben said. "Myself, the boy, two droids, and no questions asked."

Han grinned. "What is it? Some kind of local trouble?"

Ben said, "Let's just say we'd like to avoid any Imperial entanglements."

Han let that hang in the air for a moment, then said, "Well, that's the real trick, isn't it? And it's going to cost you something extra." He glanced at Luke. "Ten thousand, all in advance."

"Ten thousand?" Luke gasped. "We could almost buy our own ship for that!"

Han lifted his eyebrows. "But who's going to fly it, kid? You?"

"You bet I could," Luke said angrily. "I'm not such

a bad pilot myself!" He looked to Ben and started to rise. "We don't have to sit here and listen —"

Ben touched Luke's arm, urging him to remain seated. Then he returned his gaze to Solo and said, "We can pay you two thousand now, plus fifteen when we reach Alderaan."

Han did the math. "Seventeen, huh!" He thought about it for a few seconds, keeping his eyes on Ben and Luke, then said, "Okay. You guys got yourselves a ship. We'll leave as soon as you're ready. Docking Bay Ninety-four."

"Ninety-four," Ben repeated.

Han looked past Ben to the bar and said, "Looks like somebody's beginning to take an interest in your handiwork."

Luke glanced over his shoulder and saw that stormtroopers were talking to the bartender, who was pointing at their booth. The stormtroopers' squad leader said to the bartender, "All right, we'll check it out."

Cantina patrons stepped aside as the stormtroopers walked over to the booth that the bartender had indicated. But when the stormtroopers arrived at the booth, only Han and Chewbacca were seated at the circular table. The stormtroopers glanced at the man and Wookiee, then moved past.

When the stormtroopers were out of earshot, Han smiled at Chewbacca. "Seventeen thousand!" Han said. "Those guys must really be desperate. This could really save my neck. Get back to the ship and get her ready."

Chewbacca headed for the exit. Han stayed at the cantina to finish his drink and settle their tab.

Luke and Ben slipped out the cantina's back door. Ben raised his hood to cover his head as they walked away from the building and tried to lose themselves amidst the pedestrian traffic.

Ben said, "You'll have to sell your speeder."

"That's okay," Luke said. "I'm never coming back to this planet again."

Han Solo was stepping away from his booth at the cantina when he came face-to-face with a green-skinned Rodian aiming a blaster at him.

Speaking through his short trunk, the Rodian said, "Going somewhere, Solo?" The Rodian pushed the blaster's barrel against Han's chest, forcing him to move back to the booth.

"Yeah, Greedo," Han said as he took a seat so that his back was to the wall and the table was directly in front of him. "As a matter of fact, I was just going to see your boss. Tell Jabba that I've got his money."

"It's too late," Greedo said, after seating himself at the other side of the table. Keeping his blaster trained on Solo, he continued, "You should have paid him when you had the chance. Jabba's put a price on your head so large, every bounty hunter in the galaxy will be looking for you. I'm lucky I found you first."

"Yeah, but this time, I've got the money," Han said, slouching back to rest his left knee against the table.

"If you give it to me, I might forget I found you."

"I don't have it *with* me." Han appeared to notice something on the wall to his left, and casually reached up to pick at it with his left hand. This movement distracted the Rodian from noticing the slight shift of Han's other shoulder, as his right hand — below the table, unseen by Greedo — crept to his holstered blaster. Han continued, "Tell Jabba —"

"Jabba's through with you," Greedo interrupted. "He has no time for smugglers who drop their shipments at the first sign of an Imperial cruiser."

"Even *I* get boarded sometimes," Solo said as his right hand eased his blaster out of its holster. "Do you think I had a choice?"

"You can tell that to Jabba. He may only take your ship."

Han's expression became deadly serious. "Over my dead body."

"That's the idea." Greedo chuckled. "I've been looking forward to this for a long time."

"Yes, I'll bet you have."

No one at the bar saw what happened next, but all heads turned to Han's booth in response to a blinding flash of light and the loud report of blaster-fire. Cantina patrons and the bartender saw Han seated across from Greedo, a smoldering hole in the center of the table between them; the flash had come from the explosion of Greedo's blaster, its shattered remnants still clutched in his long-fingered hand. Greedo's blaster had been destroyed by the same laserbolt — fired by Han — that had torn up through the table. A few sharp-eyed beings also noticed a fresh scorch mark on the wall to the left of Solo's head, which indicated that Greedo might have squeezed off at least one shot. Before anyone could question the outcome of the blasterfight, Greedo's body slumped forward, collapsing dead upon the table's surface.

Some of the cantina's more monstrous patrons actually enjoyed the smell of fried Rodian.

Han rose from the table and holstered his blaster. As he walked past the bar, heading for the exit, he tossed some coins to the gaping bartender and said, "Sorry about the mess."

*   *   *

In the control room on the Death Star, Darth Vader and Grand Moff Tarkin conferred with Commander Tagge about the interrogation of the captured princess. Vader said, "Her resistance to the mind probe is considerable. It will be some time before we can extract any information from her."

Admiral Motti approached Tarkin and reported, "The final checkout is completed. All systems are operational. What course shall we set?"

Tarkin looked to Vader and said, "Perhaps she would respond to an alternative form of persuasion."

"What do you mean?" asked Vader.

Tarkin said, "I think it is time we demonstrated the full power of this station." He turned to Motti and commanded, "Set your course for Alderaan."

Motti smiled evilly as he answered, "With pleasure."

"Lock the door, Artoo," C-3PO said. The two droids were standing in an open doorway in an alleyway near the Mos Eisley cantina. They'd been waiting for Luke and Ben to return from the speeder dealer and had ducked into the doorway to avoid being seen by an approaching group of stormtroopers.

R2-D2 extended his manipulator arm to the door's locking mechanism and gave it a twist. The door slid shut just in time.

An Imperial Mark IV patrol droid hovered up the alley, preceding the stormtroopers. The stormtrooper squad leader said, "All right, check this side of the street." After another trooper checked the door that concealed the two droids, the squad leader said, "The door's locked. Move on to the next one." The stormtroopers followed the patrol droid deeper into the alley.

R2-D2 opened the door and C-3PO peeked out.

The golden droid said, "I would much rather have gone with Master Luke than stay here with you. I don't know what all this trouble is about, but I'm sure it must be your fault."

R2-D2 answered with a beeped expletive that only another droid would understand.

"You watch your language!" cried the offended C-3PO.

Facing the speeder dealer, Luke said, "All right, give it to me, I'll take it." The speeder dealer, an insectoid alien, had finally agreed to buy Luke's cherished landspeeder for two thousand credits.

Luke turned to Ben and showed him the credits. "Look at this," Luke said with dismay as they headed back for the droids. Luke had expected to get a few hundred more. He griped, "Ever since the XP-38 came out, they just aren't in demand."

"It will be enough," Ben told him.

As Ben and Luke proceeded through Mos Eisley's back alleys, they were followed by a Kubaz, an alien with a short, prehensile trunk for a nose. The Kubaz wore protective goggles and a dark cloak, and worked as an information dealer and spy for hire. One of his current clients was an Imperial stormtrooper squad leader.

The Kubaz didn't let Ben and Luke out of his sight.

*　　　*　　　*

A short walk from the Mos Eisley cantina, Docking Bay 94 was a large circular pit that had been excavated from the sandy bedrock and reinforced with duracrete. It had an open roof, high surrounding walls, and was barely large enough to contain the YT-1300 Corellian freighter that rested on its floor. The freighter was Han Solo's ship, the *Millennium Falcon*.

Several figures moved around under the *Falcon*'s hull. Most of the figures carried blasters but one didn't. He was a Hutt, a corpulent sluglike alien with a bulbous, wide-mouthed head and a tapering, muscular tail. He happened to be the most powerful crimelord in the Tatooine system, and all the other figures in the docking bay worked for him. Until very recently, he had also employed a hit man named Greedo. The gangster's name was Jabba.

"Solo," Jabba bellowed in Huttese at the *Falcon*. "Come out of there, Solo!"

"Right here, Jabba," Han called from behind the Hutt.

Jabba twisted his bulky form to see Solo and Chewbacca enter the docking bay from the passage that led up to the street. Chewbacca was casually carrying his bowcaster.

Grinning at Jabba, Solo said, "I've been waiting for you."

"Have you now?" Jabba replied.

Han sauntered forward and said, "You didn't think I was gonna run, did you?"

"Han, my boy, you disappoint me," Jabba observed. "Why haven't you paid me? Why did you fry poor Greedo?"

"Look, Jabba, next time you want to talk to me, come see me yourself. Don't send one of these twerps." Han gestured at Jabba's blaster-wielding henchmen, including a man who wore a head-concealing helmet and antique body armor: a notoriously dangerous bounty hunter named Boba Fett.

"Han, I can't make exceptions." Jabba shrugged. "What if everyone who smuggled for me dropped their cargo at the first sign of an Imperial starship? It's not good for business."

"Look, Jabba, even I get boarded sometimes. You think I had a choice? I got a nice easy charter now. Pay you back plus a little extra. I just need a little more time."

Jabba said, "Han, my boy, you're the best. So, for an extra twenty percent . . ."

"Fifteen, Jabba," Han said testily. "Don't push it."

"Okay, fifteen percent," Jabba agreed. "But if you fail me again, I'll put a price on your head so big, you won't be able to go near a civilized system."

Turning to the *Falcon*'s landing ramp, Han added, "Jabba, you're a wonderful human being." Chewbacca followed Solo into the *Falcon*.

Jabba glared at his hired thugs and said, "Come on," then turned and slithered out of the docking bay.

Ben muttered, "If the ship's as fast as he's boasting, we ought to do well." He was walking alongside Luke through an alleyway that led to Docking Bay 94. They had just recovered C-3PO and R2-D2 from their hiding place, and the droids now followed in their tracks.

They rounded a corner and found Chewbacca standing in the docking bay entrance. He looked restless, and they wasted no time following him through the doorway.

Across from Docking Bay 94, on the other side of the alley, the Kubaz spy watched from the shadows. After the droids had passed through the docking bay entrance, the Kubaz lifted a comlink to his face and summoned the stormtroopers.

Ben, Luke, and the droids followed Chewbacca down a flight of steps to the docking bay floor. When they arrived before the *Millennium Falcon,* they stopped and stared at the ship while Chewbacca headed up the ship's landing ramp.

Luke couldn't believe his eyes. The cockpit that projected out from the starboard side and the long forward mandibles made the *Falcon* recognizable as an old Corellian freighter, but the entire ship appeared to have been slapped together from used or rejected parts. To add further insult to the original design, a ridiculously oversized sensor dish was affixed to the top. The sight made Luke suddenly reconsider how he and Ben had invested their money.

Han was standing below the *Falcon*'s hull, checking the umbilicals connection as he topped off the fuel tanks. Not caring whether Han could hear him, Luke commented, "What a piece of junk."

Han heard, but he'd heard worse and didn't care. "She'll make point five past lightspeed," he said, stepping away from the umbilicals. "She may not look like much, but she's got it where it counts, kid." With pride, he added, "I've made a lot of special modifications myself. But we're a little rushed, so if you'll just get on board, we'll get out of here."

The droids followed Ben and Luke to the *Falcon*'s landing ramp. As C-3PO passed Han, he said, "Hello, sir."

Han looked away and shook his head. He didn't care much for overly polite droids.

At the top of the landing ramp, Ben, Luke, and the droids turned left through a passage tube. They passed a connecting passage tube that led to the cockpit, where Chewbacca was preparing the ship for liftoff, and arrived in the main hold. In a corner to the right, a three-passenger seat wrapped around a circular holographic game board. On the left, there was an engineering station with numerous scopes and controls, some of which appeared to have been secured with tape and glue. Most of the wall and ceiling panels were missing, leaving wires and machinery exposed.

Luke's initial reaction was that the *Falcon* looked even worse on the inside, and he didn't feel any better when he gave the engineering station a closer inspection. *These are Han's special modifications? I've never seen half of these components, and the ones I recognize aren't even compatible with one another. I'll be amazed if this thing even gets off the ground!*

The stormtrooper squad found the Kubaz spy waiting for them outside Docking Bay 94. The squad leader stopped in front of the Kubaz and said, "Which way?"

The spy pointed to the docking bay entrance.

"All right, men," commanded the squad leader. "Load your weapons!" Then the seven stormtroopers descended the steps that led to the docking bay floor.

Han was under the *Falcon*, disconnecting the umbilicals, when he saw the stormtrooper squad charge into the docking bay. One of the troopers shouted, "Stop that ship!"

Three troopers immediately opened fire. Han snapped his blaster from his holster and shot back at the troopers.

"Blast 'em!" ordered the stormtrooper squad leader.

Han aimed high to hit the duracrete ceiling above the troopers' heads. His fired bolts struck the ceiling with explosive force, sending large chunks of duracrete down upon the astonished soldiers. Han didn't stop firing until he was halfway up the landing ramp.

"Chewie, get us out of here!" Han shouted as he sealed the ramp's access hatch and bolted to the cockpit. The engines kicked on and the entire ship trembled in response.

In the main hold, R2-D2 used his magnagrips to secure himself to the deck while Luke, Ben, and C-3PO belted into the seat that wrapped around the game table. C-3PO cried, "Oh, my, I'd forgotten how much I hate space travel."

The stormtroopers continued firing as the *Falcon* — without the benefit of liftoff clearance from the spaceport authority — thrust up through the open roof of the docking bay. On a nearby street in Mos Eisley, another stormtrooper squad heard the roar of the *Falcon*'s engines. The troopers turned in time to glimpse the fleeing ship's sub-light drive exhaust blaze with intense light. The ship ascended rapidly into the pale blue sky.

As Chewbacca guided the *Falcon* up through Tatooine's atmosphere and into space, he pointed to the radar scope and barked at Han. Han glanced at the scope and said, "Looks like an Imperial cruiser. Our passengers must be hotter than I thought. Try and hold them off. Angle the deflector shield while I make the calculations for the jump to lightspeed."

Han rose from his seat to flip a series of control switches. He was still making his calculations when he jumped back into his seat. He saw two larger blips appear on the radar screen. According to the readout, each blip was an Imperial Star Destroyer.

"Stay sharp!" Han told Chewbacca. "There are two more coming in; they're going to try to cut us off."

Just then, Luke and Ben rushed into the cockpit and clung to the two seats behind Han and Chewbacca. They had heard Han's announcement regarding the incoming ships, and saw a clear field of stars beyond the cockpit window. Luke asked, "Why don't you outrun them? I thought you said this thing was fast."

Han tossed a glare at Luke and said, "Watch your mouth, kid, or you're going to find yourself floating home. We'll be safe enough once we make the jump to hyperspace. Besides, I know a few maneuvers. We'll lose them!"

The Star Destroyers fired at the *Falcon* and a

bright flash exploded outside the cockpit. Another volley of laserfire pounded the *Falcon*'s deflector shields, causing the ship to rock violently. Han grinned as he tightened his grip on the controls and said, "Here's where the fun begins!"

Ben said, "How long before you can make the jump to lightspeed?"

Han told him, "It'll take a few moments to get the coordinates from the nav computer." The *Falcon* shook again as its shields took another hit.

"Are you kidding?" Luke couldn't believe it. "At the rate they're gaining . . ."

"Traveling through hyperspace isn't like dusting crops, boy!" Han snapped. "Without precise calculations we could fly right through a star or bounce too close to a supernova and that'd end your trip real quick, wouldn't it?"

A red warning light activated in front of Chewbacca. Luke extended his arm to point at the light and asked, "What's that flashing?"

"We're losing our deflector shield," Han said, slapping Luke's hand away. "Go strap yourselves in. I'm going to make the jump to lightspeed."

Luke and Ben left the cockpit and returned to the hold. Han reached for the hyperdrive controls and threw the ignition switch.

Suddenly, the field of distant stars was transformed into long streaks of light that radiated from infinity and appeared to sweep over the ship. The *Falcon* had entered hyperspace, a dimension of space-time that allowed faster-than-light travel across the galaxy. And because it was impossible to follow a ship through hyperspace, the *Falcon* had effectively escaped the two Star Destroyers.

But as fast as the *Millennium Falcon* could travel, the little astromech droid would never be delivered to the planet Alderaan.

"We've entered the Alderaan system," Admiral Motti announced to Grand Moff Tarkin. They were in the control room on the Death Star. Tarkin stood before a wide viewscreen that displayed a small green planet. At the sound of approaching footsteps, Tarkin and Mott turned to face an adjoining corridor.

Two black-uniformed Imperial soldiers led Princess Leia through the corridor and into the control room. A pair of binders secured Leia's wrists in front of her. Behind Leia, Darth Vader followed like a malevolent shadow.

"Governor Tarkin," Leia said. "I should have expected to find you holding Vader's leash. I recognized your foul stench when I was brought on board."

Tarkin smiled. "Charming to the last." He reached out to touch Leia's chin and said, "You don't know how hard I found it signing the order to terminate your life!"

Leia jerked her head away from Tarkin's hand and said, "I'm surprised you had the courage to take the responsibility yourself!"

Tarkin said, "Princess Leia, before your execution I would like you to be my guest at a ceremony that will make this battle station operational. No star system will dare oppose the Emperor now."

If Leia was even slightly frightened, she didn't show it. She said, "The more you tighten your grip, Tarkin, the more star systems will slip through your fingers."

"Not after we demonstrate the power of this station," Tarkin informed her with confidence. "In a way, you have determined the choice of the planet that will be destroyed first. Since you are reluctant to provide us with the location of the Rebel base, I have chosen to test this station's destructive power . . . on your home planet of Alderaan." He gestured to the viewport.

At the sight of her homeworld, Leia's confident expression became suddenly fearful. "No!" she protested. "Alderaan is peaceful. We have no weapons. You can't possibly —"

"You would prefer another target?" Tarkin interrupted. "A military target? Then name the system!"

Leia thought, *He's insane. He's completely insane.*

Tarkin continued, "I grow tired of asking this. So it'll be the last time." He advanced toward Leia, forcing her to step backward into Vader. "Where is the Rebel base?"

Leia trembled against Vader. *There are billions of people on Alderaan! What can I do to save them?* She gazed past Tarkin's shoulder to look again at Alderaan on the viewport. "Dantooine," she said, then lowered her head. "They're on Dantooine."

"There," Tarkin said with satisfaction. "You see, Lord Vader, she can be reasonable." Then Tarkin turned to Admiral Motti and said, "Continue with the operation. You may fire when ready."

"What?" Leia gasped as Motti stepped away to a control console.

"You're far too trusting," Tarkin said. "Dantooine is too remote to make an effective demonstration. But don't worry. We will deal with your Rebel friends soon enough."

Leia stepped toward Tarkin and cried, "No!" Then she felt Vader's cold, tight grip on her arm, pulling her back to him and away from Tarkin.

An intercom voice announced, "Commence primary ignition."

Leia heard the sounds of generators powering up, but kept her stunned eyes on the viewscreen. Even from space, Alderaan was lushly beautiful, its grassy plains making the world resemble an emerald amidst the stars. Before Leia became a Senator, she had spent most of her youth on the green world. She knew its geography so well that she could — from her perspective on the Death Star — pinpoint the capital, Aldera, where she'd grown up . . . where her father still lived. She wondered what time it was, if he was in their home right now.

Father, I'm so sorry.

Leia couldn't believe that all her friends and loved ones, every person and every cherished place was about to be annihilated. And all because no one had opposed the Empire before the construction of the Death Star. Even as she saw the space station's green laser beam streak out at her homeworld, Leia prayed for the Death Star to fail.

But it didn't. And in one explosive instant, Alderaan was gone.

Luke was in the *Millennium Falcon*'s hold, testing his lightsaber against a small, hovering remote target globe when Ben suddenly turned away and sat down near the engineering station. Seeing that Ben seemed almost faint, Luke switched off his lightsaber and asked, "Are you all right? What's wrong?"

"I felt a great disturbance in the Force," Ben said. "As if millions of voices suddenly cried out in terror and were suddenly silenced. I fear something terrible has happened." He rubbed his eyes. Not wanting to worry Luke, he added, "You'd better get on with your exercises."

Luke nodded and turned away from Ben. He glanced to the corner seat, where Chewbacca and R2-D2 were competing at the holographic game table, with C-3PO serving as referee.

Luke stepped back to the center of the hold, activated his lightsaber, and returned his attention to the hovering remote. Ben had rightly assumed that Han kept a remote on board for quick-draw target practice, and had programmed the device to fire harmless sting bursts for Luke to deflect with his lightsaber. Luke kept his eyes on the remote and batted at two fired bursts as Han Solo entered the hold.

"Well, you can forget your troubles with those Imperial ships," Han said as he took a seat at the engineering station. "I told you I'd outrun 'em."

Han looked around the hold. Luke continued swinging his lightsaber at sting bursts from the remote. Chewie and the droids continued playing their game. Ben looked like he had a headache.

Han grumbled, "Don't everybody thank me at once. Anyway, we should be at Alderaan at about oh two hundred hours."

Han looked back to the action at the game table. From the holographic creatures that appeared to stand upon the table's gold-and-green-checkered patterned surface, Han could see Chewbacca and

R2-D2 were playing dejarik. R2-D2 moved a multi-legged blue houjix. Chewbacca countered by sending his Kintan Strider — a yellow-skinned biped that carried a club — two steps across the table. Han thought Chewie looked pleased with himself.

C-3PO said, "Now be careful, Artoo."

R2-D2 moved his Mantellian savrip — a hunched-over creature with a snakelike neck and long, powerful arms — over to Chewbacca's just-moved Kintan Strider. The savrip seized the Kintan Strider, hoisted it up, then smashed it down upon the gametable.

Chewbacca growled angrily at R2-D2.

"He made a fair move," C-3PO observed in response. "Screaming about it can't help you."

Han said, "Let him have it. It's not wise to upset a Wookiee."

Turning to face Han, C-3PO said indignantly, "But sir, nobody worries about upsetting a droid."

Han grinned. "That's because a droid don't pull people's arms out of their sockets when they lose. Wookiees are known to do that."

C-3PO looked at Chewbacca, who raised his arms and cupped his hands behind his head, flexing his hirsute muscles. C-3PO turned back to Han and said, "I see your point, sir." Leaning over to R2-D2, C-3PO advised, "I suggest a new strategy, Artoo-Detoo. Let the Wookiee win."

R2-D2 answered with a surprised beep. Chewbacca chortled happily.

When Ben felt somewhat recovered, he resumed watching Luke's practice with the remote. Luke's eyes followed the remote with intense concentration, but his movements were stiff, not relaxed. Ben said, "Remember, a Jedi can feel the Force flowing through him."

Luke said, "You mean it controls your actions?"

"Partially," Ben said. "But it also obeys your commands."

The remote hovered in a wide arc around Luke, then made a lightning-swift lunge and emitted a laser beam. At the engineering station, Han looked up just in time to see the beam strike Luke's leg.

Han laughed. "Hokey religions and ancient weapons are no match for a good blaster at your side, kid."

Luke deactivated his lightsaber and glared at Han. "You don't believe in the Force, do you?"

Han shook his head. "Kid, I've flown from one side of this galaxy to the other. I've seen a lot of strange stuff, but I've never seen anything to make me believe there's one all-powerful force controlling everything. There's no mystical energy field that controls my destiny."

Ben smiled quietly at Han's comment.

Han continued, "It's all a lot of simple tricks and nonsense."

Ben rose from his seat. "I suggest you try it again, Luke," he said, picking up a blast shield helmet from the engineering station. He placed the helmet over Luke's head and lowered the shield so it covered Luke's eyes. "This time, let go of your conscious self and act on instinct."

Luke laughed. "With the blast shield down, I can't even see. How am I supposed to fight?"

"Your eyes can deceive you," Ben said. "Don't trust them."

Luke activated his lightsaber and assumed a ready stance. The remote hovered up and moved around his body. *Don't trust my eyes? I can barely* hear *the remote! I think it's on my left. . . . No, it's . . .*

Luke was stung by another laserbolt.

. . . it's not where I thought it was.

Ben said, "Stretch out with your feelings."

Keeping the helmet on and his blade activated, Luke resumed a ready stance. He stopped thinking about the remote, just stopped thinking and relaxed, and . . . somehow, he sensed the remote's proximity. Stranger still, he seemed able to anticipate its movement through the air.

The remote fired three bursts in quick succession. Despite his blocked vision, Luke moved fast with his lightsaber and deftly parried each shot.

He switched off his lightsaber and pulled off the helmet. Ben sounded glad when he said, "You see, you can do it."

Han said, "I call it luck."

Ben replied, "In my experience, there is no such thing as luck."

Han would not be convinced. "Look, good against remotes is one thing. Good against the living? That's something else." A light flashed on a scope at the engineering station. "Looks like we're coming up on Alderaan."

Han rose from his seat and headed out of the hold to the cockpit. Chewbacca followed him.

Facing Ben, Luke said, "You know, I did feel something. I could almost see the remote."

"That's good," Ben told his new pupil, placing a hand on Luke's shoulder. "You have taken your first step into a larger world."

On the Death Star, Imperial Officer Cass, a white-haired adjutant to Grand Moff Tarkin, entered the conference room. He found Darth Vader standing at one end of the round table at the room's center, with Tarkin seated across from him at the other end. Tarkin looked up from the table's data screen and said, "Yes."

"Our scout ships have reached Dantooine," Officer Cass reported. "They found the remains of a Rebel base, but they estimate that it has been deserted for some time. They are now conducting an extensive search of the surrounding systems." Having delivered his report, Cass turned and exited the room.

"She lied!" Tarkin was outraged, rising from the table to approach Vader. "She lied to us!"

Indeed, that was just what Princess Leia had done. Vader said, "I told you she would never consciously betray the Rebellion."

Tarkin scowled at Vader. "Terminate her . . . immediately!"

Blue-and-white shimmers of energy flowed past the *Falcon* as it neared the end of its trip through hyperspace. Han and Chewbacca were seated in the cockpit. Han said, "Stand by, Chewie. Here we go." He threw a lever to kill the hyperdrive, then added, "Cut in the sub-light engines."

The *Falcon* decelerated and dropped into realspace. The energy shimmers that had been visible outside the cockpit window were replaced by a field of distant stars, along with an immediate barrage of unexpected debris.

"What the . . . ?" Han said as floating chunks of matter hammered at the *Falcon*'s particle shields. "Aw, we've come out of hyperspace into a meteor shower. Some kind of asteroid collision. It's not on any of the charts."

Responding to the hammering racket outside the ship, Luke and Ben entered the cockpit. Luke stood behind Chewbacca's seat and asked, "What's going on?"

Han explained, "Our position is correct, except . . . no Alderaan!"

"What do you mean?" Luke didn't understand. "Where is it?"

"That's what I'm trying to tell you, kid. It ain't there. It's been totally blown away."

"What? How?"

From behind Chewbacca, Ben said, "Destroyed . . . by the Empire!"

Han was doubtful. "The entire starfleet couldn't destroy the whole planet. It'd take a thousand ships with more firepower than I've —" An alarm sounded and Han glanced at a sensor scope. "There's another ship coming in."

Luke said, "Maybe they know what happened."

Without yet seeing the other ship, Ben said, "It's an Imperial fighter."

As if in response to Ben's words, a huge explosion burst outside the cockpit window, then an Imperial TIE fighter streaked past the *Falcon*. The Twin Ion Engine ship was immediately recognizable by its two hexagonal solar array wings on either side of a small, spherical command pod.

Luke said, "It followed us!"

"No," Ben observed. "It's a short-range fighter."

Han said, "There aren't any bases around here. Where did it come from?"

"It sure is leaving in a big hurry," Luke noticed as the TIE fighter sped away from the *Falcon*. "If they identify us, we're in big trouble."

"Not if I can help it," Han said, steering after the TIE fighter and away from the planetary debris. "Chewie — jam its transmissions."

"It'd be as well to let it go," Ben said. "It's too far out of range."

"Not for long . . ." Han increased power to the sub-light engines.

Ben said, "A fighter that size couldn't get this deep into space on its own."

Luke added, "Then he must have gotten lost, been part of a convoy, or something. . . ."

Han said, "Well, he ain't going to be around long enough to tell anybody about us."

"Look at him," Luke said. "He's heading for that small moon."

Han saw the moon too, and said, "I think I can get him before he gets there . . . he's almost in range."

Ben went rigid in his seat. "That's no moon! It's a space station."

Han replied, "It's too big to be a space station." But even before he'd finished, Han sounded doubtful of his own words. Like the others in the cockpit, he could now make out surface details on the object in view, and the details had an unnatural symmetry.

Luke said, "I have a very bad feeling about this."

"Turn the ship around!" Ben insisted.

"Yeah," Han agreed. "I think you're right. Full reverse! Chewie, lock in the auxiliary power."

Chewbacca did as instructed, but the *Falcon* began to shake violently and continued to travel after the TIE fighter and toward the object, which was now clearly visible as a space station.

"Chewie, lock in the auxiliary power," Han repeated, shouting over the noise of the shaking ship.

Hanging on to his seat, Luke said, "Why are we still moving toward it?"

"We're caught in a tractor beam!" Han explained. "It's pulling us in."

Tractor beams were modified force fields that immobilized objects and moved them within the range of the beam projector. Hangar bays and spaceports generally used tractor beams to help guide ships to safe landings, but the beams could also be used to capture enemy ships. And in this case, it seemed the *Falcon* was someone's enemy.

The *Falcon's* engines and deflector shields were ineffective for escape. By attempting to send the ship into full reverse, Han was only producing friction within the tractor beam, hence the shaking. The tractor beam also immobilized the *Falcon's* weapons, rendering them useless; any attempt to fire at the space station would likely cause the weapons themselves to blow up.

Luke said, "There's gotta be something you can do!"

"There's nothin' I can do about it, kid," Han said. "I'm in full power. I'm going to have to shut down. But they're not going to get me without a fight!" Han powered down the engines and the *Falcon* stopped shaking.

"You can't win," Ben told Han. "But there are alternatives to fighting."

Luke couldn't imagine what Ben had in mind, but he hoped the plan didn't require much time. At the speed the *Falcon* was traveling toward the space station, time was something they just didn't have.

The tractor beam pulled the *Millennium Falcon* straight toward the Death Star's equatorial trench. Along the trench's walls, laser turret cannons tracked the captured ship as it was drawn toward a docking bay. Because of the space station's enormous size, the docking bay — from a distance — resembled little more than a small slot that neighbored other slots within the trench. The bay was without visible doors and its interior appeared to be exposed to the vacuum of space, an illusion created by a transparent magnetic field that shielded and contained the docking bay's pressurized atmosphere.

Over an Imperial intercom, a voice announced, "Clear Bay Three-twenty-seven. We are opening the magnetic field." The field opened, allowing the *Falcon* to pass through the slotlike doorway and hover into Docking Bay 327, a wide hangar with a gleaming black deck. After the tractor beam safely deposited the *Falcon* on the deck beside a deep elevator well, the Imperial soldiers prepared to enter the docking bay.

"To your stations!" a black-uniformed Imperial officer commanded a group of stormtroopers in a chamber that adjoined the hangar. The officer turned to another officer and said, "Come with me."

The stormtroopers quickly took up position around the captured Corellian freighter. An officer ordered, "Close all outboard shields! Close all outboard shields!"

Grand Moff Tarkin and Darth Vader were still in the conference room when an intercom buzzed. Tarkin pushed a button and said, "Yes."

From the intercom, an Imperial officer announced, "We've captured a freighter entering the remains of the Alderaan system. Its markings match those of a ship that blasted its way out of Mos Eisley."

Vader said, "They must be trying to return the stolen plans to the princess. She may yet be of some use to us."

After Vader was informed of the captured freighter's location, he swept out of the conference room and headed for Docking Bay 327.

As Darth Vader entered the hangar that contained the *Millennium Falcon,* a voice over the intercom said,

"Unlock one, five, seven, and nine. Release charges." Vader walked past the elevator well and the stormtroopers who stood guard on the hangar floor, and approached the *Falcon*'s lowered landing ramp.

A gray-uniformed Imperial captain and a pair of stormtroopers stepped down the landing ramp. The captain stopped in front of Vader and said, "There's no one on board, sir. According to the log, the crew abandoned ship right after takeoff. It must be a decoy, sir. Several of the escape pods have been jettisoned."

Vader said, "Did you find any droids?"

"No, sir," the captain reported. "If there were any on board, they must also have been jettisoned."

"Send a scanning crew aboard," Vader ordered. "I want every part of the ship checked."

"Yes, sir."

Vader looked up at the ship's hull and said, "I sense something . . . a presence I've not felt since . . ."

Then it hit him.

Obi-Wan Kenobi.

He's alive.

Trusting the ship would be thoroughly checked, Vader turned fast and headed back to the conference room.

The Imperial captain turned to a stormtrooper and said, "Get me a scanning crew in here on the double. I want every part of this ship checked!"

*   *   *

While waiting for the scanning crew to arrive, two blaster-wielding stormtroopers walked in opposite directions through the *Falcon*'s passage tubes to reconnoiter the holds and cargo compartments. When the two stormtroopers reunited at the top of the landing ramp, they exited the ship satisfied that no passengers remained on board.

But inside the *Falcon,* a floor panel popped up from the passage tube; Luke and Han emerged from their hiding place, a large compartment under the floor. Han had his blaster pistol out and ready.

Luke said, "Boy, it's lucky you had these compartments."

"I use them for smuggling," Han explained. "I never thought I'd be smuggling myself in them."

Near Han and Luke, another floor panel slid back to reveal Ben hiding in the same compartment. Ben moved slowly, careful not to bump into the two droids who were squeezed in beneath him.

"This is ridiculous," Han said. "Even if I could take off, I'd never get past the tractor beam."

"Leave that to me!" Ben said.

"Damn fool," Han muttered as he lifted himself up to sit at the edge of the compartment. "I *knew* you were going to say that!"

Ben said dryly, "Who's the more foolish — the fool or the fool who follows him?"

Chewbacca raised his furry head up between Luke and Han. The Wookiee moaned with displeasure at the way he'd had to cram his large body into the compartment. Sympathetic, Han reached down and patted Chewbacca's head.

The scanning crew consisted of two gray-uniformed men with a large box of equipment. When they arrived in the hangar, two stormtrooper squads were on guard outside the *Falcon*. A stormtrooper squad leader approached the scanning crew and said, "The ship's all yours. If the scanners pick up anything, report it immediately." Then the squad leader turned to the other troopers and said, "All right, let's go."

Two remained stationed at the bottom of the *Falcon*'s landing ramp while the other troopers filed out of the hangar. A moment after the scanning crew carried their equipment box up the ramp, there was a loud crashing sound from inside the ship. Both stormtroopers assumed the scanning crew had dropped the large box.

"Hey down there!" a man's voice called from inside the *Falcon*. "Could you give us a hand with this?"

The two stormtroopers glanced at each other, then marched up the landing ramp. They had no idea that the scanning crew had already been knocked out, and that it had been the *Falcon*'s captain who'd summoned them into the ship.

Han fired his blaster pistol twice. The stormtroopers never knew what hit them.

In the command office that overlooked Docking Bay 327, a black-uniformed gantry officer noticed the two stormtrooper guards were missing from their stations at the captured ship's landing ramp. He stepped to a comm console, flipped on the comlink, and said, "TK-four-two-one. Why aren't you at your post? TK-four-two-one, do you copy?"

When no answer came, the officer stepped away from the console to a window and peered through it, looking down at the freighter on the hangar deck. A single stormtrooper stepped down the landing ramp, then stopped and looked up in the direction of the command office window. The stormtrooper tapped at the side of his helmet.

The gantry officer turned to his aide, who was seated before a wide control console, and said, "Take over. We've got a bad transmitter. I'll see what I can do."

The gantry officer walked to a closed doorway. He pressed a button, and the door slid up into the ceiling. The officer had expected to see an empty corridor that led to a lift tube that would carry him down to the hangar. To his astonishment, a hulking Wookiee filled the doorway with a stormtrooper at his side.

The Wookiee roared and lashed out at the officer, launching him across the room to smash into a row of barrel-shaped containers. The officer's aide spun in his seat and reached for his blaster, but the stormtrooper beside the Wookiee aimed his own blaster rifle at the aide and fired first. The energy charge slammed into the aide's chest, and he collapsed to the office floor.

The stormtrooper was Han in disguise. He pulled off his helmet as he and Chewbacca led Ben and the droids into the command office.

Luke, also disguised as a stormtrooper, had left the hangar deck quickly and came trotting up the corridor behind them. He had a hard time moving in his appropriated armor because he was slightly shorter than the average trooper. Entering the command office, he shut the door behind him, then pulled off his white helmet and glared at Han. "You know, between his howling and your blasting everything in sight, it's a wonder the whole station doesn't know we're here."

"Bring them on!" Han said. "I prefer a straight fight to all this sneaking around."

The droids had moved over beside the aide's vacated seat at the control console. Turning to Luke, C-3PO said, "We found the computer outlet, sir."

Ben said, "Plug in. He should be able to interpret the entire Imperial network."

R2-D2 extended a manipulator arm into the computer outlet and beeped to C-3PO, who translated, "He says he's found the main controls to the power beam that's holding the ship here. He'll try to make the precise location appear on the monitor."

Everyone looked to a small viewscreen that displayed a series of green-colored readouts. R2-D2 beeped again. C-3PO said, "The tractor beam is coupled to the main reactor in seven locations. A power loss at one of the terminals will allow the ship to leave."

Ben studied the schematics for the power generator terminal that was displayed on the viewscreen, then turned to Luke and Han and said, "I don't think you boys can help. I must go alone."

"Whatever you say," Han replied as Ben headed for the door. "I've done more than I bargained for on this trip already."

Luke stopped Ben at the door and said, "I want to go with you."

"Be patient, Luke," Ben said. "Stay and watch over the droids."

Luke gestured at Han and said, "But he can —"

Ben interrupted, "They must be delivered safely or other star systems will suffer the same fate as Alderaan. Your destiny lies along a different path from mine." Ben pressed a button on the doorway, sending the door up into the ceiling. Facing Luke, he added, "The Force will be with you . . . always!"

Ben left the command office and moved down the corridor. Luke watched Ben's departing form, then reluctantly pressed the button and sealed the doorway.

Chewbacca tilted back his head and barked.

"Boy, you said it, Chewie," Han agreed. Looking to Luke, he added, "Where did you dig up that old fossil?"

"Ben is a great man," Luke said defensively.

"Yeah," Han said, "great at getting us into trouble."

"I didn't hear you give any ideas . . ."

"Well, anything's better than just hanging around waiting for them to pick us up."

"Who do you think —"

The argument was interrupted by R2-D2, who was still plugged into the computer socket and suddenly began to whistle and beep a blue streak.

Luke turned to the droids and asked, "What is it?"

"I'm afraid I'm not quite sure, sir," C-3PO said. "He says 'I found her' and keeps repeating 'She's here.'"

Dumbfounded, Luke stepped over to the droids. "Well, who . . . who has he found?"

"Princess Leia."

"The princess?" Luke said, his eyes wide with surprise. "She's here?"

"Princess?" Han echoed from beside Chewbacca on the other side of the command office. Neither of them had heard anything about a princess.

Luke asked, "Where . . . where is she?"

"Princess?" Han repeated. "What's going on?"

R2-D2 made whirring and clicking sounds as he scanned the computer, then beeped to C-3PO.

C-3PO translated, "Level five. Detention block AA-twenty-three."

But R2-D2 wasn't finished, and emitted more beeps.

The protocol droid's voice filled with concern as he reported, "I'm afraid she's scheduled to be terminated."

"Oh, no!" Luke exclaimed. "We've got to do something."

"What are you talking about?" Han asked.

"The droids belonged to her," Luke replied. "She's the one in the message. We've got to help her."

Han and Chewbacca had never heard anything about a message either. Han warned, "No, look, don't get any funny ideas. The old man wants us to wait right here."

"But he didn't know she was here," Luke pointed out. Turning back to R2-D2, he said, "Look, will you just find a way back into that detention block?"

Han sat down and put his feet up on the console. "I'm not going anywhere," he said.

"They're going to execute her," Luke said. "Look, a

few minutes ago you said you didn't want to just wait here to be captured. Now all you want to do is stay."

"Marching into the detention area is not what I had in mind." Han wasn't budging from his seat.

"But they're going to kill her!"

"Better her than me."

I can't do this alone, Luke thought. *I've got to think of something — anything — that will convince Han to help.* Then he had it. Leaning down beside Han, he said, "She's rich."

That got Han's attention. He turned his head slightly. "Rich?"

Luke nodded. "Rich, powerful! Listen, if you were to rescue her, the reward would be . . ."

"What?"

"Well, more wealth than you can imagine."

"I don't know," Han said, "I can imagine quite a bit!"

"You'll get it!"

"I'd better!"

"You will."

"All right, kid," Han said, rising from his seat. "But you'd better be right about this!"

"All right," Luke responded. *Now we're getting somewhere!*

"What's your plan?"

Plan? Luke wondered how far he and Han might get in their stormtrooper disguises, then looked at

Chewbacca and had an idea. "Uh . . . Threepio, hand me those binders there, will you?"

The protocol droid picked up a pair of metal binders that happened to be lying on the control console and gave them to Luke.

"Okay." Luke held out the binders as he approached Chewbacca. "Now, I'm going to put these on you."

Chewbacca roared sharply and Luke stumbled backward. Luke handed the binders to Han and stammered, "Okay — Han, you . . . you put those on."

"Don't worry, Chewie," Han soothed as he carried the binders to the Wookiee. "I think I know what he has in mind."

Han placed the binders over the Wookiee's thick wrists but didn't lock them. Luke handed a small comlink transmitter over to C-3PO. Then Luke and Han picked up their helmets and headed for the door with Chewbacca.

"Er, Master Luke, sir!" C-3PO said nervously. "Pardon me for asking . . . but . . . what should Artoo-Detoo and I do if we're discovered here?"

"Lock the door!" Luke said.

"And hope they don't have blasters," Han added.

"That isn't very reassuring," C-3PO said, clapping his hand down upon R2-D2's domed head as the two men and the Wookiee left the room.

In their stormtrooper disguises, Luke and Han escorted Chewbacca through a Death Star corridor. There had been no getting around the fact that Luke looked suspiciously small for a stormtrooper, and the effect was worse when he stood next to Han. They'd agreed that Han would walk slightly ahead and to the right of Chewbacca while Luke would stay close to Chewbacca's left side. It was their hope that any casual passerby would notice the towering Wookiee, not the height of the stormtrooper beside him. This arrangement also was some relief to Luke, who was barely able to peer through the lenses of his oversized helmet. As he gripped the Wookiee's elbow, it may have looked like he was guiding a bound captive through the corridor, but in fact, Chewbacca was guiding him.

They were heading for a lift tube that would carry them to level five when Chewbacca saw a small

MSE-6 droid move toward them. The box-shaped droid traveled on four wheels and was used to deliver orders and documents. Chewbacca roared at the droid for no other reason than he felt like it. The droid shrieked and raced away from him. Chewbacca looked at the stormtrooper to his left — Luke — and barked with amusement.

They proceeded to a row of lift tubes, and passed troops, bureaucrats, and droids who were also walking through the corridor. As expected, only Chewbacca drew any stares.

As they waited for the lift tube doors to open, Luke muttered, "I can't see a thing in this helmet."

The lift opened and they stepped in. A gray-uniformed bureaucrat attempted to follow them in, but Han held up a cautioning hand to discourage him. The bureaucrat moved on to another lift.

The lift tube doors closed. Han pressed the button for level five and said, "This is not going to work."

"Why didn't you say so before?" Luke said.

"I *did* say so before!"

They'd been expecting the door to open in front of them, and were surprised when they heard it open from behind. They turned and stepped into detention block AA-23.

An Imperial lieutenant stood behind a semicircular control station of the detention security area. Behind him, two black-uniformed soldiers stood against a wall, and a short flight of steps led up to a cell corridor, where a third soldier appeared to be inspecting cell doors.

The lieutenant at the control station sneered at the sight of Chewbacca and said, "Where are you taking this . . . thing?"

Luke said, "Prisoner transfer from Cell Block one-one-three-eight."

"I wasn't notified," the lieutenant replied. "I'll have to clear it." He signaled to the two nearby guards. Both guards drew their blasters, then one guard approached Chewbacca.

Chewbacca roared and lashed out with one mighty hand, smashing the guard with enough strength to launch him off his feet. Then came total chaos.

Han shouted, "Look out! He's loose!" and tossed his blaster rifle to Chewbacca.

Luke shouted, "He's going to pull us apart!" as he fired at the startled guards. Chewbacca started shooting at the security camera eyes and laser gate controls. Laserbolts pinged and exploded all over the room.

Han shouted, "Go get him!" and grabbed a blaster from a fallen guard. The lieutenant finally realized that Han and Luke weren't real stormtroopers and reached for his own blaster. Han disabled him. Then he, Luke, and Chewbacca kept blasting until every security sensor was a shattered mess.

The lieutenant had collapsed on top of his control station, where an alarm was beeping wildly. While Chewbacca clutched his Imperial blaster rifle and watched the lift tube doors, Luke hurried into the control station and pulled the lieutenant's body aside. Han ran up beside Luke and said, "We've got to find out which cell this princess of yours is in." He scanned a data screen. "Here it is . . . twenty-one-eighty-seven. You go and get her. I'll hold them here."

Luke ran up the steps and entered the detention corridor. Han removed his stormtrooper helmet and placed it beside his blaster rifle on the console. He switched off the beeping alarm, flicked on the comlink system, and said in a calm tone, "Everything's under control. Situation normal."

Over the intercom, a voice asked, "What happened?"

"Uh . . . had a slight weapons malfunction," Han said, trying to sound official. "But, uh, everything's perfectly all right now. We're fine. We're all fine here now, thank you. How are you?" Han winced at the lameness of his own words.

"We're sending a squad up," said the voice from the intercom.

"Uh, uh, negative, negative," Han said. "We have a reactor leak here now. Give us a few minutes to lock it down. Large leak . . . very dangerous."

"Who is this?" came the intercom voice. "What's your operating number?"

Han briefly considered answering, then picked up the blaster rifle, aimed it at the comlink system, and fired at point-blank range, shattering the system. "Boring conversation anyway," he muttered, then turned to look down the detention corridor and shouted, "Luke! We're going to have company!"

Luke heard, and ran faster past the recessed doorways that lined the corridor. When he found cell 2187, he slapped a button on the wall and the cell door slid up.

And then he saw her.

Princess Leia was sleeping on the bare metal slab that served as a bed. She appeared to be wearing the same white gown that she'd worn when she'd made the holographic recording. Luke stepped down into the cell, thinking, *She's so beautiful.*

Leia opened her eyes and lifted her head. She had an uncomprehending look on her face as she said, "Aren't you a little short for a stormtrooper?"

"Huh?" Luke replied. "Oh . . . the uniform." He reached up to pull off the helmet. Shaking his hair free, he said, "I'm Luke Skywalker. I'm here to rescue you."

Leia remained on the slab and said, "You're who?"

"I'm here to rescue you. I've got your Artoo unit. I'm here with Ben Kenobi."

"Ben Kenobi!" Leia cried, jumping up. "Where is he?"

Luke said, "Come on!"

Leia ran past Luke and through the cell's open doorway, and he followed her out.

Tarkin sat at the far end of the round table in the conference room. Darth Vader stood at the other end and said, "He is here."

"Obi-Wan Kenobi!" Tarkin said. "What makes you think so?"

"A tremor in the Force. The last time I felt it was in the presence of my old Master."

Doubtful, Tarkin said, "Surely he must be dead by now."

"Don't underestimate the Force," Vader replied.

"The Jedi are extinct; their fire has gone out of the universe. You, my friend, are all that's left of their religion." A signal chimed from the comlink at the console in front of Tarkin's seat. Tarkin pressed a button on the console and said, "Yes."

On the intercom, a voice said, "We have an emergency alert in detention block AA-twenty-three."

"The princess!" Tarkin said. "Put all sections on alert!"

"Obi-Wan *is* here," Vader stated. "The Force is with him."

"If you're right, he must not be allowed to escape."

"Escape is not in his plan." Before turning for the door, Vader said knowingly, "I must face him alone."

Han and Chewbacca were still in the detention security area when they heard an ominous buzzing sound from the lift tube doors. The Wookiee growled at the noise. Han shouted, "Get behind me! Get behind me!"

Chewbacca jumped away from the lift tubes as an explosion ripped a large hole through one door. The hole's edges were still smoldering as the first stormtrooper stepped through. Han aimed and fired. The trooper fell, and another trooper pushed his way through the hole, followed by another.

Han and Chewbacca ran for the detention corridor. Behind them, one stormtrooper stopped the others and said, "Off to your left. They went down in the cell bay." The stormtroopers fired their blasters down the length of the detention corridor.

Inside the corridor, laserbolts whizzed past Luke and Leia. Because the cell doorways were recessed, the surrounding metal frames served as shallow protective alcoves. As Luke and Leia instinctively ducked against a door to avoid being hit, Han and Chewbacca came pounding up the corridor and threw themselves into neighboring doorways. Glancing back down the corridor to the security area, Han shouted, "Can't get out that way."

"Looks like you managed to cut off our only escape route," Leia said angrily.

"Maybe you'd like it back in your cell, Your Highness," Han replied.

Luke remembered C-3PO and R2-D2 were still back at the command office that overlooked Docking Bay 327. Thinking the droids might be useful, Luke reached for his comlink and said into it, "See-Threepio! See-Threepio!"

From the comlink, C-3PO replied, "Yes, sir?"

Luke said, "Are there any other ways out of the cell bay? We've been cut off!" More laserbolts zinged through the corridor. Luke shouted into his comlink, "What was that? I didn't copy!"

"I said all systems have been alerted to your presence, sir," C-3PO answered. "The main entrance seems to be the only way in or out; all other information on your level is restricted."

Just then, the droid heard someone banging on the command office's door. From the other side of the door, a stormtrooper demanded, "Open up in there! Open up in there!"

"Oh, no!" C-3PO cried.

Back at the detention cell corridor, Luke told the

others the bad news: "There isn't any other way out."

More laserfire sailed through the corridor, some blasts impacting dangerously close to Luke and his allies. Han edged out from his alcove, fired back at the stormtroopers, then said, "I can't hold them off forever! Now what?"

"This is some rescue," Leia said sarcastically. "When you came in here, didn't you have a plan for getting out?"

Han gestured to Luke and said, "He's the brains, sweetheart."

Luke said, "Well, I didn't . . ."

Leia grabbed Luke's blaster rifle and fired at a small grate in the wall next to Han. The blast tore a hole through the mesh, and Han felt the force of the explosion against the leggings of his stormtrooper armor. He shouted, "What the hell are you doing?"

"Somebody has to save our skins," Leia said, then tossed Luke's rifle back to him. "Into the garbage chute, flyboy." She jumped through the narrow opening she'd created in the grate.

Chewbacca and Han exchanged amazed glances. Neither had expected the princess to be so resourceful, let alone be bold enough to leap into a garbage chute. Chewbacca moved toward the shattered grate, then recoiled from it and yowled.

"Get in there!" Han yelled. "Get in there, you big furry oaf! I don't care what you smell! Get in there and don't worry about it." He gave Chewbacca a big kick, and the Wookiee disappeared into the tiny opening. Then Han turned to Luke's position and said, "Wonderful girl! Either I'm going to kill her or I'm beginning to like her. Get in there!"

Han continued firing back at the stormtroopers while Luke ducked laserfire and jumped through the hole. Han fired a few more blasts to create a smoky cover, then held his blaster forward as he dived into the chute.

He yelled all the way down. Like the others who'd preceded him, he landed in a deep pile of garbage.

The garbage room was a metal-walled chamber that contained heaps of trash, everything from broken metal beams and bits of plastic scrap to organic waste. A pool of foul-smelling muck completely covered the floor. Leia's white gown and Luke's stormtrooper armor were already covered with grime, and Chewbacca's fur was matted with swill.

Han leered at Leia and said, "The garbage chute was a really wonderful idea. What an incredible smell you've discovered!" Seeing Chewbacca trying to open a metal hatch, Han drew his blaster and said, "Let's get out of here! Get away from there."

Luke shouted, "No! Wait!"

Too late. Han fired at the hatch, and the laserbolt ricocheted wildly around the metal-walled chamber. Everyone dived for cover until the fired bolt's charge ended in a small explosion that didn't even dent the metal wall.

"Will you forget it?" Luke shouted to Han. "I already tried it." Gesturing to the hatch, he added, "It's magnetically sealed."

Livid at Han, Leia tilted her chin at his blaster and said, "Put that thing away! You're going to get us all killed."

"Absolutely, Your Worship," Han replied. "Look, I had everything under control until you led us down here. You know, it's not going to take them long to figure out what happened to us."

"It could be worse," Leia said.

Unexpectedly, a loud, inhuman moan worked its way up from the mucky pool. The moan echoed off the garbage room walls.

Chewbacca turned to a wall and cowered. Despite the hazard posed by the magnetically sealed walls, Luke and Han held their blasters out, ready to fire. Han said, "It's worse."

Luke said, "There's something alive in here!"

"That's your imagination," Han said.

"Something just moved past my leg!" Luke reported, then glimpsed a thick, serpentlike body twist through the muck. Luke pointed and said, "Look! Did you see that?"

"What?" Han asked.

They all looked down around their feet. No one saw the single eyestalk that rose like a periscope from the muck. The eye belonged to a dianoga, a seven-tentacled omnivorous predator that had wound up on the Death Star quite by accident. The dianoga's eye quickly surveyed the four figures who appeared to be a tasty alternative to garbage. Then the eyestalk submerged.

Suddenly, Luke was yanked under the muck.

Han shouted, "Kid! Luke!" He pushed aside some garbage, but there wasn't any sign of Luke's armored body. "Luke!" He reached into the muck but couldn't get his grip on anything. Precious seconds ticked by, and Han, Leia, and Chewbacca became more anxious. Han shouted again, "Luke!"

There was an explosion of muck as Luke broke the surface, gasping for air. A membraned tentacle was wrapped around his head, and Luke thrashed and struggled against the creature's hold.

"Luke!" Leia cried out. She grabbed a long metal pipe, extended it, and cried out, "Luke, Luke, grab hold of this."

"Blast it, will you!" Luke yelled. "My gun's jammed."

Not knowing where to shoot and afraid he might hit Luke, Han said, "Where?"

"Anywhere!" Luke hollered. Han fired downward, but the creature held Luke tight. Han fired two more blasts.

"Oh!" Luke shouted, then he was pulled under again.

Han called out, "Luke! Luke!"

Without warning, the walls of the garbage room shuddered, then went quiet. Han and Leia exchanged a worried look.

What now? Leia wondered.

With a rush of bubbles, Luke bobbed up through the muck.

"Help him!" Leia yelled as Han scrambled through the trash to lift Luke to his feet. Hoping Luke knew the cause of the walls shuddering, Leia asked, "What happened?"

"I don't know," Luke gasped. "It just let go of me and disappeared."

Han looked around at the walls and said, "I got a bad feeling about this."

The walls rumbled again, but this time they pushed inward.

"The walls are moving!" Luke shouted, then realized, *This room is a trash compactor!*

"Don't just stand there," Leia said to Han. "Try and brace it with something. Help me!"

They reached for discarded metal beams and tubelike poles, then angled them between the closing walls. Because all the garbage kept shifting and pushing up around them, it was difficult work. Despite their efforts, the poles snapped and the beams bent, and the walls continued to close in.

"Wait a minute!" Luke cried, and reached for his comlink transmitter. "See-Threepio. Come in, See-Threepio! See-Threepio!" When no answer came, Luke said, "Where could he be?"

C-3PO had accidentally left his comlink transmitter on top of a computer console in the command office for Docking Bay 327, which still contained the *Millennium Falcon*. Fortunately, when the stormtroopers finally shattered the lock and burst into the office, their attention was immediately drawn to the motionless bodies of the gantry officer and his aide lying on the floor, and they didn't notice the comlink transmitter.

The stormtrooper squad leader gestured at the abandoned computer station and said to one trooper, "Take over!" Directing another trooper's attention to the gantry officer's body, the squad leader commanded, "See to him!" Then the squad leader noticed the office's supply cabinet door was closed and said, "Look, there!"

A trooper pushed a button and the supply cabinet slid open, revealing C-3PO and R2-D2. The stormtroopers had no idea that the droids had deliberately locked themselves inside.

"They're madmen!" C-3PO exclaimed. "They're heading for the prison level. If you hurry, you might catch them." The protocol droid knew Luke and the others had already escaped from the prison level, and hoped his ruse would distract the stormtroopers.

Believing that the droids were victims and not allies of the invaders, the stormtrooper squad leader turned to five troopers and said, "Follow me!" To one trooper, he ordered, "You stand guard." The squad leader and five troopers ran out of the command office.

"Come on!" C-3PO said to R2-D2, but when they moved away from the supply cabinet, the remaining trooper raised his blaster rifle at them. Thinking fast, C-3PO faced the trooper and said, "Oh! All this excitement has overrun the circuits in my counterpart here. If you don't mind, I'd like to take him down to maintenance."

"All right," the trooper said with a nod.

C-3PO and R2-D2 hurried out of the office.

"See-Threepio!" Luke shouted into his comlink as the garbage room walls continued to rumble closer. "Come in, See-Threepio! See-Threepio!"

Chewbacca whined and pushed against a wall with his large paws. Han and Leia worked together, trying to brace a long pole between the contracting walls. All around them, garbage was snapping and popping as it was pushed together.

Leia began to slip down into the trash. Han placed his hands on Leia's hips and lifted her as he said, "Get to the top!"

"I can't," Leia said, but managed with Han's help.

Luke hung on to the comlink transmitter and tried to contact C-3PO again. "Where could he be? See-Threepio? See-Threepio, will you come in?"

After eluding the stormtroopers in the command office, R2-D2 and C-3PO returned to Docking Bay 327, where they took protective cover behind some barrels. C-3PO moved cautiously to see the *Millennium Falcon* still resting on the hangar deck. A group of stormtroopers exited the *Falcon,* carrying the bodies of the scanning crew and the two troopers who'd unwittingly donated their armor to Luke and Han. Five stormtroopers remained on guard beside the *Falcon*'s landing ramp. There was no sign of Luke and the others.

C-3PO turned to R2-D2, who stood beside a computer service panel that was embedded in a wall. "They aren't here!" said the golden droid with dismay. "Something must have happened to them." He gestured at the service panel and said, "See if they've been captured."

R2-D2 extended his computer interface arm and carefully plugged it into the service panel's socket. A complex array of electronic sounds spewed from the astromech's head.

Impatient and filled with worry, C-3PO cried, "Hurry!"

In the garbage room, the converging walls were less than two meters apart and still closing. Luke, Leia, Han, and Chewbacca struggled to avoid being crushed as they climbed the shifting heaps of trash.

"One thing's for sure," Han said. "We're all going to be a lot thinner!" Seeing that Leia was losing her footing, he shouted, "Get on top of it!"

"I'm trying!" Leia shouted back.

Luke thought, *Is this how we're going to die?!* He kept his comlink activated, but with the walls now barely a meter apart, the possibility of C-3PO being able to help was a hope that was fading fast.

R2-D2 searched the Death Star's computer banks but found no record of any intruders being captured since the *Falcon* had arrived in Docking Bay 327. The astromech rotated his dome and beeped his report to C-3PO.

"Thank goodness they haven't found them!"

C-3PO said. Glancing at the *Falcon,* he asked, "Where could they be?"

R2-D2 noticed the device that C-3PO had recovered, then beeped and whistled frantically.

"Use the comlink?" C-3PO replied, then realized he was still holding the transmitter. "Oh, my! I forgot . . . I turned it off!" He activated the comlink and said, "Are you there, sir?"

"See-Threepio!" Luke answered.

C-3PO said, "We've had some problems —"

"Will you shut up and listen to me," Luke interrupted. "Shut down all the garbage mashers on the detention level, will you? Do you copy? Shut down all the garbage mashers on the detention level."

Inside the garbage room, the walls didn't stop moving, and only seconds remained before they'd meet. Fearing C-3PO hadn't heard him, Luke repeated, "Shut down all the garbage mashers on the detention level."

R2-D2 beeped a question to C-3PO, who replied, "No. Shut them all down! Hurry!"

R2-D2's extension arm twisted in the computer socket, then he and C-3PO listened to the comlink. They'd hoped to hear that all was well, but instead, the droids heard their allies screaming.

Holding the comlink away from his head, C-3PO looked at R2-D2 and cried, "Listen to them! They're dying, Artoo-Detoo!"

Hearing more screams, C-3PO said mournfully, "Curse my metal body! I wasn't fast enough. It's all my fault! My poor master!"

But then, from the comlink, Luke's excited voice said, "See-Threepio, we're all right!"

Inside the narrow confines of the garbage room, the hollering continued, not because of injury but from the sheer joy that everyone was still alive and unharmed. Holding his comlink, Luke sat atop a pile of trash and communicated to C-3PO, "We're all right. You did great."

Chewbacca howled with relief. Despite themselves, Han and Leia embraced.

Luke saw a hatch against the far wall. To C-3PO, he said, "Hey . . . hey, open the pressure maintenance hatch on unit number . . ." He turned to Han and asked, "Where are we?"

Han checked numbers that were etched on the

hatch and read aloud, "Three-two-six-three-eight-two-seven."

C-3PO made sure R2-D2 heard the numbers correctly, and the astromech opened the hatch.

Darth Vader may have sensed Obi-Wan's presence on the Death Star, but not a single Imperial officer, stormtrooper, or droid noticed Obi-Wan's stealthy movement through the corridors as he made his way to the nearest generator trench.

Ben stepped through a doorway and surveyed the trench. It was formed by two incredibly steep facing walls, and the air between them was taut with high voltage electricity. A 1.5-meter-wide bridge without guardrails spanned the trench, and an even more narrow footbridge — only 25 centimeters wide, and also without guardrails — extended from the bridge's side to wrap around a power terminal. The power terminal stood atop a cylindrical generator tower. From the schematics that R2-D2 had conjured up back at the command station, Ben knew he'd have to step onto the footbridge to reach the generator's control panels, and that the generator tower was thirty-five kilometers tall.

Even for a Jedi Knight, that was a long way down.

Focused on his mission and fearless of the dizzying height, Ben moved across the bridge, then onto the footbridge. He edged carefully around the power terminal until he could reach the generator controls. He pressed one lever, then edged farther around the terminal until he found the controls for the tractor beam power coupling.

The hatch for trash compactor 32-6-3827 adjoined a dusty, unused hallway. Han and Luke had removed their stormtrooper armor but retained the troopers' white utility belts, each of which carried blaster power cell containers, a tool kit, and a grappling hook attached to a fibercord reel. Chewbacca sat outside the open hatch and tried to brush the grime from his matted fur. Leia smoothed out her gown and checked the pins that held her hair in place.

Handing a blaster rifle to Luke, Han glanced at Leia and said, "If we can just avoid any more female advice, we ought to be able to get out of here."

Luke said, "Well, let's get moving!"

A loud, angry moan drifted out from the open hatch. Evidently, the dianoga had survived in the garbage room and was now even more hungry. The noise caused Chewbacca to jump and run away from the hatch.

"Where are you going?" Han said, glaring at the Wookiee. Embarrassed by his copilot's behavior, Han turned toward the hatch and raised his blaster.

"No, wait," Leia said urgently. "They'll hear!"

Too late again. Han fired the blaster at the hatch, and the noise echoed throughout the hallway. Disgusted by Han's thoughtless action, Luke shook his head.

"Come here, you big coward!" Han called to the Wookiee, who stood trembling beside a nearby stack of barrels. "Chewie! Come here!"

Leia fixed her furious gaze on Han and said, "Listen. I don't know who you are or where you came from, but from now on, you do as I tell you. Okay?" She walked past Han and began to lead the group through the hallway, but Chewbacca fell into step just in front of her.

Catching up beside Leia, Han said, "Look, Your Worshipfulness, let's get one thing straight! I take orders from just one person! Me!"

"It's a wonder you're still alive," Leia said. Glaring at Chewbacca, she added, "Will somebody get this big walking carpet out of my way?" She brushed past the Wookiee.

Han shook his head and muttered, "No reward is worth this."

Ben was about to remove himself from his perilous perch upon the footbridge that ringed the generator tower's power terminal when he heard footsteps approaching. He quickly readjusted a lever on the power terminal so any passerby wouldn't notice his sabotage, then braced his body against the terminal, concealing himself from the bridge that spanned the trench.

A detachment of stormtroopers entered through a doorway and stepped onto the bridge. The commanding officer turned to two troopers and said, "Give me regular reports, please."

"Right," replied one trooper. The two troopers remained near the doorway by which they'd arrived while the other troopers marched across the bridge and through the facing doorway.

Ben intended to exit the trench by the same route. As he readjusted the lever to shut down the tractor beam, he overheard the nearby troopers speaking.

"Do you know what's going on?" asked the first trooper.

"Maybe it's another drill," the second replied.

Ben moved cautiously on the footbridge and peered around the power terminal. The two troopers were still near the far doorway, facing each other. The first trooper said, "Have you seen that new BT-sixteen?"

The second trooper said, "Yeah, some of the other guys were telling me about it. They say it's, it's quite a thing to —"

Using the Force, Ben flexed his fingers and gestured at the two troopers. Both troopers suddenly heard — or thought they heard — a muffled explosion from the doorway behind them, and turned away from the power terminal.

"What was that?" asked the second trooper.

"That's nothing," said the first trooper. "Top gassing. Don't worry about it."

Neither noticed Ben step onto the bridge and exit the generator trench.

Luke, Leia, Han, and Chewbacca entered a corridor that was on the same level as the command office for Docking Bay 327. Arriving at a window that overlooked the hangar, Han gazed down at the *Millennium Falcon* and said, "There she is."

Luke looked through the window and counted five stormtrooper sentries outside the *Falcon*. There was no sign of R2-D2 or C-3PO. Luke switched on his comlink transmitter and said, "See-Threepio, do you copy?"

"Yes, sir," C-3PO answered.

"Are you safe?" Luke asked.

"For the moment," he replied. "We're in the main hangar across from the ship."

"We're right above you," Luke said. "Stand by."

Leia tugged at Han's sleeve and gestured at the *Falcon*. "You came in that thing?" she said. "You're braver than I thought."

"Nice!" Han was thoroughly exasperated. "Come on!"

They walked fast down a hallway, making their way to the lift tube that would take them to the lower level. Han made sweeping movements with his blaster rifle, ready to fire at the first sign of trouble. But as the group rounded a corner, even Han was surprised to run straight into seven approaching stormtroopers.

"It's them!" shouted the squad leader. "Blast them!"

Han's blaster rifle was already leveled at the squad leader, and Han didn't hesitate to fire. The blast knocked the squad leader off his feet and the six remaining troopers stumbled back. Without any plan but to knock down every Imperial soldier in sight, Han fired again and charged the startled troopers, who turned and ran back up the hallway. As Han chased and fired after the troopers, he shouted to his allies, "Get back to the ship!"

"Where are you going?" Luke yelled as Chewbacca ran after Han. "Come back!"

Watching Han's departure, Leia said, "He certainly has courage."

"What good will it do us if he gets himself killed?" Luke took Leia's hand. "Come on!" They ran off in the other direction down the hallway.

*   *   *

Hollering and firing his blaster rifle, Han chased the stormtroopers through a long subhallway. At the end of the subhallway, the troopers were forced to turn left around a corner. Not thinking about where the turn might lead, Han ran after the troopers and entered a TIE fighter hangar.

Han stopped in his tracks. The hangar was filled with hundreds of stormtroopers, and it appeared that Han had interrupted their weapons drill. The stormtroopers he'd been chasing now stopped and turned with their blasters raised. The other troopers all looked his way. Han squeezed off a shot to fell one more trooper, then turned around and ran for his life.

Chewbacca had been trying to catch up with Han when he heard the hail of blasterfire up ahead, then saw Han come racing back toward him. A hail of laserbolts slammed into the wall behind Han as he ran past. Quickly sizing up the situation, the Wookiee turned and ran even faster after Han.

Before Luke and Leia could reach the hangar that contained the *Millennium Falcon,* they were spotted by yet another squad of stormtroopers. Luke fired his blaster rifle wildly as he and Leia rushed down a narrow subhallway, trying to elude the troopers who fired at them from behind.

The subhallway ended at a short ramp that led up

to an open doorway. Luke and Leia raced up the ramp and were through the doorway before they realized the floor ended at an enormous air shaft. Luke nearly lost his balance at the edge of the floor, but Leia grabbed hold of his arm and pulled him back.

"I think we took a wrong turn," Luke said, and heard his words echo as he surveyed the air shaft. The shaft's steep walls seemed to stretch to infinity. Across the chasm, another open doorway was set in the facing wall. Luke and Leia realized they were standing upon nothing more than a shallow overhang that housed a retractible bridge.

Blasterfire exploded behind them. Luke turned and fired at the advancing stormtroopers. Leia found a control panel that was embedded in the doorway. She reached to the panel, hit a switch, and the door slid shut behind them.

"There's no lock!" Leia said.

Luke aimed his blaster at the control panel and fired, frying the door's opening mechanisms. He said, "That oughta hold them for a while."

Looking to the doorway on the other side of the shaft, Leia said, "Quick, we've got to get across. Find the controls that extend the bridge."

Luke looked at the smoldering circuits on the panel in the doorway. "Oh," he said, "I think I just blasted it."

There came a grinding sound from the door behind them. Leia warned, "They're coming through!"

Luke thought, *There's got to be a way out of this!* Looking up, he spotted an outcropping of large metal pipes that jutted down from above. Then he remembered: *My stormtrooper utility belt has a grappling hook.* But as he reached to the belt, laserfire hit the wall behind him.

Luke and Leia fell back against the doorway's alcove as more laserbolts whizzed past them. Glancing out from the alcove, they saw three stormtroopers firing from an upper-level doorway on the facing wall. Luke braced himself, aimed up at the troopers, and fired back.

One trooper was hit in the chest, and fell forward into the shaft. The other troopers returned fire, and Luke threw himself back beside Leia in the alcove.

"Here, hold this," Luke said, handing the blaster rifle to Leia.

Leia bravely repeated Luke's movements, stepping out from the alcove to exchange fire with the stormtroopers before ducking back. While she kept the troopers occupied, Luke pulled the grappling hook from his belt. He was still paying out the hook's thin cable when the door behind him began to open.

"Here they come!" Leia shouted. She fired again at the stormtroopers across the shaft. One of her shots struck a trooper, and he collapsed.

Luke tossed the hook high, letting its weight carry the cable up to the metal pipes. The hook whipped around one pipe and the hook's tines locked onto the cable. Luke gave the cable a single tug to make sure it was secure, then pulled Leia to his side. Behind them, the door opened a fraction more.

Leia kissed Luke's cheek and said, "For luck!"

Keeping her grip on the blaster rifle, Leia wrapped her arms around Luke as he pushed off from the overhang. They swung across the treacherous shaft and alighted on the opposite ledge, just as the stormtroopers broke through and fired at them from behind.

Leia returned fire, then she and Luke scrambled through the doorway and ran into another hallway. This time, they wouldn't get lost on their way back to the *Falcon.*

Several stormtroopers rushed through a Death Star hallway. One trooper reported, "We think they may be splitting up. They may be on levels five and six now, sir."

Ben stood in the shadows of a narrow passageway that adjoined the hallway. When he was sure the troopers had passed, he drew his lightsaber from his belt. He did not activate the blade but held it ready. He had a feeling he would be using his weapon sooner than later. Much sooner.

Ben proceeded into the hallway.

C-3PO was becoming increasingly worried as he and R2-D2 waited for their allies to arrive in the docking bay. "Where could they be?" the protocol droid asked.

R2-D2 plugged into the computer socket and responded with a beep. He didn't know either.

Han and Chewbacca raced through a corridor with several stormtroopers hot on their trail. As the man and Wookiee approached a wide doorway, a trooper shouted out from behind, "Close the blast doors!"

Suddenly, thick metal doors began to slide out from the doorway's frame. Chewbacca maintained a breakneck pace as he ran between the converging doors. Han spun and fired back at the stormtroopers, then turned again and leaped through the closing aperture at the last possible moment before the blast doors sealed off the corridor behind him.

"Open the blast doors!" shouted the trooper. "Open the blast doors!"

On the other side, Han and Chewbacca kept running.

Ben still had his lightsaber drawn as he moved along through an access tunnel that led back to Docking Bay 327. Having disabled the tractor beam, his remaining goal was to make sure Luke and Princess Leia left the Death Star on the *Millennium Falcon*. But before he could reach the hangar, he sighted a tall, shadowy form at the end of the tunnel.

It was his former apprentice, Darth Vader.

Vader had already activated the red blade of his lightsaber. For a moment, he stood motionless. Then he approached Ben.

Obi-Wan activated his lightsaber and stepped slowly forward. He'd fought Vader before. He hadn't been afraid then either.

"I've been waiting for you, Obi-Wan," Vader said as he moved closer to the elderly Jedi Knight. "We meet again, at last. The circle is now complete."

Obi-Wan assumed an offensive position.

Vader continued, "When I left you, I was but the learner; now I am the master."

"Only a master of evil, Darth," Obi-Wan said. He made a sudden lunge at Vader but the dark lord blocked the attack. There was a loud electric crackle as their lightsabers made contact. Obi-Wan swung again and again, but each time Vader parried.

Vader said, "Your powers are weak, old man."

"You can't win, Darth," Obi-Wan said. "If you strike me down, I shall become more powerful than you can possibly imagine."

"You should not have come back," Vader said.

Their lightsabers clashed again. And again, and again. And as their battle continued, they moved closer to the main doorway that led directly to the hangar that contained the *Millennium Falcon*.

Chewbacca and Han ran through a hallway until they arrived at a side door to the hangar that housed their captured ship. Bracing themselves against the wall, they peered into the hangar and saw the same five stormtrooper sentries they'd seen earlier, from the window at the upper level. The *Falcon* looked the same as they'd left it, with the landing ramp still down.

"Didn't we just leave this party?" Han said. He glanced to his left and saw Leia and Luke rushing up from the other end of the hallway. When they arrived at his side, he said, "What kept you?"

"We ran into some old friends," Leia replied, catching her breath.

Luke asked, "Is the ship all right?"

"Seems okay, if we can get to it," Han answered. "Just hope the old man got the tractor beam out of commission."

Han was trying to think of a way to get rid of the stormtroopers in the hangar when Luke said, "Look!" Inexplicably, the stormtroopers trotted away from the *Falcon*'s landing ramp and moved past the deep elevator well.

Inside the hangar, C-3PO also saw the stormtroopers run to the other side of the elevator well. C-3PO turned to R2-D2 and said, "Come on, Artoo, we're going!"

R2-D2 extended his retractable third tread to the hangar deck and rolled forward after C-3PO, heading for the *Falcon.*

Back at the side hallway, Han said, "Now's our chance! Go!"

Chewbacca, Han, Leia, and Luke ran for the *Falcon*'s landing ramp. Luke glanced to his right and saw the stormtroopers had moved to the other side of the elevator well. They faced away from him, their attention having been drawn to a fight that was taking place in the hallway beyond the main doorway.

It was a lightsaber duel. Luke could only imagine the identity of the tall, black-clad humanoid who wielded a red lightsaber. The other duelist wore a brown cloak, and Luke thought he recognized him immediately.

"Ben?" Luke said, and came to a stop. *Who's he fighting?*

Ben looked to Luke and smiled, then he raised his lightsaber before him and closed his eyes. He looked almost serene.

Darth Vader thought Obi-Wan was surrendering, but the dark lord was without mercy. Vader's lightsaber swept through the air and sliced through Ben's form. Ben's cloak and lightsaber fell to the floor. His body was gone.

"No!" Luke shouted.

Hearing Luke's cry, the stormtroopers turned and shot at him. Luke raised his blaster rifle and returned their fire, hitting one trooper, who tumbled forward into the elevator well.

Han immediately joined in the fight, firing at the troopers while the droids and Chewbacca hurried into the *Falcon*. "Come on!" Han shouted to Luke.

Darth Vader ignored the blasterfight and looked down at the old brown cloak and lightsaber that lay on the floor. Incredibly, Obi-Wan had completely disappeared. *Where is he? How could he vanish? What sort of trickery is this?* He had assumed Obi-Wan's study of the Force had ended long ago, and that his powers had diminished over time. But Vader was wrong.

Luke and Han kept firing at the troopers. Another trooper was shot down. Leia shouted, "Come on! Come on! Luke, it's too late!"

Darth Vader looked away from Obi-Wan's cloak, then turned and strode toward the doorway to the hangar.

Han shouted, "Blast the door, kid!"

Luke fired at the controls beside the doorway, then two blast doors slid out from the walls to seal off the passage before Vader could enter the hangar. Han and Leia ran into the *Falcon*. The three remaining stormtroopers continued to fire at Luke. Luke fired again, and reduced their number to two.

Then, from out of nowhere, Luke heard Ben's voice: "Run, Luke! Run!"

Luke looked around, trying to see where the voice had come from. He saw nothing but chose to heed Ben's words and raced into the *Falcon.*

Chewbacca already had the ship's sub-light engines started when Han rushed into the cockpit. Han stowed his blaster rifle, jumped into the pilot's seat, and said, "I hope the old man got that tractor beam out of commission, or this is going to be a real short trip. Okay, hit it!"

The Wookiee punched the controls. The *Falcon* launched out of the hangar in reverse, then spun and blasted away from the Death Star. As the Corellian freighter gained distance from the Imperial space station, Chewbacca barked at Han. Even though they now knew for certain that Ben had disabled the tractor beam, they still had a problem: The destruction of the planet Alderaan had spread so much debris across the sector that it was no longer safe to use the nearest designated portal to hyperspace. They'd have to enter hyperspace by a different route.

In the *Falcon's* main hold, the droids looked at Luke, who sat at the game table with a blank expression. Leia carried a blanket over to Luke, wrapped it around his shoulders, and sat beside him. Luke just stared at the center of the game table. *Why didn't Ben defend himself? Why?*

In the cockpit, Chewbacca was still waiting for the nav computer to come up with a new route into hyperspace when Han spotted four blips on a sensor scope. "We're coming up on their sentry ships," Han said. "Hold 'em off! Angle the deflector shields while I charge up the main guns!"

Chewbacca threw switches to adjust the shields. Han pulled on a pair of skintight leather piloting gloves and bolted out of the cockpit.

Back in the main hold, Leia continued to sit by Luke. He shook his head sadly and said, "I can't believe he's gone."

R2-D2 emitted a sympathetic beep. Although C-3PO was rarely at a loss for words, he remained silent.

Leia said, "There wasn't anything you could have done."

Just then, Han rushed into the hold. Looking at Luke, he said, "Come on, buddy, we're not out of this yet!"

Leia and Luke jumped up from their seats, leaving the droids at the game table. While Leia ran to the *Falcon's* cockpit, Luke shrugged off the blanket that

Leia had given him and followed Han to the access hatch for the gunport turrets.

The access hatch opened to a narrow passage tube with a ladder that traveled between the dorsal and ventral quad laser cannons. Han climbed up the ladder and Luke climbed down. Each arrived in a windowed gunner's enclosure that contained a maneuverable seat with firing controls and targeting instrumentation. Outside each window was a large swivel-mounted quad laser cannon. Luke was pretty sure the cannons were military issue. *I don't even want to think how Han got these weapons!*

Luke and Han settled into their seats at each end of the passage tube. Han adjusted his comlink headset and spoke into the attached microphone: "You in, kid? Okay, stay sharp!"

Luke quickly familiarized himself with the controls. There was a targeting computer that worked in conjunction with the *Falcon*'s navigational computer and sensor array to calculate trajectories and attack and intercept courses. Grasping twin firing grips with built-in triggers, Luke shifted his wrists to the right; his seat automatically swiveled to the left, and the cannon's four laser barrels — visible through the ventral window — swung hard to the right. Then he pulled back on the controls and the seat lowered as the cannon raised. Each movement was accompanied by the mechanical whine from the cannon's tracking servos.

Suddenly, the *Falcon* shuddered as its shields took a laser hit from a distant attacker. In the cockpit, Leia and Chewbacca glanced from the scopes to the window, keeping their eyes peeled for the incoming Imperial sentry ships. Chewbacca spotted them first and barked. Leia said into the cockpit's comlink, "Here they come!"

The sentry ships were four TIE fighters. They came in fast, flying in a tight formation toward the *Falcon*'s cockpit before they broke away from each other and fanned out around the freighter. Then the fighters looped back and fired again at their target. Green laserbolts hammered at the *Falcon*'s deflector shields.

The *Falcon* bounced and vibrated and the ship's power surged. In the *Falcon*'s main hold, C-3PO clung to his seat beside R2-D2 as the lights dimmed and then came back on. Hoping to make himself useful, R2-D2 left the game table to inspect the engineering station. Not wanting to be left alone, C-3PO went with him.

A TIE fighter maneuvered above the *Falcon*. Han tracked the fighter and fired at it with his laser cannon, but missed. The TIE fighter looped back and streaked into Luke's view, and Luke fired, too, without effect.

Two TIE fighters spat laserfire and the *Falcon* bounced as it took more hits. Luke hung tight to his controls and fired at one of the passing TIE fighters as it soared past his window. He shouted, "They're coming in too fast!"

C-3PO and R2-D2 stumbled out of the main hold and into the passage tube just as more Imperial laserfire struck the *Falcon*. There was a small explosion at the floor. C-3PO shouted, "Oh!" as he was thrown against the passage tube's wall.

In the cockpit, Leia watched the computer readouts as Chewbacca manipulated the ship's controls. "We've lost lateral controls," she reported.

Via comlink, Han answered, "Don't worry, she'll hold together."

Near the droids, a control panel blew out in a shower of sparks beside the laser cannon access hatch. Han heard the explosion. Speaking directly to his ship, he said, "You hear me, baby? Hold together!"

R2-D2 hurried over to the smoking, sparking control panel. Among the astromech's many useful devices was a fire extinguisher. He sprayed the control panel until the fire was out.

The TIE fighters continued their attack. Luke and Han swiveled madly in their turrets as they returned fire. Han followed a TIE fighter in his sights and pumped rapid bursts of laserbolts at it. He connected, and the TIE fighter exploded. Han laughed victoriously.

A moment later, another TIE fighter swept into Luke's line of fire. Luke swung the cannon as he squeezed the firing grips and scored a direct hit, shattering the TIE fighter.

"Got him!" Luke shouted back to Han. "I got him!"

Han glanced down the passage tube, waved at Luke, and said, "Great, kid!" As he quickly returned his attention to his own targeting computer he added, "Don't get cocky."

From the cockpit, Leia reported, "There are still two more of them out there!"

The two remaining TIE fighters crossed in front of the *Falcon,* then veered away to attack from different directions. Han swiveled in his chair and followed one TIE fighter with blasts from his cannon, and Luke did the same as the other fighter streaked under the *Falcon.*

Both TIE fighters looped back, firing more rounds of green laserbolts. One fighter angled into Luke's view, and he fired a laserblast at it. The fighter exploded.

The last of the attacking TIE fighters zoomed in and fired at the top of the *Falcon.* Han swiveled behind his laser cannon and squeezed the firing grips. The fighter was instantly consumed in a massive, fiery explosion. Han blew out a relieved breath.

Luke laughed. "That's it! We did it!"

In the cockpit, Leia embraced Chewbacca and said, "We did it!"

"Help!" cried C-3PO from a tangle of sparking wires on the floor of the passage tube. "I think I'm melting!" Sighting R2-D2, he added, "This is all your fault."

R2-D2 beeped in disagreement.

The nav computer found a hyperspace portal. It was only good for a short jump, but Chewbacca seized the opportunity to gain more distance from the Death Star. He punched the controls, and the *Falcon* blasted into hyperspace.

Darth Vader stood with Grand Moff Tarkin in the Death Star control room. Tarkin looked at the wide viewscreen and said, "Are they away?"

"They have just made the jump into hyperspace," Vader said.

"You're sure the homing beacon is secure aboard their ship?" Tarkin said.

Vader didn't answer. He'd already told Tarkin that the homing beacon had been placed on the Corellian freighter and did not feel compelled to repeat himself. It had been Vader's idea to use the rescue of Princess Leia to the Empire's advantage. It had also been his idea to send the TIE fighters in pursuit of the freighter; if the princess and her allies suspected they'd been allowed to escape, they might not proceed directly to the Rebel base. The loss of the four TIE fighters and their pilots was an insignificant price for gaining the base's location.

"I'm taking an awful risk, Vader," Tarkin said. "This had better work."

Again, Vader remained silent, but he thought, *If we'd done things your way, Princess Leia would have been executed by now. And how would that have helped us find the Rebel base, Grand Moff Tarkin?*

"Not a bad bit of rescuing, huh!" Han said as he returned to the *Millennium Falcon*'s cockpit, just as Chewbacca rose to leave and check the ship for damage in the aft section. Leia remained seated behind the piloting controls.

Sliding into the Wookiee's vacated seat, Han pulled off his gloves and added, "You know, sometimes I amaze even myself."

"That doesn't sound too hard," Leia said. "They *let* us go. It's the only explanation for the ease of our escape."

"Easy!" Han said, raising his eyebrows quizzically. "You call that easy?"

"They're tracking us!" Leia insisted.

"Not this ship, sister," Han said.

Let him think what he wants, Leia thought. She said, "At least the information in Artoo-Detoo is still intact."

"What's so important?" Han asked. "What's he carrying?"

"The technical readouts of that battle station," Leia replied. "I only hope that when the data is analyzed, a weakness can be found. It's not over yet!"

"It is for me, sister!" Han said angrily. "Look, I ain't in this for your revolution, and I'm not in it for you, Princess. I expect to be well paid. I'm in it for the money!"

Leia glared at Han. "You needn't worry about your reward," she said. "When you get us to our destination, you'll receive it."

"Don't you think it'd help if you told me where we're going?"

"The fourth moon of the planet Yavin," Leia said. "That's where the base is. Then you can do whatever you like. If money is all that you love, then that's what you'll receive."

Han looked out the window. Leia rose from the pilot's seat and turned to leave just as Luke entered the cockpit. Looking at Luke, she said, "Your friend is quite a mercenary. I wonder if he really cares about anything . . . or anybody." She walked out.

"I care!" Luke said, but Leia was already walking

back to the main hold. Luke shook his head and sat down in the pilot's seat. Then he looked at Han and asked, "So . . . what do you think of her, Han?"

"I'm not trying to, kid!" Han replied.

Under his breath, Luke said, "Good."

Han glanced at Luke, who'd turned his attention to the ship's controls. Realizing that Luke might have feelings for the princess, Han decided to have some fun. He said, "Still, she's got a lot of spirit. I don't know, what do you think? Do you think a princess and a guy like me —"

"No!" Luke said sharply, then looked away, glowering.

Han grinned. Now he *knew* Luke had feelings for Leia.

Because it was impossible for a starship to change course in hyperspace, the *Falcon* had to drop back into realspace before making another jump to the Yavin system. While checking the nav computer calculations for the journey to Yavin's fourth moon, Han wondered if anyone — with or without the precious technical readouts — would be able to destroy the Death Star.

He doubted it very much.

The planet Yavin was an orange gas giant, nearly 200,000 kilometers in diameter. It had dozens of moons, three of which could support humanoid life. The innermost habitable moon was designated Yavin 4, and was covered by steamy jungles and volcanic mountain ranges. Thousands of years earlier, Yavin 4 had been the home to the Massassi, an ancient species of fierce warriors. All that remained of the Massassi were their scattered ruins, including a towering ziggurat — a terraced pyramid with successively receding stories — known as the Great Temple. It was in this long-abandoned structure that the Alliance — following their evacuation from the planet Dantooine — had relocated their primary base.

After the *Millennium Falcon* was cleared for landing, a Rebel sentry visually monitored the freighter's atmospheric descent from an observation tower, which was little more than a barrel-topped pole that extended high above the jungle floor. The *Falcon* touched down near the Great Temple, where Rebel troops greeted Princess Leia and her rescuers.

Two military speeders transported Luke and the others into the main hangar deck, a large chamber that had been excavated from the lower level of the Great Temple. The hangar contained a few dozen single-pilot starships, mostly T-65 X-wing starfighters but also some older Y-wings. The X-wings were named for their two sets of double-layered wings, which were closed during normal space flight but deployed into an X formation for combat; the end of each wingtip sported a sleek laser cannon. The Y-wing starfighters were distinguished by a forward cockpit module that housed the pilot and the weapons systems, and had two ion jet engines that swept back from the main body. Both X-wing and Y-wing designs included a socket behind the cockpit where an R2 astromech could be inserted to handle all astrogation duties.

The two military speeders came to a stop inside the hangar. The group was then approached by Commander Vanden Willard, a gray-haired leader of the Rebel Forces on Yavin 4. Willard welcomed Leia with a hug and said, "You're safe! When we heard about Alderaan, we feared the worst."

"We have no time for sorrows, Commander," Leia said. As Rebel technicians unloaded R2-D2 from the lead speeder, Leia added, "You must use the information in this Artoo unit to help plan the attack. It's our only hope."

R2-D2 was taken immediately to a computer console and debriefed. The stolen technical readouts were intact. An older, bearded Rebel general named Jan Dodonna methodically analyzed the data, searching the Death Star's design for any weakness. If there were a single chink in the space station's armor, General Dodonna was determined to find it.

Incredibly, he did.

On the Death Star, Darth Vader stood behind a chair in the conference room and watched Grand Moff Tarkin respond to a signal from the comlink on the large round table. Tarkin pressed a button and said, "Yes."

Over the comlink intercom, a voice reported, "We are approaching the planet Yavin. The Rebel base is on a moon on the far side. We are preparing to orbit the planet."

On Yavin 4, Luke was still wearing his clothes from Tatooine when he joined the orange-uniformed Rebel pilots who gathered in the base's war room briefing area. Commander Willard had told Luke that the Alliance was short of experienced pilots, and Luke had volunteered on the spot. Because the controls of T-16 skyhoppers were similar to those of the X-wing starfighters, Luke had been assigned an X-wing. Luke sat beside another pilot, a dark-haired young man who introduced himself as Wedge Antilles. C-3PO, R2-D2, and some other astromechs stood behind Luke and Wedge. Wondering if there was any chance his friend Biggs had made it all the way to Yavin 4 too, Luke looked around the room. He didn't see Biggs, but spotted Han and Chewbacca lurking against the back wall. *I didn't think they'd be here. Maybe they decided to volunteer too!*

All heads turned to the front as Princess Leia, General Dodonna, and Commander Willard entered the room. Leia moved to stand beside Jon "Dutch" Vander, leader of Y-wing Gold Squadron. Dodonna stepped before a large rectangular viewscreen and faced the gathered pilots. The viewscreen displayed the technical readouts for the Death Star.

"The battle station is heavily shielded and carries a firepower greater than half the starfleet," Dodonna said. "Its defenses are designed around a direct large-scale assault. A small one-man fighter should be able to penetrate the outer defense."

Given the Death Star's firepower, the pilots had a hard time believing they stood any chance against the superweapon. Jon Vander said, "Pardon me for asking, sir, but what good are snubfighters going to be against *that*?"

Dodonna said, "Well, the Empire doesn't consider a small one-man fighter to be any threat, or they'd have a tighter defense. An analysis of the plans provided by Princess Leia has demonstrated a weakness in the battle station."

R2-D2 — happy to have been instrumental in carrying the plans — beeped proudly to a nearby R2 unit.

"The approach will not be easy," Dodonna continued. As the viewscreen displayed a digital representation of the Death Star's equatorial trench, Dodonna said, "You are required to maneuver straight down this trench and skim the surface to this point. The target area is only two meters wide. It's a small thermal exhaust port, right below the main port. The shaft leads directly to the reactor system. A precise hit will start a chain reaction which should destroy the station."

On the viewscreen, a simulation showed a starfighter launching a projectile into what appeared to be a small hole on the floor of the Death Star's trench. As the starfighter pulled out and ascended from the trench, the projectile plummeted through a narrow shaft until it reached the reactor core at the very center of the space station. Then bright lines radiated out from the reactor core and the station's image vanished.

Dodonna continued, "Only a precise hit will set up a chain reaction. The shaft is ray-shielded, so you'll have to use proton torpedoes."

Dodonna's presentation generated a rumble of mutterings from the pilots. Wedge said, "That's impossible, even for a computer."

"It's not impossible," Luke said. "I used to bull's-eye womp rats in my T-sixteen back home. They're not much bigger than two meters."

"Then man your ships!" Dodonna ordered. "And may the Force be with you!"

The pilots rose from their seats and headed out through the door that led to the hangar. Luke caught Leia looking in his direction. He couldn't tell from her expression whether she was concerned or disappointed. Then he realized she wasn't looking at him but at someone behind him. Luke turned around, expecting to see Han and Chewbacca, but they had already left the room. The droids were still there, and R2-D2 beeped cheerfully to him. Luke looked back to Leia, but now she was gone too, along with the other Rebel leaders.

Everything's happening so fast, Luke thought. *I can't believe it was just the other day that I was watching the suns set on Tatooine, wishing I were anywhere but on that moisture farm. And here I am,*

*over halfway across the galaxy, fighting for a cause
I believe in. It's great, but . . .*

I wish I didn't feel so alone.

He thought of Ben, and Uncle Owen and Aunt
Beru, first with sadness for their loss, then with anger
at the Empire. Then he thought of the planet Alderaan, and the anger burned even more.

Luke went to get suited up for his mission.

On the Death Star, Grand Moff Tarkin and Darth
Vader watched a computer monitor that showed the
space station's position in relation to the planet Yavin
and the moon Yavin 4. As the planetary diagrams
moved over and past each other on the monitor, a
voice from the intercom announced, "Orbiting the
planet at maximum velocity. The moon with the Rebel
base will be in range in thirty minutes."

"This will be a day long remembered," Vader
said. "It has seen the end of Kenobi. It will soon see
the end of the Rebellion."

Tarkin glanced at Vader, then returned his gaze to
the monitor. He anticipated with relish delivering the
crushing blow to the Rebel Alliance.

C-3PO and R2-D2 went with Luke to the main
hangar. Luke was now wearing a bright orange
flight suit and carried a helmet adorned with Alliance emblems. In the hangar, flight crews rushed to

make last-minute adjustments to the starfighters. Over a loudspeaker, a man's voice said, "All flight troops, man your stations. All flight troops, man your stations."

Stepping down to the hangar floor, Luke found Han and Chewbacca loading small boxes onto an armored military speeder. The boxes contained precious metals, the only form of currency that Han would accept from the Alliance. Han had insisted on the payment, even though the Rebels desperately needed the materials for repairing starships and equipment. Han appeared to be completely ignoring the activity of the Rebel flight crews and pilots.

Eyeing the box in Han's hands, Luke said, "So . . . you got your reward and you're just leaving, then?"

"That's right, yeah!" Han said. "I got some old debts I got to pay off with this stuff. Even if I didn't, you don't think I'd be fool enough to stick around here, do you?"

Luke was silent, but inside, he fumed.

"Why don't you come with us?" Han said. "You're pretty good in a fight. I could use you."

"Come on!" Luke snapped angrily. "Why don't you take a look around? You know what's about to happen, what they're up against. They could use a good pilot like you. You're turning your back on them."

"What good's a reward if you ain't around to use it?" Han said as he loaded another box on the speeder. "Besides, attacking the battle station ain't my idea of courage. It's more like suicide."

"All right," Luke said. "Well, take care of yourself, Han. I guess that's what you're best at, isn't it?" He turned and started to walk off.

Han hesitated, then called out, "Hey, Luke . . ."

Luke stopped and turned. Then Han, despite himself, said, "May the Force be with you."

Although Luke may have been surprised to hear those words from the same smuggler who'd claimed not to believe in the Force, he didn't show it. He glanced down at the pile of boxes beside Han, then stared back at Solo for a moment before he turned away again.

As Luke walked off, Han caught Chewbacca's gaze and said, "What're you lookin' at?" Han loaded another box onto the speeder and muttered, "I know what I'm doing."

Scowling, Luke headed for his X-wing. Over the hangar's loudspeaker, the controller's voice announced, "All pilots to your stations. All pilots to your stations."

Leia was walking with a group of Rebel soldiers when she saw Luke. She went to him and said, "What's wrong?"

"Oh, it's Han!" Luke replied, shaking his head.

"I don't know, I really thought he'd change his mind."

"He's got to follow his own path," Leia said. "No one can choose it for him."

Luke looked away. "I only wish Ben were here."

Leia kissed Luke on the cheek, then moved off with the soldiers, heading for the war room.

Luke found his X-wing. C-3PO and R2-D2 were beside the starfighter, and two technicians were preparing to hoist R2-D2 up to the starfighter's astromech socket. Luke was about to climb up the ladder to the cockpit when he heard a familiar voice call out, "Hey, Luke!"

Luke turned to face his best friend from Tatooine. "Biggs!" he shouted with surprise. Biggs was taller and slightly older than Luke, with dark hair and a mustache. Like Luke, he wore a Rebel pilot's uniform and carried a helmet.

"Hey-ay-ay!" Biggs laughed, wrapping an arm around Luke's shoulder.

"I don't believe it!" Luke said.

"How are you?"

"Great!"

Biggs looked from Luke to the X-wing and asked, "You're coming up with us?"

"I'll be right up there with you," Luke replied with a grin. "And have I got some stories to tell you!"

Just then, a deep voice called out, "Skywalker!" Luke and Biggs stopped talking and turned to face Garven Dreis, a veteran pilot and the leader of Red Squadron, the X-wing unit that included Luke and Biggs. Dreis looked skeptically at Luke, then gestured to the X-wing and said, "You sure you can handle this ship?"

Before Luke could answer, Biggs said, "Sir, Luke is the best bush pilot in the Outer Rim territories."

Apparently, that was good enough for Dreis. He grinned at Luke and said, "You'll do all right."

"Thank you, sir," Luke said. "I'll try."

Dreis walked off to another X-wing. Biggs saw that his own X-wing was ready for liftoff and said, "I've got to get aboard. Listen, you'll tell me your stories when we come back. All right?" He started to head off.

"Biggs," Luke said, and his friend stopped and turned. Beaming with pride, Luke continued, "I told you I'd make it someday."

"Be like old times, Luke," Biggs said. "They'll never stop us!" Biggs walked fast to his starfighter.

As Luke climbed up the ladder to his own X-wing, he looked to the two crewmen who were about to ease R2-D2 into the astromech socket. The crew chief said, "That R2 unit of yours seems a bit beat-up. Do you want a new one?"

"Not on your life!" Luke said. "That little droid and

I have been through a lot together." Luke looked directly at the plucky astromech and said, "You okay, Artoo-Detoo?"

R2-D2 beeped enthusiastically.

"Good!" Luke said as he hopped into the cockpit and pulled on his helmet.

"Okay, easy!" said the crew chief as R2-D2 was lowered into his snug socket.

Still standing beside the X-wing, C-3PO looked up to R2-D2 and said, "Hang on tight, Artoo, you've got to come back."

R2-D2 beeped in agreement.

The protocol droid said, "You wouldn't want my life to get boring, would you?"

R2-D2 whistled his reply. The crewmen made some final adjustments, then climbed down to the hangar floor. Luke lowered his cockpit canopy and his X-wing lifted off to a low hover. As he followed the other starfighters toward the wide doorway, he felt a twinge of fear about his mission. *Do we really have any chance of defeating the Death Star?*

Then, from out of nowhere, Ben's disembodied voice said, "Luke, the Force will be with you."

Luke took a deep breath and guided the X-wing out of the hangar.

Outside the ancient Massassi temple, a Rebel sentry watched the starfighters rise up over the jungle and race into the morning sky.

Leia and C-3PO proceeded to the war room, where technicians and controllers monitored their illuminated tactical screens. Over the intercom, a robotic voice announced, "Standby alert. Death Star approaching. Estimated time to firing range, fifteen minutes."

Leia knew that Tarkin would order the destruction of Yavin 4 without any hesitation, just as he had done to Alderaan. *What if the Rebel pilots aren't able to carry out General Dodonna's plan?* She tried to push the thought out of her head. *We must succeed. We must!*

Leaving Yavin 4's atmosphere, the X-wing and Y-wing starfighters sped away across space. They flew in a tight formation at sub-light speed, staying in sight of one another. After they wrapped around the gas giant Yavin, they saw a strange moonlike sphere in the distance.

The Death Star.

Each pilot in Red Squadron and Gold Squadron had a comm-unit designation. Luke's designation was Red Five. Even though he knew the names of only a few other pilots, he felt a strong bond with every one of them. They were all brave men, united by their willingness to put their lives on the line against the Empire.

It's a good thing everyone isn't like Han Solo, Luke thought bitterly. He tried to shake off his disappointment. *Maybe I'm wrong. Maybe I haven't seen the last of Han.*

Over his helmet's headset, Luke heard Red Leader — Garven Dreis — say, "All wings report in."

"Red Ten standing by."

"Red Seven standing by."

"Red Three standing by." Luke thought, *That's Biggs.*

"Red Six standing by." *That's Jek Porkins.* Luke had been introduced to the burly, bearded pilot just before the mission briefing.

"Red Nine standing by."

"Red Two standing by." *Wedge.*

"Red Eleven standing by."

"Red Five standing by," Luke said. In the astromech socket behind his cockpit, R2-D2 swiveled his head and beeped.

After the other X-wing pilots reported in, Red Leader ordered, "Lock S-foils in attack position."

Staying in formation, Red Squadron unfolded their starfighters' wings and locked them into the "X" position. As they neared the Death Star, the fighters began to shudder, and the pilots bounced in their cockpits.

"We're passing through their magnetic field," Red Leader announced. "Hold tight!"

Luke concentrated on the incoming Death Star. Red Leader ordered, "Switch your deflectors on. Double front!" Luke and the other pilots adjusted the controls on their fighters' shields.

The Death Star now loomed large before the

approaching starfighters. The gargantuan space station's surface was half in shadow, and the shadowed area sparkled with thousands of lights, like a planetary city at night when viewed from space. Watching the Death Star fill his X-wing's cockpit window, Wedge gasped, "Look at the size of that thing!"

"Cut the chatter, Red Two," Red Leader said. "Accelerate to attack speed." As the starfighters increased velocity, he announced, "This is it, boys!" The X-wings angled to fly low over the Death Star's trench.

From his Y-wing, Dutch Vander said, "Red Leader, this is Gold Leader."

"I copy, Gold Leader," Red Leader answered via his headset.

Gold Leader said, "We're starting for the target shaft now."

"We're in position," Red Leader reported. "I'm going to cut across the axis and try and draw their fire."

Red Leader, his wingman, and two other X-wings peeled off and dived toward the Death Star's surface. The space station's large turbopowered laser gun emplacements became visible, and the guns rotated and fired green laserbolts at the Rebel fighters.

*　　　*　　　*

On Yavin 4, the Rebel pilots' comm transmissions were broadcast over the war room's intercom. Leia and C-3PO listened as Wedge said, "Heavy fire, boss! Twenty-three degrees."

Red Leader answered, "I see it. Stay low."

Leia wondered how Luke was doing. She looked to an illuminated tactical screen, found the blip that represented the position of his X-wing over the Death Star, and kept her eyes on the blip.

From his cockpit, Luke saw Wedge maneuver his starfighter toward the Death Star. Luke said into his comm, "This is Red Five! I'm going in!"

Luke raced down toward the space station. Laser-bolts streaked from his X-wing's cannons, creating a huge fireball explosion on the station's surface. Suddenly, Luke realized he was traveling too fast to avoid the rising flames.

Seeing Luke's situation, Biggs shouted, "Luke, pull out!"

Luke pulled hard on the controls and his fighter ascended rapidly through the fire. Glancing out his cockpit window, he could see fresh scorch marks on the leading edges of his wings.

Biggs asked, "Are you all right?"

"I got a little cooked, but I'm okay," Luke told him.

They resumed strafing the Death Star's surface with laserbolts.

*   *   *

Alarms sounded and red lights flashed within the Death Star's corridor. As stormtroopers and droids rushed to their stations, only Darth Vader appeared to remain calm amidst the chaotic activity.

A black-uniformed Imperial officer ran up to Vader. "We count thirty Rebel ships, Lord Vader. But they're so small, they're evading our turbolasers!"

"We'll have to destroy them ship to ship," Vader said. "Get the crews to their fighters."

Red Leader flew his X-wing through a heavy hail of flak. "Watch yourself!" he cautioned the other pilots. "There's a lot of fire coming from the right side of that deflection tower."

Luke sighted the deflection tower and said, "I'm on it."

Biggs said, "I'm going in. Cover me, Porkins!"

Porkins mistook Biggs for Wedge and answered, "I'm right with you, Red Three."

Biggs and Porkins angled toward the tower and fired. There was an eruption of flames from the tower's side, but the Imperials responded with a barrage of laserfire. Porkins realized he was heading straight into the barrage and said, "I've got a problem here."

Biggs shouted, "Eject!"

"I can hold it," Porkins said, angling his ship in an attempt to avoid the crisscrossing laserbolts that streaked from the station. He really thought he could make it.

Biggs saw otherwise and yelled, "Pull out!"

"No, I'm all right," Porkins said just before his fighter took a direct hit. His cockpit filled with smoke. Then his ship exploded, and Porkins was gone.

Grand Moff Tarkin watched the battle as it was displayed on a monitor in the Death Star control room. On the intercom, a voice announced, "The Rebel base will be in firing range in seven minutes."

From Tarkin's perspective, the Rebel starfighters were nothing but a slight annoyance. He couldn't imagine they would accomplish anything more than marring the surface of his space station. Still, if there were any Rebel pilots left after the destruction of Yavin 4, he would make them pay for the damage.

With their lives.

Luke was still flying low over the Death Star's surface when he heard Ben's voice again. The Jedi said, "Luke, trust your feelings."

Luke tapped his fingers against the side of his helmet. *Nothing wrong with my headset. I wish I knew what Ben meant. Right now, my only feelings are for blowing up this space station!* He squeezed his triggers and his cannons launched more laserbolts into the Death Star, then he streaked away from the explosions.

Luke was preparing for another attack when he heard a Rebel base control officer's voice on his headset. The control officer said, "Squad leaders, we've picked up a new group of signals. Enemy fighters coming your way."

"My scope's negative," Luke reported. "I don't see anything."

"Pick up your visual scanning," Red Leader advised.

In their respective cockpits, Luke and Biggs turned their heads to look outside their windows, searching for any sight of incoming Imperial fighters. Red Leader spotted the ships first and warned, "Here they come."

There were six TIE fighters. Flying in an incredibly tight formation, they raced toward the Rebel ships, then fanned out to pursue individual targets.

"Watch it!" Red Leader shouted to a young pilot named John D., whose comm-unit designation was Red Four. "You've got one on your tail."

John D. tried to evade the TIE fighter's laserfire, but ultimately failed. His X-wing shattered and exploded, scattering debris in all directions.

Red Leader visually scanned the other fighters in his squadron. "Biggs! You've picked one up. Watch it!"

"I can't see it!" Biggs answered. He sent his X-wing into a series of tight swerves but the TIE fighter followed each evasive maneuver. Green laser-fire whizzed past Biggs. "They're on me tight. I can't shake him. . . ."

"I'll be right there," Luke said, angling his X-wing to pursue the TIE fighter that was right on Biggs' tail. Glancing at his targeting computer, Luke locked his target into his sights and fired. The TIE fighter exploded in a mass of flames.

Luke thought, *I don't know how much longer we can keep this up. If the Death Star deploys even more TIE fighters, we'll really be in for it!*

Darth Vader strode purposefully down a Death Star corridor and came to a stop before two black-clad Imperial TIE fighter pilots. Like their stormtrooper counterparts, the Imperial pilots were entirely without fear.

Vader said, "Several fighters have broken off from the main group. Come with me!" He headed for a door that led to a hangar. The two pilots followed.

On Yavin 4, Leia and C-3PO continued listening to the transmissions from the Rebel pilots. Over the intercom, Biggs said, "Pull in! Luke . . . pull in!"

Then Wedge said, "Watch your back, Luke!"

Leia tried to visualize what was happening over the Death Star, and trembled.

In his cockpit, Luke heard Wedge say, "Watch your back! Fighters above you, coming in!"

Luke angled away from the Death Star's surface until he spotted the tailing TIE fighter. The Imperial pilot fired and scored a hit on Luke's X-wing, striking the port upper thrust engine. The X-wing bounced hard and flames streamed from the damaged engine.

"I'm hit, but not bad," Luke announced as he took evasive action. "Artoo, see what you can do with it. Hang on back there."

R2-D2 rotated his dome to extend a repair arm to the port engine. The brave astromech ignored the green laserfire that whizzed past the X-wing.

Red Leader lost sight of Luke. Even though Red Leader knew that Jek Porkins had already been killed, he was under the strain of combat when he called out Porkins' comm-unit designation: "Red Six . . . can you see Red Five?"

Red Ten — a young man named Theron Nett — answered, "There's a heavy fire zone on this side. Red Five, where are you?"

Luke was still trying to evade the same TIE fighter that had struck his X-wing. Soaring away from the Death Star, Luke said, "I can't shake him!"

"I'm on him, Luke!" Wedge called in. "Hold on!" Wedge dived toward Luke and the TIE fighter.

Luke increased speed, but the TIE fighter clung to his trail. Growing frantic as he waited for Wedge to come to his aid, Luke suddenly realized he'd lost sight of Biggs. Luke said, "Blast it! Biggs, where are you?"

Biggs was rapidly racing to Luke's position, but Wedge got there first. In a daring maneuver, Wedge guided his X-wing straight for the cockpit window of Luke's pursuer. Wedge fired his cannons and the TIE fighter's spherical command pod exploded into space dust. Because of his velocity, Wedge was unable to pull out, but he quickly angled his X-wing to fly through the fiery explosion, narrowly missing the two hexagonal wings that were all that remained of the destroyed TIE fighter.

"Thanks, Wedge," Luke said, breathing a sigh of relief.

"Good shooting, Wedge!" Biggs chimed in.

As Luke readjusted his controls, he heard the voice of Y-wing pilot Dutch Vander speak over his headset: "Red Leader, this is Gold Leader. We're starting our attack run."

Red Leader replied, "I copy, Gold Leader. Move into position."

*   *   *

While Gold Leader and two other Y-wings descended to the enormous space station's trench, Darth Vader and his two wingmen piloted their TIE fighters out of a Death Star hangar and into space. Vader's ship was a TIE Advanced x1 Prototype with an elongated rear deck and matching solar arrays that bent in toward the central command pod.

"Stay in attack formation!" Vader said into his fighter's comlink as he led his wingmen to the Rebel ships.

Gold Leader adjusted his scopes as he guided Gold Two and Gold Five down to the Death Star's equatorial trench, en route to the vulnerable exhaust port. Seeing the readout for their target on the nav computer, Gold Leader said, "The exhaust port is marked and locked in!"

Three Y-wings swooped down into the high-walled trench. Gold Five — an older pilot named Davish "Pops" Krail — took the lead position. Gold Leader was Krail's starboard wingman, and Gold Two — a young pilot named Tiree — was his port wingman.

Imperial cannons were along the upper edges of the trench walls, and larger cannons were mounted atop angular towers on the Death Star's surface. The cannons fired green lasers and flak exploded around the three Y-wings.

Gold Leader said, "Switch all power to front deflector screens. Switch all power to front deflector screens." Maintaining a high speed, the pilots dipped and shifted to avoid being hit. Gold Leader tried to count off the streaks of laserfire and asked, "How many guns do you think, Gold Five?"

"Say about twenty guns," Gold Five answered. "Some on the surface, some on the towers."

The Y-wing pilots' communications were broadcast over the loudspeaker at the Rebel base. There, Leia cringed when she heard the announcement over the loudspeaker: "Death Star will be in range in five minutes."

The Rebel pilots were also aware of the limited time they had left, but if they were nervous, none of them showed it. Gold Leader's voice remained steady as he said, "Switch to targeting computer."

Inside the cockpit of each Y-wing, the targeting computer scopes automatically adjusted before the pilots so they could monitor their progress to the target site. Laserfire continued to whiz past the three fighters.

"Computer's locked," Gold Two confirmed as his fighter flew through bursts of flak. A beeping sound accompanied a blinking blip on his targeting scope, and he added, "Getting a signal."

Suddenly, the barrage of Imperial laserfire came

to an abrupt end. Baffled, Gold Two said, "The guns . . . they've stopped!"

Even though the three pilots were still traveling at high speed, the trench seemed eerily calm. Gold Five glanced out of his cockpit window and said, "Stabilize your rear deflectors. Watch for enemy fighters."

Gold Leader saw the three TIE fighters first. "They're coming in! Three marks at two ten."

The three marks were Darth Vader and his two wingmen. With inhuman precision, the Imperial fighters hurtled into the Death Star trench to arrive behind the Y-wings.

As a child, Darth Vader — under a different name — had raced repulsorlift pods through the canyons of Tatooine. Then, he'd experienced not only adrenaline rushes but heightened emotions while flying, and his piloting skills had ultimately led to his liberation from the sand planet. Now, Podracing was a distant memory, a ridiculous sport for short aliens with quick reflexes. Vader's only interest in flying was if it allowed him the opportunity to exercise supreme power. In that capacity, the Rebel starfighters interested him very much.

"I'll take them myself," Vader said into his comlink. "Cover me."

"Yes, sir," answered an Imperial pilot.

Vader lined up Gold Two in his targeting computer, then pressed the trigger on his fighter's control stick. Laserfire streaked out from Vader's ship and Gold Two's Y-wing exploded in a blinding flash.

Gold Leader saw the explosion — saw his friend Tiree die in a split second — and began to panic. "It's no good," he said into his comlink. "I can't maneuver!"

"Stay on target!" Gold Five said, trying to keep Gold Leader calm.

Gold Leader tried to adjust his targeting computer and said, "We're too close."

"Stay on target!" Gold Five repeated calmly.

"Loosen up!" Gold Leader snapped.

Darth Vader adjusted his own targeting computer. He locked onto Gold Leader's ship, then pressed the control stick's trigger. The Y-wing exploded, killing Dutch Vander and throwing debris in all directions.

Gold Five was close to the target area, but with three TIE fighters on his tail, he knew he wouldn't last much longer if he remained in the trench. Guiding his Y-wing up and out of the trench, he said, "Gold Five to Red Leader — lost Tiree, lost Dutch."

The Rebel pilots knew their transmissions might be intercepted by Imperial scanners, and did not want anyone on the Death Star to know that a squadron leader had been shot down. Also, Dutch's death meant an immediate advancement of rank for Pops

Krail, who would no longer be called Gold Five. With these concerns in mind, Red Leader answered, "I copy, Gold Leader."

Pops Krail said, "They came from behind —" Before Pops could finish, one of his engines exploded. Darth Vader's TIE fighter had followed Pops out of the trench and fired a devastating blast at the Y-wing. The starfighter blazed out of control, exploded, and Pops was gone.

In the Death Star control room, Grand Moff Tarkin's aide Chief Bast left a computer console to report to his leader. Tarkin stood before the large viewscreen, watching the Death Star's progress through space, and waiting for the moment that the planet Yavin no longer obscured Yavin 4.

Chief Bast said, "We've analyzed their attack, sir, and there is a danger. Should I have your ship standing by?"

"Evacuate?" Tarkin said, outraged. "In our moment of triumph? I think you overestimate their chances!"

Tarkin returned his attention to the viewscreen. Over the Death Star's intercom, a voice announced, "Rebel base, three minutes and closing."

Thirty Rebel pilots had traveled in their starfighters from Yavin 4 to the Death Star. Standing in the Rebel base war room, Leia looked at a tactical monitor and saw that only about six X-wings and a single Y-wing remained engaged in the battle. One of the X-wings was Luke's, but with less than three minutes until the Death Star entered firing range of Yavin 4, it was hard for Leia to remain hopeful for any Rebel's future.

From over the war room's loudspeaker came X-wing pilot Garven Dreis's voice: "Red boys, this is Red Leader. Rendezvous at mark six point one."

"This is Red Two," Wedge answered. "Flying toward you."

"Red Three, standing by," said Biggs.

Leia knew Luke was Red Five. The two remaining X-wing pilots carried the comm-unit designations of

Red Ten and Red Twelve. Near Leia, General Dodonna examined the tactical screen and said into his comm, "Red Leader, this is Base One. Keep half your group out of range for the next run."

"Copy, Base One," Red Leader said. Addressing his pilots, he continued, "Luke, take Red Two and Three. Hold up here and wait for my signal to start your run."

Luke got the message. If Red Leader failed to reach the exhaust port, it would be up to Luke — with Wedge and Biggs as his wingmen — to enter the trench and make one final attempt at the target.

In his cockpit, Red Leader glanced around to watch for the TIE fighters. Beads of sweat broke out across his forehead but he dismissed the nervous reflex and tightened his grip on his control stick. "This is it!" he said, and threw his X-wing down into the Death Star's trench. Red Ten and Red Twelve followed him.

The Death Star cannons fired at the three X-wings as they raced through the high-walled trench. As laserfire streaked past them, Red Ten quickly consulted his targeting scope, then tried to sight a cannon tower that would visually indicate the target site. He said, "We should be able to see it by now."

The Imperial cannons ceased firing. Red Leader said, "Keep your eyes open for those fighters!"

Red Ten said, "There's too much interference!" Indeed, the X-wing's sensors had been designed for traveling through space, not for speeding through a space station trench, and it was difficult for Red Ten to identify the blips on his scopes. Red Ten said into his comm, "Red Five, can you see them from where you are?"

From above the trench, Luke answered, "No sign of any — wait!" He saw the three TIE fighters, and said, "Coming in point three five."

Red Ten looked up and said, "I see them."

Sunlight flared off the solar arrays of the three TIE fighters as they dived in a tight formation for the trench. Advancing on the three X-wings, Darth Vader was surprised to feel a twinge of anticipation. He was looking forward to killing more Rebel pilots.

Red Leader blocked out thoughts of the incoming enemy fighters and displayed calm as he adjusted his targeting computer. He said, "I'm in range." On his targeting scope, the blinking blip indicated he was closing in on the Death Star's thermal exhaust port. "Target's coming up!" he announced. "Just hold them off for a few seconds."

Since the X-wings were without tail guns, all Red Ten and Red Twelve could do was increase power to their rear deflector shields and maneuver to defend Red Leader against a rear attack.

From behind, Darth Vader said into his comm, "Close up formation." His wingmen complied.

Red Leader lined up the target in the crosshairs of his scope. "Almost there!" he said.

Darth Vader's targeting computer locked onto Red Twelve's X-wing. Vader pressed his control stick's trigger and his cannons spat green laserfire. The X-wing exploded and crashed against the walls of the trench.

The power of the blast nearly sent Red Ten out of control. Struggling to stay on course behind Red Leader, Red Ten said into his comm, "You'd better let her loose."

But Red Leader wasn't ready yet. All his attention was concentrated on his targeting scope, waiting for the right moment to fire his X-wing's proton torpe-does.

Red Ten said, "They're right behind me."

"Almost there!" Red Leader said.

"I can't hold them!" Red Ten yelled. He looked to his left, trying to find the position of the TIE fighters.

Vader coolly pressed the trigger on his control stick. His well-aimed shot smashed into the X-wing, and Red Ten's cockpit filled with fire and smoke. An instant later, the X-wing exploded.

Red Leader grimly watched the target line up in his scope's crosshairs, then he fired. As the two proton torpedoes zoomed down the trench, he yelled, "It's away!" He pulled up into a rapid climb just before a huge explosion billowed out of the trench.

In the Rebel base, everyone held their breath as they waited to hear the pilot's transmissions over the loudspeaker. Red Nine exclaimed, "It's a hit!"

"Negative," Red Leader said with finality. "Negative! It didn't go in, just impacted on the surface."

The announcement stunned everyone in the Rebel war room. Leia wished General Dodonna would assure her that they still had a chance, but Dodonna didn't say a word.

Luke looked down from his cockpit and sighted Red Leader's ship. The TIE fighters had followed Red Leader out of the trench and were moving up fast behind him. Luke said, "Red Leader, we're right above you. Turn to point . . . oh-five; we'll cover for you."

"Stay there," Red Leader said. Looking nervously through his cockpit window, he added, "I just lost my starboard engine. Get set up for your attack run."

Darth Vader fired at Red Leader's X-wing. The X-wing caught fire and Garven Dreis screamed as his ship plummeted to the Death Star. Luke watched helplessly as the X-wing crashed and exploded.

No time to mourn, Luke thought. *Now it's up to me, Biggs, and Wedge.*

Grand Moff Tarkin cast a sinister eye at the Death Star control room's viewscreen. Over the intercom, a voice announced, "Rebel base, one minute and closing."

In the Rebel base war room, Leia, C-3PO, General

Dodonna, and the other Rebels continued listening to the transmissions from the remaining pilots. Luke said, "Biggs, Wedge, let's close it up. We're going in. We're going in full throttle. That ought to keep those fighters off our back."

Wedge said, "Right with you, boss."

Concerned, Biggs said, "Luke, at that speed, will you be able to pull out in time?"

"It'll be just like Beggar's Canyon back home," Luke told his old friend.

Wedge and Biggs followed Luke down into the Death Star's trench. They unleashed a barrage of laserfire at the space station, and the Imperial cannons returned fire.

As Luke raced ahead, Biggs said, "We'll stay back far enough to cover you."

Wedge said, "My scope shows the tower, but I can't see the exhaust port! Are you sure the computer can hit it?"

Luke heard the question but was momentarily distracted by a Death Star cannon that slowly rotated and pumped laserbolts at the X-wings. "Watch yourself!" Luke said. "Increase speed full throttle!"

"What about that tower?" Wedge said.

"You worry about those fighters!" Luke said. "I'll worry about the tower!"

Imperial laserfire nicked one of Luke's wings and he had to struggle with his controls to steady the starfighter's flight. "Artoo," he said into his comm, "that stabilizer's broken loose again. See if you can't lock it down!"

As R2-D2 extended his repair arm once more, the Death Star's cannons ceased firing. Flying behind Luke's X-wing, Wedge looked up and saw the enemy pilots making their approach. Wedge announced, "Fighters. Coming in, point three."

The three TIE fighters swooped into the trench. Luke focused on his targeting scope, which had just marked off the distance to the target. The TIE fighters zoomed closer to the X-wings. Darth Vader fired.

"I'm hit!" Wedge shouted as his ship was blasted from behind. Although his ship was still intact, his deflector shields were lost. Realizing he wouldn't stand a chance against another attack, he said, "I can't stay with you."

"Get clear, Wedge," Luke said. "You can't do any more good back there!"

"Sorry!" Wedge said as he pulled his crippled X-wing up and out of the trench.

Darth Vader sensed one of his wingmen wanted to pursue the fleeing X-wing. "Let him go!" Vader commanded. "Stay on the leader!" The TIE fighters maintained their tight formation as they accelerated.

Biggs gazed back at the incoming TIE fighters. "Hurry, Luke," he said with worry. "They're coming in much faster this time. We can't hold them!"

Luke glanced back from his cockpit and said, "Artoo, try and increase the power!"

R2-D2 worked frantically on the engines. Swiveling his dome, he saw the TIE fighters were gaining fast on Biggs' X-wing.

Luke looked into his targeting scope. Over his headset, he heard Biggs say, "Hurry up, Luke!"

Biggs glanced at the TIE fighters and moved in to cover for Luke. Darth Vader gained on Biggs. Biggs shouted, "Wait!"

Vader fired. Luke looked back and saw the X-wing that carried his best friend suddenly explode into a million flaming bits.

Biggs!

The TIE fighters kept coming. As Luke's eyes watered, his anger grew.

Inside the Death Star, Grand Moff Tarkin felt nothing but satisfaction when the announcement came over the intercom: "Rebel base, thirty seconds and closing."

"I'm on the leader," Darth Vader told his wingmen as he adjusted his targeting computer. The three TIE fighters charged after the lone X-wing that remained in the trench.

At the Rebel base, Princess Leia glanced at C-3PO. Nervous, the droid said, "Hang on, Artoo!"

Luke adjusted the lens on his targeting scope. The

exhaust port was still some distance ahead, and the TIE fighters were coming in fast from behind. *I don't think I'm going to make it.*

Just then, he heard Ben's voice: "Use the Force, Luke."

Luke looked outside the cockpit. *Ben?*

Ben's voice said, "Let go, Luke."

Suddenly, time seemed to slow down. Luke felt not as if he were racing through the Death Star's trench at full throttle, but rather that the trench was flowing past and around him. He was aware of the pursuing TIE fighters and the weapon-laden trench walls, but he no longer felt threatened by them. He was in control, and he was not afraid.

Darth Vader sensed the change that swept over the pilot in the remaining X-wing. As Vader tried to lock onto the Rebel starfighter with his targeting computer, he said, "The Force is strong in this one!"

Luke looked at his own targeting scope.

Ben's voice said, "Luke, trust me."

Luke reached to his control panel and pressed a button. The targeting scope retracted and moved away from his helmet.

Luke's action was detected by the controllers at the Rebel base. A controller announced, "His computer's off." Addressing Luke directly, the controller said, "Luke, you switched off your targeting computer. What's wrong?"

"Nothing," Luke answered as he stayed on course for his target. "I'm all right." *I don't need the targeting computer. All I have to do is get a bit closer to the exhaust port. I can do it! I know I can do it. . . .*

Behind Luke, R2-D2 rotated his dome again to look at the incoming TIE fighters. The central TIE fighter fired a burst of laserbolts at the X-wing, and the astromech was engulfed by crackling laserfire. R2-D2 screeched, then went silent.

"I've lost Artoo!" Luke shouted.

C-3PO heard Luke over the war room loudspeaker, and the golden droid looked to Princess Leia. Like the other Rebels, she had her eyes fixed on the tactical monitor. The controller announced, "The Death Star has cleared the planet. The Death Star has cleared the planet."

There was a simultaneous announcement in the Death Star control room: "Rebel base, in range."

Tarkin turned to an officer and said, "You may fire when ready."

The Imperial officer pressed a button on an illuminated control panel. "Commence primary ignition."

While the Imperial soldiers readied the Death Star's superlaser, Darth Vader's targeting computer locked onto Luke's X-wing. Taking careful aim, Vader said, "I have you now." He pressed the trigger on his control stick.

Suddenly, an unexpected blast of laserfire angled

down into the trench and struck the TIE fighter that had been traveling alongside Vader's starboard stern. The TIE fighter exploded. Vader exclaimed, "What?" He glanced up to locate the unknown attacker.

It was the *Millennium Falcon*.

"Yahoo!" Han Solo hollered as he descended rapidly from above, guiding the *Falcon* on what looked like a collision course for the two TIE fighters.

Intending to warn Darth Vader, the startled surviving Imperial wingman cried, "Look out!" But the sight of the oncoming Corellian freighter caused the wingman to panic, and he veered radically to one side and smashed against Vader's TIE fighter. The impact sent Vader's fighter spinning up and out of the trench, while the wingman's fighter crashed into the wall and exploded. Vader fought to regain control of his fighter but it continued to tumble across space, leaving the Death Star behind.

The *Falcon* pulled out of its steep dive and Han said into his comm, "You're all clear, kid. Now let's blow this thing up and go home!"

Luke looked up and smiled, then concentrated on the exhaust port. *I can sense the target. It's right in front of me. I cannot miss.*

Luke fired the proton torpedoes. The twin high-speed concussion projectiles streaked away from his X-wing, carrying their payload of high-yield proton-scattering warheads. Both torpedoes plunged down into the thermal exhaust port, and Luke — traveling at an almost sickening speed — pulled up and out of the trench and accelerated to catch up with the *Millennium Falcon,* Wedge's X-wing, and a single Y-wing, which were already speeding away from the Death Star.

Inside the space station, the superlaser was finally ready to be fired. Grand Moff Tarkin's eyes remained fixed on the viewscreen as an Imperial controller announced, "Stand by."

The three Rebel starfighters and the *Falcon* were barely out of the danger zone when the Death Star exploded in an immense, blinding flash. From a distance, the blast resembled a small supernova.

"Great shot, kid," Han said into his comm. "That was one in a million."

Luke let out a deep breath and relaxed. Then Ben's voice said, "Remember, the Force will be with you . . . always."

Luke smiled all the way back to Yavin 4.

EPILOGUE

Darth Vader regained control of his damaged TIE fighter. As he headed for the nearest Imperial outpost, he was not preoccupied about how he would explain the loss of the Death Star to the Emperor. Tarkin had been responsible for the space station and its vulnerabilities, and the Rebels had been more cunning than anyone had anticipated. There was really nothing more to say.

But there were plenty of other things to think about. Before Vader had been knocked out of the trench, he'd recognized the Corellian freighter as the same ship that had delivered Ben Kenobi to the Death Star, reportedly from Tatooine. Vader wondered why Kenobi had been on Tatooine, and how long he'd been there.

Then Vader thought of the last X-wing pilot in the trench. *He was so strong with the Force.*

Vader wouldn't rest until he learned the truth.

*   *   *

After landing in the main hangar at the Rebel base on Yavin 4, Luke climbed out of his battered X-wing to be greeted by a throng of cheering Rebels. As he descended the ladder beside his ship, he searched the crowd for one face in particular, and then he saw her.

"Luke!" Leia shouted as she rushed to him. She threw her arms around his neck and they danced around in a circle. As Luke spun, he saw C-3PO make his way through the crowd to stand beside the X-wing, then saw Han and Chewbacca come running toward them.

"Hey! Hey!" Han said as he embraced Luke.

"I knew you'd come back!" Luke said. "I just knew it!"

Han playfully shoved Luke's face and laughed. "Well, I wasn't gonna let you get all the credit and take all the reward."

Leia beamed at Han and said, "Hey, I knew there was more to you than money."

A maintenance crew had removed R2-D2 from the X-wing and lowered him down to the hangar floor. Seeing the astromech's scorched body, Luke said, "Oh, no!"

"Oh, my!" C-3PO cried. "Artoo! Can you hear me? Say something!" When no reply came from R2-D2, C-3PO looked to the maintenance crew and said, "You can repair him, can't you?"

One of the technicians said, "We'll get to work on him right away."

"You must repair him!" C-3PO said. Turning to Luke, C-3PO added, "Sir, if any of my circuits or gears will help, I'll gladly donate them."

"He'll be all right," Luke said with great assurance. He had good reason to feel confident. He was no longer a kid with no future on a desert planet.

He was the pilot who'd just blown up the Death Star.

The next day, trumpets sounded over the Massassi temple. In the expansive ruins of the temple's high-ceilinged main throne room, hundreds of uniformed Rebel troops stood at attention and faced a long aisle. The aisle extended to the far end of the chamber and ended at steps that led up to an elevated level, upon which stood Princess Leia, General Dodonna, and the other Alliance leaders.

Luke, Han, and Chewbacca entered the throne room. Luke wore an Alliance-issue yellow flight jacket over a black tunic, brown pants, and dark leather boots. Han wore his own clothes, including a clean shirt he'd been saving for a special occasion. Chewbacca wore his bandolier.

The Wookiee followed the two men up the aisle, passing the silent troops as they marched solemnly toward the princess. When the trio arrived at the steps, Chewbacca glanced aside and barked at the troops. As if in response, the troops turned simultaneously on their heels to face the Rebel leaders.

Luke and Han ascended the steps and stopped just below Leia. Chewbacca was uncomfortable with the situation and remained on a lower step behind Han.

Princess Leia wore a white gown and a silver necklace and bracelet. She looked to Han and Luke. Luke was unable to maintain a serious expression and broke out in a big smile. Leia smiled in return.

General Dodonna handed a gold medallion to Leia. Han bowed as Leia placed the medallion around his neck. As he rose, Han winked at Leia.

Luke glanced over to C-3PO, who stood beside the Rebel leaders. The protocol droid was gleaming from head to toe, and appeared very proud. Luke nodded to acknowledge C-3PO, then returned his attention to Leia and the ceremony. He lowered his head, and Leia placed a medallion around his neck too.

Then both Han and Luke bowed to Leia, and a happy beeping sound came from beside C-3PO. It was R2-D2. The astromech had been completely refurbished, and looked better than he had when he'd been brand-new. R2-D2 wobbled back and forth with excitement, causing all to grin.

Luke, Han, and Chewbacca turned to face the assembled troops, and the ancient temple was suddenly filled with loud cheers and applause. Chewbacca surveyed the crowd and growled.

Even though friends had been lost, and the battle against the Empire was far from over, the fact remained that a small band of heroes had destroyed the Death Star against impossible odds. For that, the Rebels found cause to celebrate. And they did.

EPISODE V

THE EMPIRE STRIKES BACK

Ryder Windham
Based on the story by George Lucas and the screenplay
by Lawrence Kasdan and Leigh Brackett

A long time ago, in a galaxy far, far away. . . .

During the Battle of Yavin, Sith Lord Darth Vader piloted his own Imperial TIE fighter to defend the Death Star space station against a Rebel Alliance assault. While engaged in a dogfight with an X-wing starfighter, he sensed the enemy pilot was strong with the Force. Vader was about to fire upon the X-wing when he and his two wingmen were attacked by a Corellian YT-1300 transport. Vader survived, but his damaged TIE fighter went spinning out of control. Seconds later, the Death Star was blown into a billion pieces.

After Darth Vader brought his crippled spacecraft to an Imperial outpost, he began his investigation. He did not have to identify the Corellian transport. He'd seen it before, when it had been captured by a Death Star tractor beam and deposited in hangar 3207. The transport had been readily identified as the *Millennium Falcon*: the same ship that had eluded Imperial soldiers on Tatooine during their search for an R2 unit that had carried the plans for the Death Star.

Among the *Millennium Falcon*'s passengers from Tatooine was Vader's former Jedi Master, Obi-Wan Kenobi. On the Death Star, Kenobi's allies succeeded in their mission to rescue Princess Leia Organa, the Rebel leader who'd placed the Death Star plans in the R2 unit. Because Darth Vader had once lived on Tatooine, he was nagged by two questions: How long had Obi-Wan been there? And why?

CHAPTER 1

The lone Star Destroyer traveled silently across inter-
stellar space with the precision of a massive dart. An
Imperial-class warship, it measured 1,600 meters
long from its aft ion engines to its sharp-tipped bow,
and was equipped with enough firepower to reduce
a civilization to ashes. Even without its sixty turbolaser batteries and equal number of ion cannons, the
wedge-shaped starship looked like it was ready to
cut through anything in its path. The ship's name was
the *Avenger*; its commanding officer was Captain
Needa.

The *Avenger* arrived at its designated coordinates,
then deployed its cargo of hyperdrive pods from a recessed launch bay. Each 3.4-meter-long pod was programmed to travel thousands of light-years on a
one-way trip to a specific destination, never to return
to the *Avenger* or any other Imperial ship.

Across the galaxy, other Star Destroyers carried

out the same task, releasing hyperdrive pods into space. Soon, thousands of pods were racing off to almost as many worlds, including planets and moons that had yet to be conquered by the Empire. Each pod contained a probot, a probe droid engineered for long-range covert surveillance. Each probot had a single purpose: to find the Rebel Alliance's new base.

The *Avenger*'s pods were targeted for three planetary systems: Allyuen, Tokmia, and Hoth. The Empire had little information regarding Allyuen and Tokmia, and only slightly more for Hoth, a blue-white sun that was orbited by six planets and a wide asteroid belt. According to an old navigational chart, Hoth's inner five planets were lifeless; the outermost planet — also named Hoth — was covered entirely by snow and ice, and was orbited by three nameless moons. Because of the sixth planet's thin atmosphere and close proximity to the asteroid field, it was also frequently battered by meteors.

Speeding through space, a pod arrived in orbit of the ice world. It automatically applied emergency braking thrusters, allowing Hoth's gravity to pull it down through the thin atmosphere. The pod streaked downward until its journey ended on the planet's surface, where it smashed through layers of snow and impacted along the upper slope of a high ravine.

As smoke billowed from the impact site and darkened the surrounding snow, the pod opened to reveal the probot's armored form. Equipped with a repulsorlift and silenced thrusters, the probot had a wide, sensor-laden head that rested upon a cylindrical support body, under which dangled four manipulator arms and a high-torque grasping arm. Although the probot's primary function was to gather and transmit data for the Empire, it was also equipped with a single defense blaster.

Activating its repulsorlift, the black probot rose up through the smoke and went immediately to work. It used its sensors to scan for Alliance transmissions and to survey the terrain, seeking signs of life and habitation. The probot hovered momentarily as it gathered and analyzed data, then moved on, gliding noiselessly through the chilled air . . . unknowingly coming closer and closer to the Rebel base.

Luke Skywalker, wearing an Alliance-issued insulated patrol suit, rode his two-legged snow lizard, a tauntaun, over a windswept ice slope on Hoth. A thin layer of snow had built up on Luke's protective green-lensed goggles, so he momentarily released one gloved hand from the reins to swipe at the goggles and clear his vision.

Luke was looking for wild tauntauns, wampa ice monsters, and any other of Hoth's few indigenous creatures. Sensors were being planted for the Alliance's regional warning network, which would anticipate

Imperial or alien intruders, and it was Luke's job to make sure that no native beasts might accidentally damage them. But from what Luke could see, there wasn't any sign of life amidst the frozen wastes, not even tracks. In every direction, all he saw was white.

Luke felt about as far as he could get from his home-world, the desert planet Tatooine — not merely because of the great distance between the two planets or their dramatically different climates. So much had changed since he'd joined the Rebellion. He was no longer the boy who'd felt stuck on a moisture farm, who only dreamed of adventures on far-off worlds. He had become a warrior, a hero of the Rebel Alliance, and his adventures had exceeded his dreams.

Yet the price had been unfortunately high. Uncle Owen and Aunt Beru were dead. So was his child-hood friend Biggs Darklighter, along with many other brave Rebel pilots who'd fought in the Battle of Yavin. Luke remembered them all, but tried not to think about them too much. It was more in his nature to think of the future than dwell on the past.

But he couldn't stop thinking about Ben, the Jedi Knight, who had served so briefly as Luke's mentor in the ways of the Force.

I still miss him, Luke thought. *I wish I'd gotten to know him better on Tatooine, even though Uncle Owen would have tried to stop me. I could have learned so much. . . .*

Luke knew he needed to focus on his assignment, so he pushed aside his thoughts and guided the tauntaun along a snow-covered ridge. He reined the gray-furred beast to a stop, and it exhaled through its lower pair of nostrils, steaming the air and fogging Luke's goggles. Luke lifted the goggles over his cap's visor, then squinted at the surrounding whiteness.

His keen eyes sighted a streak of light that plummeted from the sky and slammed into the top of a nearby slope, close enough that he could hear the impact. Luke removed his electrobinoculars from his utility belt and peered through the lenses to see a magnified image of smoke rising from the impact site. Just another meteorite on Hoth? Luke wasn't sure.

He lowered the electrobinoculars and returned them to his belt, then brushed snow from the back of his left glove to reveal a comlink transmitter. As he activated the transmitter, his tauntaun shifted nervously beneath him.

"Echo Three to Echo Seven," Luke said into the comlink. "Han, old buddy, do you read me?"

Luke listened to some brief static, then heard the familiar voice of his friend, Han Solo. "Loud and clear, kid. What's up?"

Luke looked around, trying to catch sight of Han, who was also riding a tauntaun. Han's assignment had been to plant the warning sensors.

Luke said, "Well, I finished my circle. I don't pick up any life readings."

"There isn't enough life on this ice cube to fill a space cruiser," Han commented over the comlink. Luke grinned, then caught a brief glimpse of Han's mounted figure before he vanished into the snowy distance. As he departed, Han added, "The sensors are placed. I'm going back."

"Right," Luke said. "I'll see you shortly. There's a meteorite that hit the ground near here. I want to check it out. It won't take long."

Luke switched off his comlink, and his tauntaun snorted nervously. "Hey, steady, girl," he said, reining back. "Hey, what's the matter? You smell something?"

Suddenly, there was a monstrous howl. Luke turned quickly to face a massive wampa, its jaws flung open to display fiercely sharp teeth. A huge, clawed paw slammed into Luke, knocking him from his saddle. He was unconscious before he hit the snow.

Echo Base, the comm-unit designation for the Alliance's command headquarters on Hoth, was a vast network of passages and caves concealed within a glacial mountain. Some of the underground chambers had formed naturally over thousands of years, but most had been carved from the ice in a matter of weeks, thanks to the Alliance Corps of Engineers and their industrial lasers. The base had quickly become home to several thousand Rebel soldiers, technicians, and pilots. It also served as the temporary accommodations for two lapsed mercenaries: Han Solo, captain of the *Millennium Falcon*, and his first mate, Chewbacca the Wookiee.

Although Han and Chewbacca had worked steadily with the Alliance in the three years since the Battle of Yavin, neither had formally enlisted. This was one reason why Han, unlike Luke, wore a dark, fur-lined heavy-weather parka instead of an Alliance uniform. The other reason was that Han thought he looked better in his own clothes.

Returning from his assignment, Han rode his tauntaun up to the mouth of an enormous ice cave, the north entrance of Echo Base. He kept the tauntaun moving at a fast trot as they entered.

The cave had been transformed into a low-ceilinged hangar for starships. Dozens of Rebel soldiers were at work, some busily securing the base while others worked on vehicles. Han steered his tauntaun past a group of Rebel troopers who were unloading supplies, and brought the tauntaun to a stop next to a pair of waiting handlers. They grabbed the beast's reins, and Han dismounted in one smooth motion. Landing on the snow-covered floor, he felt a stinging sensation in his legs, which — despite his insulated boots and leggings — were cold and stiff from riding. As he stepped away from his tauntaun, he pushed his parka's hood back, removed his snow goggles, and kept moving to get the blood circulating in his legs.

Han walked deeper into the hangar. He passed teams of technicians who were adding repulsor-coil heaters to T-47 airspeeders to prevent the motors from freezing, effectively transforming the vehicles into what the Rebels had nicknamed "snowspeeders." A battle-damaged X-wing was also under repair. Han had to be careful not to bump into any Rebels or trip over an astromech droid as he stepped over the power cables that snaked across the floor.

Han finally reached his own ship, the heavily modified Corellian transport. From the hangar floor, he looked up to see Chewbacca sitting atop the *Falcon*'s starboard mandible. Chewbacca, a tall, brown-furred Wookiee, was using one hand to shield his eyes with a pair of welding goggles — the goggles' strap was too small to fit around the Wookiee's broad head — while the other hand operated a fusioncutter. Sparks flew where the fusioncutter's plasma beam met the *Falcon*'s hull.

"Chewie!" Han called out, but the Wookiee didn't stop working. "Chewie!" he called again — to no avail. Either the surrounding noise was too much or the Wookiee was ignoring him. "Chewie!" he yelled a third time.

The Wookiee lowered the goggles and unleashed a series of harsh, irritated growls.

"All right, don't lose your temper," Han said. "I'll come right back and give you a hand."

Han changed out of his cold-weather gear, which reeked of the tauntaun's oily fur, and put on fresh clothes, including a black, long-sleeved jacket that went well with his frame. After changing, he walked through a narrow-walled passage and stepped down into the Echo Base command center.

Laser-cut skylights in the low, icy ceiling provided natural illumination for the room. Han looked around and saw Rebel controllers and droids setting up electronic equipment and monitoring radar signals. Most of the comm-scan computer stations, flat-screen monitors, and even the chairs had been used on Yavin 4, but because of Hoth's climate, the command center was more tightly packed to conserve heat. All the Rebels wore white insulated uniforms, gloves, and gray snowboots.

Han caught sight of Princess Leia Organa, who wore a heated vest over her white jumpsuit. She looked away from her console and spotted him immediately. He held her gaze for a second before he broke eye contact.

The commander of the Alliance ground and fleet forces in the Hoth star system, General Rieekan, glanced up from a console and said, "Solo?"

"No sign of life out there, General," Han reported. "The sensors are in place. You'll know if anything comes around."

Rieekan, looking tired and older than his years, read the data displayed on the console as he asked, "Commander Skywalker reported in yet?"

"No," Han said. "He's checking out a meteorite that hit near him."

"With all the meteorite activity in this system, it's going to be difficult to spot approaching ships," Rieekan said, his eyes still on the console.

"General, I've got to leave," Han said. "I can't stay here anymore."

"I'm sorry to hear that."

"Well, there's a price on my head. If I don't pay off Jabba the Hutt, I'm a dead man." Han didn't have to explain further. Everyone at Echo Station knew that Han had been a smuggler, and that one former client — a notorious Hutt crimelord on Tatooine — had placed a bounty on his head after he'd failed to reimburse the Hutt for a spice shipment he'd dumped to avoid Imperial arrest. The Alliance had given Han more than enough credits to repay Jabba, but the Rebels had also kept him very busy since the Battle of Yavin. Unfortunately, Hutts were not known for their patience.

"A death mark's not an easy thing to live with," Rieekan commented. Looking away from the console, he faced Han. "You're a good fighter, Solo. I hate to lose you." The two men shook hands.

"Thank you, General," Han said. As he turned away from Rieekan, he caught the gaze of Princess Leia again. There was tension in her face, somehow made more severe by the way her hair was braided and tied across her head. Looking at her expression, Han had no trouble imagining she was concerned about him.

Han approached Leia and said, "Well, Your Highness. I guess this is it."

"That's right," Leia replied, her voice cooler than the air.

Taken aback, Han said, "Well, don't get all mushy on me. So long, Princess." He turned away and walked straight for an adjoining laser-cut corridor.

"Han!" Leia shouted, following him into the hall.

Han stopped and turned to face her. "Yes, Your Highnessness?"

"I thought you had decided to stay," Leia said, her voice betraying her disappointment in his decision.

"Well, the bounty hunter we ran into on Ord Mantell changed my mind."

"Han, we need you!"

Han gave her a quizzical look, and echoed, "*We* need?"

"Yes."

"Oh, what about *you* need?"

"I need?" Leia said, apparently baffled. "I don't know what you're talking about."

Fed up, Han shook his head. "You probably don't." He turned away and headed off through the corridor.

Walking fast to follow Han, Leia said, "And what precisely am I supposed to know?"

Without breaking his stride, Han kept his eyes forward and said, "Come on! You want me to stay because of the way you feel about me."

"Yes," Leia said from behind. "You're a great help to us. You're a natural leader —"

Han stopped and whirled on Leia. "No!" he said, jabbing a finger at her for emphasis. "That's not it. Come on." Leia gaped. Han grinned, then raised a thumb to gesture at his face and said, "Aahhh — uh-huh! Come on."

Leia stared at him for a moment, then said, "You're imagining things."

"Am I?" Han said. "Then why are you following me? Afraid I was going to leave without giving you a good-bye kiss?"

Outraged, Leia spat out, "I'd just as soon kiss a Wookiee."

"I can arrange that," Han replied. As he turned and stormed off down the corridor, he added, "You could use a good kiss!"

Struck speechless, Leia stood there and watched him go. What could she say to him that she hadn't said before? *We're at war with the Empire,* she thought. *There's so much at stake for the Rebellion. I don't have time for . . . for Han Solo's nonsense!*

Later at Echo Station, the golden droid C-3PO and his astromech counterpart, R2-D2, walked through a corridor that led to the main hangar. As they rounded a corner, R2-D2 emitted a flurry of accusatory beeps.

"Don't try to blame me," C-3PO replied testily. "I didn't ask you to turn on the thermal heater. I merely commented that it was freezing in the princess's chamber."

R2-D2 rotated his domed head and responded with a defensive beep, prompting C-3PO to exclaim, "But it's *supposed* to be freezing. How are we going to dry out all her clothes? I really don't know."

R2-D2 beeped in protest, which only made C-3PO more agitated. "Oh, switch off," he said as they entered the hangar.

They approached the *Millennium Falcon,* where they found Han and Chewbacca working on the freighter's central lifters. Han was back in his cold-weather gear, which was now soiled with grime and oil as well as smelling of tauntaun.

"Why did you take this apart now?" Han yelled at Chewbacca. "I'm trying to get us out of here, and you pull both of these —" Words failing him, he gestured at the lifters.

"Excuse me, sir," C-3PO interrupted.

Han said to Chewbacca, "Put them back together right now."

C-3PO tried again. "Might I have a word with you, please?"

"What do you want?" Han snapped, not bothering to hide his irritation.

"Well, it's Princess Leia, sir. She's been trying to get you on the communicator."

"I turned it off," Han said, staring down the droid. "I don't want to talk to her." The way Han said it, he made it clear that he wanted this conversation to end immediately.

"Oh," said C-3PO. "Well, Princess Leia is wondering about Master Luke. He hasn't come back yet. She doesn't know where he is."

"I don't know where he is either," Han fumed, angered that the droid wasn't gone already.

"Nobody knows where he is," C-3PO stated.

That got Han's attention. "What do you mean, 'nobody knows'?"

C-3PO stammered, "Well, uh, you see . . ."

"Deck officer!" Han called out, looking away from C-3PO to find the Rebel officer in charge of docking bay operations. "Deck officer!"

"Excuse me, sir," C-3PO interjected. "Might I inqu —"

Han abruptly put his hand over C-3PO's mouth as

the deck officer ran to them. The deck officer looked at Han and said, "Yes, sir?"

"Do you know where Commander Skywalker is?"

"I haven't seen him. It's possible he came in through the south entrance."

"'It's possible'?" Han repeated skeptically, and the deck officer realized how feeble his statement had sounded. Han continued, "Why don't you go find out? It's getting dark out there."

"Yes, sir," answered the deck officer, who ran off to find his assistant.

Han removed his hand from C-3PO's mouth. The droid said, "Excuse me, sir. Might I inquire what's going on?"

Concerned and not really listening, Han replied, "Why not?"

Han sauntered off, leaving Chewbacca and the droids behind. C-3PO shook his head and said, "Impossible man. Come along, Artoo, let's find Princess Leia. Between ourselves, I think Master Luke is in considerable danger."

Han made his way to the chamber where the tauntauns were stabled, near the base's north entrance. Several exhausted Rebel scouts rested in the ice-walled chamber . . . but Luke wasn't among them. Han was trying to think of where else Luke might be when the deck officer and his assistant hurried toward him.

"Sir," said the deck officer. "Commander Sky-walker hasn't come in the south entrance. He might have forgotten to check in."

"Not likely," Han said. "Are the speeders ready?"

"Er, not yet," said the deck officer. "We're having some trouble adapting them to the cold."

"Then we'll have to go out on tauntauns," Han said. Before anyone could protest, Han turned and headed for the snow lizards.

The deck officer was aghast. Tauntauns were in-digenous, but they were hardly invulnerable to the cold, and what Han Solo was about to do was pure madness. Hoping to maintain some control of the sit-uation, the deck officer called after Solo, "Sir, the temperature's dropping too rapidly."

"That's right," Han said without looking back. "And my friend's out in it."

As Han approached the tauntaun he'd ridden ear-lier, the assistant officer said, "I'll cover sector twelve. Have comm control set to screen alpha."

The deck officer watched Han climb onto the snow creature's back and said, "Your tauntaun'll freeze before you reach the first marker."

"Then I'll see you in hell!" Han replied. He dug his heels into the tauntaun's side, and raced out of the cave into the bitter night.

CHAPTER 2

Luke Skywalker didn't know if he'd emerged from unconsciousness on his own or in response to the wampa's echoing howl. As he opened his eyes and took in his surroundings, he knew he was in serious trouble.

He was hanging upside down. In a cave. His entire body hurt. And he was very, very cold.

He struggled to get his bearings. A chill against the back of his neck suggested the cave's entrance was behind him. Icy stalactites and stalagmites, resembling many rows of teeth, obscured his view of the cave's dim interior. He couldn't see the wampa, but he could hear the snap of bones breaking, and chewing sounds. Judging from what he heard, Luke knew the wampa wasn't very far away.

Straining his aching muscles, Luke twisted his torso and neck to look up at the cave's ceiling. His booted feet were embedded in the ice. He strained his arms up and tried to work his legs out, but the ice was too thick, and he didn't have any leverage. He let his body slump and stretched his arms down, but he was suspended just high enough that he couldn't touch the floor. To free himself, he'd have to blast his way out, or . . .

He remembered his lightsaber. He reached to his belt, but the lightsaber was gone. *Oh, no! Don't tell me it's lost!* Luke angled his head, and spotted the lightsaber half buried in the snow on the floor below him.

He stretched out his arm, but the lightsaber was beyond his reach. Fortunately, Luke had another resource: the Force.

According to Ben, the Force was an energy field created by all living things. It surrounded and penetrated everything, binding the galaxy together. Since the Battle of Yavin, Luke had also learned that the Force could be utilized for moving small objects.

Still suspended from the cave's ceiling, Luke extended his right hand toward the lightsaber. He tried to envision the weapon rising from the snow and arriving into his waiting glove. But nothing happened.

Luke was far from mastering the Force, or even fully understanding it, but he had a feeling that he might be trying too hard. He closed his eyes and relaxed his muscles. He also did his best to remain calm, for in the recesses of his awareness, he sensed that the wampa was moving in the cave. *Did the wampa hear me trying to wrench myself free of the ice?* Luke no longer heard the sound of the creature's chewing.

Luke stopped thinking about the wampa. Again, he extended his hand and gazed upon the lightsaber in the snow. *The Force binds us. . . .*

He heard the approaching wampa's heavy footsteps.

The Force calls my lightsaber to me. . . .

The lightsaber shot out of the snow and into Luke's hand. Luke activated the weapon, and its blue energy beam blazed to life. As he raised the blade to cut through the ice that bound his legs, the wampa lunged for him.

The lightsaber sliced through the ice, and Luke kept the weapon activated as he tumbled to the cave's floor. He sprang to his feet just as the wampa was about to pounce, and swung the lightsaber hard. In a single motion, he cut off the monster's right arm. The severed limb landed on the snow with a muffled thud. Howling in pain, the wampa clutched at its open wound.

Not wasting a precious second, Luke deactivated the lightsaber and scurried away from the wailing beast. He moved by instinct, pushing his way through snow and ice until he tumbled out through the mouth of the cave and into . . .

A blizzard.

When I wanted to leave Tatooine, I never bargained for this.

Dazed and lost, Luke pressed on, leaving the cave far behind as he moved deeper into the storm.

The snowfall was increasingly heavy at Echo Base, where R2-D2 stood just outside the base's north entrance. Ignoring the cold flakes that were collecting on his cylindrical body, the astromech adjusted the slender scanner antenna that protruded up from a panel on his domed head. The antenna was topped by a life-scan sensor, and even though he hadn't picked up any signals so far, R2-D2 wasn't ready to give up. Still, he couldn't help but emit some worried beeps.

"You must come along now, Artoo," said C-3PO, who'd been standing watch with his friend. "There's really nothing more we can do. And my joints are freezing up."

R2-D2 beeped, long and low.

"Don't say things like that!" C-3PO cried. "Of course we'll see Master Luke again. And he'll be quite all right, you'll see." As C-3PO turned and headed back through the hangar entrance, he muttered, "Stupid little short-circuit. He'll be quite all right."

R2-D2 let out a mournful beep, but remained outside, sensors on full alert.

*   *   *

Except for his own gloved hands and the back of his tauntaun's head, Han Solo could barely see anything but falling snow. He knew that finding Luke in this environment was next to impossible, but if he didn't try, Luke was as good as dead.

So Han continued looking and kept the tauntaun moving. Eventually, they arrived near a glacial rise that shielded them slightly from the wind. There, Han let the animal rest while he dismounted, carrying a portable scanner from his utility pack.

Han extended the scanner's antennae and tried to pick up any readings. There were no life-forms within the scanner's limited range and no incoming comm transmissions, but there was plenty of interference from the storm. Han carried the scanner back to the tauntaun and climbed onto his saddle.

In the hangar at Echo Base, a Rebel lieutenant walked up to his commanding officer, Major Derlin, and said, "Sir, all the patrols are in. Still no —"

Major Derlin raised a hand to caution the lieutenant, who then noticed that Princess Leia stood nearby, watching them and listening. The lieutenant gulped, chose his words carefully, and said, "Still no contact from Skywalker or Solo."

Chewbacca, R2-D2, and C-3PO were near the cave's entrance. Hearing the lieutenant's report, C-3PO turned and approached the princess. "Mistress Leia,

Artoo says he's been quite unable to pick up any signals, although he does admit that his own range is far too weak to abandon all hope."

Major Derlin said, "Your Highness, there's nothing more we can do tonight. The shield doors must be closed."

Leia wished she could blink her eyes and wake up from this nightmare, but she knew she wasn't dreaming. Luke and Han really were out there somewhere in sub-freezing temperatures, and unless she wanted the cold to spread throughout Echo Base, the shield doors couldn't remain open. She found herself speechless, and cast her gaze at the floor as she nodded to Major Derlin. It had to be done.

"Close the doors," Derlin ordered.

"Yes, sir," said the lieutenant.

At the mouth of the cave, two thick metal doors rumbled along their tracks as they converged to close off the entrance. Chewbacca moaned, and R2-D2 spat out a complex series of beeps.

Addressing Leia, C-3PO said, "Artoo says the chances of survival are seven hundred and twenty-five . . . to one."

With a loud boom, the doors locked in place and sealed off the cavern. Chewbacca threw his head back and let out a suffering howl.

C-3PO reconsidered his last statement, and

added, "Actually, Artoo has been known to make mistakes . . . from time to time."

Leia walked off, and C-3PO returned to R2-D2. "Oh, dear, oh, dear," said the golden droid. He patted R2-D2's dome, trying to comfort the distressed astromech. "Don't worry about Master Luke, I'm sure he'll be all right. He's quite clever, you know . . . for a human being."

Luke lay facedown in the snow, nearly unconscious. He didn't want to give up, but the cold had given him little choice. Unable to move or feel, and barely able to think, he was waiting for the inevitable when he heard a voice.

"Luke . . . Luke."

Luke recognized the voice. He hadn't heard it since the Battle of Yavin, when it had urged him to trust his feelings and use the Force to destroy the Death Star. Slowly, Luke raised his head. A short distance away from him stood the shimmering, spectral form of Obi-Wan Kenobi. To make sure he wasn't hallucinating, Luke said aloud, "Ben?"

"You will go to the Dagobah system," Ben said.

"Dagobah system?" Luke repeated. *I'm not hallucinating. I'm sure of it.*

"There you will learn from Yoda, the Jedi Master who instructed me."

Luke groaned as he tried not to go into shock. "Ben . . . Ben."

Ben disappeared — but a lone tauntaun rider materialized where he had been and approached Luke's position. Luke's eyes closed and he passed out in the snow.

Fortunately for Luke, the tauntaun rider was not a hallucination, either. Han Solo slid off his mount and trudged as fast as he could to Luke's motionless body. Behind him, his tauntaun let out a low, pitiful bellow.

"Luke!" Han said, taking hold of his friend. "Luke! Don't do this, Luke. Come on, give me a sign here." He leaned close to Luke's face to make sure he was still breathing. He was, but just barely.

Han was trying to think about what to do next when he heard a rasping sound. He turned in time to see his tauntaun stagger and fall dead to the snow-covered ground.

Temporarily stunned, Han stared at the fallen tauntaun. Then he grabbed Luke's arms and dragged him to the tauntaun's body. "Not much time," he muttered. He knew he'd have to work fast, before the tauntaun's corpse froze.

Luke moaned, "Ben . . . Ben . . ."

Han figured Luke was delirious. "Hang on, kid," he said. He took Luke's lightsaber, ignited its blade, and cut the dead Tauntaun's belly wide open.

"Dagobah system . . ." Luke mumbled. "You will go to Dagobah . . ."

Struggling to get Luke inside the carcass, Han explained, "This may smell bad, kid . . . but it will keep you warm . . . till I can get the shelter built."

Oblivious to everything, Luke moaned, "Yoda . . ."

"Agh!" Han gasped as the gutted beast's rancid stench swam over him. "Agh . . . I thought they smelled bad on the outside! *Agh!*"

With Luke tucked more or less into the tauntaun's body cavity, Han removed a pack and took out a shelter container. The shelter would offer pitiful protection against the bitter cold . . . but it was all Han had.

The next morning offered clear blue skies for the Rebel pilots who raced over Hoth in the four snub-nosed T-47 snowspeeders — enclosed two-man craft that allowed a pilot and gunner to be seated back-to-back. Each of these four carried only a single pilot, to allow room for Luke Skywalker and Han Solo, should either be found. After skirting a high plateau, the snowspeeders veered off in different directions to search for the missing men.

Rebel pilot Zev Senesca's comm-unit designation was Rogue Two. Zev had been on Hoth long enough to have a hard time believing anyone could've survived the previous night's blizzard. Also, the war had claimed too many lives for Zev to be much of an optimist. He was grimly concentrating on the scopes that ringed his cockpit when he heard a low beep from a monitor. Activating his transmitter, he called out, "Echo Base . . . I've got something! Not much, but it could be a life-form. . . ."

Zev banked his craft, made a slow arc, then raced off in a new direction. Switching to a different transmission frequency, he said, "Commander Skywalker, do you copy? This is Rogue Two." No response. "This is Rogue Two. Captain Solo, do you copy?"

"Good morning," Han's voice sounded from a speaker in Zev's cockpit. "Nice of you guys to drop by."

It had been weeks since Zev had felt any reason to smile, but the one that broke out across his face went from ear to ear. "Echo Base . . . this is Rogue Two. I found them. Repeat, I found them." He steered the snowspeeder to follow the source of Han's transmission, and soon sighted Han's emergency shelter. Han stood beside the shelter and waved, safe at last.

Luke wondered, *Am I dead?*

His whole body felt empty, drained of life, yet there was a lightness about him. *I feel like I'm floating. But what's that pressure over my mouth and . . . is something pinching my nose? And what are those whirring noises?* Opening his eyes, he saw blurred lights and rising air bubbles, and thought, *I'm drowning!*

He had emerged from unconsciousness to find himself submerged in a transparent cylindrical tank filled with warm liquid. A breathing mask was strapped over his mouth and a small clamp sealed his nostrils. From Luke's perspective, the tank's shape produced a distorted view of strange figures moving outside. But as his vision adjusted, Luke recognized the figures as 2-1B, an older medical droid that served the Rebel Alliance, and his assistant, the multiarmed droid FX-7. It was FX-7 who was responsible for the whirring sounds.

Luke realized he was in the Echo Base medical center, and that the liquid in the tank was bacta, a synthetic chemical that made wounds heal quickly and left no scars. Luke's last conscious memory was of Ben, appearing before him in the snow. *Who rescued me? And how?*

Then he saw his friends. Leia, Han, Chewbacca, R2-D2, and C-3PO were gathered on the other side of the medical center's window. They waved to him. Still groggy, Luke returned the gesture, then felt his body being lifted out of the tank.

It was time to return to the world.

"Master Luke, sir, it's so good to see you fully functional again," C-3PO said to Luke, who now sat on a bed in the medical center's white-walled recovery room. Leia smiled as R2-D2 rolled up beside Luke's bed and beeped.

"Artoo expresses his relief also," C-3PO translated.

Luke was by no means fully functional. He was tired and sore, and his battered features were nasty evidence of his encounter with the wampa. But he was alive and he would heal.

Behind Luke, the door slid open with a soft hiss, and Han and Chewbacca entered.

Han asked, "How you feeling, kid? You don't look so bad to me. In fact, you look strong enough to pull the ears off a gundark."

Luke grinned. "Thanks to you."

"That's two you owe me, junior," Han said, referring to the Battle of Yavin, when he'd prevented Darth Vader from shooting down Luke's starfighter.

Han swiveled to lean against the foot of Luke's bed and face Leia. "Well, Your Worship, looks like you managed to keep me around for a little while longer."

"I had nothing to do with it," Leia retorted. "General Rieekan thinks it's dangerous for any ships to leave the system until we've activated the energy shield." Indeed, the Rebels had been working round-the-clock on the power generators so the energy shields would be ready when needed.

"That's a good story," Han said. "I think you just can't bear to let a gorgeous guy like me out of your sight."

In bed, Luke grimaced. Han was his friend, but the *Millennium Falcon*'s captain was also so full of himself that he could be unbearable. *How can Han talk to Leia that way? She's a princess! Sometimes I wish he would just keep his mouth shut.*

Coolly glaring at Solo, Leia slowly shook her head and said, "I don't know where you get your delusions, laserbrain."

Chewbacca tilted his head back and produced an amused, gurgling bark.

"Laugh it up, fuzzball," Han said reproachfully. "But you didn't see us alone in the south passage." He moved toward Leia and slinked an arm around her back. "She expressed her true feelings for me."

Stunned, Luke's eyes darted from Han to Leia and back to Han. *Is Han serious? Does Leia really want . . . ?*

"My . . . !" Leia gasped, her temper boiling over. Han eased away from Leia as she released a barrage: "Why, you stuck-up . . . half-witted . . . scruffy-looking . . . *nerf herder!*"

"Who's scruffy-looking?" Han asked, looking genuinely insulted. Then he turned to Luke and said, "I must have hit pretty close to the mark to get her all riled up like that, huh, kid?"

But Luke wouldn't meet Han's gaze. He was too angry. Even the droids sensed the tension in the air.

Leia composed herself, then moved closer to

Luke's bed. Looking at Han, she said, "Why, I guess you don't know everything about women yet." Then she leaned over Luke and kissed him on the lips.

Luke thought, *Huh?*

C-3PO, who had been standing just behind Han, nearly tripped over himself to get a better view. After seeing that Leia and Luke were indeed in an embrace, the baffled droid redirected his gaze from Chewbacca to Han to see their reaction. Chewbacca made a curious whimpering sound. Han did his best to keep his expression relaxed and neutral, as if seeing Leia and Luke interested him only mildly.

The kiss lasted about three seconds.

Leia pulled away from Luke. She looked at Han, who kept his expression neutral as he met her gaze. Then, without any further word, Leia walked to the door and left the room.

Han turned his casual gaze to Luke. Luke put his hands behind his head and leaned back into his bed, trying hard to keep a smug smile from his face. *Well, Han, do you have anything to say now?*

From a loudspeaker, a voice announced, "Headquarters personnel, report to command center."

Han glanced at Chewbacca, who tilted his furry head at the door. Trying not to look relieved at the opportunity to make an exit, Han tapped Luke's arm and said, "Take it easy," then followed Chewbacca out of the room.

Ever polite, C-3PO added, "Excuse us, please," and trotted after R2-D2, leaving Luke alone.

Walking fast, Han arrived first at the command center, followed by Leia, Chewbacca, and the droids. Inside the dim, low-ceilinged room, General Rieekan stood beside Wyron Serper, the center's senior controller, who was seated before a console screen. Seeing Leia, General Rieekan said, "Princess . . . we have a visitor."

The group gathered around the console screen and examined a comm-scan display map of Echo Base and its surrounding areas. On the map, a small, unidentified blip appeared to the north. Rieekan said, "We've picked up something outside the base of zone twelve, moving east."

"It's metal," Serper reported.

"Then it couldn't be one of those creatures," Leia said, referring to the wampas.

"It could be a speeder, one of ours," Han suggested.

Serper raised a hand to adjust a control on his headset. "No," he said. "Wait — there's something very weak coming through." Serper switched on an audio speaker, allowing the others to hear the intercepted transmission, a strange series of choppy electronic noises.

Looking to Rieekan, C-3PO said, "Sir, I am fluent in

six million forms of communication. This signal is not used by the Alliance. It could be an Imperial code."

With that possibility in mind, the gathered Rebels listened even more attentively to the signal. After several seconds, Han decided, "It isn't friendly, whatever it is." Without waiting for the general or anyone else to issue an order, Han turned to his first mate and said, "Come on, Chewie, let's check it out."

As Han and Chewbacca headed for the hangar, Rieekan thought they might require backup. To Serper, Rieekan said, "Send Rogues Ten and Eleven to station three-eight."

Trouble had arrived.

When the Imperial probot was finished sending its message, it retracted its two high-frequency transmission antennae down into its sensor head. Then the droid hovered away from its hiding place behind a wide snowdrift, where its telescopic sensors had maintained an unobstructed view of the Rebels' power generator.

The probot was heading down a ridge toward the Rebel base when its sensors detected movement by a nearby snowbank. The probot spun its sensor head and directed its primary visual sensors at the snowbank, where a Wookiee's snow-covered head had popped up.

Chewbacca ducked as the droid fired three rapid laser bursts. The laser bolts missed the Wookiee and bored into the snowbank.

But Chewbacca was just a decoy, and Han — concealed behind a rise of glacial rock — was right behind the droid. While the droid was still distracted, Han rose and snapped off a quick shot at the droid's hovering form. Unlike the droid, Han didn't miss.

The fired bolt slammed into the droid but barely dented its metal plating. The droid responded by quickly rotating its cylindrical body in midair and firing back at Han. But Han had already ducked and the droid missed again.

Han came up fast and fired a second blast at the droid, again meeting his mark. After the way the droid had taken his first shot, Han knew he'd be lucky if he could disable it. So he was surprised when — a moment after his second shot hit the droid — the droid exploded into smoke and flames, leaving nothing behind but a fine spray of black-metal dust across the snow.

In the command center, General Rieekan stood next to Leia, who sat at a comm console and listened to Han's report. From the comlink, Han's voice said, "'Fraid there's not much left."

"What was it?" Leia asked.

"Droid of some kind," Han answered. "I didn't hit it that hard. It must have had a self-destruct."

"An Imperial probe droid," Leia deduced.

Han said, "It's a good bet the Empire knows we're here."

It had been anything but easy for the Rebels to establish a base on Hoth. But if there were even a slight possibility that the Empire knew the location of Echo Base, no one was safe on the ice planet. With grim resolve, Rieekan said, "We'd better start the evacuation."

CHAPTER 3

Many light-years away from Hoth, five Imperial Star Destroyers and their respective TIE fighter escorts rendezvoused in space. Despite the immense size of each Star Destroyer, all fell under the shadow of an even more enormous ship: the *Super*-class Star Destroyer, *Executor*.

At 8,000 meters long, the *Executor* was the largest traditional starship constructed by the Imperial Navy. Only the Death Star space station had been larger. Equipped with more than a thousand weapons, the *Executor* carried 144 TIE fighters and 38,000 stormtroopers. And all were at the disposal of the ship's commander: Darth Vader, Lord of the Sith.

Clad entirely in black, with a helmet that completely concealed his head and a cape that reached the floor, Darth Vader was darker than deepest space. On the *Executor*'s bridge, he stood before a transparisteel viewport and surveyed his fleet. Because the *Executor* was protected by a powerful shielding force field, the bridge was positioned at the bow — usually the most vulnerable area of a starship — and offered Vader a panoramic view unobstructed by any part of his ship.

Behind Vader, a long walkway extended to the captain's control station. The walkway was without railings, and on either side the floor dropped off to expose the bridge's lower level. There, gray-uniformed Imperial technicians operated their console stations, and tried not to look up to find themselves eye level with Darth Vader's boots.

A door opened near the captain's station, and Vader's two chief officers — the pompous Admiral Ozzel and the younger, powerfully built General Veers — entered the bridge. Like all high-ranking Imperial officers, Ozzel and Veers wore gray uniforms and caps, as well as black leather gloves, belts, and boots. They were approaching the walkway that led to Vader when the *Executor*'s captain called out, "Admiral."

"Yes, Captain?" Ozzel answered, turning with Veers to face Captain Piett, a lean man with eyes that appeared tired from staring at monitors.

"I think we've got something, sir," Piett informed him. "The report is only a fragment from a probe droid in the Hoth system, but it's the best lead we've had."

Unimpressed, Ozzel snapped, "We have thousands of probe droids searching the galaxy. I want proof, not leads!"

But Piett wasn't finished. He added, "The visuals indicate life readings."

"It could mean anything," Ozzel said, growing impatient with Piett. "If we followed up every lead . . ."

"But sir," Piett interrupted, "the Hoth system is supposed to be devoid of human forms."

"You found something?" Darth Vader's deep, mechanically tinged voice rumbled, his black mask looking down at Piett. None of the officers had heard or seen his tall, dark form approach.

"Yes, my lord," said Piett, directing Vader's attention to a lower console monitor. The monitor displayed the transmitted image of a snow-base power generator.

"That's it," Vader said with conviction. "The Rebels are there."

Admiral Ozzel saw nothing on the monitor that specifically indicated a Rebel presence, and he did not believe in expending time and energy on a mere hunch. Employing what he considered his most diplomatic manner, Ozzel still sounded condescending when he spoke: "My lord, there are so many uncharted settlements. It could be smugglers, it could be . . ."

"That is the system," Vader interrupted. His tone was

filled with restrained menace, making it clear that he would not tolerate any questioning of his actions. "Set your course for the Hoth system. General Veers, prepare your men." Darth Vader turned and stalked off the bridge.

Veers looked at Ozzel, who appeared stung by Vader's lack of respect for military protocol. Hoping to restore his commanding officer's confidence, Veers said, "Admiral?"

Ozzel nodded, giving *his* permission for Veers to prepare the soldiers, as if his permission even mattered. Veers walked off quickly, and Ozzel — furious over his treatment by Vader — threw a threatening gaze at Piett before he left in a huff.

If Captain Piett was afraid of Admiral Ozzel, he didn't show it. In Piett's experience, it was smarter to be afraid of Darth Vader.

On Hoth, everyone at Echo Base was preparing to evacuate. In the transport bay, several transports were being loaded by soldiers carrying heavy boxes of equipment and supplies. The soldiers moved quickly, but not in panic. Near one transport, two Rebels faced their captain.

"Groups seven and ten will stay behind to fly the speeders," the captain ordered, prompting one soldier to walk off quickly. Turning to the remaining soldier, the captain said, "As soon as each transport is loaded, evacuation control will give clearance for immediate launch."

"Right, sir," answered the soldier.

In the main hangar deck, Han was atop the *Millennium Falcon*, trying frantically to complete the welding on the lifters. In the *Falcon*'s cockpit, Chewbacca sat ready at the controls. After finishing a weld, Han stood up and shouted, "All right, that's it. Try it . . ."

Chewbacca threw a switch. Unfortunately, the switch accidentally triggered a minor explosion on the problematic lifter, and nearly launched Han from the *Falcon*'s hull.

"Off!" Han shouted as he leaped away from another small explosion. "Turn it off! Turn it off! Off!"

Chewbacca howled as his furry fingers darted from one switch to the next. When he realized Han had stopped shouting, the Wookiee looked from the cockpit to see if he was all right. At first, all he saw was smoke.

The smoke cleared. Han was unhurt but exasperated as he surveyed the new damage. Sometimes, being captain of the fastest ship in the galaxy was not as thrilling as it could be.

In the medical center, Luke got into his bright-orange pressurized g-suit. He was almost ready to leave when 2-1B turned his skull-like metal head in time to see his departing patient. Luke had the impression that 2-1B had genuinely enjoyed hearing about the technical challenges of converting T-47 airspeeders into snowspeeders, and wasn't surprised when the droid commented, "Sir, it will take quite a while to evacuate the T-47s."

"Well, forget the heavy equipment," Luke said. "There's plenty of time to get the smaller modules on the transports." He grabbed his flight gear and headed for the door.

2-1B said, "Take care, sir."

During his recovery, Luke had gotten to observe the droid well enough to know he meant it. Luke smiled and said, "Thanks."

Leaving the medical center, he proceeded through the laser-cut corridors to the main hangar. Pilots, gunners, and astromech droids scurried about as he walked toward Chewbacca, who was now working under the *Millennium Falcon.*

"Chewie, take care of yourself, okay?" Luke said, and reached up to scratch the Wookiee's neck. Luke turned to walk away, but Chewbacca threw his arms around Luke and gave him a tight hug before letting him go. Luke looked up to find Han standing atop the *Falcon* with a small repair droid.

"Hi, kid," Han said from his elevated position, then turned to the repair droid and scolded, "There's got to be a reason for it. Check it at the other end. Wait a second." While the droid rotated its visual sensors, Han looked back down at Luke and asked, "You all right?"

"Yeah," Luke said. There were so many things he wanted to tell Han. How much their friendship meant, how he hoped Han wasn't hurt by Leia's rejection, how he wished him safety and happiness . . . but everything he thought of saying somehow sounded like the one thing he didn't want to say: *Good-bye.* So Luke just nodded, then started to walk away.

"Be careful," Han said.

Glancing back, Luke said, "You, too."

In the command center, a Rebel controller urgently gestured for General Rieekan and reported, "General, there's a fleet of Star Destroyers coming out of hyperspace in sector four."

Rieekan leaned over the controller's shoulder to examine the monitor display of sector four, then ordered, "Reroute all power to the energy shield." Turning from the controller, Rieekan faced a Rebel officer and said, "We've got to hold them till all the transports are away. Prepare for ground assault."

While the *Executor* and five Star Destroyers had traveled through hyperspace to arrive in orbit of the ice planet Hoth, Darth Vader had been inside his meditation chamber. A spherical enclosure with a black exterior, the chamber was pressurized to keep Vader comfortable, even with his helmet off.

General Veers entered Vader's private quarters and carefully approached the chamber. Veers stood at attention as jawlike clamps unlocked at the sphere's side, allowing its upper half to rise.

Darth Vader was seated in the center of the chamber's bright white interior. His black helmet was already facing the general, as if he'd been anticipating this meeting.

"What is it, General?" Vader asked.

"My lord, the fleet has moved out of lightspeed," Veers reported. "Comm-scan has detected an energy field protecting an area of the sixth planet of the Hoth system. The field is strong enough to deflect any bombardment."

Vader seethed. "The Rebels are alerted to our presence. Admiral Ozzel came out of lightspeed too close to the system."

Hoping to explain Admiral Ozzel's decision, Veers said, "He felt surprise was wiser. . . ."

"He is as clumsy as he is stupid," Vader interrupted. "General, prepare your troops for a surface attack."

"Yes, my lord," Veers said, then left.

Vader's seat rotated, allowing him to face a wide

viewscreen. It flicked on and displayed an image of Admiral Ozzel and Captain Piett on the *Executor*'s bridge. Ozzel turned his face and said, "Lord Vader, the fleet has moved out of lightspeed, and we're preparing to — aaagh!"

On the viewscreen, Ozzel was touching his throat with his left hand. Vader, using the Force, had constricted Ozzel's windpipe.

"You have failed me for the last time, Admiral," Vader said.

Admiral Ozzel took a step backward but remained on the viewscreen.

Vader said, "Captain Piett."

"Yes, my lord," said Piett, tearing his eyes away from the choking admiral to face Vader.

"Make ready to land our troops beyond their energy field and deploy the fleet so that nothing gets off the system." As Admiral Ozzel's strangled form fell to the bridge's deck with an audible thud, Vader added, "You are in command now, *Admiral* Piett."

Piett straightened and said, "Thank you, Lord Vader." He looked to some nearby soldiers and jerked his head slightly, silently instructing them to remove Ozzel's corpse. Piett had always strived to learn from the mistakes of others, but he had not expected a promotion so soon.

*   *   *

There was a sense of urgency at Echo Base. No one knew when the Imperials would strike, but everyone was certain that an attack was inevitable. And because the Rebels' energy shield would protect the base from aerial attack, the Rebels knew the assault would come from the ground.

In the center of the main hangar, Princess Leia and Major Derlin briefed a group of pilots. Leia told them, "All troop carriers will assemble at the north entrance. The heavy transport ships will leave as soon as they're loaded. Only two fighter escorts per ship. The energy shield can only be opened for a short time, so you'll have to stay very close to your transports."

"Two fighters against a Star Destroyer?" said a young pilot who everyone called Hobbie. He sounded more than a little doubtful.

Turning to Hobbie, Leia explained, "The ion cannon will fire several shots to make sure that any enemy ships will be out of your flight path. When you've gotten past the energy shield, proceed directly to the rendezvous point." She gestured to all the pilots. "Understand?"

In unison, the pilots replied in the affirmative. Leia knew, despite any doubts, they would do everything they could to make the plan work. "Good luck," she wished them.

"Okay," said Major Derlin, clapping his gloved hands for attention. "Everybody to your stations. Let's go!" The pilots went to their vehicles, and Leia ran to the command center.

Outside the ice cave, Rebel soldiers carried weapons and positioned them along snow trenches, while others loaded power packs into gun turrets. Near the base power generators, troops rushed to set up their heavy battle equipment. And all around Echo Base, Rebel lookouts trained their eyes and macrobinoculars to the surrounding ice plains, scanning for any sign of the anticipated Imperial troops.

Leia arrived in the command center to find General Rieekan with his eyes glued to the comm-scan display. At their consoles, the Rebel controllers were tense, and everyone was trying hard not to show any fear.

Rieekan said, "Their primary target will be the power generators." He turned to a controller and said, "Prepare to open shield."

The Rebels' protective energy shield was opened, allowing two X-wing starfighters to escort a bulky, 90-meter-long transport up and away from Hoth's surface, leaving Echo Base at least temporarily exposed to the Imperials.

Now all the three Rebel ships had to do was get past the hulking Star Destroyers.

As expected, the two X-wings and the Rebel transport did not go unnoticed as they rose quickly through Hoth's atmosphere. On the bridge of one Imperial Star Destroyer, an Imperial controller approached his captain, who was regarding the ice world through the main viewport.

"Sir," said the controller. "Rebel ships are coming into our sector."

"Good," said the captain. "Our first catch of the day."

Inside the Echo Base command center, a female controller kept her eyes on the comm-scan display, watching the three rising blips that indicated the transport and its two X-wing escorts. On their present course, the vessels were heading almost straight for a Star Destroyer.

"Stand by, ion control," the controller said into a

transmitter while she watched the blips. When she knew the Rebel ships were almost within visual range of the destroyer, she gave the command: "Fire!"

Outside the Rebel base, a giant ball-shaped ion cannon made pumping motions as it blasted three consecutive red energy beams skyward. Each energy beam streaked past the escaping Rebel ships and didn't stop until they smashed into the waiting Star Destroyer.

The scarlet bolts took out the destroyer's missile launchers and conning tower, and caused a series of fiery explosions to spread across its metal hull. The destroyer veered, then spun out of control. As the Imperial ship careered into deep space, the Rebel transport and X-wings raced onward to safety.

Back at Echo Station, Rebel pilots, gunners, and ground troops were hurrying to their stations and vehicles when they heard a controller announce over loudspeakers: "The first transport is away." Throughout the base, the Rebels cheered. It was hardly time to celebrate, but the battle had gotten off to a promising start.

In the main hangar, pilots and gunners were scrambling into their snowspeeders, which were lined up in rows with their cockpit canopies raised. When Luke arrived at his speeder, he found his gunner — a fresh-faced, eager kid named Dack Ralter — already in the speeder's aft-facing gunner's seat.

Dack turned his head to see Luke and asked, "Feeling all right, sir?"

"Just like new, Dack," Luke said as he climbed into the pilot's seat. "How about you?"

"Right now I feel like I could take on the whole Empire myself."

Luke grinned. "I know what you mean." He pulled on his helmet as Dack lowered the cockpit canopy. With the canopy in place, Luke glanced through its transparisteel windows to look at the other pilots of Rogue Group, who would be under his command. The pilots included Zev Senesca, who'd been first to locate Han and Luke after their long night out in the snow; Wedge Antilles, who'd also seen combat at the Battle of Yavin; and Hobbie, who'd known Luke's friend Biggs Darklighter.

Luke hoped all the Rebel pilots would survive the day.

Outside the hangar, hundreds of Rebel troops took up their positions in a series of long snow trenches. There was a tense silence among the soldiers as they braced their blaster rifles along the upper banks of the trenches and gazed out over the bleak landscape, watching the horizon for any movement.

They didn't have to wait long. Small dot-sized objects began to appear on the horizon. The dots were moving in the direction of the Rebel base.

A Rebel officer lifted a pair of macrobinoculars to

his eyes. Through the lens, he saw a very close view of a giant battle machine that traveled on four long, jointed legs. He adjusted the view to zoom back and saw three more of the armored behemoths. The trench officer had no difficulty identifying the machines as Imperial AT-ATs: All Terrain Armored Transports.

At 20 meters long and over 15 meters tall, AT-ATs were heavily armored and almost unstoppable weapons platforms. Although the AT-ATs resembled robot quadrupeds, they were manned vehicles, operated from within the command section that extended from the front like a head, and had the capacity to carry up to forty troopers. Each AT-AT command section was armed with two side-mounted medium blaster cannons and two heavy laser cannons that jutted out from under the command section's "chin."

The AT-ATs were still distant, but the rhythmic pounding of their lumbering footsteps was already causing the ground to vibrate at Echo Base. The trench officer lowered his macrobinoculars and spoke into his comlink: "Echo Station Three-t-eight. We have spotted Imperial walkers!"

Back at the command center, the trench officer's report was received and relayed by a controller: "Imperial walkers on the north ridge."

The snowspeeder pilots responded immediately. The speeders lifted from the hangar floor, raced out of the cave, and flew above the ice field at full throttle. Accelerating away from the base, they headed toward the distant Imperial walkers.

From the trenches, there were now five walkers visible. The lead walker did not pause its advance as it opened fire, blasting red energy beams at the Rebel troops. Fire and ice exploded around the trenches, sending the Rebels diving for cover.

Flying past a Rebel battlement, Luke sighted the walkers and said, "Echo Station Five-seven. We're on our way."

The snowspeeders flew low over trenches, where Rebel troops were now firing at the approaching walkers. Luke addressed the other pilots via his helmet's comlink: "All right, boys, keep tight now."

The walkers' heads were attached to flexible armored necks, and the heads angled to fire at the incoming snowspeeders. Red energy bolts whizzed past the evasive speeders, but the Rebel pilots kept heading for their targets.

Behind Luke, Dack adjusted his targeting system to aim for the walker's forward laser cannons. Dack warned, "Luke, I have no approach vector. I'm not set."

"Steady, Dack," Luke replied. "Attack pattern delta. Go now."

Luke banked his speeder to the right of one walker, knowing he was trailed by the speeder flown by Hobbie. Then Luke angled back toward the walker and said, "All right, I'm coming in."

As Luke threw his speeder into a steep dive toward the walker's left side, Dack squeezed the triggers for the laser cannons. Luke watched the speeder's cannons fire and score several direct hits, all ineffective, then steered the speeder between the walker's left legs and under the machine's belly. He pulled back on his flight controls to bring the speeder into a rapid ascent over another walker, and Dack fired at that walker, too, without making a dent.

Luke shouted into his comlink, "Hobbie, you still with me?"

Hobbie was, and kept his speeder close on Luke's wing. The two speeders raced directly at the head of a walker, fired their cannons, then split and flew past it. From his aerial position, Luke made a quick survey of the battle below and all around him. A speeder banked through and away from the legs of a walker, then the walker swiveled and fired, striking a snowspeeder and sending it crashing into the snow.

Luke looked back at the walker and said, "That armor's too strong for blasters."

On the horizon, another walker moved up past Luke's cockpit window. Luke banked and began to make another run. Into his comlink, he said, "Rogue Group, use your harpoons and tow cables. Go for the legs. It might be our only chance of stopping them." Luke guided the speeder straight for the walker and said, "All right, stand by, Dack."

"Oh, Luke, we've got a malfunction in fire control," Dack reported with concern. "I'll have to cut in the auxiliary."

"Just hang on," Luke said. He wished he could see what Dack was doing, but the cockpit's back-to-back seating made that virtually impossible. Keeping his eyes focused on the walker, Luke assured his gunner again, "Hang on, Dack. Get ready to fire that tow cable."

Energy bolts streaked from the walker and exploded in midair bursts, creating a deadly obstacle course for Luke. The flak buffeted the snowspeeder. Dack was struggling to set up his harpoon gun when Luke heard an explosion from behind.

"Dack?" Luke said. When no answer came, he repeated louder, "Dack!"

But Dack was lost, his body slumped over his smoldering controls.

General Veers stood at his station inside the command section of the lead AT-AT. In front of him, two pilots sat behind their controls and faced a wide, viewport. Through the thin viewport, Veers saw a Rebel speeder bank in from the side and head straight at the command section. The speeder's cannons fired, blasting away at the AT-AT's viewport. An explosion rippled across the walker's windows, then quickly dissipated, causing no damage.

Veers guided his impregnable war machine closer to a line of trenches and fired the AT-AT's laser cannons. A Rebel gun turret was hit and exploded. A handful of Rebels held their ground and returned fire, for all the good it did them, while the rest scattered away from the burning turret.

When the smoke cleared, Veer and his pilots sighted the Rebel power generators in the distance. Once the generators were destroyed, the energy shield would be down and the Rebels would be completely vulnerable. However, Veers's AT-AT was not yet within firing range.

Veers's command console was equipped with a compact HoloNet transceiver, which could transmit and project holograms: three-dimensional images produced by beams of light. The shallow bowl-shaped transceiver activated to display a flickering blue hologram of Darth Vader.

"Yes, Lord Vader," Veers addressed the holographic image. "I've reached the main power generators. The shield will be down in moments. You may start your landing."

*   *   *

Luke knew there was nothing he could do about Dack. He also knew he had to keep flying and not leave the fight, doing whatever he could to stop the Imperial walkers. If he couldn't launch his speeder's harpoon and tow cable, then he'd help another pilot execute the plan.

Luke spotted a snowspeeder flying off his port wing. It was Wedge. Into his comlink, Luke said, "Rogue Three."

"Copy, Rogue Leader," Wedge answered from his speeder.

"Wedge, I've lost my gunner," Luke said as he angled back to the walker. "You'll have to make this shot. I'll cover for you." Luke began a wide sweep around the walker and instructed, "Set your harpoon. Follow me on the next pass."

"Coming around, Rogue Leader," Wedge replied, steering after Luke. Behind Wedge sat his gunner, Wes Janson. With steely nerves, Janson readied his harpoon gun.

Trying to distract the walker's crew, Luke flew past the command section's viewport. As more flak exploded around his speeder, he glanced from his cockpit to see Wedge fly his own speeder under the same walker. "Steady, Rogue Two," Luke warned another pilot.

Wedge's speeder had barely passed under the

walker's belly when Wedge ordered: "Activate harpoon."

Janson pressed the firing switch, and the harpoon launched. The harpoon — tipped with a fusion disk that would adhere to any metal surface — flew straight at one of the walker's ankles and embedded itself. As Wedge banked hard to the left, Janson could see a thin line of the retractable flexisteel tow cable trailing behind them.

"Good shot, Janson," Wedge said. He continued banking until he circled the walker, wrapping the tow cable around the Imperial machine's enormous legs. Janson clung to the harpoon gun and watched the tow cable. If Janson didn't detach the cable at just the right time . . . Wedge didn't even want to think about it.

"One more pass," Wedge said as he banked around the front of the walker.

"Coming around," Janson said. "Once more."

Wedge swung the speeder between the legs of the giant walker, and Janson shouted, "Cable out! Let her go!"

"Detach cable," Wedge ordered.

Janson pressed a switch, and the cable release on the back of the speeder snapped loose. As the cable dropped away, Janson said, "Cable detached."

Wedge accelerated away from the walker. The enormous war machine attempted to step forward, but the cable had so thoroughly tangled its legs that it began to topple. It teetered for a moment, then crashed heavily onto the icy ground.

In the trenches, the Rebel troops cheered at the sight of the fallen walker. A trench officer shouted, "Come on!"

But it wasn't necessary for the ground troops to charge the downed walker. From overhead, Wedge and another Rebel pilot descended in their speeders and fired energy charges at their Imperial target. At least one of the charges penetrated the AT-AT's armor plating, for in the next moment, the entire walker was consumed in a massive explosion, launching bits of metal in all directions.

From his cockpit, Wedge shouted, "Woo-ha! That got him!"

"I see it, Wedge," Luke said, watching the spectacle from his own speeder. "Good work."

The battle was taking its toll on the Rebels' command center, where large chunks of ice tumbled from the walls and ceiling. C-3PO stood nervously beside Princess Leia in front of a comm-scan display as another shock wave rocked the room.

General Rieekan approached Leia and said, "I don't think we can protect two transports at a time."

"It's risky," Leia admitted, "but we can't hold out much longer. We have no choice."

With reluctance, Rieekan ordered, "Launch patrols."

Leia turned to an aide and said, "Evacuate remaining ground staff."

Hearing this, C-3PO did not bother to excuse himself as he exited the command center. He knew every detail of the evacuation plan, including R2-D2's assignment. R2-D2 was to guide Luke's X-wing starfighter out of the hangar through the south entrance of Echo Base, then meet Luke on the slope near the ion cannon. C-3PO walked quickly through the laser-cut corridor, hoping he'd be able to say good-bye to his friend before he left the hangar.

As the golden droid entered the hangar, he saw many Rebel soldiers running to their ships. He was walking toward Luke's X-wing when he overheard Han Solo shouting, "No, no! No!"

C-3PO glanced up to see Chewbacca atop the *Millennium Falcon*, sitting half in the starboard mandible's maintenance access bay. Apparently, the *Falcon*'s repairs were not yet finished. Then C-3PO saw Han appear next to Chewbacca. Han gestured with his hand into the access bay and snarled, "This one goes there, that one goes there. Right?"

C-3PO walked past the *Falcon* until he arrived at Luke's X-wing, just in time. A tubular hoist was secured to R2-D2's dome, and a technician was already raising the plucky astromech from the floor.

"Artoo, you take good care of Master Luke now, understand?" C-3PO said. R2-D2 answered with affirmative beeps and whistles as the technician guided and lowered his cylindrical body into the X-wing's astromech socket, just behind the cockpit. C-3PO added, "And . . . do take good care of yourself."

R2-D2 replied with another round of beeps.

C-3PO shook his head and walked away from the X-wing. "Oh, dear, oh, dear," he said as he headed back to the command center.

On the vast snow plains of Hoth, the battle raged on. The Imperial walkers fired lasers as they lumbered onward and continued their slow, steady assault on the Rebel base. Another Rebel gun tower was destroyed, then another, and another.

Inside his own AT-AT's command section, General Veers studied various readouts on his control console. His AT-AT was almost near firing range of the Rebels' generator. Veers turned to a white-armored Imperial snowtrooper and said, "All troops will debark for ground assault." Then Veers turned back to the AT-AT's two pilots and said, "Prepare to target the main generator."

Flak burst around Luke's snowspeeder as it hurtled through the cold skies of Hoth. Glancing to a speeder that was traveling through the air to his left, he sighted Zev in the cockpit. Into his comlink, Luke asked, "Rogue Two, are you all right?"

"Yeah," Zev replied. In fact, there was some blood on Zev's face, but the brave pilot was still alert. "I'm with you, Rogue Leader."

"We'll set harpoon," Luke said. "I'll cover for you."

Luke and Zev raced their speeders toward the giant walkers. As Zev prepared for the attack he said, "Coming around."

The Imperial walkers fired red laser bolts that streaked past the snowspeeders. Cautioning his fellow pilots, Luke said into his comlink, "Watch that cross fire, boys."

Zev said, "Set for position three." He angled his speeder for the harpoon tactic, then said to his gunner, "Steady."

Luke flew fast alongside Zev and warned him to stay tight and low.

Suddenly, Zev's speeder was hit by a laser bolt. Zev yelled as his ship bucked violently, then his cockpit exploded and his flaming speeder fell from the sky.

Luke was flying through flak. He tried to stabilize, but then there was a sound like a thunderclap as an explosion rocked his speeder. The noise caused Luke to reflexively close his eyes. When he opened them, there was a nasty crack across his cockpit window. His speeder was filling with smoke, and electrical sparks rippled over his controls. Luke shouted into the comlink, "Hobbie, I've been hit!"

Smoke poured out of the back of Luke's speeder. He gripped the controls and struggled with them, but they were useless. As he hurtled faster toward the oncoming Imperial walker, he knew he was going to crash.

Luke braced himself as his speeder — now totally out of control — veered to the right of the oncoming Imperial walker and went down. Fortunately, the snow was deep where the speeder crashed — but he still landed hard, and felt the safety harness dig into his torso before he came to a dead stop.

Thick black smoke billowed from the snowspeeder's main thrusters. Luke pushed up the speeder's damaged canopy in time to see another walker advancing toward him. He slipped out of his harness, turned to the backseat, and grabbed hold of Dack's shoulder. He'd hoped to haul his gunner's body out of the cockpit, but when he glanced again at the walker, he knew he'd never make it.

Then he looked to a slot beside his seat:

EMERGENCY SURVIVAL STORAGE.

Still in the cockpit, Luke risked another glance at

the approaching walker, which would be on top of him in one more step. Desperately reaching into the storage slot, he grabbed two items, then threw his body out of the cockpit just as one of the walker's massive footpads came crashing down on his ruined snowspeeder.

Luke clutched the two items he'd hastily selected. One was a portable harpoon gun. The other was a concussion charge.

Luke started running after the Imperial walker.

Han Solo dodged broken steam pipes and crumbling ice ceilings as he raced through the underground corridors from the hangar to the Echo Base command center. When he burst into the command center, it was a shambles, but he was not surprised that a few people remained at their posts. He spotted C-3PO, then saw Leia just beyond the golden droid. She was at one of the control consoles, standing beside a seated controller, still trying to help others.

Han shouted, "You all right?"

C-3PO looked in Han's direction. Leia nodded and yelled back, "Why are you still here?"

"I heard the command center had been hit."

C-3PO turned to Leia to hear her response, which was: "You got your clearance to leave." She returned her attention to the console. C-3PO looked back at Han.

"Don't worry, I'll leave," Han said. "First I'm going to get you to your ship."

"Your Highness," C-3PO pleaded, "we must take this last transport. It's our only hope."

Brushing past debris that had fallen in the middle of the command center, Leia went to another controller and said, "Send all troops in sector twelve to the south slope to protect the fighters." She thought, *That'll give Luke and the other pilots a better chance of reaching their ships.*

Just then, a blast rocked the command center, and C-3PO was thrown backward into Han's arms. Over a loudspeaker, a controller announced, "Imperial troops have entered the base. Imperial troops have entered —"

Han righted C-3PO, then stepped over to Leia, grasped her upper arm, and said, "Come on . . . that's it."

Leia held Han's gaze for a moment before the realization hit her: *We've lost the base.* She then turned back to the seated controller and said, "Give the evacuation code signal. And get to your transports!"

Into a comlink, the controller said, "K-one-zero . . . all troops disengage."

Han could see Leia was exhausted. Keeping his grip on her arm, he started to lead her out of the command center to the corridor. Behind them, C-3PO cried, "Oh! Wait for me!"

*   *   *

Back in the trenches, the situation had become dire.

"Begin retreat!" shouted the Rebel trench officer.

A second officer commanded, "Fall back! Fall back!"

The troops responded, fleeing from the battle as the snow-covered ground exploded around them. The Imperial walkers fired their lasers at the running Rebels, continuing their advance toward Echo Base.

But Luke — still on the battlefield — wasn't ready to retreat. The way he saw things, the Rebel soldiers would have a better chance of making it to their transports if he could bring down one more Imperial walker.

Luke watched a nearby walker's foot rise, then ran under it. He fired his harpoon gun at the walker's underside, and a thin cable trailed after the rising, fusion-tipped projectile. The harpoon struck the metal hull and attached firmly.

Still running, Luke clipped the harpoon gun's cable drum to his belt buckle. Instantly, his feet left the ground and he was pulled up by the cable until he came to a stop just under the walker's lower plating.

Hanging precariously near a solid metal hatch, Luke reached to his utility belt for his lightsaber and activated its blade. In a swift motion, he cut through the hatch, then deactivated his lightsaber and returned it to his belt, where he'd also attached the concussion charge. Snapping the concussion charge from his belt, he hurled it up through the open hatch, then released his belt clip from the cable drum.

Luke plunged and landed hard, facedown. Fortunately, the deep snow broke most of his fall. The Imperial walker continued forward and one of its rear footpads nearly struck Luke. Then the walker stopped mid-step, and a muffled explosion came from within. Luke raised his head in time to watch the AT-AT's body rupture, blasting black smoke from its seams and every narrow opening. The smoldering behemoth teetered, then became the second Imperial walker to fall on Hoth.

General Veers saw the second AT-AT fall, then guided his own walker past its burning bulk. Without taking his eyes from the viewport, he addressed the pilot to his right: "Distance to power generators?"

"One-seven, decimal two-eight," the pilot answered.

A Rebel snowspeeder flew into Veers's path, and Veers took over the weapons controls to angle his walker's cannons, then fired. The blast slapped the speeder out of the sky and sent it into a spiral that ended with a fiery explosion in the snow.

Veers reached for the electrorangefinder and lined up the main generator. "Target," he said. "Maximum firepower."

The AT-AT spat out energy beams from its laser cannons, and blew the generator sky high.

With C-3PO several paces behind them, Han and Leia were running through an ice corridor, heading for Leia's transport, when the power generator exploded. They didn't actually see the explosion, but from the muffled roar that echoed throughout the base, they knew something big had blown up. As Han and Leia rounded a corner, the corridor's ice walls buckled and large chunks of ice fell from the ceiling, directly in their path.

Han threw himself at Leia, becoming a human shield as he knocked her to the corridor floor. Snow fell and filled the space, covering them with icy dust. Leia remained on the floor while Han rose quickly to find that the route to Leia's transport was now blocked by the cave-in.

Han pulled a comlink from a pocket on his jacket and said, "Transport, this is Solo. Better take off — I can't get to you. I'll get her out on the *Falcon*." He took Leia's arm and urged, "Come on!" as he pulled her up from the floor. Together they hurried back in the other direction —

— and nearly ran straight into C-3PO. The protocol droid had been far enough behind them that he had not seen the cave-in. As Leia and Han bolted past him, C-3PO turned and stammered, "But . . . but . . . but . . . where are you going?" They neither stopped nor answered, so C-3PO ran after them and called, "Oh . . . come back!"

The white-armored Imperial snowtroopers had to blast through the ice and a collapsed doorway to gain entrance to the command center. Two snowtroopers stepped past the broken remains of the tactical screens and comm consoles, and were followed by the dark, menacing form of Darth Vader.

Vader had arrived on Hoth in his personal shuttle. As snowtroopers swarmed into the command center, he paused to survey the shattered machinery, searching for anything that might tell him more about the Rebel insurgency.

"Wait!" C-3PO wailed as he ran after Leia and Han. "Wait for me! Wait! Stop!" The two humans ran through an open doorway, but as the droid followed, the door slid shut in his face. "How typical," C-3PO fumed at the closed door.

Before he could complain further, however, the door slid open and Han seized the droid. "Come on," Han said as he yanked C-3PO after him.

They ran through the cavernous hangar, making their way past abandoned cargo containers until they saw the *Millennium Falcon*. Chewbacca stood at the base of the *Falcon*'s landing ramp and waved his arms urgently at the running figures. But the engines still weren't fired up, so the Wookiee — not wanting to waste any precious seconds — didn't bother waiting at the ramp.

C-3PO ran as fast as he could. Han turned and shouted, "Hurry up, Goldenrod, or you're going to be a permanent resident!"

"Wait! Wait!" the droid cried as he followed Han and Leia up the landing ramp. He was halfway up when he felt the ramp start to rise from the hangar floor, nearly sending him sprawling into the ship.

The hangar was filled with a tortured, whirring sound of the *Falcon*'s engines. Inside the ship's main hold, Han stood before a control panel, flipping switches, while Chewbacca kept his blue eyes on a troublesome gauge. Leia watched as the Wookiee was suddenly struck by an unexpected blast of steam. Han flipped a different switch and said, "How's this?"

Leia gaped at Solo and said, "Would it help if I got out and pushed?"

C-3PO interrupted to say, "Captain Solo, Captain Solo —"

Ignoring the droid, Han answered Leia: "It might."

Still trying to get Han's attention, C-3PO said, "Sir, might I suggest that you —"

Han cut off the droid with a devastating glare. Quickly but reluctantly, C-3PO said, "It can wait."

Leia followed Han as he ran from the hold to the cockpit, where she watched him attempt to activate the cockpit's instruments. The instrument lights came on briefly, then dimmed. Angered and frustrated with his ship's temperamental technology, Han raised a fist and gave the instrument panel a solid whack. The lights illuminated again and stayed on.

Behind Han, Leia watched in disbelief and said, "This bucket of bolts is never going to get us past that blockade."

"This baby's got a few surprises left in her, sweetheart," Han promised as his hands darted across the switches and buttons on the cockpit's instrument panels.

Through the cockpit's transparisteel windows, they saw a squad of Imperial snowtroopers enter the hangar. Most wielded standard-issue blaster rifles, but one team carried a heavy repeating blaster cannon and a tripod. Leia guessed the snowtroopers would have their cannon set up in less than a minute, and she had a hard time believing the *Falcon* would be out of the hangar that soon.

Fortunately, one of the *Falcon*'s surprises was still functioning: An autoblaster — concealed above a panel in the ship's lower hull — popped out of its recess and swiveled to aim at the snowtroopers. The autoblaster spat out a rapid series of laser bolts, cutting down the nearest snowtroopers.

Han slid into the pilot's seat. Behind him, Leia got into the navigator's seat. She felt a thumping vibration as Chewbacca approached, his large feet pounding up the tubular corridor that led to the cockpit.

"Come on! Come on!" Han shouted to the Wookiee, who ducked as he hurried through the cockpit's open hatch. The hatch door slid shut and Chewbacca scrambled into the copilot's seat to Han's right. "Switch over," Han said, ready to give the ignition another try. "Let's hope we don't have burnout."

A blaster bolt struck and glanced off the window near Chewbacca and he let out a nervous yelp. Through the cockpit's window, they saw the snowtroopers had almost completed their assembly of the tripod-mounted cannon. Unlike the Imperial blaster rifles, the cannon had enough firepower to punch holes in the *Falcon*'s hull.

The *Falcon*'s engines fired. Han flashed a grin at Leia and said, "See?"

Not impressed, Leia leaned forward in her seat and said, "Someday you're going to be wrong, and I just hope I'm there to see it."

The snowtroopers were about to fire their cannon when the *Falcon*'s autoblaster swiveled again and unleashed a steady stream of laser fire. The energized projectiles smashed into the cannon, and the

Imperial weapon blew up, throwing the snowtroopers in all directions.

"Punch it!" Han ordered, and Chewie hit the accelerator. Han, Chewbacca, and Leia sank back against their seats as the ship launched forward.

Darth Vader arrived in the hangar just in time to see the *Millennium Falcon* soar out the mouth of the cave and vanish into the sky.

On the south slope outside Echo Base, Luke was making his way to his waiting X-wing starfighter when he heard the sound of a familiar starship's engine. He looked back to see the *Millennium Falcon* race away from the base and travel over the snow, then angle up and away from Hoth's surface.

Luke arrived at the evacuation site as the last Rebel transport was lifting off and the surviving pilots were running to their X-wings. Luke sighted his own X-wing, with R2-D2's blue-domed head poking up from the ship's astromech socket.

"Artoo!" Luke shouted.

Rotating his visual sensors to see Luke, R2-D2 let out some happy beeps.

"Get her ready for takeoff," Luke said. He watched as R2-D2 initiated the X-wing's repulsorlift, opened the cockpit canopy, and guided the vessel over the snow to Luke. As Luke stepped up to the X-wing, he saw Wedge heading for another X-wing.

"Good luck, Luke," Wedge said. "See you at the rendezvous."

R2-D2 made a long whimpering beep as Luke climbed into the cockpit and lowered its canopy. "Don't worry, Artoo," Luke said. "We're going, we're going."

The X-wing ascended through Hoth's atmosphere and Luke kept his eyes open for Imperial ships. But as he entered space, he was surprised not to see even one of the Star Destroyers that had brought the Imperial soldiers to Hoth. He supposed it was possible the destroyers were on the other side of Hoth, beyond his visual range. And he hoped that the Rebel transports and the *Millennium Falcon* had also escaped Hoth without difficulty.

The X-wing was cruising at sublight speed when Luke began to flip a series of control switches. Then he guided the starfighter into a steep turn and continued flying in a different direction.

R2-D2 beeped, and Luke glanced down at a monitor screen on his control panel. On the screen, R2-D2's beep was neatly translated into a text-format question. Luke read the question and replied into his comlink, "There's nothing wrong, Artoo. Just setting a new course."

R2-D2 beeped again, and Luke's monitor displayed another question.

Luke answered, "We're not going to regroup with the others."

R2-D2 whistled in protest.

Luke continued, "We're going to the Dagobah system."

R2-D2 was quiet while Luke checked his readouts and made a few adjustments. In the cockpit, the only sound was the soft hum of the instruments until R2-D2 finally chirped up.

Luke said, "Yes, Artoo?"

R2-D2 uttered a carefully phrased stream of beeps and whistles.

Luke read the translation on his monitor and chuckled. "That's all right. I'd like to keep it on manual control for a while."

The astromech droid let out a defeated whimper. Luke smiled and continued on his course for Dagobah.

The *Millennium Falcon* was not leaving Hoth so easily. The moment the ship entered space, it had four small TIE fighters and one enormous Star Destroyer on its tail. Green laser fire streaked from the TIE fighters, hammering the *Falcon*'s shields.

Inside the *Falcon*'s cockpit, Chewbacca checked a

monitor to confirm the status of the deflector shields, which were taking a pounding from the flak that exploded around the ship. The Wookiee let out a loud howl.

Han answered, "I saw 'em! I saw 'em!"

"Saw what?" Leia said from the seat behind.

"Star Destroyers," Han explained. "Two of them, coming right at us."

Leia spotted the Star Destroyers as the door behind her slid open and C-3PO stumbled into the cockpit. "Sir, sir!" C-3PO called to Han. "Might I suggest —"

"Shut him up or shut him down!" Han snapped at Leia, and C-3PO was pushed to the rear of the cockpit. To Chewbacca, Han shouted, "Check the deflector shields!"

Chewbacca readjusted an overhead switch and barked a reply that didn't sound good.

"Oh, great," Han said. "Well, we can still outmaneuver them."

Han increased power to the thrusters. With one Star Destroyer still directly behind it, the *Millennium Falcon* headed straight for the two oncoming destroyers. When the *Falcon* was practically between the two vessels, he threw his ship into a steep dive. The Star Destroyer that had been behind him was too unwieldy to follow his maneuver, and continued to travel on a collision course with the other Star Destroyers.

Alarms sounded within the three Star Destroyers. Inside one destroyer, an Imperial officer shouted, "Take evasive action!" But it was too late for the two of them. As their hulls made brushing contact, the ugly sound of shredding metal could be heard on the bridges of both ships.

With four TIE fighters still in hot pursuit, the *Millennium Falcon* raced away from the colliding destroyers. Inside the *Falcon*'s cockpit, Leia hung on to her seat and C-3PO braced himself against the hatch as Han and Chewbacca guided their ship through a dizzying spiral to evade the laser-firing TIE fighters.

To Chewbacca, Han shouted, "Prepare to make the jump to lightspeed!"

"But sir!" C-3PO cried to no avail. Han was already reaching for the hyperdrive controls.

Leia saw the TIE fighters appear as incoming blips on a monitor and shouted, "They're getting closer!"

"Oh, yeah?" Han said with a gleam in his eye. "Watch this." He pulled back on the hyperdrive shift. All eyes looked forward through the cockpit's windows, to the starfield beyond. Han waited for his ship to hurtle forward into hyperspace and transform the view into long streaks of starlight . . . but out-side the cockpit, the distant stars remained fixed against the darkness of space.

"Watch what?" Leia asked.

Han examined the controls and muttered, "I think we're in trouble."

"If I may say so, sir," C-3PO said, "I noticed ear-lier, the hyperdrive motivator has been damaged. It's impossible to go to lightspeed!"

"We're in trouble!" Han decided as he switched to autopilot and rose from his seat. Chewbacca fol-lowed Han out of the cockpit and ran to the hold, where the mighty Wookiee bent to the deck and raised a metal plate to reveal a systems access area: a pit filled with a complex tangle of metal pipes, ca-bles, and wires. Han hastily lowered himself into the pit while Chewbacca turned his attention to a nearby systems monitor panel.

In the pit, Han wrapped his body around a hori-zontally stretched pipe and reached out to adjust a cir-cuit switch. He shouted, "Horizontal boosters . . . !"

From the far side of the hold, Chewbacca an-swered with a loud, negative bark.

Han twisted his body around the metal pipe to reach for some different switches. He shouted, "Allu-vial dampers! Now?" Another negative bark came from Chewbacca. Han said, "That's not it."

A moment later, Chewbacca heard Han call from

the pit: "Bring me the hydrospanners!" The Wookiee picked up a toolbox that had been resting on top of a metal barrel, then shuffled across the deck and placed the toolbox at the edge of the open pit. Han climbed up to select a hydrospanner from the toolbox and said, "I don't know how we're going to get out of this one." He had just lowered himself from Chewbacca's view when the *Falcon* was struck by something that caused a bone-jarring jolt, sending the toolbox sliding into the pit.

"Oww!" Han yelled as the toolbox landed on him. "Chewie!" Han raised himself half out of the pit and felt another jolt, accompanied by a rumbling noise. "Those were no laserblasts!" Han realized. "Something hit us."

As Han scrambled out of the pit, Leia's voice called from a comlink, "Han, get up here!"

"Come on, Chewie!" Han said, racing from the hold.

As Han and Chewbacca rushed into the cockpit, Leia greeted them with a single word: "Asteroids!" Her statement was confirmed by the nightmarish view outside the cockpit window. The *Falcon* had accidentally traveled into the Hoth system's asteroid belt, and thousands of asteroids — pieces of stray matter and planetary debris — drifted through space. Some were small chunks of rock, but others were many times larger than the *Falcon*. Even worse, many asteroids were drifting at different speeds and trajectories.

"Oh, no," Han mumbled. He and Chewbacca pushed their way past Leia and C-3PO to jump back into their respective seats. Solo quickly glanced at the sensor monitors. So far, the *Falcon*'s particle shields were holding up against the debris, but the four TIE fighters and a single Star Destroyer were coming up fast behind them. As if to remind Han of their presence, the TIE fighters fired their cannons, and flak buffeted the *Falcon*'s shields.

Without hesitation, Han said, "Chewie, set two-seven-one."

The *Millennium Falcon* accelerated, temporarily increasing the distance from the pursuing TIE fighters. But through the *Falcon*'s cockpit window, asteroids that were already too close for comfort appeared to grow larger.

"What are you doing?" Leia said to Han. "You're not actually going into an asteroid field?"

"They'd be crazy to follow us, wouldn't they?" Han pointed out, guiding his ship past more asteroids and deeper into the field.

"You don't have to do this to impress me," Leia said, tightening her grip on her seat. She expected Han to respond with some cocky comment, and was dismayed when he didn't. He kept his hands on the controls and his eyes on the sickening view in front of him.

Protocol droids were not programmed to panic, but as C-3PO looked at the asteroids in the *Falcon*'s path, the feeling came to him naturally. Addressing Han, he said, "Sir, the possibility of successfully navigating an asteroid field is approximately three thousand seven hundred and twenty to one."

"Never tell me the odds!" Han said with bravado.

A large asteroid whizzed past the cockpit, then another flew past from a different direction. Han made the *Falcon* drop and weave to avoid being hit. Just off his starboard side, several small asteroids crashed into a larger one. The so-called asteroid field was more like an all-out asteroid storm.

The *Falcon* veered around the large asteroid and raced past the explosion of smaller rocks. The four pursuing TIE fighters tried to swerve around the rocks, but one TIE fighter swooped straight into an asteroid and exploded.

Two huge asteroids tumbled toward the *Millennium Falcon*, which quickly banked around both of them. The three TIE fighters followed but one of them scraped an asteroid and went tumbling out of control and smashed into another asteroid.

Leia risked a glance at one of Han's sensor screens. She saw there were only two TIE fighters still after them, but the pursuing destroyer had also entered the asteroid field. Before she could take any comfort in knowing that the Star Destroyer must be taking a severe beating, she became more concerned with the new bunch of asteroids that appeared to be racing toward the cockpit.

She sat stone-faced, staring through the window as an enormous asteroid dropped past the cockpit and narrowly missed the *Falcon*. Chewbacca barked in terror. C-3PO's hands covered his eyes.

Han gave Leia a quick look. "You said you wanted to be around when I made a mistake; well, this could be it, sweetheart."

"I take it back," Leia gasped. More asteroids raced past the cockpit. "We're going to get pulverized if we stay out here much longer."

"I'm not going to argue with that," Han said.

"Pulverized?" C-3PO repeated, too afraid to process the word.

Han said, "I'm going closer to one of those big ones."

"Closer?" Leia cried in astonishment.

"Closer?" C-3PO echoed.

Louder than Leia and C-3PO, Chewbacca barked the word in his own language.

Han threw the *Millennium Falcon* into a steep dive, aiming toward a moon-sized asteroid. The two remaining TIE fighters followed, and the Imperial pilots fired at the *Falcon* every chance they had.

Seconds later, the *Falcon* was flying dangerously fast and low over the asteroid's crater-pitted surface. Suddenly, the terrain dropped off to reveal a wide, high-walled canyon. As the TIE fighters continued to spit green laser fire after the *Falcon*, Han spotted a jagged, vertical shadow at the far end of the canyon that suggested a ravine between two high cliffs. Without any warning or explanation to his friends, Han raced for the gap. The TIE fighters kept after him.

The *Falcon* sped into the ravine, but the distance between the two cliff walls narrowed rapidly. Banking hard past jagged rock, Han swiftly elevated his ship's port side while dropping the starboard, effectively transforming the *Falcon*'s profile so its height became its width, and allowing the *Falcon* to fly sideways through the ravine.

Although the two TIE fighters were smaller than the *Falcon*, their pilots weren't nearly as skilled as Han Solo. In quick succession, both TIE fighters smashed into the ravine walls and exploded.

Still traveling sideways, the *Millennium Falcon* blasted out of the ravine to emerge in another canyon. As Han stabilized the ship, C-3PO cried, "Oh, this is suicide!"

Han noticed something on his main scope. He

nudged Chewbacca and pointed to a circular shadow on the canyon floor. "There," Han said. "That looks pretty good."

"What looks pretty good?" Leia asked.

"Yeah," Han said. "That'll do nicely."

Baffled, C-3PO turned to Leia and said, "Excuse me, ma'am, but where are we going?"

Out the cockpit window, they saw the same circular shadow: a large crater on the asteroid's surface. Han circled back, then swung the *Falcon* into a dive that deposited them into the crater . . . and total darkness.

At the very tips of the *Falcon's* extended mandibles, the forward floodlights came on. From what the crew could see, the crater they'd entered was really a deep tunnel.

To Han, Leia said, "I hope you know what you're doing."

All Han could reply was, "Yeah, me too."

Luke Skywalker gazed at the strange, cloud-covered world that now filled the view from his X-wing. Behind him, R2-D2 beeped from his astromech socket, and Luke read R2-D2's words as they were translated on the console monitor.

"Yes, that's it," Luke replied into his comlink. "Dagobah."

R2-D2 beeped a hopeful question.

Luke said, "No, I'm not going to change my mind about this." Examining his sensor scopes, Luke seemed slightly apprehensive. "I'm not picking up any cities or technology. Massive life-form readings though. There's something alive down there. . . ."

Again, R2-D2 beeped, but this time his question was filled with worry.

Luke said, "Yes, I'm sure it's perfectly safe for droids."

It was twilight above Dagobah as Luke began his descent. He entered the atmosphere and his view was soon obscured by clouds. He turned his focus to his sensor scopes . . . and discovered they weren't working.

An alarm began to buzz, and R2-D2 beeped and whistled frantically.

"I know, I know!" Luke said. "All the scopes are dead. I can't see a thing! Just hang on. I'm going to start the landing cycle."

R2-D2 squealed, but his cries were drowned out by the deafening roar of the X-wing's retrorockets. Luke flipped on the landing lights, but he still couldn't see the planet's surface through the dense atmosphere. Suddenly, there was a series of thrashing, cracking sounds, and Luke realized his ship was crashing through the upper branches of tall trees. Then, with a sudden jolt, the X-wing came to a stop.

Luke had landed in a watery peat bog. The X-wing was half-submerged, but from what Luke could see through the fog, his ship was still in one piece.

Luke opened the cockpit canopy and he got his first taste of Dagobah's humid climate. The smell of rot permeated the air. As he pulled off his gloves, he heard the caws and croaks of mysterious, unseen creatures. Behind him, R2-D2 beeped nervously.

Luke climbed out of his cockpit and stepped carefully onto the X-wing's long nose as R2-D2 removed himself from his socket to have a better look at their fog-shrouded surroundings. The X-wing's landing lights barely penetrated the fog, but R2-D2 was able to make out some of the giant, twisted gnarltrees that loomed around them. The gnarltrees had huge roots that rose out of the boggy terrain and gathered into wide trunks. Under and between the roots, cave-sized hollows had formed, leaving natural shelters for creatures of the swamp. Everything appeared to be covered with green moss or slime.

R2-D2 whistled anxiously. Luke turned and said, "No, Artoo, you stay put. I'll have a look around."

Still standing on the X-wing's nose, Luke checked to make sure his blaster was secure in the holster at his right hip, then bent slightly as he removed his helmet. The movement was enough to make his starfighter shift, and R2-D2 was thrown off balance. The droid let out an electronic yelp as he fell into the bog with a loud splash.

Luke spun and called, "Artoo?" He dropped to his knees and leaned out from the X-wing, trying to locate the droid, but the water's surface was blanketed by mist. "Artoo! Where are you? Artoo!" Luke held his breath and waited for some sign of —

A small periscope rose up through the mist. From underwater, R2-D2 made a gurgly beep.

At the sight of the little astromech's periscope, Luke let out a long breath. The periscope rotated so R2-D2 could glimpse his relieved master as he said, "You be more careful."

The periscope began to move through the mist, but Luke saw that R2-D2 wasn't heading in the most direct route to the bog's shore. "Artoo," he said, and the periscope glanced back at him. Luke pointed toward shore and said, "That way!" R2-D2 beeped, then moved off again, following Luke's instruction.

Luke tossed his helmet into the X-wing's open cockpit, then jumped into the murky water. He was right next to the shore and had no difficulty climbing some underwater roots to the muddy ground. But as he emerged with his g-suit covered in muck, he heard R2-D2's pathetic electronic scream.

Luke spun in time to see R2-D2's periscope drop and vanish into the mist, as he caught a glimpse of a large serpentlike creature rolling through the water just behind the droid's position. As suddenly as the creature had revealed its form, it disappeared underwater.

"Artoo!" Luke shouted as he drew his blaster fast, ready to fire at the first sight of the beast when it resurfaced. But seconds passed, and it didn't resurface. Luke watched the mist over the water and waited. *Come on, Artoo. Make a noise. Do something!*

Without warning, there was an explosion of bubbles and mud, and R2-D2 was launched like a missile from the water. Luke watched in stunned silence as the ejected droid sailed through the air, screeching all the way, and dropped out of sight between two trees.

The crash sounded awful.

Luke scrambled over slippery moss and odorous plants to find R2-D2 coated with slime and mud, resting upside down against some gnarled roots.

"Oh, no!" Luke said. "Are you all right?"

R2-D2 beeped and flailed his upturned legs against the vines. Luke noticed some alien bones on the ground nearby, and he wondered if they'd been expectorated by the same creature that had tried to make a meal of R2-D2.

"Come on," Luke said, gently righting the poor droid to his feet. "You're lucky you don't taste very good. Anything broken?"

Nothing appeared to be damaged, but R2-D2 responded with a beep that sounded soggy and miserable.

Luke wiped mud from R2-D2's body. "If you're saying coming here was a bad idea, I'm beginning to agree with you." He stood up and looked around, then squatted down beside the droid. "Artoo, what are we doing here? It's like . . . something out of a dream or . . . I don't know." He pried more mud from the primary photo receptor on R2-D2's domed head and added, "Maybe I'm just going crazy."

R2-D2 beeped, popped open a cranial access port, and spat mud onto the ground.

On the *Executor*, Admiral Piett hesitated as he entered Darth Vader's inner sanctum. From where Piett stood, just at the doorway, he could see Vader's spherical meditation chamber was partially open, but the sphere's interlocking mechanical jaws obscured the view of Vader himself. Piett moved cautiously forward, and when he was able to see the seated figure within the meditation chamber, he gulped in astonishment.

Darth Vader was not wearing his helmet. He sat facing away from Piett, who shivered at the sight of the back of Vader's head; it was pale, hairless, and heavily scarred.

Take a good look, Admiral, thought Vader. *Imagine the worst, and let your fear fuel my power.*

Piett watched a robotic clamp lower from the sphere's ceiling and place the familiar black helmet over Vader's head. He quickly composed himself as Vader's seat rotated to face him.

Vader said, "Yes, Admiral?"

"Our ships have sighted the *Millennium Falcon*, Lord. But . . . it has entered an asteroid field, and we cannot risk —"

"Asteroids do not concern me, Admiral," Vader interrupted. "I want that ship, not excuses."

"Yes, Lord," Piett said as the meditation chamber's upper half descended.

The *Millennium Falcon* had touched down inside the asteroid cave. A sensor scan had detected a warm, pressurized atmosphere outside the ship, but the *Falcon*'s crew was more concerned with repairing their ship than speleological anomalies. Leia, C-3PO, and Chewbacca were checking instruments in the cockpit when Han entered and said, "I'm going to shut down everything but the emergency power systems."

Hearing this, C-3PO said, "Sir, I'm almost afraid to ask, but . . . does that include shutting me down, too?"

"No," Han said with a smile as he flipped several switches to *off* positions. "I need you to talk to the *Falcon* and find out what's wrong with the hyperdrive."

Suddenly, the ship lurched, causing the cockpit's occupants to stumble into one another. A moment after it happened, the ship stabilized.

Facing Han, C-3PO said, "Sir, it's quite possible this asteroid is not entirely stable."

"Not entirely stable?" Han said with annoyance. "I'm glad you're here to tell us these things." He pushed C-3PO toward Chewbacca and said, "Chewie, take the professor in the back and plug him into the hyperdrive."

"Oh!" C-3PO exclaimed as Chewbacca guided him out of the cockpit. "Sometimes I just don't understand human behavior. After all, I'm only trying to do my job in the most —" The hatch slid shut, cutting off C-3PO's words.

Leia and Han were still inside the cockpit when the *Falcon* suddenly lurched again. Leia was thrown across the cockpit into Han, and he stumbled back into the navigator's seat. His arms encircled Leia protectively as she landed on his lap. Then, abruptly, the lurching motion stopped.

"Let go," said Leia.

"Shh!" Han said, trying to listen for any unusual sounds outside the ship as he kept his arms around Leia.

"Let go, please," Leia insisted.

"Don't get excited," Han said as he released his hold.

Leia fumed. "Captain, being held by you isn't quite enough to get me excited."

"Sorry, sweetheart," Han replied with a smirk. "We haven't got time for anything else." He opened the hatch and left the cockpit.

Leia turned to look out the window, but she was so flustered she couldn't see straight. *Why does he have to be such a jerk?* she thought. *And why do I let him get to me?* She felt almost dizzy with anger as her brain fumbled for words that she might have used to tell off Han, once and for all. Then she realized her lips were moving, mumbling words that just wouldn't come out right.

I don't know what's worse, Leia thought. *Feeling furious at Han, or feeling . . . something else.*

Something she didn't want to acknowledge.

She raised her white-gloved hand and whacked the cockpit's wall.

On Dagobah, the mist had dispersed a bit, but the swamp remained a gloomy place. Luke had retrieved a box of emergency provisions from his X-wing and set up his camp in a clearing. As he ignited a compact fusion furnace that he'd placed on a rotten log beside R2-D2, the droid beeped at him.

"What?" Luke said. "Ready for some power? Okay. Let's see now." He ran a power cable from the furnace to the droid. "Put that in there," he said to himself as he plugged the cable into R2-D2's socket. "There you go."

R2-D2 beeped, apparently content for the moment.

Luke patted R2-D2's domed head and said, "Now all I got to do is find this Yoda . . . if he even exists." To himself, he thought, *I don't even know what Yoda looks like. Since he taught Ben, he must be very old. And strong, too, if he can survive in this environ-*

ment. For the first time, Luke realized he'd been assuming Yoda was male, when in fact he didn't have any idea.

Luke sighed as he stood and looked around. "It's really a strange place to find a Jedi Master. This place gives me the creeps."

R2-D2 beeped. Even though Luke didn't have a portable droid translator, he had a feeling that the little droid agreed with him.

Luke sat down on a rock beside R2-D2 and removed a box of food rations from his stack of supplies. As he bit into a dehydrated nutrition bar, he continued, "Still . . . there's something familiar about this place."

R2-D2 beeped, wondering what Luke meant.

"I don't know . . ." Luke said, glancing at the surrounding trees. "I feel like . . ."

"Feel like what?" a strange, croaking voice interrupted.

Luke's blaster flashed from its holster and he was suddenly aiming at a short, squat alien who sat on a nearby stump. "Like we're being watched!" Luke finished.

"Away put your weapon!" the creature said as he threw his arms up over his face. "I mean you no harm." He wore a ratty old robe and clutched a small gimer stick that he held up defensively. He lowered his arms to peek over his sleeves, allowing Luke to get a better look at him. He had wrinkled green skin, long tapered ears, and large eyes that looked somehow alert and sleepy at the same time. His manner of speech was unusual and his words came out in a rhythmic croak. Luke didn't recognize the creature's species, but he appeared harmless.

The creature asked, "I am wondering, why are you here?"

"I'm looking for someone," Luke answered warily.

"Looking?" the creature said with amusement. "Found someone, you have, I would say, hmmm?" He chuckled.

Luke tried to keep from smiling as he answered, "Right."

"Help you I can. Yes, mmmm."

"I don't think so," Luke replied. Looking away as he holstered his blaster, he didn't see the creature smile slyly. Luke added, "I'm looking for a great warrior."

"Ahhh! A great warrior," the creature said, then laughed and shook his head. "Wars not make one great." Easing himself down to the ground, he held his gimer stick forward as he hobbled on his stubby tridactyl feet over to Luke's supplies. Luke had placed his nutrition bar on top of a box, and the creature picked up the bar and examined it.

"Put that down!" Luke said. "Now . . . hey!" Much to Luke's surprise, the creature had just taken a tiny bite from the bar. Luke said, "That's my dinner!"

As Luke snatched the bar and a box of rations, the creature's face twisted with disgust at the bar's taste. He said, "How you get so big, eating food of this kind?"

Luke considered finishing the nutrition bar, then thought better of it and tossed it into the swamp. "Listen, friend," he said, "we didn't mean to land in that puddle, and if we could get our ship out, we would, but we can't, so why don't you just —"

"Aww, can't you get your ship out?" the creature asked.

Luke turned to see that the creature had set aside his gimer stick and had crawled headfirst into an open container. Luke couldn't believe it. *He's rummaging through my supplies!*

"Hey, get out of there!" Luke shouted.

"Ahhh!" said the creature as he dug out an electronic device.

Luke grabbed the device and said, "Hey, you could have broken this."

Ignoring Luke, the creature dug faster, considered an item, then said, "No!" and tossed it over his shoulder. He picked out another object and tossed it after the other.

"Don't do that," Luke said. "Ohhh . . . you're making a mess."

"Oh!" cried the creature as he pulled out a tiny power lamp and regarded it with delight. He flicked it on and moved the light around his face.

"Hey, give me that!" Luke said.

"Mine!" the creature said, clutching the tiny lamp. "Or I will help you not."

"I don't want your help," Luke said. "I want my lamp back. I'm gonna need it to get out of this slimy mudhole."

The creature glared at Luke. "Mudhole? Slimy? My home this is."

While the creature faced Luke, R2-D2 opened an access panel and extended one of his manipulator arms, then clamped onto the lamp and tried to snatch it from the creature's tight grip. "Ah, ah, ah!" said the creature as he and R2-D2 began a tug-of-war contest with the lamp as the prize.

"Oh, Artoo, let him have it!" Luke said. But the droid ignored him and continued to tug.

With his free hand, the creature reached for his gimer stick and began whacking R2-D2 as he shouted, "Mine! Mine! Mine!"

"Artoo!" Luke cried out, prompting the droid to release his grip and allow the creature to win. As R2-D2 retracted his manipulator, the creature reached out with his gimer stick and playfully tapped the droid's access panel shut.

Tired of the creature, Luke said, "Now will you move along, little fella? We've got a lot of work to do."

"No! No, no!" said the creature, wielding the tiny lamp as he hobbled over to Luke. "Stay and help you, I will." The creature laughed and added, "Find your friend."

"I'm not looking for a friend," Luke said. "I'm looking for a Jedi Master."

The creature's eyes went wide and his tapered ears dipped. "Oohhh, Jedi Master. Yoda. You seek Yoda."

Now it was Luke who was surprised. Bending down so his eyes were almost level with the creature's, he said, "You know him?"

"Mmm. Take you to him, I will." The creature laughed. "Yes, yes. But now we must eat. Come. Good food. Come." The creature walked away from Luke's camp, then turned back and repeated, "Come, come."

Luke didn't trust the creature, but he wasn't afraid of him either. He turned to the astromech and said, "Artoo, stay and watch after the camp."

R2-D2 watched his master follow the creature deeper into the swamp. The droid slowly rotated his domed head clockwise, looking for any other life-forms that might be lurking in the darkness or the trees. He kept looking until he'd completed a full rotation and spotted Luke again, now farther away.

R2-D2 beeped an electronic sigh.

"Oh, where is Artoo when I need him?" C-3PO said with dismay as he shook his head. The golden droid was standing inside the *Falcon*'s main hold, and the ship was still in the cave on the moon-sized asteroid. C-3PO had just attempted to communicate with the ship's computer by whistling and beeping into a control panel on the main hold's wall. The control panel had responded with a mystifying whistle that left C-3PO slightly baffled.

Han entered the hold to check on some wires and cables. C-3PO said, "Sir, I don't know where your ship learned to communicate, but it has the most peculiar dialect. I believe, sir, it says that the power coupling on the negative axis has been polarized. I'm afraid you'll have to replace it."

Han grimaced at the droid. "Well, of *course* I'll have to replace it," he said, then walked across the hold and looked up to an open access compartment in the ceiling. Chewbacca's head peeked out to gaze down at Han, who handed a wire coil to the Wookiee and said, "Here! And Chewie . . ."

Chewbacca whined, waiting for Han to continue.

Han glanced back at C-3PO, who was still facing the control panel on the other side of the hold. Hoping only Chewbacca would hear his words, Han said in a low voice, ". . . I think we'd better replace the negative power coupling."

Chewbacca responded with an affirmative bark.

From the main hold, Han stepped through an open hatch into the adjoining circuitry bay, a narrow-walled cluster of switches and valves that also served as a shortcut — via a second hatch — to the port side cargo hold. Inside the circuitry bay, Leia had just finished welding a valve. She had removed her white gloves, and was now struggling with a lever. Her back was to Han, and she was so focused on the lever that she didn't hear his approach. But as he extended his arms past hers to reach for the lever, Leia was startled. And when she quickly realized it was Han who'd come up behind her, she was suddenly outraged. Still gripping the lever with both hands, she turned it hard with a thrust of her elbows to send Han back a step.

"Hey, Your Worship," Han said. "I'm only trying to help."

"Would you please stop calling me that?" Leia snapped, and tried turning the lever again.

Han shrugged. "Sure, Leia."

Leia broiled. She'd been putting up with Han's jibes about her royal title for so long that it seemed unfair that he should speak her name so easily. Still infuriated, she leaned into the lever and said, "Oh, you make it so difficult sometimes."

"I do, I really do," Han agreed. "You could be a little nicer, though. Come on, admit it. Sometimes you think I'm all right."

Suddenly, her hands slipped on the lever and her bare knuckles smacked against the metal. She reflexively raised one hand to her mouth, as if she might kiss away the pain, then turned to face Han and said, "Occasionally, maybe . . . when you aren't acting like a scoundrel."

"Scoundrel?" Han repeated, and took her hands in his and examined them. "Scoundrel? I like the sound of that."

Leia realized he was massaging her hands. She said, "Stop that."

"Stop what?" Han replied, trying to look innocent.

"Stop that! My hands are dirty."

"My hands are dirty, too. What are you afraid of?"

"Afraid?" The question caught Leia off guard.

Han said, "You're trembling."

"I'm not trembling," Leia countered, and realized, *He's still holding my hands.*

The space between them closed. Han said, "You like me because I'm a scoundrel. There aren't enough scoundrels in your life."

"I happen to like nice men," Leia told him. She hadn't meant to whisper, but she did.

Han replied softly, "I'm a nice man."

"No, you're not. You're . . ."

And then their lips met. For a few seconds, Leia stopped thinking about whether her hands were clean, or about the Empire, or about . . .

"Sir, sir!" C-3PO said from behind Han, and tapped him on the shoulder. "I've isolated the reverse power flux coupling."

Neither Leia nor Han had heard the droid enter the circuit bay from the main hold. Han eased out of Leia's embrace, slowly turned, and advanced toward C-3PO, blocking the droid's view of Leia and forcing him to step backward through the open hatch. Han said icily, "Thank you. Thank you very much."

Not comprehending Han's sarcasm, C-3PO said happily, "Oh, you're perfectly welcome, sir," then turned and walked away.

Han turned back to face the circuit bay's interior, but if he'd hoped to find Leia waiting for him to get rid of C-3PO, he was too late. Leia had already left through the other hatch.

At Darth Vader's command, the fleet of Imperial Star Destroyers was escorting *Executor* through the asteroid field. The warships fired at the obstacles in their path, but the asteroids far outnumbered the combined weaponry of all the warships, and the Star Destroyers were taking a severe pummeling. Incredibly, the *Executor* remained unscathed.

A large asteroid slammed into one Star Destroyer's conning tower, and the ship was instantly engulfed by massive explosions. Evidence of the ship's loss was immediately played out on the bridge of the *Executor*, where Darth Vader stood before hologram images of the commanding officers of his escort; one hologram, an Imperial captain, quickly faded and disappeared as his transmission — along with his ship — came to a violent end.

Vader ignored the vanished hologram and faced

the three-dimensional projection of the *Avenger's* Captain Needa, who reported, ". . . and that, Lord Vader, was the last time they appeared in any of our scopes. Considering the amount of damage we've sustained, they must have been destroyed."

"No, Captain, they're alive," Vader said. "I want every ship available to sweep the asteroid field until they are found."

With that, the conference was over. As the holograms faded out, Admiral Piett walked hurriedly onto the bridge and was almost breathless when he came to a stop before the *Executor's* commander. Piett gasped, "Lord Vader."

One look at Piett's pallor, which was white as a sheet, and the Sith Lord knew the man was scared. "Yes, Admiral, what is it?"

Piett took a gulp of air, then tried to keep his voice from trembling as he said, "The Emperor commands you to make contact with him."

"Move the ship out of the asteroid field so that we can send a clear transmission."

"Yes, my lord," Piett said as Vader's menacing form swept off the bridge.

Vader proceeded to his personal quarters. When the *Executor* was out of the asteroid field, he stepped down from his meditation chamber to stand upon a circular black panel, a HoloNet scanner that allowed him to transmit communications across the galaxy. As the dark lord dropped to his left knee and bowed his helmeted head, the panel's outer ring was illuminated. Vader slowly raised his gaze to the empty air before him, and the emptiness was instantly filled by flickering blue light.

The light assembled to form a hologram that was nearly as tall as the room itself: a large three-dimensional image of a cloaked head with eyes that blazed wickedly from shadowy, pitted features.

There was no mistaking the face of Emperor Palpatine.

Still kneeling before the immense hologram, Vader said, "What is thy bidding, my Master?"

From light-years away, on the planet Coruscant, the Emperor said, "There is a great disturbance in the Force."

"I have felt it," Vader said.

The Emperor continued, "We have a new enemy. The young Rebel who destroyed the Death Star. I have no doubt this boy is the offspring of Anakin Skywalker."

"How is that possible?" Darth Vader managed to ask through his shock. Could it be . . . true?

"Search your feelings, Lord Vader. You will know it to be true. He could destroy us."

"He's just a boy," Vader pointed out, the belief rising within him that Anakin's son could exist. He thought, *If the Emperor knows about the boy, then he also knows the fate of Obi-Wan Kenobi.* Vader added, "Obi-Wan can no longer help him."

"The Force is strong with him," the Emperor said. "The son of Skywalker must not become a Jedi."

The Emperor had not said, in so many words, that the young Skywalker must die, which was fortunate because Vader had something else in mind. He told his master, "If he could be turned, he would become a powerful ally."

"Yes," said the Emperor, his expression thoughtful, as if he had not previously considered this possibility. Sith Lords had long maintained a rule of limiting their number to only two: one master and one apprentice — but now, the Emperor's eyes seemed to ignite, and he repeated, "Yes. He would be a great asset. Can it be done?"

"He will join us or die, Master," Vader said. He bowed, and the Emperor's hologram faded out.

Nothing will stand in my way, Darth Vader thought. *Nothing will stop me from achieving my goal. If I must search the farthest reaches of the galaxy, I will find Luke Skywalker.*

R2-D2 found Luke inside a small house made out of mud.

It was raining, and it had been easy for R2-D2 to track Luke's water-filled footprints from their camp near the spot where they'd landed on Dagobah. Although the astromech had been cautious to travel through the swampy forest on his own, he'd been even more rattled by the idea of remaining alone at the camp. Luke's footprints had led the droid to the house that had been constructed under the overhanging roots of a towering gnarltree. With its sloping outer walls, the house appeared almost organic, as if it were growing from the ground. Only the windows — smallish oval portals — and a sculpted chimney indicated the moss-covered dwelling was not a natural formation.

The structure was not much taller than the astromech himself. As the rain pelted off his domed head, R2-D2 rose up on the tips of his treads, peeked into a window, and listened. Inside, the small green-skinned creature was cooking something in a pot on a stove while Luke squatted under the low mud-packed ceiling.

"Look, I'm sure it's delicious," Luke said, eyeing the food in the pot. "I just don't understand why we can't see Yoda now."

"Patience!" the creature exclaimed. "For the Jedi it is time to eat as well. Eat, eat. Hot."

Luke moved with difficulty in the cramped quarters, but managed to sit down near the fire and serve himself from the steaming pot. He tasted the strange food and wished he hadn't.

"Good food, hm?" asked the creature. "Good, hmmm?"

But Luke wasn't interested in the food. "How far away is Yoda? Will it take us long to get there?"

"Not far," said the creature. "Yoda not far. Patience. Soon you will be with him." He tasted the food directly from the pot. "Rootleaf, I cook. Why wish you become Jedi? Hm?"

"Mostly because of my father, I guess," Luke admitted.

"Ah, father," the creature said. "Powerful Jedi was he, mmm, powerful Jedi, mmm."

"Oh, come on," Luke said, angry with the creature. "How could you know my father? You don't even know who I am. Oh, I don't know what I'm doing here. We're wasting our time."

The creature looked away from Luke and sounded disappointed as he said, "I cannot teach him. The boy has no patience."

From out of nowhere, Ben's voice answered, "He will learn patience."

Startled, Luke looked around, searching for Ben as if he might appear within the mud house.

"Hmmm," mumbled the creature. He turned

slowly, studied Luke, and said, "Much anger in him, like his father."

Ben's voice replied, "Was I any different when you taught me?"

"Hah," the creature said. "He is not ready."

Luke looked at the creature, who returned his gaze with wise old eyes. Then Luke suddenly realized the truth, and gasped, "Yoda!"

Yoda nodded.

"I *am* ready," Luke said. "I . . . Ben! I . . . I can be a Jedi. Ben, tell him I'm ready." Trying to see Ben, Luke started to get up — only to smack his head against the hut's ceiling.

"Ready, are you?" Yoda said, fixing Luke with a severe glare. "What know you of ready? For eight hundred years have I trained Jedi. My own counsel will I keep on who is to be trained! A Jedi must have the deepest commitment, the most serious mind." Yoda tilted his head slightly to address Ben, who remained invisible, as he gestured to indicate Luke. "This one a long time have I watched. All his life has he looked away . . . to the future, to the horizon. Never his mind on where he was. Hmm? What he was doing. Hmph." Yoda raised his gimer stick and jabbed Luke. "Adventure. Heh! Excitement. Heh! A Jedi craves not these things." Lowering his gimer stick, he stared at Luke. "You are reckless!"

Ben's disembodied voice said, "So was I, if you re-member."

"He is too old," Yoda replied. Before the fall of the Old Republic, Jedi began their training as infants — before they could know about fear and anger — and were raised at the Jedi Temple on the planet Coruscant. One rare exception had been Luke's father, who'd been nine years of age when he'd arrived at the Jedi Temple. Yoda had been extremely reluctant to allow Luke's father to become a Jedi, and given everything that had transpired, he was even more hesitant to teach Luke. Yoda added, "Yes, too old to begin the training."

Desperate for Yoda to reconsider, Luke said, "But I've learned so much."

Yoda sighed. Addressing the invisible Ben, he asked, "Will he finish what he begins?"

Instead of allowing Ben to answer, Luke said, "I won't fail you." As Yoda's gaze returned to him, Luke felt compelled to add, "I'm not afraid."

Yoda said, "Oh," his eyes widening, and his voice dropping to a low, threatening tone, "you will be. You *will* be."

Under the command of Captain Needa, the Imperial Star Destroyer *Avenger* cruised along the edge of the asteroid field, firing at every piece of drifting matter that strayed too close to the immense ship. Because there had been no sign that the *Millennium Falcon* had been destroyed or had left the asteroid field, Darth Vader maintained the Rebels had to be hiding on one of the larger asteroids. If they were, the *Avenger* would flush them out.

Captain Needa had dispatched Imperial TIE bombers with TIE fighter escorts, and the pilots soon arrived upon a moon-sized asteroid. There, the double-podded bombers dropped free-falling thermal detonators that exploded and left new craters on the asteroid's ravaged terrain.

Tucked away in the depths of the asteroid cave, the crew of the *Falcon* heard the distant explosions on the surface of their hiding place. While Han,

Chewbacca, and C-3PO made repairs in the main hold, Leia sat alone in the cockpit, thinking.

She wasn't thinking about how they'd get out of the cave or asteroid field, or even if they'd escape the Imperial ships. She was thinking about Han. And Luke. And how she felt about them, which was complicated. Luke was sweet and shy. He'd never told her in so many words that he was fond of her, but even before their kiss on Hoth, she knew he cared for her deeply. They had an indescribable bond.

And Han was . . . well, for all of his occasionally good qualities, he was arrogant and incredibly self-centered. Leia resented Han's behavior, the way he seemed bent on having her choose between him or Luke. *As if I don't have any more pressing concerns than Han's ego.* And Han knew Luke was fond of her, which only put more of a strain on their friendship. *Honestly, what kind of a friend is Han? I just don't know. . . .*

But he is a good kisser.

She looked at her hands. She couldn't remember when she'd put her white gloves back on, but she was wearing them now. It wasn't that cold in the *Falcon*, but gloves were good for other things, like discouraging bare-handed massages. *Why invite trouble?* Still, she'd been surprised by the warmth and gentleness of Han's touch. . . .

This is madness! What am I, a schoolgirl? There's

a war on and I have a job to do. I don't have the time or energy for this! I should just tell Han to —

She saw something move outside the cockpit window. She thought, *Maybe my eyes are getting tired?* Leaning forward in her seat, she peered into the darkness.

Suddenly, a leathery, flying creature appeared and suctioned its face against the window with a loud slap. Startled, Leia screamed and fell back against her seat, then turned and hurried out of the cockpit.

In the main hold, C-3PO was trying yet again to engage Han's attention. "Sir, if I may venture an opinion —"

"I'm not really interested in your opinion, Three-pio," Han interrupted.

Leia ran into the hold, past the droid, and found Han and Chewbacca facing a wall, making repairs to exposed cables. She said, "There's something out there."

Chewbacca and Han, both wearing welding goggles, looked almost comical as they turned to face Leia. Han raised his goggles and asked, "Where?"

"Outside, in the cave."

As if in response, there came a sharp banging on the hull.

C-3PO cried, "There it is! Listen! Listen!"

The noise came again. Chewbacca barked anxiously.

"I'm going out there," Han said. He stepped over to a wall-mounted rack of supplies.

Leia said, "Are you crazy?"

"I just got this bucket back together," Han said. "I'm not going to let something tear it apart." He reached to a nearby supply rack and grabbed a breath mask, a portable life-support unit that would allow him to breathe in the cave.

Leia said, "Oh, then I'm going with you." She took a breath mask and hurried after Han, then Chewbacca did the same.

C-3PO stood nervously in the hold. To the departing figures, he said, "I think it might be better if I stay behind and guard the ship." Another mysterious noise echoed off the hull, causing the droid to tremble and mutter, "Oh, no."

At the top of the ship's landing ramp, Han, Leia, and Chewbacca placed their breath masks over their noses and mouths. The landing ramp extended to the cave floor, and Han walked down it, followed by Leia and Chewbacca. Han had his blaster pistol out and Chewbacca carried his Wookiee bowcaster. Leia held her empty hands out at her sides and thought, *Shouldn't I be carrying a glow rod or something?*

There was a heavy mist in the cave, which was illuminated only by the *Falcon*'s landing lights. Han stepped cautiously onto the cave floor. While his eyes searched for anything unusual on his ship's shadowy exterior, Leia followed. Testing her footing, she said, "This ground sure feels strange. It doesn't feel like rock."

Han looked at the swirling mist and said, "There's an awful lot of moisture in here."

"I don't know," Leia remarked vaguely, then added, "I have a bad feeling about this."

"Yeah," Han agreed.

Suddenly, Chewbacca barked through his face mask and pointed toward the *Falcon*'s cockpit. Han moved fast, firing his blaster at the indicated spot. There was a loud screech, then Han yelled to Leia, "Watch out!"

A leathery creature tumbled from the cockpit to the ground. Han stepped over and bent down to examine the dead beast, saying, "It's all right. It's all right."

Chewbacca walked over to Han and whimpered.

Han said, "Yeah, what I thought. Mynock." Han and Chewbacca had encountered mynocks before: silicon-based parasites that feed on energy from starships. Han said, "Chewie, check the rest of the ship, make sure there are no more attached. They're chewing on the power cables."

"Mynocks?" Leia asked. *I've never heard of them.*

"Go on inside," Han said. "We'll clean them off if there are any more."

But before Leia could return to the landing ramp, a swarm of mynocks swooped past her. She raised her arms in front of her head to protect herself, then more mynocks flew at Chewbacca, who swung his bowcaster at them.

Inside the *Falcon*, C-3PO entered the cockpit to see what was going on outside. The droid nearly jumped out of his metal plating when several mynocks flapped their wings against the cockpit window. "Ohhh!" C-3PO shouted. "Go away! Go away!" He waved his arms at them. "Beastly thing. Shoo! Shoo!"

Chewbacca fired at one, and the fired bolt of energy slammed into the cave wall — causing the entire cave to rumble.

Han stood still, listening to the sounds in the cave. The mynocks had suddenly flown away, but why? Han thought about it, then said, "Wait a minute . . ." He aimed his blaster at the cave floor and fired.

More rumbling, only worse. The entire cave suddenly tilted hard to the side, nearly launching Han, Leia, and Chewbacca off their feet. As the cave rocked around them, they rushed across the misty floor and up the landing ramp.

Running for the main hold, Han tore off his breath mask and shouted, "Pull her up, Chewie. Let's get out of here!"

Chewbacca ran to the cockpit. Leia followed Han

into the hold, where they nearly fell into C-3PO. As Han checked the scopes on a control panel, Leia said, "The Empire is still out there. I don't think it's wise to —"

"No time to discuss this in committee," Han interrupted.

"I am not a committee!" Leia protested as Han bolted for the cockpit. The *Millennium Falcon*'s main engines began to whine. Leia went after Han, stumbling into the corridor walls as another quake rocked the ship.

When Leia and Han entered the cockpit, Chewbacca was already hanging on to his seat. As Han jumped behind his controls and pulled back on the throttle, Leia insisted, "You can't make the jump to lightspeed in this asteroid field!"

"Sit down, sweetheart," Han replied. "We're taking off!"

The cave quake diminished as the ship moved forward. C-3PO stepped into the cockpit just as Chewbacca noticed something ahead. The Wookiee barked.

C-3PO pointed to the cockpit window and exclaimed, "Look!"

Han said, "I see it, I see it."

They were fast approaching a row of jagged white stalagmites and stalactites that surrounded the cave's entrance. But as the ship hurtled forward, the jagged formations appeared to be closing in on each other, and the entrance grew smaller.

Han pulled hard on the throttle to increase speed.

"We're doomed!" the droid cried.

"The cave is collapsing!" Leia shouted.

"This is no cave," Han said.

Leia gasped, "What?" Then she realized Han was right. They weren't looking at the mouth of the cave, but the mouth of an enormous monster. The jagged rock formations were really teeth.

Chewbacca howled as the *Millennium Falcon* zoomed forward and rolled on its side to pass — just barely — between two of the gigantic white teeth. The jaws quickly slammed closed behind them. The ship ascended, and the monster — a space slug — raised its head after them and tried for another bite but missed. The *Falcon* was too fast. As the ship sped away from the asteroid, the space slug tilted its massive head, then withdrew and slid back into its cave.

The *Falcon* headed once more into the asteroid belt.

Yoda was riding in a pack strapped to Luke's back. Already sweating in his sleeveless tunic, Luke grabbed hold of a thick vine that stretched down from a high tree to the Dagobah swamp. He pulled himself up, hand over hand, carrying Yoda with him. Winged creatures flew through the humid air, but Luke ignored them.

At a designated branch, Luke turned, grabbed another vine, and swung away from the tree, down to the ground. He landed on solid soil, flipped his body forward over a broad root, and began to run through the swamp. As Luke raced in and out of the heavy ground fog, Yoda spoke to the back of Luke's head, urging him on.

"Run!" Yoda said as he clung to Luke's shoulders. "Yes. A Jedi's strength flows from the Force. But beware of the dark side. Anger . . . fear . . . aggression. The dark side of the Force are they. Easily they flow, quick to join you in a fight. If once you start down the dark path, forever will it dominate your destiny, consume you it will, as it did Obi-Wan's apprentice."

Luke came to an abrupt stop and said, "Vader." Breathing hard, he turned his head slightly to address Yoda and asked, "Is the dark side stronger?"

Yoda answered, "No . . . no . . . no. Quicker, easier, more seductive."

"But how am I to know the good side from the bad?"

"You will know," Yoda assured his new pupil, his voice a soothing rasp in Luke's ear. "When you are calm, at peace. Passive. A Jedi uses the Force for knowledge and defense, never for attack."

"But tell me why I can't —"

"No, no, there is no why," Yoda interrupted. "Nothing more will I teach you today. Clear your mind of questions. Mmm. Mmmmmmm."

Luke closed his eyes to meditate.

R2-D2 beeped in the distance as Luke lowered Yoda to the ground. While the aged Jedi settled himself on a wide root, Luke stepped over to a tree branch, where he'd placed his shirt and weapon belt.

As Luke pulled on his shirt, he sensed something strange and deadly in the air. He turned to see a huge, dead, black tree, its trunk surrounded by a few feet of water. Giant, twisted roots formed a dark and sinister-looking cave on one side. Luke stared at the tree and a chill ran down his spine.

"There's something not right here," he said. "I feel cold, death."

"That place . . ." Yoda said from his seat, "is strong with the dark side of the Force. A domain of evil it is. In you must go."

Luke thought, *He actually wants me to go in?* But he also somehow knew the journey was necessary. It seemed the place was silently calling to him, beckoning. Hesitant, Luke asked, "What's in there?"

Yoda said, "Only what you take with you."

Luke looked warily between the tree and Yoda, then started to strap on his weapon belt.

Seeing this, Yoda said, "Your weapons . . . you will not need them."

Luke gave the tree a long look, then shook his head and strapped on his belt. Yoda shrugged. As Luke walked away, the little droid trembled.

Luke brushed aside some hanging vines, then lowered himself into a hole. In the darkness, he could barely make out the passage that lay before him, but he proceeded deeper into it. There were roots, tangled and twisting up the walls, and the smell of rot and decay was everywhere. Could these roots bring life to the tree above? Somehow it seemed doubtful.

The space widened around him, and then he saw

something move in front of him. There was a shadowy form, then mechanical breathing sounds, and a sense of dread.

Darth Vader.

The dark lord appeared from the blackness, and Luke took a few steps back. Time seemed to slow down, but Luke's mind raced: *How did Vader get to Dagobah? Is he looking for Master Yoda? Or is he here for . . . me?* Then he remembered his lightsaber, and in an instant, the cave was illuminated by its blue blade.

Vader drew and activated his own red lightsaber, crossing his blade with Luke's. Luke tried to concentrate but felt himself being distracted, drawn into the sound of labored breathing that came from Vader's helmet. Then Vader attacked.

But Luke was ready. He angled his blade defensively to block Vader's blade, and there was a loud, electric clash between the two lightsabers. The dark lord pulled back and swung again; Luke parried and prepared for Vader's next assault. Their lightsabers again connected with a loud crackle of energy, until Luke broke free, swung hard —

— and cut off Vader's head.

Sparks showered up from the neck of Vader's decapitated form, his body toppled, and his helmet rolled across the cave floor.

Luke stared at the helmet, and its black oval lenses

seemed to stare back. Then there was another shower of sparks, and the helmet's faceplate burned away. The smoke cleared to reveal a face, cradled in the smoldering, broken shell of Vader's helmet.

The face was Luke's own.

This isn't really happening, Luke thought as he stared at the head, into its cold, dead eyes. *It's all some kind of a hallucination or nightmare. But . . . what could it possibly mean?*

While Luke made his way out of the cave, Yoda remained seated on the root. He looked at the ground and shook his head. Although Luke did not yet comprehend what had happened in the cave, Yoda knew that it had been a test. And that Luke had failed.

On the bridge of the *Executor*, Darth Vader approached an assembly of six bizarre figures. Each had Vader's clearance to be on the *Executor*, but none were entirely welcome.

"Bounty hunters," Admiral Piett muttered to two Imperial controllers on the bridge's lower level. "We don't need that scum."

"Yes, sir," agreed one controller.

"Those Rebels won't escape us," Piett added as he turned away from the controllers. He was immediately distracted by a growl from above. He looked up to see one of the bounty hunters, a tall humanoid reptilian whose long, clawed arms stuck out from an ill-fitting flight suit, which Piett guessed had once belonged to a human pilot. The hunter stared down from the upper level and bared his fangs at Piett.

Piett stared back, hesitant to make a move that the creature might interpret as sudden. But the staring contest came to an end when another controller approached Piett and said, "Sir, we have a priority signal from the Star Destroyer *Avenger*."

"Right," Piett answered as he tore his gaze from the hunter and followed the controller to a console.

The menacing reptilian's name was Bossk, and he remained standing at the edge of the bridge's upper level while Darth Vader surveyed the other bounty hunters. There was Dengar, a brutal-looking man with a bandaged head who wore Imperial surplus armor; IG-88, an assassin droid that resembled nothing more than an ambulatory arsenal; Zuckuss, an insectlike alien whose face was partially concealed by a breathing mask, and his partner 4-Lom, a late-model protocol droid.

Finally, there was the hunter who was widely regarded as the most dangerous of all: Boba Fett.

Fett was clad in old green battle armor that he wore over a pale gray reinforced double-layer flight suit. His head was completely concealed by a green helmet with a T-shaped macrobinocular viewplate and a retractable targeting rangefinder that allowed him to view his surroundings without turning his head. He carried numerous concealed weapons, and openly clutched a late-model modified EE-3 blaster rifle. On his back, he wore a missile-firing jetpack.

All the bounty hunters listened as Darth Vader said,

"There will be a substantial reward for the one who finds the *Millennium Falcon*. You are free to use any methods necessary, but I want them alive." Vader extended a black-gloved finger at Boba Fett and stressed, "No disintegrations."

"As you wish," Fett said, his voice a nasty rasp. He was already on retainer for Jabba the Hutt, the Tatooine-based gangster who'd placed a bounty on Han Solo. Jabba also wanted the *Falcon*'s captain alive, so Fett had no intention of killing him. If he did the job right, he would be rewarded by the Empire *and* the Hutt.

Boba Fett had another reason for wanting to capture Solo. Until recently, he'd had a perfect record for getting the job done. Any job, no matter how dirty or tough. But several weeks earlier, Fett had made a mistake: Another assignment had left him temporarily unable to follow a tip on Solo's whereabouts, so he'd subcontracted Dengar, Bossk, and another bounty hunter named Skorr to search for Solo. The hunters not only found and captured Solo, but delivered him to the planet Ord Mantell, where Fett had arranged to meet them. But shortly after Boba Fett arrived on Ord Mantell, Skorr was dead — and Han Solo was gone.

Both Dengar and Bossk had failed enough bounty hunts to assure that neither would ever have a perfect record, but Boba Fett was different. He had his reputation to maintain.

Darth Vader turned as an excited Admiral Piett ascended to the upper level. "Lord Vader!" Piett said. "My lord, we have them."

The *Avenger* had the *Millennium Falcon* on the run. The destroyer fired lasers at the smaller ship, which weaved to evade not only the blasts from behind but the few asteroids that remained in its path.

Inside the *Falcon*'s cockpit, Leia and C-3PO sat in the rear seats and watched nervously as Han and Chewbacca prepared for the jump to hyperspace. Glancing out the cockpit window, the droid said, "Oh, thank goodness we're coming out of the asteroid field."

"Let's get out of here," Han said. "Ready for lightspeed?" He reached for the throttle. "One . . . two . . . three!"

On "three," Han pulled back on the throttle. Outside the cockpit, the view of distant stars remained unchanged. Again.

"It's not fair!" Han protested.

Leia rolled her eyes and gaped. Chewbacca whimpered and raised his furry hands in defeat.

"The transfer circuits are all working," Han said, then insisted, "It's not my fault!"

Leia couldn't believe it. "No lightspeed?"

"It's not my fault," Han said again.

Suddenly, the *Falcon* was slammed hard as Imperial laserfire struck the stern.

C-3PO glanced at a sensor scope and said, "Sir, we just lost the main rear deflector shield. One more direct hit on the back quarter and we're done for."

Han looked to Chewbacca and said, "Turn her around."

Chewbacca barked in puzzlement.

"I said turn her around!" Han said, jumping out of his seat to throw a set of switches on the cockpit wall. "I'm going to put all power in the front shield."

"You're going to attack them?!" Leia said with alarm as Han jumped back behind the controls.

When Han didn't reply, C-3PO informed him, "Sir, the odds of surviving a direct assault on an Imperial Star Destroyer —"

"Shut up!" Leia shouted.

Han banked hard to port, then made a steep, twisting turn. In the next moment, the *Falcon* was racing toward the infinitely more powerful Destroyer.

Standing on the *Avenger*'s bridge, watching the *Falcon* through the viewport, Captain Needa couldn't believe his eyes. "They're moving to attack position!" he exclaimed. "Shields up!"

The Star Destroyer's laser cannons fired at the on-coming ship, but none hit their target. From Needa's position, it looked like the *Falcon* was coming straight for the bridge.

Out of pure human reflex, Needa and his men ducked as the Rebel ship roared past the viewport. But instead of the expected collision, there was suddenly silence. Needa looked out the viewport.

The *Falcon* was nowhere to be seen.

Needa turned to the tracking officer and ordered, "Track them. They may come around for another pass."

The tracking officer checked his console screen, then said, "Captain Needa, the ship no longer appears on our scopes."

"They can't have disappeared," Needa said. "No ship that small has a cloaking device."

Consulting his screen again, the tracking officer said, "Well, there's no trace of them, sir."

The *Avenger*'s communications officer looked up from his console. "Captain, Lord Vader demands an update on the pursuit."

Needa drew a breath, then turned to his first officer and said, "Get a shuttle ready. I shall assume full responsibility for losing them and apologize to Lord Vader. Meanwhile, continue to scan the area."

"Yes, Captain Needa," said the officer.

As Captain Needa left the bridge and headed for

the shuttle hangar, the *Avenger* changed course to rendezvous with the Imperial fleet.

On Dagobah, Luke's muscles strained as his palms pressed against the dry mud. He was standing on his hands, with his legs extended up into the air and Yoda perched on his right foot. Then Luke slowly lifted his right hand and felt his weight shift down the length of his left arm.

Still balanced on Luke's foot, Yoda instructed, "Use the Force, yes. Now . . . the stone."

A short distance from Luke, two rocks rested in the dirt. Luke stared at them and concentrated. One of the rocks lifted from the ground.

"Feel it," Yoda intoned.

And even though Luke wasn't touching the rock, he could sense its texture and weight. *It's dry on the top, slick on the bottom . . . not heavy at all.* The rock hovered, then came to a gentle rest on the other.

R2-D2 was standing at the water's edge, watching Luke and Yoda with fascination, when he heard a bubbling noise from behind. The astromech rotated his domed head and saw the source of the sound: Luke's X-wing was rapidly sinking into the mucky water.

The little droid beeped frantically, distracting Luke.

"Concentrate!" Yoda scolded, but it was too late. The upper rock slid off the lower, and Luke collapsed, sending Yoda tumbling across the ground.

Luke rose quickly and hurried over to R2-D2, who was now chirping wildly. Luke watched his ship sink under the water until only the upper starboard wing remained visible above the surface.

"Oh, no," Luke said. "We'll never get it out now."

"So certain are you," Yoda replied. He had righted himself from the fall to sit facing Luke, and he wore an expression of mild contempt. "Always with you it cannot be done. Hear you nothing that I say?"

"Master, moving stones around is one thing," Luke said, then gestured to the X-wing. "This is totally different."

"No!" Yoda said. "No different! Only different in your mind. You must unlearn what you have learned."

"All right," Luke said. "I'll give it a try."

"No!" Yoda protested fiercely. "Try not. *Do*. Or do not. There is no try."

Luke turned his body to face the water. He closed his eyes as he extended his right hand, aiming his outstretched fingers at the submerged X-wing. He concentrated.

He sensed the X-wing's dimensions and sharp contours, felt the weight of the ship and the water's pressure against its hull. Was the starfighter underwater so different from a small rock on dry land? Eyes still closed, Luke felt a stirring from within, and knew the X-wing was rising.

As the starfighter's nose lifted from the muck, Yoda's eyes went wide with anticipation. But then Luke grimaced . . . *It's too big . . . too heavy* . . . and the X-wing sank again.

Looking defeated and drained, Luke turned away from the shore and dropped to the ground beside Yoda. He told the Jedi Master, "I can't." Then he added, "It's too big."

"Size matters not," Yoda said. "Look at me. Judge me by my size, do you? Mm?"

Luke shook his head.

"Mmmm," Yoda murmured. "And well you should not. For my ally is the Force. And a powerful ally it is. Life creates it, makes it grow. Its energy surrounds us and binds us. Luminous beings are we . . ." He pinched Luke's shoulder. ". . . not this crude matter."

Yoda made a sweeping gesture and continued, "You must feel the Force around you. Here, between you . . . me . . . the tree . . . the rock . . . everywhere! Yes, even between the land and the ship!"

Thoroughly discouraged, Luke said, "You want the impossible." He got up and started to walk away.

Yoda sighed. Slowly, he bowed his head and closed his eyes. Then he raised his small right hand in the direction of the sunken X-wing.

The starfighter began to rise again.

R2-D2 watched the displaced water flow off the

starfighter as it lifted from the swamp. Long strands of moss and weeds dangled from the ship as it rose higher. The little droid began beeping wildly.

Luke heard R2-D2's cries and turned back. The X-wing was hovering high over the water's surface. He looked to Yoda, then back to the X-wing. The ship slowly traveled through the air, then descended to land on an area of moss-covered ground.

Luke examined the starfighter, brushing some muck from its hull to convince himself this wasn't another hallucination. The X-wing was real, all right. Luke turned back to Yoda. He knelt before the Jedi Master and gasped, "I don't . . . I don't believe it."

With a touch of sadness in his voice, Yoda said, "That is why you fail."

After the *Avenger* met up with the Imperial fleet, Captain Needa traveled by shuttle to board the *Executor*. Minutes later, on the *Executor*'s bridge, Captain Needa spoke the words that would be his last. As Vader choked him from afar, he clutched desperately at his throat. But it was no use. He dropped to his knees, lifted his head, and tried to rise, then collapsed at the feet of Darth Vader.

Vader said, "Apology accepted, Captain Needa."

As two black-uniformed Imperial soldiers lifted Needa's lifeless body and carried it from the bridge, the Sith Lord walked to the nearby command console, where Admiral Piett and his aides were examining data. Seeing Vader approach, Piett stepped away from his console and stood at attention.

"Lord Vader," Piett said, "our ships have completed their scan of the area and found nothing. If the *Millennium Falcon* went into lightspeed, it'll be on the other side of the galaxy by now."

"Alert all commands," Vader said. "Calculate every possible destination along their last known trajectory."

"Yes, my lord," Piett said. "We'll find them."

Vader loomed over Piett and warned, "Don't fail me again, Admiral."

Piett swallowed hard, then turned to an aide and ordered, "Alert all commands. Deploy the fleet."

The *Millennium Falcon*'s possible destination routes were quickly computed by the Imperials. As the *Executor* and Star Destroyers prepared to leave the area, every Imperial helmsman, navigator, controller, and technician kept their keen eyes on their consoles and monitors. And because all sensors had already indicated the *Falcon* had vanished from the sector, not one Imperial soldier thought to look out a window.

But even if anyone had looked directly at the port aft of *Avenger*'s command tower, they might not have immediately spotted the *Millennium Falcon*, which rested flat against the destroyer's hull, right where Han Solo had landed it. Because of the *Falcon*'s faded white exterior, the Corellian transport blended right in with the Imperial ship.

"Captain Solo, this time you have gone too far," C-3PO said from his seat behind Chewbacca in the cockpit.

Chewbacca growled at the golden droid. C-3PO answered, "No, I will not be quiet, Chewbacca. Why doesn't anyone listen to me?"

Leia leaned forward in her seat behind Han. Both were looking out the cockpit window, watching the Star Destroyers move off in different directions.

"The fleet is beginning to break up," Han said. He glanced at Chewbacca and said, "Go back and stand by the manual release for the landing claw."

"I really don't see how that is going to help," the droid said as Chewbacca climbed from his seat and moved out of the cockpit. "Surrender is a perfectly acceptable alternative in extreme circumstances. The Empire may be gracious enough —"

C-3PO's sentence was cut short by Leia, who'd reached behind the droid's neck to switch him off. The droid slumped forward against his seat belt and remained silent.

"Thank you," Han said.

Leia felt the need to ask, "What did you have in mind for your next move?"

Gesturing at the Star Destroyers, Han replied, "Well, if they follow standard Imperial procedure, they'll dump their garbage before they go to lightspeed, and then we just float away."

"With the rest of the garbage," Leia said, which made Han wince. "Then what?"

"Then we've got to find a safe port somewhere

around here." Han activated a mapscreen on his control panel, and Leia leaned closer to him to study the map. Han asked, "Got any ideas?"

"No. Where are we?"

"The Anoat system."

"Anoat system," Leia repeated thoughtfully. "There's not much there."

"No," Han said, then noticed something on the map. "Well, wait. This is interesting. Lando."

"Lando system?"

Han grinned and said, "Lando's not a system, he's a man. Lando Calrissian. He's a card player, gambler — scoundrel." He glanced at Leia and added, "You'd like him."

Leia smirked. "Thanks."

Han returned his attention to the mapscreen. "Bespin," he said, giving the destination more consideration. "It's pretty far, but I think we can make it."

Reading the displayed data on Bespin, Leia said, "A mining colony?"

"Yeah," Han said. "A Tibanna gas mine. Lando conned somebody out of it." He leaned back in his seat and added, "We go back a long way, Lando and me."

From Han's tone, Leia got the impression that his history with Lando wasn't entirely friendly. "Can you trust him?" she asked.

"No," Han admitted. "But he has got no love for the Empire, I can tell you that."

Chewbacca barked over the ship's intercom and Han quickly changed his readouts. Then he stretched to look out the cockpit window and saw a wide, rectangular hatch open on the Star Destroyer's hull. Speaking into the intercom, Han said, "Here we go, Chewie. Stand by." He waited for several large bits of metal refuse to float out of the open hatch, then said, "Detach!"

The *Falcon*'s landing claw released, and the transport drifted away along with the debris that trailed from the Imperial cruiser. As they drifted farther from the ship, Leia felt increasingly elated. Granted, she would have been more relieved if the *Falcon*'s hyperdrive had actually kicked in when it was supposed to, but if it hadn't been for Han's quick thinking and cunning piloting skills . . . *I have to give him some credit.*

As Han kept his eyes on the departing Star Destroyer, Leia touched his shoulder and said, "You do have your moments. Not many of them, but you do have them." She kissed his cheek, then settled back into her seat.

The destroyer's three main ion engines flared brightly, then the ship launched forward and vanished into the distance. Han fired the *Falcon*'s sub-light engines and veered away from the debris, heading in the opposite direction of the Imperial ship's trajectory.

As the *Falcon* sped away from the debris trail, there was a sudden flare from behind a large piece of drifting scrap — which wasn't scrap at all. It was *Slave I*, a highly modified *Firespray*-class patrol-and-attack ship, equipped with numerous hidden weapons. And it was the personal transport for the bounty hunter Boba Fett.

Fett had correctly calculated that the *Millennium Falcon* had never actually escaped from the *Avenger*, and had only avoided detection. Now, as he accelerated after Han Solo's ship, it seemed his calculations would pay off.

Slave I had long-range sensor scopes and an illegal masking-and-jamming system that made it virtually invisible on most scanners. The special technology had allowed Boba Fett to infiltrate the Imperial Fleet, locate the *Millennium Falcon*, and maneuver *Slave I* into the *Avenger*'s debris trail without alerting anyone to his presence. Fett was so confident in *Slave I*'s supreme stealth that he kept the escaping *Falcon* within visual range as he computed its trajectory.

Fett checked his computer readout: The Rebel ship was heading for the Bespin system. As the *Falcon* was traveling at sublight speed, the bounty hunter concluded there was something wrong with the ship's hyperdrive. And because *Slave I*'s hyperdrive was fully operational, Fett knew he'd be able to reach Bespin before Solo.

The bounty hunter considered his next move, then transmitted a coded message to the *Executor*.

On Dagobah, R2-D2 stood near some equipment cases and watched as Yoda continued to instruct Luke. The Jedi trainee was yet again standing on his hands with his feet extended up, but R2-D2 noticed Yoda had refrained from perching on one of Luke's feet this time, opting instead to remain on the ground.

Yoda said, "Concentrate."

Luke closed his eyes. Two equipment cases rose from the ground, then hung suspended in the air.

"Feel the Force flow," Yoda said, his voice soothing. "Yes."

The astromech droid felt himself being lifted, and momentarily thought he might have unwittingly stepped on the back of a rising creature. When he realized the only thing between him and the ground was Luke's will, the little droid beeped nervously.

"Good," Yoda said. "Calm, yes. Through the Force, things you will see."

Still standing on his hands, Luke opened his eyes, then closed them again.

"Other places," Yoda continued. "The future . . . the past. Old friends long gone."

Suddenly, Luke's mind was overwhelmed by an unexpected vision. His eyes opened wide and he shouted, "Han! Leia!"

The suspended objects fell to the ground. Unlike the equipment cases, R2-D2 screeched on the way down. Luke tumbled and rolled over onto his side.

Yoda shook his head. "Hmm. Control, control. You must learn control."

Luke looked dazed and rattled. He wanted to tell Yoda about the vision, but wasn't sure how to put it into words. Hesitantly, he said, "I saw . . . I saw a city in the clouds."

"Mmm," Yoda muttered. "Friends you have there."

Luke looked anguished as he recalled, "They were in pain."

Yoda nodded. "It is the future you see."

"Future?" Luke said with alarm. "Will they die?"

Yoda closed his eyes, meditated briefly, then opened his eyes and gazed at Luke. "Difficult to see. Always in motion is the future."

Luke thought, *If I saw the future, is it also possible for me to change it?* He pushed himself up from the ground and said, "I've got to go to them."

Yoda sighed. "Decide you must how to serve them best. If you leave now, help them you could. But you would destroy all for which they have fought and suffered."

Luke couldn't stand the thought of his friends suffering. He thought, *Could Yoda be right? If I try to help, would I really be doing the wrong thing?* He gazed hard at Yoda, hoping the Jedi Master would suggest other alternatives for action, or interpret brighter possibilities for the future.

Yoda remained silent. And in the silence, Luke knew there was nothing left to say, because Yoda was right: The future was difficult to see.

Luke nodded sadly.

And Yoda knew Luke had already decided what to do.

CHAPTER 13

The Cloud City Control Wing Guard pilot was getting on Han Solo's nerves.

"No, I don't have a landing permit," Han snarled into the *Millennium Falcon*'s cockpit comlink.

Behind Han, Leia leaned forward and looked left, past Chewbacca and out the cockpit window, to see the two twin-pod cloud cars that had appeared from out of nowhere. The cloud cars were so close that Leia could distinguish the Wing Guard pilot whose mouth moved in synchronization with the voice from the comlink.

Leia thought, *Welcome to Bespin.*

Bespin was a giant, gaseous planet, a world of billowing clouds and endless sky. Its atmosphere was a prime source of valuable Tibanna gas, which was used as either a conducting agent to boost blaster firepower or a hyperdrive coolant. The world was also home to Cloud City, the largest of the airborne Tibanna factories, and the *Falcon*'s destination.

The *Falcon* had descended through Bespin's upper altitudes until it entered a narrow band of breathable air. Not only breathable, but breathtaking for its sweeping views of cloud formations. The initial sight of Bespin had seemed warm and inviting, especially to those who'd so recently endured the frigid climate of Hoth. But when the two twin-pod cloud cars had suddenly swooped into view, it had become quickly evident that the Bespin skies were far from entirely friendly.

Han said into the comlink, "I'm trying to reach Lando Calrissian." He'd barely uttered Lando's name when the nearest cloud car fired a blaster cannon and flak exploded outside the *Falcon*. "Whoa!" Han shouted. "Wait a minute! Let me explain."

From the *Falcon*'s intercom, the Cloud City Wing Guard pilot said, "You will not deviate from your present course."

"Rather touchy, aren't they?" a reactivated C-3PO commented from the seat behind Chewbacca.

To Han, Leia said, "I thought you knew this person."

Chewie barked and growled at Han. Han replied, "Well, that was a long time ago. I'm sure he's forgotten about that."

From the intercom, the Cloud City Wing Guard

said, "Permission granted to land on Platform three-two-seven."

Han wanted to say something else into the comlink, but instead he said, "Thank you," and switched off.

Chewbacca looked at Han and grunted. Han glanced back at Leia and C-3PO and said, "There's nothing to worry about. We go way back, Lando and me."

"Who's worried?" said Leia, clinging to her seat.

The two cloud cars escorted the *Falcon* across the sky, and it wasn't long before Cloud City came into view. Sixteen kilometers in diameter and seventeen kilometers tall, the 392-level floating city resembled an immense wheel lying on its side. The entire city was held aloft by 3,600 repulsorlift engines, and had a long central stalk that dropped down beneath it and ended in a unipod. The unipod used tractor beams to draw Tibanna gas up into the city's gas refineries.

As the *Falcon* neared the city, Leia could see it was slowly rotating, and that the cityscape had a rounded, decorative design with tall towers and wide plazas. The long shadows of streamlined skyscrapers swept over the *Falcon*'s exterior as it passed over the city. The two cloud cars stuck with the Corellian transport.

Platform 327 was a circular platform at the end of

an extended walkway that was connected to an upper level of a skyscraper. The *Falcon*'s landing jets fired, and the ship touched down neatly. The cloud car escorts flew off.

Steam vented from the jet exhausts as the ship's landing ramp lowered. Han stepped down to the platform, followed by Chewbacca, Leia, and a very hesitant C-3PO. They looked to the far end of the platform, where a rectangular door was visible against the high wall of the skyscraper. The door was closed.

"Oh," C-3PO said. "No one to meet us."

They remained at the bottom of the landing ramp, watching the distant door and waiting. A warm wind moaned softly across the city.

Leia said, "I don't like this."

"Well, what would you like?" Han snapped, as if they had any options.

Hoping to sound optimistic, C-3PO stated, "Well, they *did* let us land."

"Look, don't worry," Han said, turning to Leia. "Everything's going to be fine. Trust me."

At the end of the platform, the rectangular door slid up to reveal two men engaged in a discussion. Because of the distance and the light from inside the open doorway, the two appeared as silhouettes, but Han's keen eyes recognized one of them.

"See?" Han said to Leia, gesturing to the doorway. "My friend."

The two men exited the door and were followed by six uniformed guards. Together, they headed up the walkway toward the *Falcon*.

Han stepped over to Chewbacca and muttered, "Keep your eyes open, huh?"

Chewbacca let out a growl as Han headed down the walkway.

As the figures approached, Leia was able to make out the two who walked in front of the six guards. The taller one was a dashing brown-skinned man with wavy black hair and a thin mustache; a silk-lined blue cape was draped across his shoulders and, from the way he moved, he looked like the man in charge. The other man was bald with pale white skin, and was primarily distinguished by the computer bracket that was wrapped around the back of his hairless head.

Han smiled at the approaching couple and said, "Hey?"

The caped man stopped two meters shy of Han. He fixed Han with an angry glare, then shook his head and said, "Why, you slimy, double-crossing, no-good swindler! You've got a lot of guts coming here after what you pulled."

Han pointed to himself innocently, and silently mouthed, *Me?*

The caped man walked slowly toward Han until the two men were face-to-face. Then, without warning, he moved fast and threw a jab at Han. Han blocked with his arm, but the jab was a fake, and the man threw his arms around Han and embraced him. Clearly, whatever gripe Lando Calrissian had with Han was a thing of the past.

Lando laughed and his face broke into the most incredibly winning smile. He said, "How you doing, you old pirate?"

The bald man with the computer bracket around his head saw that the situation was under control. He turned to the guards and pointed at the door behind them. The guards filed back with the bald man.

Holding Han at arm's length, Lando said, "So good to see you! I never thought I'd catch up with you again. Where you been?"

From the *Falcon*'s landing ramp, the golden droid observed, "Well, he seems very friendly."

Leia said, "Yes . . . very friendly." She followed close to C-3PO as he stepped away from the ramp, and couldn't help but think, *He's almost too friendly.*

"What are you doing here?" Lando asked Han.

"Ahh . . . repairs," Han said, indicating the *Falcon.* "I thought you could help me out."

Lando wore an expression of mild panic as he looked at the *Falcon* and said, "What have you done to my ship?"

"*Your* ship?" Han said, trying not to lose his cool. "Hey, remember, you lost her to me fair and square."

Lando grinned. Looking past Han, he caught the Wookiee's gaze. "And how are you doing, Chewbacca? You still hanging around with this loser?"

Chewbacca growled a reserved greeting and maintained his distance. Leia thought, *Chewie doesn't trust this guy either.*

Then Lando took sudden notice of the young woman who moved up behind Han with a protocol droid. Smiling at Leia, he said, "Hello. What have we here?" He moved close to her and said in his most engaging voice, "Welcome. I'm Lando Calrissian. I'm the administrator of this facility. And who might you be?"

"Leia."

"Welcome, Leia," Lando said with a bow; he then smoothly took Leia's left hand, cupped it in his own, and kissed the back of her glove.

Leia threw a desperate glance at Han. Returning her gaze to Lando, who still held her hand, she thought, *So much for gloves discouraging kisses.*

"All right, all right, you old smoothie," Han said as he took Leia's hand and steered her away from Lando.

Seeing Lando's now-empty hand, C-3PO stepped right up and took it. "Hello, sir. I am See-Threepio, Human Cyborg Relations. My facilities are at your —"

The protocol droid would have continued, but the still-smiling Lando had already released the mechanical hand and was walking after Han and Leia, who were moving down the walkway and heading for the door. Outraged, C-3PO exclaimed, "Well, really!" Then he noticed Chewbacca was also heading for the door, and started after him. C-3PO paused only briefly on the walkway to gaze at the city skyline. Cloud City was a very impressive sight, even to a droid.

Lando caught up alongside Han and asked, "What's wrong with the *Falcon*?"

"Hyperdrive."

"I'll get my people to work on it," Lando promised.

"Good," Han said.

Without breaking his stride, Lando turned to Leia and said, "You know, that ship saved my life quite a few times. She's the fastest hunk of junk in the galaxy."

"How's the gas mine?" Han asked, wanting to change the subject from his ship. "Is it still paying off for you?"

"Oh, not as well as I'd like," Lando admitted as they walked through the open doorway and proceeded through a white-walled corridor. "We're a small outpost and not very self-sufficient. And I've had supply problems of every kind. I've had labor difficulties. . . ."

Han laughed.

Lando asked, "What's so funny?"

"You," Han said. "Listen to you — you sound like a businessman, a responsible leader. Who'd have thought that, huh?"

Lando looked at Han and grinned. "You know, seeing you brings back a few things."

"Yeah," Han said, and tossed what he hoped was a reassuring glance to Leia, who was right behind him with Chewbacca and C-3PO.

"Yeah," Lando echoed. "I'm responsible these days. It's the price you pay for being successful."

Han and Lando laughed as the group passed a closed door on the corridor wall. C-3PO was walking right behind Chewbacca when the door slid open to reveal a silver-metal protocol droid. Despite its different color, the silver droid appeared to be the same model as C-3PO. C-3PO stopped in his tracks.

"Oh!" C-3PO said. "Nice to see a familiar face."

The silver droid glanced at the golden droid and mumbled, "E chu ta!" Then the silver droid stepped from the open doorway and brushed past.

"How rude!" C-3PO exclaimed as the droid walked off. C-3PO was about to turn and catch up with Chewbacca and the others when he heard a beeping sound come from the open doorway. Curious, C-3PO entered a narrow room, then heard another round of beeps from an adjoining chamber.

"That sounds like an Artoo unit in there," C-3PO said. "I wonder if . . ."

He followed the beeping noise into the next chamber, which had walls that were covered with pipes, gauges, and complex mechanisms. Not immediately seeing anyone, C-3PO called out, "Hello? Hello?" No response. Then he glanced around the room and commented, "How interesting."

"Who are you?" snapped a man's voice from the other side of the chamber.

C-3PO had to turn his head to face the speaker. And after he turned, he suddenly wished he had never entered the room. He tried to sound calm as he replied, "Who am I?" He wanted to get out immediately, and started to back up as he continued, "Oh, I'm terribly sorry. I . . . I didn't mean to intrude." He took a few more cautious steps backward and gestured pleadingly with his arms. "No, no, please don't get up." Then he threw his arms up defensively and cried, "No!"

There was a sudden explosion of blaster fire. A laser bolt slammed into C-3PO's chest. His upper torso smashed into the wall behind him and his head launched into the air. The rest of his body went everywhere else.

A smoldering gold metal foot and part of one leg clattered across the floor and skidded to a stop just shy of the doorway that remained opened to the corridor. The door slid shut a moment before Chewbacca —

having retraced his own steps — came back looking for C-3PO.

Chewbacca sniffed the air and smelled blaster fumes. Was that an unusual smell in a city that processed Tibanna gas for use in blasters? Chewbacca wasn't sure, but he did know that the protocol droid had been right behind him just a moment ago. So where had the droid gone?

The Wookiee growled. Something didn't smell right, and it wasn't just the scent of blasters. But since he couldn't see any sign of C-3PO, he turned and headed back down the corridor to rejoin his other friends.

It was night on Dagobah. R2-D2 was on top of the X-wing starfighter, moving into his socket behind the cockpit. Luke, wearing his orange g-suit, was loading a case onto the ship. Yoda stood on a nearby knoll and watched Luke. The Jedi Master didn't look happy.

"Luke!" Yoda said. "You must complete the training."

"I can't keep the vision out of my head," Luke replied as he hastily inspected his ship. "They're my friends. I've got to help them."

"You must not go!" Yoda insisted.

Luke faced Yoda and said, "But Han and Leia will die if I don't."

From out of the darkness, Ben Kenobi's voice spoke: "You don't know that."

To Luke's amazement, a slightly shimmering light began to glow in the air behind Yoda. Then the light materialized into the form of old Ben. The luminous Jedi wore a grave expression as he said, "Even Yoda cannot see their fate."

"But I can help them!" Luke argued. "I feel the Force!"

"But you cannot control it," Ben said. "This is a dangerous time for you, when you will be tempted by the dark side of the Force."

Yoda agreed, "Yes, yes. To Obi-Wan you listen. The cave. Remember your failure at the cave!"

"But I've learned so much since then, Master Yoda," Luke said as he returned his attention to his X-wing. "I promise to return and finish what I've begun. You have my word."

Ben explained, "It is you and your abilities the Emperor wants. That is why your friends are made to suffer."

"That's why I have to go," Luke said.

Ben said, "Luke, I don't want to lose you to the Emperor the way I lost Vader."

"You won't," Luke assured him. He thought back to his first meeting with Ben, back on Tatooine. Ben had told Luke that Darth Vader had been one of his pupils until he'd been seduced by the dark side of the Force. According to Ben, Vader had helped the Empire to destroy the Jedi Knights, including Luke's own father. *I'll never be anything like Darth Vader*, Luke thought. *And I won't be lost to the Emperor.*

Yoda said, "Stopped they must be. On this all depends. Only a fully trained Jedi Knight with the Force as his ally will conquer Vader and his Emperor." As Luke stowed the last of his gear onto the X-wing, Yoda continued, "If you end your training now, if you choose the quick and easy path, as Vader did, you will become an agent of evil."

"Patience," Ben said with great emphasis, as if it was the one word Luke should remember.

Patience? Luke couldn't believe anyone would encourage patience right now. Facing Ben, he snapped, "And sacrifice Han and Leia?"

Yoda answered, "If you honor what they fight for . . . yes!"

Luke reached for the lower rung of the X-wing's retractable ladder and looked away from Ben and Yoda.

Ben said, "If you choose to face Vader, you will do it alone. I cannot interfere."

"I understand," Luke muttered. Then he climbed the ladder to the starfighter's open cockpit and said, "Artoo, fire up the converters."

As the X-wing's engines fired up, Ben warned, "Luke, don't give in to hate — that leads to the dark side."

"Strong is Vader," Yoda added. "Mind what you have learned. Save you it can."

"I will," Luke said as he pulled on his helmet. "And I'll return. I promise." The cockpit canopy lowered, and the X-wing lifted off from the ground and ascended into the night sky.

As Yoda raised his gaze to watch the departing X-wing, Ben's apparition faded into the darkness. Yoda sighed, looked down at the ground, and shook his head sadly. "Told you, I did," he said. "Reckless is he. Now matters are worse."

Ben's disembodied voice said, "That boy is our last hope."

Yoda returned his gaze to the sky and said mysteriously, "No. There is another."

Leia paced before the wide window that offered a magnificent view of Cloud City. She was within the living quarters that had been assigned to her and she wore fresh clothes, all courtesy of Lando Calrissian. From the skylight that dominated the circular room's ceiling, natural light poured in and illuminated the interior and its comfortable furnishings. The entire room and all its contents were white and immaculately clean.

Leia didn't like the place one bit.

The room's main door slid open and Han entered. "The ship's almost finished," he said as Leia crossed the room to him. "Two or three more things and we're in great shape."

"The sooner the better," Leia said. "Something's wrong here. No one has seen or knows anything about Threepio. He's been gone too long to have gotten lost."

"Relax," Han said. He took Leia by the shoulders and gently kissed her forehead. "I'll talk to Lando. See what I can find out."

"I don't trust Lando." Leia pulled away from Han and sat on a plush white couch.

"Well, I don't trust him, either," Han said as he sat down beside Leia. "But he is my friend. Besides, we'll soon be gone."

Trying to keep the sadness from her voice, Leia said, "And then you're as good as gone, aren't you?"

Han looked away, then looked back to Leia's troubled face. He didn't know how to respond to her question, so he just gazed into her eyes and remained silent.

Like any large metropolis, Cloud City had to deal with unwanted junk. But because Cloud City was not built upon solid ground and had no land-based natural resources, dumping was not an economical option. Virtually everything — from outmoded technology to broken appliances — was recycled into usable materials. And the recycling process began in the junk rooms.

Chewbacca found the junk rooms on a level below Lando Calrissian's headquarters. The Wookiee had already visited every other accessible part of the building. He was determined to find C-3PO. As

Chewbacca entered a junk room and saw the piles of scrap metal that were heaped throughout, he wished C-3PO hadn't wound up here, of all places. But where else could C-3PO be?

Chewbacca made his way past the scrap heaps, keeping his eyes peeled for gold-plated metal. He picked up several pieces, but nothing was from a protocol droid. He tossed the scraps aside and kept searching.

Then he heard a roar. Not an animal sound, but a noise made by intense fire.

Chewbacca edged around a high stack of crushed metal and found a conveyer that moved scrap from a garbage chute to the other side of the room. Four small, porcine humanoids — Chewbacca recognized them as Ugnaughts — were stationed on both sides of the long conveyer, from which they selectively removed valuable scrap. Anything the Ugnaughts didn't want was fed through an open oval-shaped door into a blazing furnace, the source of the roaring sound.

Chewbacca sighted a flash of gold on the conveyer and realized he was looking at the blaster-scorched remains of C-3PO. The Wookiee pushed his way past the scrap heaps and Ugnaughts to grab C-3PO's headless torso. Then he quickly knocked the droid's other dismembered parts off the conveyer.

One of the Ugnaughts had seized C-3PO's head.

Chewbacca barked a command at the Ugnaught, but rather than hand over the head, the Ugnaught tossed it to one of his fellow workers. Chewbacca tried to intercept the catch but missed, and failed to prevent the droid's head from being thrown to another Ugnaught. That Ugnaught threw it to another, who missed, and C-3PO's head clattered against the floor.

Chewbacca howled with rage. And the Ugnaughts quickly learned the hard way that it's pure foolishness to play keep-away with a Wookiee.

Leia and Han were still in the bright white living quarters when Chewbacca entered, carrying a packing case. The case was crammed with C-3PO's parts.

"What happened?" Leia gasped, rising from the couch.

Chewbacca set the case onto the circular table at the center of the room, then grunted an explanation.

"Where?" Han said.

Chewbacca repeated himself.

Han said, "Found him in a junk pile?"

Leia shook her head as she peered into the case. "Oh, what a mess. Chewie, do you think you can repair him?"

Chewbacca examined some of C-3PO's pieces, looked at Leia, then shrugged.

Han said, "Lando's got people who can fix him."

"No, thanks," Leia said, a bit surprised that Han had even considered the idea. From what she'd seen so far, Lando dealt with most of his responsibilities through his aide Lobot, the bald cyborg with the cranial computer bracket. According to Lando, Lobot's headband kept in constant contact with Cloud City's central computer. She had as much reason to trust Lobot as she did Lando, which was not at all.

Just then, an electronic chime sounded and Lando stepped down into the room. Standing in the doorway, he said, "I'm sorry. Am I interrupting something?"

"Not really," Leia said.

Lando cast a long, appreciative glance at Leia, then beamed and said, "You look absolutely beautiful. You truly belong here with us among the clouds."

"Thank you," Leia said coolly, thinking, *I wonder how many times he's used that line.*

Lando said, "Will you join me for a little refreshment?"

Han looked at Lando suspiciously. Chewbacca answered with a hungry bark.

Lando added, "Everyone's invited, of course." He offered his hand to Leia, but Han stepped in and Leia took his arm. Lando was turning to lead them out of the room when he noticed the gold-metal limbs in the case on the table. With a quizzical expression, Lando said, "Having trouble with your droid?"

Leia and Han exchanged a quick glance, then Han looked at Lando and said, "No. No problem. Why?"

Han and Leia exited the room, and Lando and Chewbacca followed, leaving C-3PO's parts behind. The group proceeded into a window-lined corridor, where long shafts of light fell across white walls and columns. As they walked past a group of uniformed laborers, Lando gestured at the surroundings and said, "So, you see, since we're a small operation, we don't fall into the . . . uh . . . jurisdiction of the Empire."

Leia said, "So you're part of the mining guild, then?"

"No, not actually," Lando said, leading the way down another corridor. "Our operation is small enough not to be noticed . . . which is advantageous for everybody, since our customers are anxious to avoid attracting attention to themselves."

Han asked, "Aren't you afraid the Empire's going to find out about this little operation and shut you down?"

"That's always been a danger looming like a shadow over everything we've built here," Lando said as he approached a closed pair of doors, "but things have developed that will ensure security." Chewbacca sniffed the air and growled. That rotten smell again.

Lando stopped at the double doors and said, "I've just made a deal that will keep the Empire out of here forever."

The doors parted at the middle and slid sideways into the wall to reveal a white-walled dining room with a long, neatly arranged banquet table. At the far end of the table, rising from his seat, was Darth Vader.

Chewbacca roared. Leia froze. And Solo made his move, quick-drawing his blaster pistol to fire at Vader. But the dark lord, moving with incredible speed, raised his right black-gloved hand and deflected the fired bolt into the wall. Han rapidly squeezed off three more shots, but all were just as easily nullified by Vader. Then Han felt an invisible tug as his blaster was torn from his grip. The weapon flew through the air, straight at Vader, who caught it by the barrel.

Facing Leia and her allies, Vader lowered the blaster to the table and said, "We would be honored if you would join us."

A figure stepped out from an alcove behind Vader. It was Boba Fett. Clutching his blaster rifle across his armored chest, the masked bounty hunter moved so he was just off to Vader's left side.

Leia, Han, and Chewbacca were still standing in the open doorway when they heard a clattering of footsteps behind them. A squad of blaster-wielding stormtroopers had taken up position outside the dining room. Near them stood Lobot, who was unarmed.

Even though Leia had already expressed her mistrust for Lando, and heard his talk of deals that would keep the Empire out of Cloud City, it was only upon seeing Lobot with the stormtroopers that she realized . . . *Lando set us up!*

She looked at Lando, as did Han and Chewbacca. Lando looked Han square in the eye and said grimly, "I had no choice. They arrived right before you did. I'm sorry."

"I'm sorry, too," Han said, his expression blank. He took Leia's arm, and together they turned, stepped toward the banquet table, and faced Darth Vader. After all, there was nowhere else to go. Then Chewbacca and Lando entered the dining room, and the double doors slid closed behind them.

Luke's X-wing starfighter raced across space. Although no one had told him the location of his friends, his vision had been crystal clear. They were in a city in the clouds. He was certain he would find them on Bespin.

Through his cockpit window, Luke sighted the giant gaseous planet in the distance. Behind him, R2-D2 beeped and whistled. Luke consulted the scope that displayed the translation for the astromech's language, then answered, "No. Threepio's with them."

Sounding more distressed, R2-D2 whistled again.

"Just hang on," Luke said. "We're almost there."

Luke couldn't stop thinking about his vision, how his friends were in pain. He accelerated toward Bespin and hoped he would arrive in time to help them.

CHAPTER 15

Chewbacca was in agony.

The Wookiee was in a Cloud City prison cell and a high-pitched siren was screeching and echoing off the cell's durasteel walls. He pressed both hands hard against the sides of his hairy head, trying in vain to protect his sensitive ears. He felt like his skull was about to split wide open.

Chewbacca started pacing back and forth within the large cell, his arms flailing in useless effort to ward off the violent din. Desperate to escape, he reached up to grab the thick, black metal bars that crisscrossed overhead and separated him from the upper ceiling. He tugged at the bars but they wouldn't yield. Suddenly, the siren ended, but it took Chewbacca a moment to comprehend it was over. The noise was still ringing in his ears.

The Wookiee shook his head and moaned, waiting for the pain to drain off. Exhausted, he looked down to a metal bench, on which rested the case that contained C-3PO's parts. Who had taken the case from Leia's living quarters and delivered it to his cell? Why hadn't the stormtroopers just returned the parts to the Cloud City junk room? Chewbacca had no idea. He was more relieved that the parts hadn't been smelted than curious about how they'd arrived in the cell. And now that the siren was silenced, he could concentrate on reassembling the droid.

He reached into the case and removed one of C-3PO's hands, then set the hand aside and picked up the droid's head. He contemplated it for a moment, looking into the droid's dead eyes as if they held some secret. Without any tools at his disposal, Chewbacca doubted he could do much for the droid. But he could try.

He reached for the droid's torso and placed it on his lap. Then he examined the scorched metal at the bottom of the head and found the neck ring was unbroken. He stuck C-3PO's head into the torso's neck socket and began to reconnect the wires and adjust the circuits.

The lights in C-3PO's eyes sparked on and then flickered out. Chewbacca made another adjustment and the eyes switched on again. This was followed by a flurry of almost unintelligible words, uttered at varying speeds and tones, from C-3PO's mouth: "Mmm. Oh, my. Uh, I, uh — Take this off, uh, don't mean to intrude here. I, don't, no, no, no . . . please don't get up. No!"

Chewbacca twisted a wire and C-3PO's eyes switched off. Then he squeezed a circuit as he pulled a wire, and the eyes illuminated again. But this time, C-3PO's head moved from side to side in the torso's neck socket and the droid spoke clearly: "Stormtroopers? Here? We're in danger. I must tell the others."

Then C-3PO tried to move, and realized the awful truth. "Oh, no!" he cried. "I've been shot!"

Darth Vader watched as two stormtroopers prepared an elaborate mechanism in the prison entry area. The mechanism consisted of an adjustable rack that stood vertically and faced a slanted panel of assorted instruments, including chemical injectors, microsurgical vibroscalpels, diagnostic scanners, and an electroshock assembly. All the instruments were designed to induce pain, which was appropriate since the mechanism was engineered for torture.

Han Solo was strapped to the rack. Unable to move his arms or legs, he studied the pain-inducing instruments on the facing panel and tried to brace himself for the worst. From what he'd heard about

Imperial torture devices, the diagnostic scanners would be used to anticipate loss of consciousness and the chemical injectors would keep him awake. That way, he wouldn't pass out, and would experience every measure of pain.

Darth Vader walked around the instrument panel and stood close to Han. Because the rack elevated Han's body, Vader had to tilt his own head back slightly to stare directly — through the lenses of his black helmet — into Han's eyes. Han glared at Vader and clenched his bound fists.

A red light illuminated on the slanted panel, and the rack tilted forward. Han's head and neck were not restrained, so he twisted his face away and squeezed his eyes shut as the rack lowered his upper body into direct contact with the horrendous instruments. Vader leaned in closer and watched Han's facial responses with interest.

A spark flashed at the top of the instrument panel, and Han winced.

A second spark flashed, and Han screamed. The pain was overwhelming.

The third spark came, and Han learned there was pain beyond overwhelming.

Han didn't pass out. And the torture mechanism was just getting started.

*   *   *

Solo's piercing cries filtered through the closed door that separated the prison entry area from the holding chamber. In the holding chamber, the closed door was guarded by two stormtroopers. Lando Calrissian and Lobot stood a short distance from the stormtroopers, as did Boba Fett. Hearing Han's screams, Lando and Boba Fett slowly turned to look at each other. Lando tried to keep his face as expressionless as Fett's helmet.

The door slid open. Darth Vader ducked his head as he strode through the doorway and entered the holding chamber.

Lando said, "Lord Vader."

Brushing past Lando, Vader stopped to face Fett and said, "You may take Captain Solo to Jabba the Hutt after I have Skywalker." Then he walked off.

"He's no good to me dead," Boba Fett said, following Vader into a corridor with Lando and Lobot in their wake.

"He will not be permanently damaged," Vader assured him, passing two stormtroopers as he entered an open lift tube.

"Lord Vader," Lando repeated. "What about Leia and the Wookiee?"

Turning to face Lando, who stood just outside the lift tube, Vader said, "They must never again leave this city."

Lando was stunned. "That was never a condition of our agreement, nor was giving Han to this bounty hunter!"

"Perhaps you think you're being treated unfairly," Vader said.

Lando knew there was only one answer he could give. "No," he said.

"Good," Vader replied. "It would be unfortunate if I had to leave a garrison here." The lift tube door slid shut.

Boba Fett turned and headed back to the holding chamber, leaving Lando and Lobot standing in the corridor near the lift tube. Watching Boba walk away, Lando muttered, "This deal is getting worse all the time."

In the large cell, working without tools, Chewbacca had managed to make some progress with C-3PO. More wires had been sorted, some had been reconnected, and the droid's right arm — like his head — had been reattached to his upper torso. Chewbacca had the torso propped up on his lap as he adjusted the circuits that were housed in the middle of the droid's back. C-3PO's audio and visual sensors seemed to be working fine and, as he faced the cell's far wall, he was able to comment on the Wookiee's handiwork.

"Oh, yes, that's very good," C-3PO said as the Wookiee tweaked a circuit. "I like that." Suddenly, the lights in the protocol droid's eyes flashed off. "Oh! Something's not right because now I can't see." After Chewbacca made another adjustment, C-3PO continued, "Oh. Oh, that's much better."

Then C-3PO tried to wiggle the fingers on his right hand, but something about the action felt awkward. "Wait," he said, and twisted his head to look down at his chest. "Wait! Oh, my!" he cried. Where he'd expected to see his chest, he instead saw the exposed circuits on his back, and was suddenly livid. "What have you done? I'm backward, you flea-bitten furball. Only an overgrown mophead like you would be stupid enough —"

Chewbacca threw the circuit breaker at the base of C-3PO's neck, and the droid's eyes and voice switched off. The Wookiee was about to resume the repairs when he smelled something in the air, then heard the sound of approaching footsteps. As he placed C-3PO's upper body with the rest of his parts, the cell's door slid up into the ceiling. Turning to the doorway, he watched as two stormtroopers hauled in Han.

Han's arms were draped over the stormtroopers' shoulders. His eyes were open, his jaw hung loose, and the toes of his boots dragged along the floor behind him. The troopers dumped him into the cell and left, sealing the door behind them.

Chewbacca barked with concern as he kneeled down to hug Han.

"I feel terrible," Han mumbled.

The Wookiee gently lifted Han to his feet, then helped him over to a bare metal slab, a retractable resting platform that projected from the wall. Han winced as Chewbacca lowered his aching body upon the slab.

A second door slid open, and two stormtroopers shoved Princess Leia into the cell. Instead of the clothes that Lando had given her, she was back in the same insulated jumpsuit she'd worn when she'd arrived at Cloud City. She saw Chewbacca standing beside Han's prone form. Chewbacca whimpered a sad greeting.

Leia moved to the metal slab, then knelt beside Han and gently pushed her fingers through his hair. His eyes briefly locked on hers. She said, "Why are they doing this?"

"They never even asked me any questions," Han said.

Leia kissed his forehead. Then the door slid open behind her. Leia turned to see two blue-uniformed Cloud City guards enter, followed by Calrissian.

At the sight of the caped man, Chewbacca roared.

Han was having difficulty raising his head, so Leia

turned back to him and whispered, "Lando." She remained beside Han as Lando and the two guards walked to the center of the cell. Leia noticed Lando wasn't wearing his customary smile, and that his expression was downright grim. But after the way he'd handed them over to Darth Vader, she didn't much care whether Cloud City's administrator was having a bad day.

Han struggled to rise from the slab and said, "Get out of here, Lando!"

"Shut up and listen!" Lando shouted. "Now, Vader has agreed to turn Leia and Chewie over to me."

"Over to you?" Han said with disbelief.

Leia wondered, *What's Lando trying to pull this time?*

Lando said, "They'll have to stay here, but at least they'll be safe."

"What about Han?" Leia asked.

"Vader's giving him to the bounty hunter," Lando said.

Leia glared at Lando. "Vader wants us all dead!"

"He doesn't want you at all," Lando said. "He's after somebody called, uh . . ." Lando had to search his memory for the name Vader had said in the holding chamber, but quickly remembered. ". . . Skywalker."

"Luke?" Han said, sitting up on the slab.

"Lord Vader has set a trap for him," Lando said.

"And we're the bait," Leia immediately concluded.

Lando said, "Yeah, well, he's on his way."

"Perfect," Han said as he slowly rose to his feet. On shaky legs, he stepped toward Lando and said, "You fixed us all real good, didn't you? My friend!"

Han moved fast for a man who'd just come off an Imperial torture rack. His right fist connected with Lando's jaw, sending Lando stumbling back into one of his guards. But Han's coordination and sense of balance were all off, and he tried to grab Lando as he fell forward. He only managed to snare Lando's cape before he hit the floor.

There wasn't any trouble with the guards' coordination. Han tried to push himself up from the floor, but one guard drew a blaster and slammed the weapon's butt into Han's back. The other guard drew his blaster and aimed it at Chewbacca. The Wookiee roared and Lando shouted, "Stop!"

The guards held their fire and Leia moved beside Han's fallen form. Lando pulled his cape back around his shoulders and said, "I've done all I can. I'm sorry I couldn't do better, but I got my own problems."

Han looked up from the floor and sneered, "Yeah, you're a real hero."

Lando, looking more grim than ever, walked out of the cell with his two guards. After the door slid shut, Chewbacca knelt down beside Han. As Han caught his breath, Leia shook her head and said, "You certainly have a way with people."

Han tried to offer a smile, but after everything he'd been through, even smiling hurt.

Even without Darth Vader's sinister presence, the windowless carbon-freezing chamber was among the least inviting places on Cloud City. The dark chamber was an effective but inelegant device, used to mix Tibanna gas with carbonite, then flash-freeze the mixture into solid blocks that could be easily transported. The mixing and freezing were done in a deep pit at the center of an elevated circular platform that dominated the chamber, and the carbonite blocks were removed by retrieval tongs — large retractable manipulator claws — that were housed in the high ceiling above the central pit.

Steam blasted and billowed from various vents throughout the chamber, which was ringed by a narrow catwalk. Two stairways descended from the catwalk to the elevated platform's surface: a concentric design of embedded red lights, air intakes, and black metal. The combination of the red-illuminated metal floor and rising steam made the platform resemble an immense heating element that was set on "hot." If the chamber's inhospitable design were not enough to discourage tourism, the platform's perimeter was also without a guardrail.

Darth Vader stood at the platform's edge, gazing down at the sheer drop to the metal pipes and hoses that laced across the chamber floor. He turned and walked through rising steam to the platform's center, where Lando, Lobot, and two stormtroopers stood near the open pit. In the pit, two Ugnaughts busily readied the control casing for the mixing and freezing process.

Vader said, "This facility is crude, but it should be adequate to freeze Skywalker for his journey to the Emperor."

An Imperial soldier stepped onto the platform and approached the dark lord. "Lord Vader," said the soldier, "ship approaching, X-wing class."

"Good," Vader said. There were many carbon-freezing chambers on Cloud City, but Vader had chosen this one for its strategic position: It had the advantage of being closest to Platform 327, where the *Millennium Falcon* would be easily sighted by Skywalker. Confident that Luke would walk right into his trap, Vader ordered, "Monitor Skywalker and allow him to land."

The soldier nodded, then walked quickly from the platform.

Lando said, "Lord Vader, we only use this facility for carbon freezing. You put him in there . . . it might kill him."

"I do not want the Emperor's prize damaged," Vader said. "We will test it . . . on Captain Solo."

Vader moved across the platform, and the two stormtroopers followed. As they passed by Lobot and Lando, one stormtrooper gave Lando a mild shove to stand aside.

Understandably, Lando didn't shove back.

In his X-wing starfighter, Luke descended through Bespin's upper atmosphere. Behind him, R2-D2 beeped with excitement as the X-wing flew through beautiful white clouds and emerged within visual range of a great, floating metropolis.

Cloud City was straight ahead.

CHAPTER 16

Boba Fett led the procession along the catwalk that wrapped around the wall of the carbon-freezing chamber. The sinister bounty hunter was followed by Han Solo, whose hands were manacled before him, then Princess Leia and Chewbacca. Strapped to the Wookiee's back, a cargo net carried C-3PO's parts. The droid was upset that only his head and right arm had been reattached, and seemed even more dismayed that his head faced the opposite direction of Chewbacca's. In this manner of travel, the droid was unable to see where they were going, and was forced to face the two stormtroopers who followed the Wookiee.

C-3PO saw more stormtroopers stationed around the chamber, and tried to twist his head around to see where Chewbacca was heading. "If only you had attached my legs, I wouldn't be in this ridiculous position," the droid complained. "Now, remember,

Chewbacca, you have a responsibility to me, so don't do anything foolish."

The group followed Fett down the stairs to the chamber's elevated platform. On the way down, Leia noticed Lobot standing at the bottom of the stairway. Then she saw Lando, standing near the platform's center, looking down into a pit where some Ugnaughts were working.

Two stormtroopers preceded Darth Vader into the chamber via the second stairway. As Vader descended to the elevated platform, he saw that the Ugnaughts were making final adjustments to the control casing into the central pit. It appeared the carbon-freezing apparatus was all in place.

Han came to a stop behind Lando and said, "What's going on . . . buddy?"

Without turning to face Han, Lando said, "You're being put into carbon freeze."

Leia and Han were standing just a short distance apart, but when they turned to face each other, Leia felt the distance like a chasm. Across from them, Fett approached Vader and said, "What if he doesn't survive? He's worth a lot to me."

"The Empire will compensate you if he dies," Vader said. Then he turned to the stormtroopers and commanded, "Put him in!"

Realizing what was about to happen, Chewbacca let out a wild howl. He threw his right arm out to his side, striking a stormtrooper with enough force to launch the figure from the elevated platform. Before anyone thought to react, Chewbacca lashed out with his left arm and disposed of a second stormtrooper in the same fashion. Across the platform, Boba Fett brought up his blaster rifle, but Vader — hoping to preserve his other captives — lashed out and grabbed the rifle's barrel, forcing the bounty hunter to aim away from the melee.

"Oh, no!" C-3PO cried from Chewbacca's back as more stormtroopers rushed the Wookiee. "No, no, no! Stop!"

"Stop, Chewie, stop!" Han shouted. "Stop!"

Chewbacca threw a third stormtrooper from the platform.

Glad to have Han's support for once, C-3PO pleaded, "Yes, stop, please! I'm not ready to die."

Han shouted louder, "Hey, hey! Listen to me. Chewie!"

Chewbacca howled. The stormtroopers swarmed around the Wookiee, trying to fit a pair of durasteel binders over his thick wrists in case he attacked again. Still enraged, the Wookiee was considering falling back over the side of the platform and dragging as many stormtroopers as he could with him when Han said, "Chewie, this won't help me."

Realizing the Wookiee was still considering doing something drastic, Han shouted, "Hey!" He gave

Chewbacca a stern look. "Save your strength. There'll be another time. The princess — you have to take care of her."

Leia glanced at Darth Vader and Boba Fett, then edged past the stormtroopers to stand close between Chewbacca and Han.

Han looked up at Chewbacca and said, "You hear me? Huh?"

Whimpering, Chewbacca nodded. As the stormtroopers secured the binders to the Wookiee's wrists, Leia and Han looked sorrowfully at each other. Both knew it might be their last moment together. Han moved forward and Leia raised her mouth to his for one final kiss.

The stormtroopers pulled Han away and made him walk backward until he stood upon a hydraulic lift at the platform's center. Han kept his eyes on Leia.

Leia called out, "I love you!"

To which Han said, "I know."

Two Ugnaughts approached Han, removed the manacles from his wrists, then stepped away from him. Leia watched the lift descend, carrying Han down into the central pit. From where Leia stood, only Han's head was visible. His gaze never strayed from her.

Lando looked from Han to Leia, then back to Han. Chewbacca howled.

Darth Vader gestured to an Ugnaught at a nearby control panel. The Ugnaught threw a switch, and only then did Han look away, flinching once before he appeared to vanish within a powerful blast of steam that exploded from the pit.

From behind Chewbacca, C-3PO said, "What . . . what's going on? Turn around. Chewbacca, I can't see."

Chewbacca whimpered. The steam was still clearing as the large retrieval tongs descended from the ceiling to the pit. The tongs locked onto the solid block of carbonite, then raised the heavy block from the pit to the platform.

Colored a lustrous dark gray, the carbonite block was 81 centimeters wide, 203 centimeters high, and 25 centimeters deep. It weighed over 100 kilograms, not including the weight of Han Solo, who was frozen solid within it. His face and the front of his body protruded slightly from the block's flat surface, with sharp, clearly defined creases on his shirt and pants. His hands and forearms — raised defensively — protruded the most. In all, he had the appearance of an unfinished statue, its form only partially emerged from a slab of black metal. But in this case, the statue looked as if it had been fighting to escape.

Two Ugnaughts stepped up to inspect the carbonite block's control casing, a frame with slender monitors embedded in its sides. After checking the monitors for gas ratio and carbonite integrity, one Ugnaught reached up to place his small, strong hands against the block's front, then pushed. The block fell back against the metal platform with a loud clang, and the noise made Leia jump back against Chewbacca.

But she couldn't tear her gaze from Han's frozen form, which now faced the ceiling. Prone on the floor with his hands clutching at the air, Han looked as if he were perpetually drowning. Devastated, Leia shuddered, and Chewbacca turned his body to her.

The Wookiee's movement allowed a very curious C-3PO to finally get a glimpse of what had transpired. From Chewbacca's back, the dismembered droid said, "Oh . . . they've encased him in carbonite. He should be quite well protected — if he survived the freezing process, that is."

While Fett and Vader watched, Lando stepped over to the prone block, knelt beside it, and examined the control casing's monitor for life systems. He pushed a button, listened to the monitor, then checked the illuminated readout.

Vader said, "Well, Calrissian, did he survive?"

"Yes, he's alive," Lando replied. "And in perfect hibernation."

As Lando rose and stepped away from the carbonite block, Vader turned to Boba Fett and said, "He's all yours, bounty hunter."

Fett responded with a single nod.

Vader looked to the Ugnaughts and ordered, "Reset the chamber for Skywalker."

Just then, an Imperial officer descended to the chamber platform. Stopping in front of Vader, he said, "Skywalker has just landed, my lord."

"Good," Vader said. "See to it that he finds his way in here."

The officer hurried out. Vader turned and watched Lando approach Leia and attempt to take her arm, apparently with the hope she would allow him to escort her from the chamber. Leia jerked her arm away.

Vader said, "Calrissian, take the princess and the Wookiee to my ship."

Lando was outraged. "You said they'd be left in the city under my supervision."

"I am altering the deal," Vader said. "Pray I don't alter it any further."

As Vader swept out of the carbon-freezing chamber, Lando's hand instinctively went to his throat. He knew what Vader would do to him if he pushed his luck.

Lando looked at Lobot. Lobot returned the gaze with a sidelong glance. And with that single, silent communication, Lobot knew what he had to do.

Luke had landed his X-wing starfighter without any difficulty, but as he and R2-D2 moved carefully down a white-walled, high-ceilinged corridor, he knew that something was very wrong on Cloud City. He didn't understand why there hadn't been anyone to greet or confront him on the landing platform.

Where is everybody?

Moving quietly forward, Luke arrived at a side hallway. He peered around the corner to see that the hallway connected with another corridor. He was about to enter the hallway when he heard footsteps.

Luke pulled back quickly, drew his blaster pistol, and flattened against the wall. With his blaster held tight in his right hand, he leaned forward, took a cautious peek down the hallway, and saw Boba Fett walking down the corridor.

Boba Fett?! What's that bounty hunter doing here? He saw Boba Fett's helmet shift slightly, as if he were about to turn to face Luke, but he didn't turn his head as he kept walking. Then Luke remembered the bounty on Han. *Maybe Yoda and Ben were wrong. Maybe my vision had nothing to do with Darth Vader and the Emperor. Maybe it was all about Boba Fett capturing Han.*

Fett was followed by a floating slab of metal that Luke couldn't make out. The floating slab was followed by two blue-uniformed Cloud City guards, who held the end of the slab and appeared to be guiding it through the hallway. Luke realized the slab was resting on a thin repulsor sled, an antigravity device used to transport heavy objects. The guards were followed by a pair of Imperial stormtroopers.

Stormtroopers! Luke suddenly realized that the Empire was definitely involved with whatever was going on at Cloud City. *Looks like Ben and Yoda were right.*

The procession passed out of Luke's viewing range. Keeping his blaster out, Luke moved quickly down the hallway until he'd arrived at the next corridor. Peering around the corner, he saw the end of the procession — the backs of the departing stormtroopers — just before they rounded a corner and he lost sight of them again.

R2-D2 had followed Luke through the hallway, and beeped as he arrived at his master's side. Luke raised a hand, signaling the droid to be silent and stay put. R2-D2 obediently stopped beeping and rolled back from him.

Trusting that the procession was now far enough ahead of him that he could follow unnoticed, Luke stepped forward into the corridor. Which was a mistake.

Boba was positioned near the same corner where Luke had lost sight of the two stormtroopers. The bounty hunter's blaster rifle was aimed at Luke. Boba fired.

Luke fell back into the hallway as the laser bolt whizzed past him and impacted at the hallway wall.

He realized too late that he must have been spotted by Fett's targeting rangefinder as the hunter had led the others past the hallway. Fett quickly fired two more bolts, which smashed into the corridor wall near Luke's position, then fired a fourth bolt that followed the first into the hallway wall.

Leia was walking down a corridor with Chewbacca and C-3PO — the droid's pieces still strapped to the Wookiee's back — when she heard four blaster shots. The shots sounded like they'd come from behind, so Leia looked back, but all she saw were two of the four stormtroopers in her escort. The other two were in front of her, and in the lead were a gray-uniformed Imperial lieutenant and Lando Calrissian.

Lando heard the fired blasters, too. He continued walking without missing a step but adjusted his cape slightly so neither the lieutenant nor anyone behind him was able to see what he did next. With his left hand, Lando reached to a thin comlink that was strapped to his right wrist, tapped a key sequence, and sent a signal to Lobot.

R2-D2 beeped frantically. Luke patted R2-D2's dome, trying to reassure the astromech that he'd be all right. Around the corner from Luke, the two shots that had struck the corridor wall had left smoldering scorch marks.

Luke held his blaster pistol and edged out into the corridor. *No sign of Fett.* He pressed forward, trying to pick up the bounty hunter's trail.

As Luke approached another side hallway, he heard more footsteps. He passed a window as he entered the hallway and did not consider that the light from the window might cast his shadow onto the hallway's wall.

The Imperial lieutenant was walking just behind Calrissian when he saw a shadow glide across the wall of an adjoining hallway. The lieutenant stopped, gestured at Lando to open a nearby door, then signaled the stormtroopers under his command. As the stormtroopers took up firing position, the lieutenant grabbed Princess Leia and yanked her after Lando.

Luke jumped back against the hallway wall as the waiting stormtroopers fired their blaster rifles at him. After several laser bolts whizzed past him, he risked a quick glance up the hall and was almost overwhelmed by what he saw.

Four stormtroopers. Chewbacca and Leia! That Imperial officer's holding Leia like a body shield! Is that C-3PO on Chewie's back? Who's the caped man opening that door?

The stormtroopers kept shooting at him, but Luke held his fire and watched as the caped man stepped through the open doorway. As three of the storm-troopers shoved Chewbacca through the doorway, Leia saw Luke and shouted, "Luke! Luke, don't — it's a trap!"

The Imperial officer dragged Leia after Chew-bacca, but Leia gripped the doorway and shouted again, "It's a trap!" Then Leia was pulled through. One stormtrooper fired two more shots at Luke, then exited the same way as the others.

The doorway remained open.

So it's a trap, Luke thought. *But what happens to my friends if I don't try to rescue them?*

Luke headed for the open doorway.

CHAPTER 17

His blaster pistol at the ready, Luke stepped through the open doorway and into a dark antechamber. R2-D2 tried to follow, but a moment after Luke entered, the door slid down and locked behind him, leaving the little droid in the outer corridor.

There wasn't any sign of Luke's friends or the stormtroopers in the antechamber. Except for the locked door behind Luke, the only visible exit was an open lift tube. The lift's floor was circular, and only large enough to carry a single passenger.

Luke stepped onto the lift, and was instantly transported up through a hole in the ceiling. He'd been delivered to the top of an elevated platform in a large chamber. There was steam everywhere. Luke looked around at the pipes and hoses that lined the walls and ceiling, and he tried to determine the chamber's function. As he stepped off the lift, a metal grate slid over the lift and locked in place.

Luke realized an unseen enemy was controlling his movements, drawing him into a predetermined path and sealing off his avenues of retreat. He looked at his blaster pistol. *How effective will a blaster be against someone I can't even see?* Uncertain of where to proceed, he kept his blaster drawn as he moved away from the sealed lift.

"The Force is with you, young Skywalker," a deep voice rumbled from behind him, causing Luke to turn fast. "But you are not a Jedi yet."

It was Darth Vader.

The dark lord was positioned above Luke, standing on a grated floor that was connected to the elevated platform by a stairway. Luke holstered his blaster as he climbed the steps to stand before Vader, then drew his lightsaber and ignited its blue blade.

Vader activated his own red-bladed lightsaber. Luke stepped forward and raised his weapon. There was a mild electrical crackling sound as the two men crossed sabers.

Luke swung first, but Vader blocked the blow with ease. Luke pulled away and swung again, but Vader blocked and pushed back with considerable strength, knocking Luke to the floor. Keeping his lightsaber angled up toward Vader, Luke rose to his feet and assumed a defensive position. Vader swung at Luke, but Luke blocked and swung back, and soon their lightsabers were sweeping and clashing faster than the eye could follow.

The duel had just begun.

What's happening to Luke? Leia wondered. She and the droid-toting Wookiee were being led through yet another corridor, with two stormtroopers behind them, two in front, and Lando and the Imperial lieutenant back in the lead. Glancing at the back of Lando's head, she swore, *If I ever get out of this, I'll fix Lando so he never smiles again.*

As the group proceeded past an intersection in the corridor, Leia glanced to her right and saw Lobot approaching with a group of Cloud City guards from a connecting hallway. To her surprise, more guards suddenly materialized from adjoining hallways, then drew and aimed their sleek blaster pistols at the Imperial lieutenant and stormtroopers. Outnumbered and unprepared, the stormtroopers raised their armored arms and held out their blaster rifles in surrender.

Lando shoved the Imperial lieutenant toward one of the guards, then turned to the two stormtroopers behind them and took their weapons. Leia gaped as Lando stepped past her and handed both blaster rifles to Lobot.

"Well done," Lando said to his aide, then turned to the two stormtroopers behind Leia and Chewbacca and took away their blaster rifles. Turning back to Lobot, Lando said, "Hold them in the security tower — and keep it quiet. Move."

As Lobot and the Cloud City guards escorted their Imperial captives out of the corridor, Lando handed the two blaster rifles to Leia, then turned his attention to the binders that were locked around Chewbacca's wrists.

Surprised by this turn of events, Leia asked Lando, "What do you think you're doing?"

"We're getting out of here," Lando replied.

From the net at Chewbacca's back, C-3PO chimed in, "I knew all along it had to be a mistake."

The moment Chewbacca's binders were unlocked, he reached out and wrapped his hairy fingers around Lando's neck. Leia glared at Lando and said, "Do you think that after what you did to Han we're going to trust you?"

"I had no choice. . . ." Lando gasped.

"What are you doing?" C-3PO cried, twisting at Chewbacca's back in a desperate effort to see the others. "Trust him, trust him!"

Leia said, "Oh, so we understand, don't we, Chewie? He had no choice."

Chewbacca tightened his grip on Lando and leaned forward, forcing Lando to his knees. Lando's voice was a choked whisper: "I'm just trying to help —"

"We don't need any of your help," Leia said.

Lando gasped, "H-a-a-a . . ."

"What?" Leia said.

"It sounds like *Han*," said C-3PO, who had the best ear for languages.

Lando clutched at Chewbacca's wrists and rasped, "There's still a chance to save Han . . . at the East Platform."

Leia said, "Chewie," and the Wookiee released Lando. Still on his knees, Lando breathed hard, taking in deep lungfuls of air. As Leia and Chewbacca started running out of the corridor, he looked up to see C-3PO's parts bouncing in the net at Chewbacca's back.

"I'm terribly sorry about all this," C-3PO said as he moved away from Lando. "After all, he's only a Wookiee."

Even though he hadn't completely gotten his breath back, Lando rose from the floor and started running after the others. Leia was right: They had no reason to trust him. But if there was any chance of saving Han, Lando wanted to be there when it happened.

"Put Captain Solo in the cargo hold," Boba Fett instructed the two Cloud City guards. The guards guided the floating carbonite block up *Slave I*'s sloped landing ramp and through a narrow access hatch. Fett stood beside a stormtrooper on the landing ramp and kept his gaze on the walkway that extended from the landing platform. There was a door at the end of the walkway. If anyone came through the door before *Slave I* lifted off, Fett would see them.

Boba had already received payment from the Empire for tracking the *Millennium Falcon* to Cloud City, and he looked forward to collecting the bounty that Jabba the Hutt had placed on Solo. But Fett was well aware of the fact that other bounty hunters were still hoping to collect that bounty, and a lot could happen between Cloud City and Jabba's palace on Tatooine.

The guards exited the hatch and left with the stormtrooper. Boba Fett entered *Slave I*, locked the hatch behind him, and went to the cargo hold to secure his valuable merchandise.

With C-3PO's parts clattering in the net against his back, Chewbacca ran behind Leia as Lando led them around a curved terrace that overlooked the city. Leia and Chewbacca were armed with the blaster rifles that Lando had taken from the stormtroopers. The sky was red.

As they ran toward another corridor, C-3PO spotted a familiar droid in a nearby alcove. "Artoo!" the droid cried. "Artoo! Where have you been?"

Hearing C-3PO's words, Chewbacca stopped and turned around to bark at R2-D2, but his sudden action left C-3PO staring at the corridor wall.

C-3PO said, "Wait, turn around, you woolly —!" As Chewbacca turned to catch up with Leia and Lando, C-3PO was again able to see R2-D2, who was racing after the Wookiee. "Hurry, hurry!" C-3PO cried. "We're trying to save Han from the bounty hunter!"

R2-D2 whistled frantically after C-3PO.

"Well, at least you're still in one piece!" C-3PO replied, bouncing along at Chewbacca's back. "Look what happened to me!"

Leia was the first to reach the door to the East Platform. She ran through the doorway, followed by Chewbacca, but they stopped in their tracks as *Slave I* began to lift and rise away from the platform. Chewbacca roared and fired his blaster rifle, but the laser bolts glanced off the ship's energized shields.

Leia watched *Slave I* blast into the sky. The bounty hunter was getting away, doubtlessly heading for Tatooine. Leia had a horrible feeling that she might never see Han again.

"Oh, no!" C-3PO cried. "Chewie, they're behind you!"

Leia spun, and for once she was glad that C-3PO's

parts were dangling at Chewbacca's back. Otherwise, they might not have been aware until too late that they had been followed by the two stormtroopers.

The two were visible through the open doorway, in the corridor that had led to the East Platform. Lando jumped away from the doorway just as the stormtroopers fired, sending red blaster bolts over R2-D2's domed head and past Leia and Chewbacca. The Wookiee returned fire and felled a stormtrooper on his first shot, then squeezed off a series of bolts at the remaining stormtrooper while Lando and Leia darted back through the doorway, heading for a lift tube.

R2-D2 beeped nervously as the laser bolts sailed past his body. Chewbacca kept firing at the stormtrooper and moved fast after Leia and Lando. As the group hurried for a lift tube, Leia wondered again about Luke's fate.

Luke thought, *Doesn't Vader ever get tired?* He'd been engaged in battle with Darth Vader for several minutes, and the dark lord had not let up at all. Luke, on the other hand, was already sweating hard, and not just from the physical effort of the duel. All the steam was making the air in the chamber feel more humid than Dagobah's oppressive climate.

Yet Luke was holding up, matching Darth Vader's fighting prowess blow for blow. As steam billowed around them, Vader said, "You have learned much, young one."

"You'll find I'm full of surprises," Luke replied. He swung his lightsaber at Vader, and Vader swung back with enough power to knock Luke's weapon from his grip. Luke's lightsaber spun and fell away, then automatically deactivated as it clattered against the upper surface of the elevated platform.

Hoping to recover his lightsaber, Luke threw himself down the stairway, rolling painfully upon the metal steps until he landed on the metal platform. Darth Vader leaped into the air, passing over the steps to land with a loud *clang* near his opponent. Luke flinched at the sound, and looked up to see the tip of Vader's lightsaber dangling in front of his face.

Luke rose to his feet and backed away from Vader. *Where's my lightsaber? I can hardly see a thing down here!*

"Your destiny lies with me, Skywalker," Vader said as he slowly advanced toward Luke. "Obi-Wan knew this to be true."

"No!" Luke cried, then backed right into the open pit at the center of the raised platform.

"All too easy," Vader intoned.

At the bottom of the pit, Luke quickly struggled to his feet. He instantly recognized the metal columns inside the pit as freezing coils, and just as quickly knew he had to get out of the pit. Fast.

Still atop the elevated platform, Vader gestured at the nearby carbon-freezing controls and used the Force to pull a lever. Had Vader not looked away from the sudden blast of steam that erupted from the freezing pit, he might have seen Luke's form shoot from the pit to the ceiling.

Vader returned his gaze to the pit, waiting for the billowing steam to clear. Thinking Luke was frozen and that his words would go unheard, Vader said, "Perhaps you are not as strong as the Emperor thought."

There was a loud *clank* from overhead, and Vader looked up to see Luke clutching at a tangle of pipes and cables. "Impressive . . . most impressive," Vader commented, then raised his lightsaber and swung at a dangling hose. Steam blasted from the sliced ends of the hose, temporarily clouding Luke's vision.

But Luke flipped away from the ceiling and — on his way down — reached out with his left hand to grab a length of the sliced hose. Landing on his feet, he twisted the hose to spray steam directly into Vader's helmeted face. As the dark lord snarled and recoiled, Luke spotted his own lightsaber, resting on the other side of the platform. He extended the fingers of his right hand, and the lightsaber launched through the air and smacked into his palm. Vader swung his red-bladed lightsaber through the steam just as Luke ignited the blue beam of his own weapon. The lightsabers clashed as more steam flooded the chamber.

"Obi-Wan has taught you well," Vader said. "You have controlled your fear . . . now release your anger." He launched another attack, trying to goad Luke into unleashing his emotions. "Only your hatred can destroy me," he continued, swinging again at his opponent. But Luke leaped and executed a mid-air somersault, landing behind Vader. Vader was caught off guard as Luke lashed out with his lightsaber, and the dark lord backed up, stepping past the edge of the elevated platform.

Vader snarled as he fell to the darkness below.

With all the steam and noise on the platform, Luke was not surprised that he didn't hear Vader's impact. Luke peered over the edge and looked down, but saw no sign of Vader or his red lightsaber.

Luke thought, *Should I go after him?* Then he remembered Yoda's words: *Stopped they must be.*

Luke deactivated his lightsaber, clipped it to his belt, and jumped down into the darkness. Landing on the floor of the freezing chamber, he edged past a wall until he stood before a circular metal vent. The vent slid open, revealing a narrow, tubular tunnel that descended at a slight angle. *Another opening hatch and passage,* Luke observed. *Vader wants to lure me in.*

He entered the tunnel, walked through its short

length, and stepped down into a wide room. Behind him, a double hatch slid over the tunnel's opening. *He's trying to rattle my nerves. But I won't be rattled. If that tunnel's my only way out, my lightsaber will slice through the hatch.*

Luke moved across the room, searching for Darth Vader.

Vader stood in the shadows of the reactor control room and watched Luke walk toward a large circular window. Beyond the window was Cloud City's reactor shaft, a central wind tunnel nearly a kilometer in diameter.

Vader thought, *You were unwise to follow me down here. It would have been so much easier on you if you'd allowed yourself to be frozen in carbonite.*

Yes. Search the room for me. I'm not hiding. I'm right here. You see me now? Good.

Go on. Activate your lightsaber. The blue blade still looks so pure. Do you know I'm familiar with that particular weapon? The very one you're holding? The one that Obi-Wan must have given you. No, I don't believe you know that. Not yet.

Allow me to activate my own lightsaber. That's right . . . gaze at it, and believe that I'm preparing to strike. Don't mistake me . . . I am preparing to strike, but not with my lightsaber. I shall use the Force.

Pay no attention to the crack of metal behind you. That's just the sound of a pipe snapping from the wall and flying toward you. Ah! You dodged it. How clever.

But can you dodge this metal case? No, for it just struck the back of your head. Can you dodge this piece of machinery? No, it seems you could not. Can you dodge this . . . ?

A long, heavy piece of metal pipe traveled through the air, missing Luke's battered body but smashing through the large window. There was a sudden rush of air as the room depressurized, and a fierce wind tore at anything that wasn't bolted down, including Vader and Luke. As Vader's black cape tugged at his neck and shoulders, he reached out to grip the wall and watched as the wind lifted Luke off his feet and sucked him out through the shattered window, into Cloud City's reactor shaft.

Moments later, the wind died down, and Vader was able to release the wall. He stepped forward to the window, leaned over its jagged shards, and peered down to see Luke dangling from a gantry. He watched Luke pull himself up onto the gantry, and noticed that Luke had not lost his lightsaber during the fall.

Vader withdrew from the window. He thought, *The Emperor did not underestimate Luke Skywalker's strength. But I underestimated his will to live. I won't make that mistake again.*

As Vader made his way to a nearby lift tube, he decided it was time to relieve Luke of his lightsaber.

Leia saw more stormtroopers coming up the corridor. She fired a burst of laser bolts at them, then darted up a short flight of steps to the waiting lift tube, which fortunately managed to hold her, Lando, Chewbacca, C-3PO's parts, and R2-D2.

The lift tube carried them to the corridor next to the *Millennium Falcon*'s landing platform. There was a control panel on the wall beside the door to the platform, and Lando ran to the panel and quickly punched in a coded sequence. Unfortunately, the code failed to open the door.

"The security code has been changed!" Lando exclaimed.

From Chewbacca's back, C-3PO said, "Artoo, you can tell the computer to override the security system."

R2-D2 beeped and scooted toward what appeared to be a computer terminal at the base of the control panel. The astromech popped open a panel and extended his computer interface arm as fast as he could, but not fast enough for the nervous C-3PO, who cried, "Artoo, hurry!"

Lando crossed the corridor to a comlink console, then entered his security code to address all parts of Cloud City. Holding the comlink, he said, "Attention! This is Lando Calrissian. The Empire has taken control of the city. I advise everyone to leave before more Imperial troops arrive."

As Lando turned from the comlink, there was a bright spark where R2-D2's arm met with the socket. R2-D2 screamed and smoke seeped out from under his domed head. Chewbacca grabbed hold of R2-D2 and tore him away from the wall.

"This way," Lando said, urging the group to follow him up the corridor.

R2-D2 beeped angrily and tried to move after the others, but accidentally smacked into the wall.

"Well, don't blame me," C-3PO said, bobbing along behind Chewbacca. "I'm an interpreter. I'm not supposed to know a power socket from a computer terminal."

R2-D2 regained control of himself but was still beeping with fury as he sped after his friends.

If Lando had wondered whether his broadcast message had reached the citizens of Cloud City, all doubts were dismissed as he ran into a crowded plaza, filled with people running for the public transport ships. Lando led Leia, Chewbacca, and R2-D2 to another door, and the astromech wasted no time in plugging his computer interface arm into a proper terminal socket.

Suddenly, they sighted approaching stormtroopers. As Leia and Chewbacca opened fire on the Imperial soldiers, R2-D2 rotated his dome and beeped at C-3PO, who — flailing against Chewbacca's back — was more immediately concerned about the blaster bolts that were whizzing past his head. "We're not interested in the hyperdrive on the *Millennium Falcon*," C-3PO shouted over the blaster fire. "It's fixed! Just open the door, you stupid lump."

More stormtroopers arrived, and Chewbacca, Leia, and Lando had to retreat down the corridor. They hadn't traveled far when R2-D2 let out a triumphant beep. The door slid open.

C-3PO shouted, "I never doubted you for a second. Wonderful!"

R2-D2 retracted his arm from the socket and waited until his friends had made it through the door. When he saw the stormtroopers advance from the corridor, he deployed his built-in fire extinguisher and sprayed opaque gas into the air. While the stormtroopers blundered through the smokescreen, R2-D2 moved through the door to the landing platform.

Despite R2-D2's efforts, a few stormtroopers managed to find their way to the open doorway. As Chewbacca neared the *Falcon*'s landing ramp, he tossed his pilfered blaster rifle to Lando. Lando took cover under the ship and fired at the stormtroopers, allowing Leia and R2-D2 time to make it to the ship.

The *Falcon*'s landing ramp was down. Unfortunately, Chewbacca forgot that C-3PO was strapped to his back. The droid's squirming didn't help either.

"Ouch!" C-3PO shouted as the back of his head struck the *Falcon*'s hull. "Oh! Ah! That hurt. Bend down, you thoughtless — ow!"

While Chewbacca and C-3PO bumped their way up the ramp, Leia turned to fire at the stormtroopers, who were now pouring out through the doorway. Lando saw R2-D2 scoot up the ramp and shouted, "Leia! Go!" Leia ran into the ship, with Lando at her heels.

Chewbacca had deposited the cargo net with C-3PO's parts on the floor before he ran into the cockpit and started flipping switches, energizing shields, and preparing for liftoff. As R2-D2 entered the *Falcon*, he extended a retractable claw to grab the cargo net and dragged C-3PO to a safer location.

C-3PO said, "I thought that hairy beast would be the end of me."

R2-D2 beeped.

"Of course, I've looked better," C-3PO grumbled.

Outside the *Falcon*, laser bolts glanced off the ship's shields as the stormtroopers continued to fire. But before the Imperials could do any serious damage, the *Falcon* lifted off the landing platform and roared away into the twilight sky.

Inside the Cloud City reactor shaft, Luke moved carefully along the gantry that was secured to a large, rudderlike vane. The vane was used to create desired changes in airflow, controlling the city's movements through Bespin's skies while routing Tibanna gas to processing facilities. Even though the gantry had a protective railing, Luke kept close to the vane and tried to shield his body from the strong, continuous wind that whipped through the deep shaft.

Luke edged around the vane to an open doorway that led into a narrow control room. The room was dark, only illuminated by the winking lights on the control consoles that lined the walls. Knowing that an activated lightsaber would reveal his position, Luke kept his weapon off as he stepped in.

Vader's close, he thought as he walked past the control consoles. *Dangerously close.*

Vader emerged sooner than Luke expected, leaping out from the shadows with his red lightsaber blazing. Luke jumped back and activated his own lightsaber's blue beam in time to block the attack.

But Vader swung wildly, slicing into machinery on either side of the narrow room as he drove Luke back through the open doorway.

Vader followed Luke onto the gantry, then brought his lightsaber down hard against Luke's blade. Luke stumbled and fell back against the metal-floored walkway that extended out to a cantilevered platform. He raised his gaze to find himself staring up the length of Vader's extended lightsaber.

"You are beaten," Vader said, looming above Luke. "It is useless to resist. Don't let yourself be destroyed as Obi-Wan did."

Remembering how Darth Vader had cut down Obi-Wan, Luke felt a sudden surge of strength, his face twisting with anger. He flicked his wrist and his lightsaber's blade whipped up, smacking Vader's blade aside and allowing Luke to quickly scramble to his feet. Vader lunged again with his weapon, and the two men exchanged a swift series of blows.

Luke swung hard and connected with the black armor plate on Vader's right shoulder. The Sith Lord snarled in pain as bright sparks exploded from the shoulder plate. But Vader never lost his grip on his lightsaber, and he swung again at Luke. Luke dodged the attack, darted past a vertical array of weather sensors at the platform's outer edge, then leaped to a beam that extended from the platform to another tall sensor array. Below the beam, the immense shaft fell away farther than his eyes could see.

Balancing on the beam, Luke turned as Vader's lightsaber sliced through the weather sensors. Luke raised his lightsaber to block another blow from Vader, but as his left hand clung to the damaged sensors and he struggled to maintain his footing, Vader's lightsaber lashed out again —

— and cut off Luke's right hand.

Luke screamed. His hand arced away from his right arm, carrying his lightsaber with it. The lightsaber automatically deactivated, and the weapon fell with the severed hand down into the shaft.

Vader moved forward to the edge of the platform and gazed down at Luke. Luke clutched his wounded arm to his chest and slumped down upon the beam.

"There is no escape," Vader said as Luke moved away from him, crawling backward to the outermost sensor array. "Don't make me destroy you."

But Luke kept crawling. He felt dizzy and sick. His only goal was to put distance between himself and Vader.

Seeing that Luke was utterly defeated, Vader switched off his lightsaber. "You do not yet realize your importance," Vader continued. "You have only begun to discover your power. Join me and I will complete your training. With our combined strength, we can end this destructive conflict and bring order to the galaxy."

Reaching the end of the beam, Luke wrapped his arms around the outermost sensor array. Turning to face Vader, he screamed, "I'll never join you!"

"If only you knew the power of the dark side," Vader said, reaching out to clutch the air with his black-gloved fist. "Obi-Wan never told you what happened to your father."

"He told me enough!" Luke said as he wrapped his arms around the sensor array and lowered his feet to a metal ring. Wincing, he added, "He told me you killed him."

"No," Vader said, his fist still clenched. "I *am* your father."

Luke's eyes went wide. *My father? But Ben told me . . .*

"No," Luke whimpered. "No. That's not true! That's impossible!"

"Search your feelings," Vader said. "You know it to be true."

"No!" Luke shouted. "No!"

The wind picked up, and Vader's black cape rippled at his back. "Luke. You can destroy the Emperor. He has foreseen this. It is your destiny." He opened his left hand and held it out to Luke. "Join me, and together we can rule the galaxy as father and son."

His voice is so hypnotic, Luke thought, and felt part of himself falling under Vader's spell. But only part of him. Luke looked down into the deep shaft that seemed to stretch down to forever.

"Come with me," Vader urged. "It is the only way."

Luke looked directly at Vader and felt a certain calmness as he thought, *No. It's not the only way.*

Then Vader watched in astonishment as Luke released his arms from the sensor array and fell, down, down into the reactor shaft.

There was nothing to break Luke's fall. As he tumbled through the air, he looked up, half expecting to see Darth Vader leap down after him. But all he saw of Vader was a rapidly receding black speck at the edge of the already distant vane.

Suddenly, Luke was aware that he was no longer falling straight down. Twisting his body, he saw that he was caught in a powerful air current that was drawing him toward an open exhaust pipe in the shaft's wall.

Luke sailed into the exhaust pipe, a metal-lined tubular tunnel that twisted down and away from the reactor shaft. The pipe's walls were smooth, sending Luke on an uncontrolled slide until he entered what seemed to be a dip in the pipe, and slowed to a stop. But before he could plan his next move, a trap-door dropped open beneath him, plunging him down another pipe.

Luke's mind raced, trying to figure out where the second pipe would carry him. As the pipe twisted into an almost vertical slope, he guessed the pipes were designed to expel stray matter from the reactor shaft. He extended his limbs in an attempt to slow his descent, but the effort was too much for his drained, battered body. He continued to slide.

The pipe terminated at a retractable hatch, and as Luke's body neared it, the hatch opened. Luke fell through the open hole and slammed into some spindly horizontal metal bars. He desperately grabbed at the bars and caught them.

He realized he was clutching at an electronic weather vane that was secured to the wide under-side of Cloud City. Below Luke, there was nothing but clouds.

Luke felt so helpless. Then he thought of the spirit of Obi-Wan, who had come to his aid before, and he gasped, "Ben . . . Ben, please!"

But Ben had said he could not interfere if Luke chose to face Vader, and so there would be no response.

Luke's muscles strained as he struggled to get a better hold on the weather vane. He looked up to the hatch from which he'd been ejected. The hatch was still open. He began to shimmy up the weather vane, but as he reached for the hatch door, the door automatically lifted and locked in place.

Then Luke slipped down the weather vane, but somehow caught the horizontal bars with his legs so that he dangled upside down. The pain was almost unbearable.

"Ben," Luke cried again. But when Ben did not answer, Luke thought of the one other person who might be able to help him. "Leia!" he cried out.

He didn't even know if Leia was still on Cloud City, or if she was in any position to help him. Still, he clung to the weather vane, searched the surrounding clouds, and yelled, "Hear me! Leia!"

The *Millennium Falcon* was flying fast away from Cloud City but had not yet left Bespin's upper atmosphere when Leia heard Luke's voice. She was sitting in the pilot's seat, looking through the cockpit window, and at first she thought the voice was just some trick of her imagination. But then an image formed in her mind, an image of Luke, injured and dangling from some kind of metal array at the bottom of Cloud City.

"Luke . . ." Leia said. Then she turned to her right, where Chewbacca sat behind his controls. She said, "We've got to go back."

Lando was standing in the area behind Chewbacca's and Leia's seats. Lando had just informed Leia that the *Falcon*'s sensors had detected the approach of TIE fighters, so he was surprised by Leia's sudden decision. He said, "What?"

"I know where Luke is," Leia said.

"But what about those fighters?" Lando asked.

Leia commanded, "Chewie, just do it."

As Chewbacca reset his controls, Lando said, "But what about Vader?"

Chewbacca roared at Lando.

"All right, all right, all right," Lando said, knowing better than to argue with the Wookiee.

The *Falcon* looped around a wide cloud formation and sped back to Cloud City.

Darth Vader strode through a white-walled corridor in Cloud City. An Imperial officer and a squad of stormtroopers traveled in his wake as he headed for his shuttle's landing platform. "Alert the Star Destroyer to prepare for my arrival," he said to the officer, then walked toward his tall *Lambda*-class shuttle.

Vader knew Luke had not perished in the reactor shaft. *If he had, I would have sensed it.* Vader would have searched for Luke himself, but upon learning that Princess Leia and Lando Calrissian had escaped in the *Millennium Falcon*, and that Imperial scanners had detected the *Falcon* was now returning to Cloud City, Vader had revised his plan. He would return to the *Executor*, and allow the princess to rescue Luke.

Then Darth Vader would capture them all.

The *Falcon* soared closer to Cloud City, and Lando was the first to sight the figure that dangled like a broken doll from the electronic weather vane. "Look, someone's up there," he said, pointing a finger to direct Chewbacca's and Leia's gaze.

"It's Luke," Leia said. He looked like he was about to fall. Leia tried to remain calm as she said, "Chewie, slow down. Slow down and we'll get under him. Lando, open the top hatch."

As Lando ran out of the cockpit and went to the hydraulic lift, Chewbacca jockeyed the ship under Luke. Luke caught a brief glimpse of Leia in the cockpit, then saw the top hatch slide open to reveal Lando.

"Okay," Leia said as the Wookiee closed the distance between the *Falcon*'s hull and Cloud City's bottom. Chewbacca barked, and Leia said, "Easy, Chewie."

Luke didn't know Lando, but because he'd arrived with Leia, Luke trusted he was an ally. The moment the *Falcon*'s hatch was positioned beneath him, Luke let go of the weather vane and fell into his arms.

"Lando?" Leia said into the ship's comm.

Lando answered, "Okay, let's go."

Leia watched Chewbacca paw the controls and the *Falcon* dropped away from the bottom of Cloud City. Just then, the Wookiee saw three Imperial TIE fighters approaching at high speed.

Leia climbed out of her seat and found Lando supporting Luke in the passage tube behind the cockpit. Lando had wrapped a blanket around Luke, and Leia felt crushed as she imagined the beating Luke had obviously endured. She took Luke in her arms, allowing Lando to enter the cockpit and scramble into the pilot's seat.

Luke moaned, "Oh, Leia."

Suddenly, Imperial-fired flak exploded outside the ship.

"All right, Chewie," Lando said. "Let's go."

The Wookiee aimed for some distant clouds, increased power to the thrusters, and launched the ship away from the oncoming TIE fighters.

As the *Falcon* hurtled forward, Leia moved Luke to a bunk and broke out the ship's emergency medical supplies. She worked fast and did her best to treat his wounds, and didn't ask for details when she placed the autotourniquet on his right arm. But Leia suspected she'd be needed in the cockpit, so when Luke was stabilized, she kissed him and said, "I'll be back."

Leia entered the cockpit and took the navigator's seat behind Lando. Both Chewbacca and Lando were flipping switches and adjusting controls as they tried to shake off the TIE fighters that were now hammering the *Falcon*'s deflector shields with their lasers. As the *Falcon* entered space, Leia saw a large, wedge-shaped ship in orbit of Bespin, and said, "Star Destroyer."

It was Vader's ship, the *Executor*.

"All right, Chewie," Lando said. "Ready for lightspeed."

"*If* your people fixed the hyperdrive," Leia pointed out. After all, she'd been disappointed by the *Falcon*'s hyperdrive twice before.

Ignoring Leia's remark, Lando said, "All the coordinates are set. It's now or never."

Chewbacca barked.

Lando ordered, "Punch it!"

The Wookiee pulled back on the throttle. The engine sounded like it was winding up, then it cut off.

"They told me they fixed it," Lando said as Chewbacca let out a frustrated howl. "I trusted them to fix it."

More flak exploded outside the *Falcon*. Leia sat

back in her seat and glared at Lando. Chewbacca jumped out of his seat and stormed out of the cockpit.

"It's not my fault!" Lando insisted.

After returning to the *Executor*, Darth Vader proceeded to the bridge and walked directly to Admiral Piett's command station. Snapping to attention at the sight of Vader, Piett announced, "They'll be in range of our tractor beam in moments, lord."

Vader asked, "Did your men deactivate the hyperdrive on the *Millennium Falcon*?"

"Yes, my lord," Piett reported. He knew if his men hadn't done their job, he'd be a dead man.

"Good," Vader said. "Prepare a boarding party and set your weapons for stun."

"Yes, my lord."

Seated on a crate in the *Millennium Falcon*'s main hold, C-3PO was almost entirely reassembled except for his lower left leg, which he held across his lap. Since boarding the *Falcon*, R2-D2 had been working as fast as he could to put his friend back together, and was now using a retractable tool to repair C-3PO's right foot.

Chewbacca ran into the hold and grunted loudly to himself. C-3PO remarked, "Noisy brute. Why don't we just go into lightspeed?"

While Chewbacca lifted the deck plates to uncover the access pit, R2-D2 beeped his explanation.

"We can't?" C-3PO said. "How would you know the hyperdrive is deactivated?"

As Chewbacca jumped into the pit, R2-D2 whistled knowingly.

"The city's central computer told you?" said C-3PO, surprised. "Artoo-Detoo, you know better than to trust a strange computer."

R2-D2's extended repair tool sparked against the golden droid's right foot.

"Ouch!" C-3PO cried. "Pay attention to what you're doing!"

In the pit, Chewbacca confronted the hyperdrive with a fusioncutter. There was an unexpected flash of electric current, triggering a surge that caused sparks to fly in the *Falcon*'s cockpit.

On the bridge of the *Executor*, Vader gazed through the viewport and watched the *Falcon* attempt to evade the pursuing TIE fighters. Focusing his attention on the ship that carried the young Skywalker, he said aloud, "Luke."

On the *Falcon*, Luke's head lifted from his bunk. He said, "Father."

Son, Vader said from across space, *come with me.*

Luke's head fell back to the bunk. "Ben," he moaned, "why didn't you tell me?" Then the ship's hull shuddered. Luke rose from his bunk, taking the blanket with him, and proceeded to the cockpit.

In the cockpit, Lando shouted into the comm, "Chewie!"

In the main hold's access pit, Chewbacca heard Lando and angrily smashed the fusioncutter against the hyperdrive mechanism.

Back in the cockpit, Lando and Leia looked up in surprise as Luke entered. Wrapped in the blanket, he gazed out the cockpit at the *Executor* and said, "It's Vader."

Then Luke heard Vader's voice again from across space: *Luke . . . it is your destiny.*

Luke sank back into the seat behind Leia. He closed his eyes and groaned again, "Ben, why didn't you tell me?"

The *Executor* was closing in on the *Millennium Falcon*. Admiral Piett turned to a lieutenant and said, "Alert all commands. Ready for the tractor beam."

"Artoo, come back at once!" C-3PO cried in the *Falcon*'s main hold. "You haven't finished with me yet!" Indeed, C-3PO was still holding his left leg. As R2-

D2 scooted past the access pit that contained the furious Chewbacca and over to the main engineering console, C-3PO said, "You don't know how to fix the hyperdrive. Chewbacca can do it. I'm standing here in pieces, and you're having delusions of grandeur!"

R2-D2 extended his manipulator arm to move a circuit on a control panel. Suddenly, the control panel lit up, and the hyperdrive kicked in.

"You did it!" C-3PO shouted as the entire ship tilted up, sending R2-D2 rolling backward into the open pit to fall on top of Chewbacca. The hyperdrive engines roared.

In the cockpit, Luke was already seated, but Leia and Lando were nearly thrown off their feet as the ship blasted into hyperspace.

In the blink of an eye, the *Millennium Falcon* was gone. On the *Executor*'s bridge, Admiral Piett gasped, then looked at Darth Vader and cringed.

Vader was still facing the viewport, gazing at the area where the *Millennium Falcon* had been just moments before escaping into hyperspace. He turned slowly, then proceeded across the walkway, away from the viewport. Below Vader, the technicians in the bridge's lower level looked up at him, waiting for him to react to the situation.

Maintaining his slow stride, Vader glanced to his

right and barely noticed Admiral Piett. The Sith Lord could practically taste the Imperial officer's fear, but as angry as he was at losing Luke, he knew that Piett — unlike some recently deceased Imperial officers — was not at fault. Vader had much to contemplate, so he looked away from Piett and kept walking.

Without a word, he left the bridge.

The Rebel fleet was traveling through space, en route to what the Rebel Alliance hoped would be their new secret base. X-wing and Y-wing starfighters cruised past some of the larger vessels, including a three-hundred-meter-long Nebulon-B escort frigate, which had been converted for medical duty.

A single ship was attached to the Nebulon-B's docking tube: the *Millennium Falcon*. In the *Falcon*'s cockpit, Lando Calrissian was in the pilot's seat. As Chewbacca entered the cockpit, Lando spoke into his comlink, "Luke, we're ready for takeoff."

Luke's voice answered, "Good luck, Lando."

Lando said, "When we find Jabba the Hutt and that bounty hunter, we'll contact you."

Luke answered into his own comlink, "I'll meet you at the rendezvous point on Tatooine." Showered and wearing a clean white robe, Luke was sitting on an elevated bed in the Nebulon-B's surgery suite. The bed was adjusted to an upright position so he could watch 2-1B, the medical droid, who stood to his right. At the foot of his bed, Leia stood quietly, listening to Luke's conversation with Lando.

From Luke's comlink, Lando's voice said, "Princess, we'll find Han. I promise."

Luke thought Leia might say something, but she remained silent, so he said into his comlink, "Chewie, I'll be waiting for your signal."

The Wookiee wailed over the comlink.

Luke said, "Take care, you two. May the Force be with you."

Chewbacca's wail was heard again over the comlink, which brought a smile to Leia's face. Luke grinned back at her, but then Leia's smile seemed to melt away into an expression of sadness.

No, not sadness, Luke thought as she stepped away from him. *She's devastated. Devastated about Han.*

Leia moved across the room to join R2-D2 and the fully repaired C-3PO, who were facing a wide viewport. Luke turned his attention back to 2-1B's surgical work. At Luke's right wrist, there was an open panel that exposed the working mechanisms for his new hand, a realistic-looking synthetic replica that the droid had already attached to the end of Luke's arm.

Testing the hand's artificial nerve connections, 2-1B prodded the fingers with a thin metal pin. "Ow!" Luke said, feeling the pin's contact. Luke wriggled the fingers, made a fist, then relaxed his hand. It was completely functional.

Luke rose from the bed and stepped over beside Leia and the droids. He followed their gaze out the viewport and watched the deployed *Millennium Falcon* glide past and away from the medical frigate. He put his arm around Leia's back and held her to his side, hoping to comfort her, then he realized he was touching her shoulder with his new hand.

R2-D2 whistled as the *Falcon* flew out of sight. Still standing by Leia, Luke thought about the future. *Will we be able to rescue Han? Why didn't Ben tell me the truth? And what will I do if . . . no, not if. What will I do when I next meet Darth Vader?*

My father.

The future had once seemed so promising to Luke, but now everything seemed uncertain and complicated. What had Yoda said? *Always in motion is the future.*

The medical frigate and the rest of the Rebel fleet slowly veered onto a different course, then continued on into space.

Like his father, Anakin Skywalker, Luke Skywalker had a future to think about.

EPISODE VI

RETURN OF THE JEDI

Ryder Windham
Based on the story by George Lucas and the screenplay
by Lawrence Kasdan and George Lucas

A *long time ago, in a galaxy far, far away. . . .*

After the destruction of the Death Star, the Sith Lord Darth Vader became obsessed with finding Rebel pilot Luke Skywalker. Vader almost caught him on the ice planet Hoth, but Luke — hoping to learn more about the Jedi arts — fled to Dagobah, where he trained with the aged Jedi Master Yoda.

With the aid of the bounty hunter Boba Fett, Darth Vader captured Luke Skywalker's friends and used them as bait to lure Luke into a trap on Cloud City. Despite Yoda's admonishments, Luke went to save them, only to be brutally wounded in a lightsaber duel with Vader. The Sith Lord further stunned his adversary with the declaration that he was really Luke's father. Vader's claim was all the more shocking because Luke's trusted mentor Ben Kenobi — the Jedi Master formerly known as Obi-Wan Kenobi —

had once told Luke that his father had been murdered by Vader.

Luke managed to escape Vader's clutches, but not before his friend Han Solo — a slightly reformed smuggler — had been frozen in a block of carbonite and turned over to Boba Fett. After several run-ins with competing bounty hunters, Boba Fett delivered Han's frozen form to the vile gangster Jabba the Hutt on the sand planet Tatooine.

While Luke and his allies prepared to rescue Han, the evil Emperor Palpatine sent Darth Vader to a remote sector of space, where the Empire's most powerful secret weapon was now under construction. . . .

CHAPTER 1

The second Death Star was far from finished.

Suspended in a synchronous orbit of the gas giant Endor's forest-covered moon, the space station was — at its present stage — an immense exposed superstructure, only partially covered by armored plating. Enormous skeletal girders curled away from the completed areas, wrapping protectively around the internal reactor core that ran between the station's poles. Even in its unfinished state, it was obvious that the station would be sphere-shaped.

And like its predecessor, the station had a superlaser focus lens positioned in its upper hemisphere and a trench that ringed the equator. However, it had none of the former Death Star's design flaws. The redesigned superlaser would require mere minutes — not hours — to be recharged, and could be focused more finely, allowing it to fire at moving targets, such as capital ships. With a projected diameter of 160 kilometers and a substantial increase in firepower, the new Death Star would be not only larger than the original but also much more lethal.

An Imperial Star Destroyer arrived near the building site, then a *Lambda*-class shuttle and two TIE fighters dropped out of the Star Destroyer's main hangar. As the shuttle and its escorts traveled toward the Death Star, its captain spoke into a comlink: "Command station, this is ST Three-twenty-one. Code Clearance Blue. We're starting our approach. Deactivate the security shield."

From the Death Star, a controller answered, "The security deflector shield will be deactivated when we have confirmation of your code transmission. Stand by . . . you are clear to proceed."

"We're starting our approach."

On the shuttle, Darth Vader peered through a window at the monstrous assemblage. He thought, *Even if it succeeds where the previous Death Star failed, it is an infant's trinket compared to the power of the Force.*

As Vader's shuttle neared the space station's equatorial trench, its hinged port and starboard wings raised in preparation for landing. The TIE fighters peeled off, and the shuttle proceeded to enter a wide hangar, where it touched down on a gleaming black deck.

In the Death Star control room, the shield operators sat rigidly behind their consoles. A control officer turned from a viewport, faced one of the shield operators, and said, "Inform the commander that Lord Vader's shuttle has arrived."

"Yes, sir," the shield operator quicky replied.

The Death Star's commanding officer was Moff Jerjerrod, a tall, confident technocrat who had risen through the ranks of Logistics and Supply. Jerjerrod hurried to the hangar and walked quickly past the Imperial officers and white-armored stormtroopers who stood at attention before the landed shuttle. Despite his confidence, Jerjerrod swallowed nervously as the shuttle's landing ramp lowered. There wasn't a single Imperial soldier who hadn't heard about Darth Vader's predilection for strangling those who'd failed to carry out his orders. Jerjerrod had no intention of having his name added to Vader's list of kills.

Darth Vader strode down the ramp. From his head-concealing helmet to his shin-armored boots, he was a nightmarish figure, clad entirely in black. An outer robe fell from his shoulders to the floor behind him, and he swept onto the hangar deck like a malevolent shadow.

"Lord Vader," Jerjerrod said, "this is an unexpected pleasure. We're honored by your presence."

"You may dispense with the pleasantries, Commander," Vader said, not breaking his stride as he moved past the gathered troops. "I'm here to put you back on schedule."

Walking fast to keep abreast with the dark lord, Jerjerrod said, "I assure you, Lord Vader, my men are working as fast as they can."

"Perhaps I can find new ways to motivate them."

Jerjerrod stopped walking and promised, "I tell you, this station will be operational as planned."

Vader stopped, too. Turning to face Jerjerrod, he said, "The Emperor does not share your optimistic appraisal of the situation."

"But he asks the impossible," Jerjerrod replied. "I need more men."

"Then perhaps you can tell him when he arrives."

Jerjerrod was aghast. "The Emperor's coming here?"

"That is correct, Commander," Vader stated. "And he is most displeased with your apparent lack of progress."

Jerjerrod had been standing straight, but tried to stand even straighter as he said, "We shall double our efforts."

"I hope so, Commander, for your sake. The Emperor is not as forgiving as I am."

Vader turned and walked out of the hangar, leaving Jerjerrod behind.

Back on Tatooine, C-3PO had troubles of his own.

"Of course I'm worried," the protocol droid

replied to a question his astromech companion R2-D2 had asked. "And you should be, too. Lando Calrissian and poor Chewbacca never returned from this awful place."

The awful place was their destination: Jabba the Hutt's palace, a large fortress near the southwestern border of the Western Dune Sea. But as the droids trudged once again across the desert world's desolate terrain, R2-D2 was more optimistic about the fate of their friends. For one thing, Lando could take care of himself pretty well. Also, the droid knew that Chewbacca hadn't even arrived yet at Jabba's palace, although he didn't bother mentioning this detail to C-3PO. Sometimes, the less C-3PO knew, the better. The astromech droid rotated his domed head to whistle a timid response to his gold-plated companion.

"Don't be so sure," C-3PO said. "If I told you half the things I've heard about this Jabba the Hutt, you'd probably short-circuit."

Indeed, Jabba Desilijic Tiure was legendary for his vicious temper, endless greed, gruesome appetite, and fondness for violent entertainment. He had been the reigning crime lord in the Outer Rim Territories for hundreds of years, and his illegal enterprises included smuggling, glitterstim spice dealing, slave trading, assassination, and piracy.

Jabba's palace had been built around the ancient monastery of B'omarr monks, a mysterious religious order that believed in isolating themselves from all physical sensation to enhance the power of their minds; to achieve this, enlightened monks had their brains transplanted into nutrient-filled jars. Rumor had it that B'omarr monks still existed in the palace's lower levels. C-3PO wasn't in any hurry to find out if the rumors were true.

The palace was a cluster of domed cylindrical towers. The largest structure was an enormous citadel with a massive rust-encrusted iron door at its base. Hesitantly approaching the door, C-3PO asked, "Artoo, are you sure this is the right place?"

R2-D2 answered with an affirmative beep.

C-3PO looked for some kind of signaling device — a chime, bell, or comlink panel — but saw none. Glancing at R2-D2, he said, "I'd better knock, I suppose." C-3PO tapped lightly on the door, then stepped back and observed, "There doesn't seem to be anyone here. Let's go back and tell Master Luke."

A small circular hatch slid open on the door and a long mechanical arm rapidly extended through the hatch. At the end of the arm, there was a large electronic eyeball with a built-in vocoder. The eyeball — set within a bronze optical shutter — belonged to a surveillance droid, which glared at C-3PO and snapped, "Tee chuta hhat yudd!"

"Goodness gracious me!" C-3PO said. Facing the

electronic eyeball, he gestured to R2-D2 and said, "Artoo Detoowha . . ."

The surveillance droid's arm pivoted to turn its gaze on the R2 unit. R2-D2 beeped, and the eyeball jutted forward unexpectedly for a closer look. R2-D2 beeped and jumped back.

". . . bo Seethreepiowha," C-3PO continued, indicating himself, "ey toota odd mishka Jabba du Hutt."

Hearing his master's name, the surveillance droid made an inhuman chuckling sound. Then the mechanical arm and eyeball zipped back into the door, and the hatch slammed shut.

"I don't think they're going to let us in, Artoo," C-3PO said, turning to walk away. "We'd better go."

R2-D2 could tell C-3PO was eager to get away from the palace, but the astromech didn't budge from the closed door. Suddenly, there was a horrific metallic grinding noise and the door began to rise. The door was still opening as R2-D2 scooted under it and into the citadel's dark, cavernous entry.

"Artoo, wait," C-3PO called. "Oh, dear!" Reluctantly, he followed the little droid into the citadel, and saw his friend was already far ahead of him. "Artoo, Artoo, I really don't think we should rush into all this."

Suddenly, a spiderlike robot with spindly legs lurched out from the shadows and scuttled past

C-3PO. The robot carried a jar that contained a brain: a disembodied B'omarr monk. Frightened by the sight, C-3PO cried, "Oh, Artoo! Artoo, wait for me!"

As R2-D2 moved forward, hidden sensors in the hallway walls scanned his body. The sensors pinpointed the many sophisticated tools that were housed in R2-D2's frame, but didn't detect any concealed explosives or blasters. The sensors did notice what appeared to be a non-standard cylindrical device in R2-D2's dome, but since the object was not a projectile weapon or a bomb, the sensors let it pass.

R2-D2 kept moving through the darkness until he struck something hard. Backing up, he adjusted his optical sensors to see that he'd bumped into a large Gamorrean, a green-skinned porcine alien with a large-nostriled cartilaginous snout and upturned tusks. Suited in heavy armor, the Gamorrean loomed over the droid and grunted.

C-3PO came up fast behind R2-D2 and said, "Just you deliver Master Luke's message and get us out of here." Stopping beside R2-D2, C-3PO saw the Gamorrean guard, then saw a second Gamorrean guard emerge from the shadows and said, "Oh, my!" The iron door slammed shut behind them. C-3PO added, "Oh, no."

"Die Wanna Wanga!" rasped an alien voice from nearby. C-3PO turned to see the speaker: a tall, pale-skinned male Twi'lek with blazing red eyes. The Twi'lek wore a black silk robe and his two long *lekku* — tail-like appendages that grew out from the back of his head — were draped around his sloped shoulders.

"Oh, my!" C-3PO repeated. He bowed to the Twi'lek, then replied, "Die Wanna Wauaga. We — we bring a message to your master, Jabba the Hutt."

R2-D2 let out a series of quick beeps, prompting C-3PO to add, "And a gift." Surprised by this last detail, C-3PO glanced at R2-D2 and said, "Gift, what gift?"

The Twi'lek shook his head. "Nee labba no badda." Then he smiled, revealing a mouth filled with sharp teeth, and stepped closer to R2-D2. The Twi'lek's hands had long fingernails, and he reached down to caress the little droid's dome, clearly indicating that he would like to possess the gift himself with the words, "Me chaade su goodie."

R2-D2 recoiled from the Twi'lek's touch. The droid rotated his dome back and forth, effectively shaking his head, and let out a protesting array of squeaks.

C-3PO faced the Twi'lek and translated, "He says that our instructions are to give it only to Jabba himself!"

One of the Gamorreans grunted and snarled menacingly at the Twi'lek, making it clear that Jabba would be angered if he didn't receive the droid's message. The Twi'lek's eyes went wide with fear and anger.

Facing the Twi'lek, C-3PO gestured to R2-D2 and said, "I'm terribly sorry. I'm afraid he's ever so stubborn about these sort of things."

The Twi'lek glared at the droids, then said, "Nudd chaa," and motioned them toward a dark doorway. One of the Gamorrean guards tagged along as the droids followed the Twi'lek to a tunneled stairway.

C-3PO said, "Artoo, I have a bad feeling about this."

The Twi'lek's name was Bib Fortuna, and he was Jabba's chief lieutenant. But Bib was hardly loyal to his master, and secretly anticipated the day the Hutt would croak his last. Grumbling to himself, Bib led the droids and Gamorrean guard down a flight of steps and into the Hutt's throne room.

The throne room was a dimly illuminated chamber that was literally crawling with grotesque creatures, most of whom were intoxicated. Numerous aliens cavorted on an elevated bandstand and various smoke-filled nooks. Jabba himself rested his bulky, gluttonous form upon a broad dais, and lazily sucked on a pipe linked to a naal thorn burner.

Beside the burner sat Salacious Crumb, a small Kowakian monkey-lizard with small beady eyes, long pointed ears, and a nasty laugh. Behind Jabba stood a short Jawa, who held a long-stalked palm and gently fanned the air around the Hutt. To Jabba's right, a lovely green-skinned female Twi'lek named Oola perched at the edge of the dais. Oola was one of Jabba's many slaves, and she wore a collar around her neck — Jabba held the leash.

Bib left the droids standing beside a wide metal grating on the floor in front of Jabba, then stepped up onto the dais and whispered to the Hutt. Jabba chortled and blinked his bulbous eyes. When he was done laughing, he let his gaze settle on the two.

C-3PO bowed and said, "Good morning." Turning to R2-D2, he said, "The message, Artoo, the message."

Impatient, Jabba exclaimed, "Bo shuda!"

R2-D2 rotated his dome and aimed his holographic message projector into the air behind him. All eyes turned to see a light-generated three-dimensional image of a black-uniformed human male materialize within the throne room. Because of the way R2-D2 had positioned himself, the hologram appeared to be facing Jabba. At approximately three meters tall, the hologram was larger than life.

"Greetings, Exalted One," the figure in the hologram said. "Allow me to introduce myself. I am Luke Skywalker, Jedi Knight, and friend to Captain Solo. I know that you are powerful, mighty Jabba, and that your anger with Solo must be equally powerful. I seek an audience with Your Greatness to bargain for Solo's life."

Hearing this, Jabba and his crowd laughed heartily.

"With your wisdom," Luke's hologram continued, "I'm sure that we can work out an arrangement which will be mutually beneficial and enable us to avoid any unpleasant confrontation. As a token of my goodwill, I present to you a gift: these two droids."

"What did he say?" C-3PO asked with alarm.

Luke's hologram continued, "Both are hardworking and will serve you well." With that, the hologram flickered off.

"This can't be!" C-3PO cried. "Artoo, you're playing the wrong message."

Bib whispered again to Jabba. In Huttese, Jabba replied loudly, "There will be no bargain."

Hearing this, C-3PO muttered, "We're doomed."

Jabba continued, "I will not give up my favorite decoration. I like Captain Solo where he is." The Hutt gestured with his meaty right hand to the other side of the throne room. The two droids followed the direction of Jabba's gesture to a display alcove. There, a dark gray rectangular slab was suspended vertically by a force field, and a man's figure — the same color as the slab — was set like a low-relief statue. The man's eyes were squeezed shut, and his mouth a silent cry.

"Artoo, look!" C-3PO said. "Captain Solo. And he's still frozen in carbonite."

C-3PO had been present in the Cloud City carbon-freezing chamber when Darth Vader had orchestrated the freezing of Han Solo. Vader had used Han as a test subject to determine whether a human could survive the freezing process, as Vader had intended to freeze Luke as well. Luke had evaded freezing and had been rescued by his allies, but they'd been unable to stop Boba Fett from fleeing Cloud City with Han's frozen form.

Obviously, Boba Fett had collected Jabba's bounty for Han Solo. And Han had been hanging on Jabba's wall ever since.

R2-D2 let out a worried beep.

Jabba instructed the Gamorrean guard to take C-3PO and R2-D2 to the cyborg operations supervisor. Leaving the throne room, the Gamorrean marched the two droids down a shadowy passageway that was lined with holding cells. Cries from imprisoned creatures echoed off the cold stone walls.

"What could possibly have come over Master Luke?" C-3PO wondered aloud. "Is it something I did? He never expressed any unhappiness with my work." C-3PO saw a repulsive hand reach out between the bars of a cell door and try to grab him. "Oh! Oh!" the protocol droid exclaimed. "How horrid!" Trying to avoid the hand, he moved to the other side of the passage. A long tentacle snaked out from between the bars of another cell door, and C-3PO felt the tentacle wrap around his neck.

"Ohh!" he wailed as he pulled himself free.

R2-D2 beeped pitifully as they moved to a thick metal door at the end of the passage. The door slid up into the ceiling, revealing a boiler room filled with steam and noisy machinery. The guard motioned R2-D2 and C-3PO into the boiler room, where a second guard awaited them.

Proceeding through the chamber, C-3PO noticed a white-metal 8D8 smelting droid who operated a rotating vise; the vise held a power droid, and the 8D8 rotated the power droid into an inverted position. When the power droid's two legs were positioned above its upside-down body, the 8D8 lowered red-hot branding irons onto its blocky feet. C-3PO cringed as the power droid let out an agonized electronic screech.

A few steps beyond the rotating vise, they arrived before Jabba's cyborg operations supervisor: a tall, skeletal robot named Eve-Ninedenine, who stood before an ancient, rickety computer console. C-3PO was distracted by the horrific sight of a nearby humanoid droid who was stretched out on what appeared to be a vertical torture rack, which was slowly pumping up and down, tugging at the unfortunate victim's manacled limbs.

Looking up at C-3PO and R2-D2, Eve-Ninedenine said, "Ah, good. New acquisitions." The robot's synthesized female voice sounded as if it had been stolen from an elderly prison matron, and as she spoke, her hinged vocoder flapped up and down beneath her sharp metal chin. Sizing up C-3PO, Eve-Ninedenine said, "You are a protocol droid, are you not?"

"I am See-Threepio, Human Cy —"

"Yes or no will do," Eve-Ninedenine interrupted.

"Oh," C-3PO said. "Well, yes."

Ninedenine said, "How many languages do you speak?"

"I am fluent in over six million forms of communication and can readily —"

"Splendid!" Eve-Ninedenine said, cutting off C-3PO again. "We have been without an interpreter since our master got angry with our last protocol droid and disintegrated him."

Hearing this, and remembering the incident, one Gamorrean guard clutched his broad belly and chuckled.

"Disintegrated?" C-3PO gasped, his voice filled with panic. Then he heard a snapping sound from the torture rack, and turned to see the upper rack had lifted higher than its mechanical victim's limbs could extend. Sparks exploded from the poor droid's arm and leg sockets.

Eve-Ninedenine rotated her head to one of the Gamorreans and said, "Guard! This protocol droid might be useful. Fit him with a restraining bolt and take him back up to His Excellency's main audience chamber."

The Gamorrean shoved C-3PO toward the door. The golden droid yelled, "Artoo, don't leave me! Ohhh!"

R2-D2 let out a plaintive cry as the door closed. Then he rotated his dome and beeped angrily at Eve-Ninedenine.

"You're a feisty little one," Eve-Ninedenine said, "but you'll soon learn some respect. I have need for you on the master's sail barge. And I think you'll fill in nicely."

The smelting droid lowered the branding irons again on the upside-down power droid's feet, and again the power droid screeched. R2-D2, who'd visited many inhospitable places in his long lifetime, decided that Jabba's palace was the absolute worst.

If any other crime lord had received a slightly threatening holographic message from someone who claimed to be a Jedi Knight, the crime lord might have prepared to negotiate, flee to another planet, or surrender entirely. But Jabba was not just any other crime lord, so he decided to throw a party.

It was a lewd and noisy affair, with semi-clad alien females gyrating to the rhythms of the Max Rebo band. On the bandstand, Max Rebo — a blue-skinned Ortolan who played a Red Ball Jett organ — performed a relatively slow tune; he was accompanied by a froglike Shawda Ubb named Rapotwanalantonee — everyone called him Rappertunie — who played the growdi, a combination flute and water organ. While the music played, the nubile Twi'lek Oola danced evocatively beside the fleshy rumblings of Yarna d'al Gargan on the floor in front of Jabba's dais. From his dais, Jabba kept his grip on

Oola's leash as he drooled and watched her green body move.

Although Jabba may have appeared carefree, he had taken at least two precautions against the possible arrival of Luke Skywalker. First, he had instructed Bib Fortuna to make sure Skywalker didn't set foot inside the palace. Second, he'd made sure that his party included one particularly well-armed guest: Boba Fett.

Wearing the helmet he'd inherited from his father, Boba Fett was completely concealed within his weapon-laden suit, which included wrist-rocket gauntlets, kneepad rocket dart launchers, spring-loaded boot spikes, a turbo-projected grappling hook, and a bulky missile-firing jet backpack. His preferred weapon was a BlasTech EE-3 blaster rifle that he'd modified to fire with one hand; it was rarely out of his grip.

Fett had done various jobs for Jabba over the years, starting when he was a young boy, primarily as an enforcer. To most debtors, the very idea of receiving a visit from the merciless bounty hunter was good enough reason to make sure they paid Jabba on time. Boba Fett stood near the alcove that displayed the carbonite-frozen Han Solo and surveyed the throne room.

To the bounty hunter, everyone in the palace was

a suspicious character, so all he could really do was stand back and watch for Skywalker. But Fett watched the band's three female alien backup singers, too. One of them, a beautiful red-haired ungulate in a form-fitting body glove, looked down from the stage and winked at him.

Boba Fett's presence was also noticed by C-3PO. Having encountered him before, the golden droid kept his distance.

The music came to a close and Rappertunie bowed his small, chubby head to the audience. Jabba tugged at Oola's leash and said in Huttese, "Ah! Do that again!"

One of Max Rebo's singers, a short, furry alien named Joh Yowza, thought Jabba was demanding another tune. In a deep, raspy voice, Yowza called out, "One, two, three!"

This prompted Rappertunie to start playing another song, but it wasn't the one Yowza wanted. Yowza shouted, "No, daddy, no! One, two, three!"

The entire band kicked in, and the three backup singers slinked onto the stage. The drunken audience hooted and yowled when lead singer Sy Snootles — a spindly-legged temptress with blue-spotted yellow-green skin — strutted out from behind the other singers and seized the microphone. Snootles' most notable physical feature was her mouth, which was at the end of a thirty-centimeter-long protrusion extending from her brightly mottled head. Her full, luscious lips were painted bright red.

Although Max Rebo had been leading his ensemble through a variation on a popular jizz-wailer standard, Sy Snootles slyly batted her long eyelashes and began belting out improvised lyrics that would have been officially banned by the Empire. Members of the audience found this amusing, except for the prudish Bib Fortuna, who was mortified. As for C-3PO, the protocol droid was completely bewildered by Sy Snootles' blatant misuse of several verbs.

While the music played, Jabba — with a lascivious gleam in his eye — beckoned Oola to come sit with him. The Hutt bellowed, "Da eitha!"

Oola stopped dancing and backed away, shaking her head. "Na chuba negatori Na! Na! Natoota . . ."

Furious, Jabba pulled hard at the leash, pointed to his dais, and commanded, "Boscka!"

Oola pulled back on the taut leash and continued to protest.

Jabba slammed his fist down on a button. Before Oola could step aside, a trapdoor opened beneath her and she plummeted through the floor. The musicians and singers went silent and looked to the spot where Oola had vanished. The trapdoor snapped shut and Jabba's cretinous friends hurried to peer down through the metal grating to view a deep pit below the floor.

Oola tumbled out of the hole and onto the dirt floor of the deep, high-walled pit. She rose quickly and stood to face a large iron door that was set into one of the pit's walls. Oola trembled as the door began to rise, and a muffled growl came from the other side. She knew what was coming, and that she was about to die, but she had already decided that death was preferable to spending one more moment as Jabba's slave.

While Jabba's friends looked down through the grating to watch Oola meet her doom, C-3PO shook his head and turned away. He glanced wistfully at the carbonite form of Han Solo, and wondered if he'd ever leave Jabba's palace in one piece.

Suddenly, there was the sound of blasterfire from a nearby stairway. C-3PO and everyone else turned to face the steps that led up to the citadel's main entrance. One of Jabba's bolder goons ran up the steps to find the source of the blasterfire, but a moment later he came falling back and landed in an unconscious heap on the floor.

Fett had heard the blast and seen the goon fall, but that sort of violence wasn't unusual in the palace. He returned his attention to Rystáll, the alluring singer who'd captured his attention and now stood close beside him, admiring his helmet. Using his helmet's targeting rangefinder, he kept an eye on the nearby stairway.

Two figures descended the steps and entered the throne room. The first was a bounty hunter completely clad in leather, including a head-concealing helmet with a metal speech scrambler and head bracket; the bracket was equipped with a vision-plus scanner and built-in targeting laser. In one leather-gloved hand, the hunter carried a long lance tipped with a shock blade. The other hand held a leash that was secured to a collar around the neck of the second figure: a tall, furry Wookiee, who appeared weak and dazed.

Keeping a firm grip on the leash, the masked hunter bowed to Jabba. Then, in a digitally scrambled male voice that sounded like a scratchy, guttural monotone, the hunter said in Ubese, "I am Boushh. I have come for the bounty on this Wookiee."

Hearing this, C-3PO peeked out from behind Jabba's henchmen and quietly cried, "Oh, no! Chewbacca!"

Jabba didn't speak Ubese, but he did recognize the captive Wookiee. From his dais, Jabba grinned and said, "At last we have the mighty Chewbacca."

The Hutt summoned C-3PO. Stepping up beside him, the protocol droid said, "Oh, us, yes, uh, I am here, Your Worshipfulness. Uh . . . yes!"

Jabba made a statement in Huttese. C-3PO turned to Boushh and translated, "Oh, the illustrious Jabba bids you welcome and will gladly pay you the reward of twenty-five thousand."

Boushh answered in Ubese, "I want fifty thousand. No less."

Turning to Jabba, C-3PO translated, "Fifty thousand. No less."

Aghast, Jabba flew into a rage. One of his thick arms lashed out and pushed the protocol droid, who fell off the dais and clattered to the floor below. Boushh casually transferred the lance from one hand to the other, so both the lance and leash were held in the hunter's right glove.

Rising from the floor, C-3PO muttered, "Oh, oh . . . but what, what did I say?"

Jabba addressed Boushh. As Jabba spoke, Boba Fett stepped away from Rystáll and moved to stand where he had a clear view of both Boushh and the Wookiee.

Jabba finished talking and looked at C-3PO. Switching back to Ubese, C-3PO faced Boushh and said, "Uh, the mighty Jabba asks why he must pay fifty thousand."

Boushh's left hand reached into an ammo pocket, removed a metal orb, and thumbed a switch on the orb. As a small light flashed at the switch's base, Boushh answered.

Cringing, C-3PO nervously translated, "Because he's holding a thermal detonator!"

Max Rebo covered his eyes with his stubby blue fingers, and Salacious Crumb — along with almost everyone else — dived for protective cover.

But Fett didn't hesitate, drawing his blaster rifle with incredible speed and aiming its barrel at Boushh. He recognized the thermal detonator as a Class-A type that would yield a blast radius of about twenty meters. He could also determine from the detonator's activation indicator light that Boushh had the trigger's control pins programmed to act as a deadman's switch: if Boushh's thumb came off the detonator's trigger, everyone and everything within the throne room — except for maybe a few pieces of Fett's armor — would be instantly disintegrated. Despite his reflexes, Boba Fett knew he wouldn't make it out of the room fast enough, but he wasn't about to die cowering on the floor.

A tense silence filled the throne room. Then Jabba the Hutt tilted his massive head back and began to laugh. When he caught his breath, he gestured to Boushh and said in Huttese, "This bounty hunter is my kind of scum . . . fearless and inventive."

Seeing that Jabba seemed to be in control of the situation, Fett lowered his blaster rifle slightly. Jabba made an offer to Boushh, which C-3PO translated: "Jabba offers the sum of thirty-five." Facing Boushh, the golden droid added, "And I *do* suggest you take it."

Boushh deactivated the thermal detonator and said, "Zeebuss."

"He agrees!" C-3PO exclaimed with immense relief. The throne room was filled with cheers and applause, and the raucous party resumed.

A pair of Gamorrean guards grabbed Chewbacca and hauled him out of the room. Boushh spoke briefly to C-3PO, then Bib Fortuna leaned in and muttered something about financial arrangements to Boushh. Bib stepped away, then both Boushh and C-3PO turned to see Boba Fett watching them from across the room. Fett slowly nodded his helmeted head to mutely acknowledge the other hunter.

Time and again, Fett had proven that he didn't have any real competition in the bounty hunter trade. However, Boushh had just demonstrated that even he could be caught unprepared.

Boba Fett was determined it wouldn't happen again.

The Gamorrean guards led Chewbacca down a curved stairway to the dungeon. But before the Wookiee left the throne room, he caught sight of an armored man who wielded a large vibro-ax. A bizarre helmet with a fang-adorned strap concealed the man's features, but Chewbacca saw through Lando Calrissian's disguise.

Lando had used an old underworld contact on Tatooine to secure a guard job at Jabba's palace, where he'd been assigned work — under the name Tamtel Skreej — on one of the Hutt's sand skiffs. It had pained Lando to watch the Gamorreans shove Chewbacca toward the doorway that led to the dungeon, but he let it happen because he knew the time had not yet come to fight.

Night fell on Tatooine, and darkness flooded Jabba's palace. When the drinks had all been poured and the last reveler had either left or passed out, a single figure stepped silently through the throne room. It was Boushh.

Boushh moved stealthily past a group of snoring, drunken creatures. Arriving before the display alcove, the bounty hunter looked up at the carbonite slab that contained Han Solo's frozen form. Below the slab, the floor was covered with sand. If there were any concealed security devices, Boushh did not see them.

Boushh stepped into the alcove and found two illuminated buttons on the wall, just below a curtained lift shaft. A press of the lower button deactivated the force field that held the slab suspended in the air. The slab slowly lowered to the floor — at least until it unexpectedly teetered and fell back, smacking against the wall with a loud thud.

Boushh glanced around and made sure that the nearby creatures were still sleeping. They were, and Boushh's attention returned to the slab that now leaned upright against the wall.

Control panels were set along the outer side edges of the carbonite frame. Boushh pressed a button beside the carbonite flux monitor, then slid the decarbonization lever and watched a green light flicker on the life system monitor.

The case began to emit a sound as the hard shell that covered the contours of Han's face began to melt away. Boushh watched bright energy spill out of the broken carbon shell. Sooner than expected, the metallic coat of carbonite drained off, and Han's slack body fell forward, away from the slab, collapsing on the sandy floor.

Boushh knelt beside Han and struggled to raise him. His hair and skin were wet and cold, and he was shaking all over.

Speaking in Basic, Boushh's scratchy, digitized voice said, "Just relax for a moment. You're free of the carbonite."

Han opened his eyes and reached for Boushh's mask.

"Shhh," Boushh said. "You have hibernation sickness."

"I can't see," Han said.

"Your eyesight will return in time," Boushh replied, helping him up to a sitting position.

Han continued to shake. "Where am I?"

"Jabba's palace."

"Who are you?"

Boushh reached up to remove the leather and metal helmet, revealing the face of Princess Leia. In her own voice, she said, "Someone who loves you."

"Leia!"

Leia kissed Han. She'd feared she'd never see him again, at least not alive, but here he was in her arms. For all the lost time, and because time was precious, she had to kiss him.

Then she remembered where they were. Her lips left his and she said, "I gotta get you out of here." She wrapped her arms around his torso and pulled him up to his feet.

Then they both heard a sound: a low, rumbling guffaw.

"What's that?" Han asked, straining his temporarily blinded eyes to seek out the source of laughter in the darkness. "I know that laugh."

Above the alcove, a curtain slid back from the lift shaft, revealing Jabba the Hutt and his chortling minions. Han and Leia slowly turned to face the crime lord. Salacious Crumb sat within the folds of Jabba's curved, meaty tail. Behind Jabba, C-3PO stood between Bib Fortuna and a three-eyed Gran named Ree-Yees. C-3PO had been unable to caution Leia because Ree-Yees' right hand was plastered over his vocoder.

Leia held Han close to her. Behind them, another curtain slid away from a stairway that led up to the palace's guest quarters. From the stairs, Boba Fett and Jabba's guards moved forward to the display alcove.

Han blinked his eyes and said, "Hey, Jabba. Look, Jabba. I was just on my way to pay you back, but I got a little sidetracked. It's not my fault."

"It's too late for that, Solo," Jabba said in Huttese. "You may have been a good smuggler, but now you're bantha fodder." Jabba laughed again, and Salacious Crumb joined in, cackling wildly.

Han said, "Look —"

"Take him away," Jabba ordered.

"Jabba . . ." Han said as he was seized by two guards and pulled away from Leia. "I'll pay you triple! You're throwing away a fortune here. Don't be a fool!"

As Han was hauled out of the room, a Gamorrean guard and the disguised Lando Calrissian came up on either side of Leia and gripped her arms. Jabba said, "Bring her to me."

The guards obeyed and escorted the princess so she was nearly up against the Hutt. Glaring at

Jabba, Leia said boldly, "We have powerful friends. You're going to regret this."

"I'm sure," Jabba slobbered. His tongue lolled out of his wide mouth and brushed against the side of her face and clothes.

"Ugh!" Leia said, recoiling.

C-3PO trembled and looked away. "Ohhh, I can't bear to watch," he cried.

Jabba thought Leia had a pleasant flavor, but he didn't care much for her drab, dusty clothes. He ordered Bib Fortuna to fetch some garments that were more to his taste. . . .

Jabba's guards brought Han down to the dungeon, shoved him into a cell, and locked the door behind him. In the middle of the cell's floor, there was a dirty puddle; Han splashed through it and nearly stumbled, but his groping hands caught the stone wall and he steadied himself. He still felt painfully cold and he couldn't stop trembling.

Suddenly, a growl came from the far side of the cell. Startled, Han jerked away from the sound, then he blinked his sightless eyes and said, "Chewie? Chewie, is that you?"

Chewbacca barked and stepped out from his shadowy corner. The Wookiee flung his furry arms around his friend.

Han said, "Chew — Chewie!"

Chewbacca barked some more.

"Wait, I can't see you, pal," Han explained. "What's goin' on?"

Chewbacca barked his reply.

There wasn't anything wrong with Han's hearing, and he couldn't believe what the Wookiee had just told him. "Luke?" Han said. "Luke's crazy. He can't even take care of himself, much less *rescue* anybody."

Chewbacca barked more.

"A — a Jedi Knight?" Han said with disbelief. "I'm out of it for a little while, everybody gets delusions of grandeur."

The Wookiee growled insistently. Then he hugged Han close to his chest and patted his head, trying to warm him.

"I'm all right, pal," Han said. "I'm all right."

But Chewbacca hadn't finished bringing Han up-to-date. He quickly informed Han that Lando Calrissian — who'd betrayed them to Darth Vader on Cloud City — had become their ally, and that Lando had already secretly infiltrated Jabba's palace.

If the information had come from anyone other than Chewbacca, Han would've never believed it. He found it difficult to imagine he could ever trust Lando again. But if they all got out of this mess alive, he was willing to give it a try.

The next morning, two Gamorrean guards were stationed in the dark entrance of Jabba's palace when the massive iron door began to rumble open. As the door lifted, bright sunlight poured in, revealing a solitary, silhouetted figure standing outside. The figure stepped through the doorway and into the cavernous hallway.

The hallway's hidden sensors scanned the figure: a human male who wore a black hooded robe. Beneath, the man was clad in a black tunic, pants, a leather belt, and boots. The sensors quickly determined he was not carrying any weapons . . . but he *did* have one unusual feature: his right hand appeared externally normal but was actually a fully functional mechanical replica. If this detail concerned Jabba's security system, it didn't stop the iron door from sliding shut behind the man.

When the man was halfway through the entrance hall, the two Gamorreans stepped out of the shadows and raised their axes to block his path. They'd expected him to surrender or run away, and were surprised when he stopped, raised a hand, and gestured at them. Both guards were instantly compelled to lower their weapons and fell back to their stations.

Luke Skywalker proceeded into the palace.

Once again, there was silence in Jabba's throne room. There had been another party, and more drinks and brain cells had gone the way of those previous. Behind Jabba's dais, C-3PO maintained a nervous watch over the sleeping bodies sprawled throughout the multileveled lair.

Leia, eyes closed, lay slumped beside Jabba's slumbering form. She had replaced Oola as Jabba's slave dancer, and was worried about the acrobatic dances she might have to perform. She wore a collar around her neck that was secured to a long chain. She also wore a skimpy costume that left very little of her unexposed to view. Salacious Crumb — who remained awake — leaned over from his resting spot within the curve of Jabba's tail and peeked at Leia's bare stomach.

Bib Fortuna was also awake. Hearing the sound of footsteps descending the stairway from the main entrance, he ran up and saw Luke coming down. The Twi'lek muttered in Huttese, telling Luke to leave immediately.

Luke simply said, "I must speak with Jabba."

Hearing these words, Leia opened her eyes and sat up. *Luke!*

On the stairway, Bib tried to hold off Luke. Shaking his tailed head, he said, "Shh. Ee toe seet. Jabba no two zand dehank obee. No pahgan."

Luke stared hard at Bib and said, "You will take me to Jabba now!"

Bib did not realize that Luke was using the Force to influence his thoughts. Reacting as if it had been his own idea to bring Luke to Jabba, Bib said, "Et tu takku u Jabba now," and motioned for Luke to continue down the stairs.

As Luke descended after Bib into the throne room, he said, "You serve your master well."

"Eye sota va locha," Bib agreed.

Luke added, "And you will be rewarded."

Leia saw Luke approach the dais but remained silent. From behind Jabba, C-3PO cried out, "At last! Master Luke's come to rescue me!"

Jabba's guards also noticed Luke's arrival and edged toward him cautiously. Bib Fortuna stepped up onto the dais, leaned close to the side of Jabba's broad head, and whispered, "Master."

Jabba's heavy eyelids slid back and he let out a wet snort. The noise awakened others in the room, who looked over to the dais to see what was going on. Jabba shifted his weight slightly, and Leia felt the slave collar tug against her throat.

Gesturing to Luke on the floor below the dais, Bib continued, "Luke Skywalker, Jedi Knight."

Outraged, Jabba said in Huttese, "I told you not to admit him."

"I must be allowed to speak," Luke insisted.

In Huttese, Bib said, "He must be allowed to speak."

"You weak-minded fool!" Jabba scowled. "He's using an old Jedi mind trick." Bib yelped as Jabba shoved him off the dais.

Luke sighted the disguised Lando among Jabba's guards. Several Gamorreans had moved up behind

Luke, but he remained outwardly calm and composed. He pulled back his hood to reveal his face. On the dais, Boba Fett emerged to stand beside the Hutt.

Staring hard at Jabba, Luke said, "You will bring Captain Solo and the Wookiee to me."

Jabba laughed. "Your mind powers will not work on me, boy."

He's stronger than I imagined, Luke realized. Moving closer to Jabba, he said, "Nevertheless, I'm taking Captain Solo and his friends. You can either profit by this . . . or be destroyed. It's your choice. But I warn you not to underestimate my powers."

C-3PO saw that Luke had stepped directly onto the trapdoor. "Master Luke," the droid called out, "you're standing on —"

But Jabba interrupted, "There will be no bargain, young Jedi. I shall enjoy watching you die."

Jabba's guards advanced toward Luke. Luke extended his right hand, and a guard's blaster suddenly jumped out of its holster and flew into Luke's waiting hand. As Luke raised the blaster to Jabba, a Gamorrean lunged at him, grabbing his arm.

Jabba shouted, "Boscka!" and brought his hand down on the trapdoor's control button. As the trapdoor opened, the Gamorrean squeezed Luke's arm and the blaster fired into the ceiling. Both Luke and the Gamorrean plunged into the pit beneath the throne room.

Jabba's dais slid forward across the floor, sealing the trapdoor.

Tumbling through the hole, Luke lost the blaster. He landed amidst the skeletal remains of various creatures. Expecting to fight the Gamorrean who'd fallen into the pit with him, he whipped off his black robe and rose to his feet. The Gamorrean was still rising when Luke glanced up at the bottom of the grating, where Jabba and his courtiers gazed down at him and laughed.

Luke saw Leia and C-3PO through the grating far above him. There was fear in Leia's eyes. Luke thought, *Don't be afraid, Leia! We're going to get out of here.*

Then there was a rumbling sound, and Luke looked to the pit's far wall, where a large iron door began to rise up into a slot in the rocky ceiling. A horrific growl echoed from a holding cave beyond the door, and the Gamorrean started squealing hysterically. From above, C-3PO cried out, "Oh, no! The rancor!"

Luke thought, *What am I up against now?* The door was still rising when he had his first glimpse of the monster's massive claws. Luke sensed that the rancor's ferocity matched its size, and his eyes went wide with alarm as the rancor hunched its form and pushed its way through the doorway.

Lurching into the pit on two powerful legs, the rancor revealed itself to be a reptile-like beast, roughly five meters tall. It had an enormous, fanged maw set beneath a pair of small glowing eyes. Its head and jaws seemed to take up most of its body; its two long arms ended in absurdly long, sharp talons. A broken chain dangled from a manacle at its right wrist.

The rancor opened its wide mouth and roared at the Gamorrean, who tried futilely to scramble out of the pit. Luke noticed the pit's walls bore deep scratches and claw marks from others who'd tried to escape the rancor and failed.

While Jabba and his cohorts cackled and jeered, the rancor reached out and snatched up the Gamorrean. The smaller creature kicked and squealed as the rancor popped him into its mouth. *Crunch!* The rancor tilted its head back and swallowed the guard, armor and all.

Then the monster turned for Luke. Above them, Jabba the Hutt smiled grotesquely.

The rancor swiped at Luke, but the young man jumped aside. A long arm-bone from an earlier victim lay on the pit floor, and Luke seized it. Suddenly, the rancor's talons wrapped around Luke's body and lifted him off his feet.

Luke clung to the bone as the rancor drew him to

its salivating mouth. The rancor's fangs were still slick with the Gamorrean's blood, and the stench of gore was almost overwhelming. With a sharp twist, Luke wedged the bone into the rancor's mouth, forcing its jaws back. Startled, the beast reflexively released Luke, who fell to the floor.

There was a loud snap, and Luke glanced up to see the rancor had crushed the bone. Luke found a small crevice in the pit wall and scurried into it. Gazing past the monster to the holding cave beyond, he spotted a utility door. *If I can just get to it . . .*

The hungry rancor saw Luke and reached into the crevice. Luke grabbed a large rock and smashed it down on the rancor's talon. The rancor howled.

Luke rolled out of the crevice and ran for the holding cave, which was littered with even more bones. He reached the utility door and pushed a button. The door slid open, but a heavy barred gate separated him from the adjoining chamber, in which two guards — the rancor's keepers — were playfully fighting over their dinner. They stopped fighting when they saw Luke. Luke turned to see the monster was still in the pit. He pulled with all his might on the gate but with no effect. On the other side of the gate, the two guards picked up spears and laughed as they poked at Luke, forcing him away.

As the rancor hunched down and prepared to enter the holding cave, Luke noticed a control panel halfway up the wall beside the doorway. Thinking fast, he picked up a skull from the cave floor and hurled it. The rancor was just ducking its head through the doorway when the thrown skull smashed against the control panel, destroying the iron door's lifting mechanism. The heavy door came crashing down upon the rancor's head, its sharp stakes pinning the monster to the floor.

There was a collective gasp from the watchers above. The rancor wasn't merely pinned; the door's pointed base had actually pierced and crushed the monster's skull. Its left talon flexed once, then went slack. The rancor was dead.

Breathing hard, Luke fell back against the wall of the holding cave. The rancor's keepers opened the gate and entered, passing Luke to examine their dead beast. One of the keepers broke down and wept. The other glared menacingly at Luke, who was unfazed.

Several guards immediately rushed into the holding cave and took Luke away. The guards were surprised and disappointed when Luke didn't resist.

Up in the throne room, Jabba was fuming. He couldn't believe that Luke had killed his prized rancor. Glowering at his guards, he commanded in Huttese, "Bring me Solo and the Wookiee. They will all suffer for this outrage."

The guards hurried out, and soon returned with

the two prisoners. From a different stairway, other guards — including Lando — dragged Luke into the throne room. As they were hauled before Jabba's dais, Luke shouted, "Han!"

"Luke!" Han called back. He still couldn't see, but he was pretty sure he could smell Jabba nearby.

"Are you all right?" Luke asked.

"Fine," Han replied. "Together again, huh?"

"Wouldn't miss it."

"How are we doing?"

Luke grinned. "The same as always."

"That bad, huh? Where's Leia?"

"I'm here," Leia said from Jabba's side. With the slave collar still tight around her neck, and Jabba stroking her like a domestic pet, she was almost relieved that Han was still blinded.

Boba Fett remained near Jabba and kept an alert watch on the captives while the Hutt began speaking in Huttese. C-3PO listened and said, "Oh, dear." As Jabba continued, C-3PO translated, "His High Exaltedness, the great Jabba the Hutt, has decreed that you are to be terminated immediately."

"Good," Han said. "I hate long waits."

Jabba prattled on, and C-3PO conveyed, "You will therefore be taken to the Dune Sea and cast into the Pit of Carkoon, the nesting place of the all-powerful Sarlacc."

Han leaned closer to Luke and muttered, "Doesn't sound so bad."

"In his belly," the protocol droid continued, "you will find a new definition of pain and suffering as you are slowly digested over a thousand years."

"On second thought," Han interjected, "let's pass on that, huh?"

As the guards hauled Chewbacca, Han, and Luke out of the throne room, Luke glared at the Hutt and said, "You should have bargained, Jabba. That's the last mistake you'll make."

Jabba laughed heartily and tugged the chain that held Leia, forcing her back against his slimy bulk. Leia thought, *This isn't going to end well, Jabba. Not for you!*

Under a clear blue sky, a herd of wild, thick-furred banthas trekked across the western Dune Sea, the large area of sandy desert that stretched across the Tatooine wastes. Bound for a distant mesa, the banthas ignored the three repulsorlift vessels that passed in the distance. The vessels — one large and two small — glided several meters above the sand, heading north. Even the banthas knew better than to travel that way across the Dune Sea, if only to avoid the Great Pit of Carkoon.

The three craft were owned by Jabba the Hutt. The two smaller repulsorlifts were matching nine-meter-long open-topped cargo skiffs, which Jabba had had armor plated. Hardly more than flying platforms, the skiffs were without seats, so the pilot and passengers all stood on an exposed deck that was edged with a low protective railing. The first skiff flew as escort to the larger vessel and carried a group of Jabba's goons; the second skiff carried six guards — including Lando, in disguise — and three bound captives: Luke, Han, and Chewbacca.

The larger repulsorlift was Jabba's sail barge. Thirty meters in length, the *Khetanna* had been designed as a luxury pleasure craft, although most of its expensive trappings had been stripped years ago. Its two bright orange sails — primarily used as awnings to protect those on deck from the glare of Tatooine's suns — had faded considerably, and its hull and interior were mostly bare metal. What it lacked in comforts, however, it made up for with armor plating, a custom-mounted deck blaster cannon, plenty of room for Jabba's guests, and an extremely well-stocked kitchen. By any standards, the barge had style.

But Leia's standards were higher than most. *The sooner I get off this stinking death trap, the better.* She was inside the banquet room, located on the deck below the privacy lounge at the barge's stern. Because Jabba preferred the dry heat of Tatooine, the barge's air-conditioning system had been removed long ago and replaced with retractable window shutters. Still scantily clad, Leia sat beside an open window on the barge's port side and gazed at her captured friends on the skiff traveling alongside.

Jabba and his cronies were laughing and drinking heavily. Bounty hunter Boba Fett paced, instinctively eyeing the horizon for any signs of trouble. R2-D2 had been outfitted as an ambulatory bar, and was serving drinks — mostly spice-spiked flameouts and pink-and-green bantha blasters — from an elaborately decorated gold tray that wrapped around the back of his domed head. The Hutt downed another drink, then tugged at the chain attached to Leia's collar, just to remind her who was boss. Leia winced at the sharp jerk from the chain but clung to the edge of the window to keep her eyes on the skiff.

On the skiff, the captive trio stood close to one another behind a guard who was acting as lead lookout on the prow. Han squinted at the desert sky and said, "I think my eyes are getting better. Instead of a big dark blue, I see a big light blur."

"There's nothing to see," Luke said. "I used to live here, you know."

"You're gonna *die* here, you know," Han said. "Convenient."

"Just stick close to Chewie and Lando," Luke said, scanning the desert before them. "I've taken care of everything."

Sounding very unconvinced, Han said, "Oh . . . great!"

On the barge, Jabba pulled hard this time at the chain that bound Leia, yanking her away from the window and up against his side. She tried to pull away, but Bib Fortuna moved in behind her and pressed his long-fingered hand against her bare back, pushing her against the drooling Hutt. Jabba raised a goblet to Leia and drunkenly burbled in Huttese, "Soon you will learn to appreciate me."

C-3PO was also traveling on the barge. As he made his way past a group of intoxicated aliens, he bumped into a shorter droid who was carrying a tray of drinks. The tray and goblets clattered to the floor, and the droid immediately let out a series of angry beeps and whistles. Looking down, C-3PO said, "Oh, I'm terribly sor — Artoo! What are you doing here?"

R2-D2 thought his appearance spoke for itself, but the astromech beeped a quick reply.

"Well, I can *see* you're serving drinks," C-3PO said. "But this place is dangerous. They're going to execute Master Luke and, if we're not careful, us, too!"

Unconcerned, R2-D2 whistled a singsong response.

"Hmm," C-3PO said. "I wish I had your confidence."

The barge and skiffs arrived at the Great Pit of Carkoon, which was a huge sand basin. While the escort skiff circled the perimeter, the sail barge came to a hovering stop above the rim at one side of the depression. The prisoners' skiff stopped in the air above the pit's center.

Luke peered down over the skiff's railing and saw

a mucous-lined hole — just over two meters in diameter — at the bottom of the deep cone of sand. The hole was actually a mouth, and the mouth belonged to the Sarlacc, an omnivorous subterrestrial monster. Staggered rows of inward-pointing needle-shaped teeth ringed the mouth's upper area, and long tentacles stretched outward, trying to snag the skiff. A long appendage emerged from the mouth, rising like an angry serpent; at the end of this appendage was a sharp beaked mouth that snapped and bit at the dusty air.

A long, narrow metal plank was extended from the edge of the prisoners' skiff. The spear-wielding guards then released Luke's bonds and shoved him onto the plank.

On the barge, Jabba kept Leia against his side as he gazed across the pit to the prisoners' skiff. At Jabba's urging, C-3PO picked up a bulky comlink that was hooked up to a loudspeaker. The golden droid's amplified voice announced, "Victims of the almighty Sarlacc: His Excellency hopes that you will die honorably. But should any of you wish to beg for mercy, the great Jabba the Hutt will now listen to your pleas."

As Jabba took the comlink from C-3PO, no one noticed R2-D2 heading for a nearby stairway that led to the upper deck. Clutching the comlink close to his mouth, Jabba laughed and said, "Jedi . . ."

Before Jabba could continue, Han shouted back, "Threepio, you tell that slimy piece of worm-ridden filth he'll get no such pleasure from us." Han glanced at Chewbacca and added, "Right?"

Chewbacca growled in agreement.

Luke saw R2-D2 roll out onto the barge's exposed upper deck. The droid had shed the heavy tray of drinks and took his position beside the railing that overlooked the Sarlacc pit.

"Jabba!" Luke called out. "This is your last chance. Free us or die."

Hearing this seemingly ludicrous threat, Jabba and his motley companions were almost overcome by their own mocking laughter. Because Jabba was holding the comlink right up to his mouth, the barge's loudspeakers made his laughter rumble over the area. When the hysteria subsided, Jabba said in Huttese, "Move him into position."

A guard prodded Luke to the edge of the plank until he stood almost directly above the Sarlacc's gaping maw. Luke looked to Lando and nodded. Lando nodded back.

Luke lifted his gaze to R2-D2 on the barge's deck, then gave the droid a jaunty salute. It was the signal R2-D2 had been waiting for. A panel slid back from the astromech's domed head, revealing Luke's concealed lightsaber. Luke's original lightsaber had been lost during his duel with Darth Vader on Cloud

City, but he'd constructed a new one on Tatooine. He'd already used it, and knew that it worked.

Oblivious to the silent exchange between Luke and R2-D2, Jabba faced the prisoners' skiff and commanded in Huttese, "Put him in."

At that moment, Luke jumped off the plank and turned, catching the end of the plank by his fingertips. The plank bent down with Luke's weight, then sprang back up, catapulting him skyward.

R2-D2 simultaneously launched the lightsaber from his dome. As the weapon arced up and away from the barge, Luke executed a midair somersault and landed on the skiff beside Han and Chewbacca. He casually extended his left arm, and the lightsaber landed in his waiting palm.

Luke instantly ignited the lightsaber and attacked the two guards behind Han and Chewbacca. At the skiff's stern, Lando tore off his own helmet and swung it hard at the pilot behind the controls. Luke's lightsaber flashed furiously — two guards dropped their weapons as they toppled overboard, screaming as they slid down the pit's sandy slope into the Sarlacc's mouth.

Jabba exploded with rage and Leia trembled. The Hutt ordered the guards around him to go to their battle stations, and the guards went running. As a Gamorrean knocked C-3PO to the floor, Boba Fett raced for the stairway to the upper deck.

Luke swung his lightsaber again and sent two more guards into the deadly pit. Stepping over a spear and a blaster pistol that had fallen to the skiff's deck, he hurried to untie the bonds on Chewbacca's wrists. The Wookiee barked anxiously. Luke said, "Easy, Chewie."

Lando was still struggling with the skiff pilot when some guards appeared on the barge's upper deck. Jabba had not anticipated trouble from Luke and his allies, so heavy canvas tarpaulin had been secured over the custom-mounted laser cannon to keep the weapon free of sand. While a pair of Gamorreans hastily removed the tarp, a flat-faced Nikto with multiple nostrils slapped a portable blaster cannon onto the deck's railing. The Nikto fired at the armored skiff, and the power of the blast sent both Lando and the pilot overboard.

A length of rope fell away from the side of the skiff, and Lando grabbed for it, then swung out, dangling over the pit. The pilot wasn't so lucky and plunged into the Sarlacc.

"Whoa!" Lando shouted, clinging to the rope. "Whoa! Help!"

On the barge's upper deck, Fett took two swift strides from an open hatch, fired the jets on his backpack, and blasted away from the barge. As Chewbacca untied Han's bonds, Fett flew over the pit, landed on the prisoners' skiff, and brought his blaster rifle up fast. But before he could fire, Luke spun with his lightsaber and hacked off the blaster's barrel.

The skiff was rocked by another blast from the Nikto on the barge. The impact sprayed shards of metal everywhere, and Chewbacca threw himself protectively in front of Han, knocking him to the deck.

"Chewie!" Han shouted. "You're hit?"

Rolling away from Han, Chewbacca clutched at his left leg and howled.

Han grabbed at the air and said, "Where is he?"

Concerned for his friends, Luke looked away from Boba Fett for just an instant, and the bounty hunter took full advantage of the distraction. He launched a strong metal cable from his wrist gauntlet, and the cable whipped rapidly around Luke, pinning his arms against his sides. But Luke was holding his lightsaber in his right hand, and his wrist was still free; bending it, he brought the lightsaber's blade straight up and sliced through the cable.

As the cable fell away from Luke, another blast struck the skiff, knocking Boba Fett to the deck. The bounty hunter remained motionless as Lando, still dangling below the skiff, shouted, "Han! Chewie!"

"Lando!" Han called back.

Just then, laserfire from a different direction whizzed past Luke's head. He turned to see it came from the blaster-wielding guards on the escort skiff, which had swung in over the Sarlacc pit. Thinking Fett was disabled and that Han and Chewbacca could take care of Lando, Luke sprang through the air to land on the other skiff.

As Luke swung his lightsaber, Chewbacca barked at Han, directing him to pick up a dropped spear. Then Chewbacca saw Boba Fett, who was badly shaken, pushing himself up from the deck. The Wookiee barked desperately to Han.

"Boba Fett?!" Han answered, startled, as he picked up the spear.

Fett saw Luke fighting on the neighboring skiff. Using his right arm to steady his left, the dazed bounty hunter raised his wrist gauntlet and aimed at Luke. Fett fired, but the shot went high. Behind him, Han repeated, "Boba Fett?! Where?" He turned blindly, swinging the spear hard.

By sheer luck, the spear whacked the middle of the bounty hunter's backpack. The impact caused the jetpack to ignite, and Fett was launched from the skiff like a missile. His flight sent him smashing against the side of the sail barge, then he fell back, tumbling to the pit below. The weight of his armor and pack caused him to slide that much faster down the pit's slope and into the Sarlacc's mouth. A moment later, the Sarlacc burped loudly.

Jabba was so stunned by the sight of Boba Fett's

apparent demise that he finally dropped his bulky comlink. Leia snatched it up and brought it down hard upon an instrument panel that housed the barge's power circuits. All the shuttered windows slammed shut at the same time as the lights went out.

Leia leaped up behind Jabba, draping her chain over his head and around his bulbous neck. Hanging on to the chain, she then threw herself backward, letting her weight pull the chain taut against his throat. She put her muscle into it and twisted the chain hard. The Hutt's flaccid neck contracted under the tightening chain, and his eyes bulged out from their sockets.

Leia kept on tugging with all her might. *Now you know how it feels to have cold iron around your throat, Jabba!*

The Hutt's tail twitched, then his scum-coated tongue flopped out of his head.

He was dead.

Outside the barge, Luke continued to fight the guards on the escort skiff while Han extended his spear down to Lando's dangling form below the other skiff. Stretching the spear out as far as he could, Han said, "Lando, grab it!"

"Lower it!" Lando said as Luke sent more guards into the pit.

"I'm trying!" Han replied.

The Nikto fired again from the barge and an explosive blast struck the skiff, knocking the repulsorlift craft on its side. Although the skiff's steering vanes dug into the sand and prevented the craft from sliding into the pit, virtually everything on deck — including Han, Chewbacca, and a few scattered weapons — started to slide overboard. The rope snapped, and Lando fell to the sandy slope above the Sarlacc's open mouth, but he dug his heels into the sand and managed to stop his descent.

One of Han's feet snagged the skiff railing and he found himself dangling upside down above Lando and the pit. "Whoa! Whoa! Whoa!" Han shouted. Above him, the wounded Chewbacca hung on to the skiff for dear life. Han called, "Grab me, Chewie! I'm slipping!"

The Wookiee grabbed Han's feet, and Han extended the spear again toward Lando, who was clutching at the side of the pit, trying to dig a handhold. On the other skiff, Luke had dispensed with the last guard when he looked up to see more armed thugs running out onto the barge's deck, where the Gamorreans had finally removed the tarp from the laser cannon. As the figures on the barge fired at his friends, Luke leaped from the skiff to the bare-metal side of the sail barge. His body slammed against the hull but he caught hold of the edges of a closed window.

Suddenly, a hatch opened to his left and a leathery-skinned Weequay popped out, holding a menacing blaster pistol. Luke reached over, grabbed the Weequay's wrist, and yanked him straight out of the hatch. The alien yelled as he fell past Lando to the waiting Sarlacc, who hadn't eaten so well in a long time.

Lando lay motionless to avoid slipping further. Above him, Chewbacca continued to cling to the upside-down Han, who extended the spear again to Lando and said, "Grab it!" Lando reached carefully. Han said, "Almost . . . you almost got it!"

But the Nikto and other gunners fired yet again from the barge, striking the front of the tilted skiff and causing Lando to let go of the spear. Lando shouted, "Hold it! Whoa!"

The gunners were about to release another barrage when Luke leaped onto the barge's deck. He activated his lightsaber and made quick work of the Nikto, then moved fast toward the other guards, alternately cutting down their weapons and deflecting fired laserbolts back at the shooters.

Han extended the spear to Lando again. "Gently now," Han said. "All . . . all right. Easy. Hold me, Chewie."

Lando screamed. One of the Sarlacc's tentacles had coiled itself tightly around his ankle and was dragging him down.

Hanging onto the spear, Han glanced up and

hazily saw the barrel of a guard's fallen blaster sticking out from the skiff. "Chewie!" Han shouted. "Chewie, give me the gun." The Wookiee passed the blaster down to Han's free hand. Han said, "Don't move, Lando."

"No, wait!" Lando cried. "I thought you were blind!"

"It's all right," Han said. "Trust me. Don't move."

Lando saw that Han, still fuzzy-eyed, was unintentionally aiming the blaster's barrel at Lando's legs. "A little higher!" Lando shouted. "Just a little higher!"

Han adjusted his aim and fired. The laserbolt struck the tentacle, and the Sarlacc let out a pained shriek as it released Lando, who grabbed the spear and held tight.

"Chewie, pull us up!" Han shouted. "All right . . . up, Chewie, up!"

Chewbacca began pulling Han up, but his muscles were strained. Fortunately, Lando was able to work his way up the steep slope, and he climbed back onto the skiff to help the Wookiee.

During all this commotion, R2-D2 had managed to avoid being hit or trampled and had returned to the banquet room to find Leia still chained to Jabba's corpse. From his cylindrical body, R2-D2 readily deployed and extended his laser torch, then fired a controlled burst at the chain, neatly cutting it and freeing Leia.

"Come on," Leia said to R2-D2. "We gotta get out of here."

As they raced for the exit, R2-D2 found C-3PO lying on the floor, kicking and screaming. Salacious Crumb was on top of him and had pulled the droid's right photoreceptor straight out of his eye socket.

"Not my eyes!" C-3PO yelled. "Artoo, help! Quickly, Artoo. Oh! Ohhh!"

Deploying his laser torch again, R2-D2 bravely raced over and zapped Salacious Crumb. The monkey-lizard screamed and leaped to the upper rafters.

"Beast!" C-3PO exclaimed before he hurried after R2-D2, heading for the hatch to the upper deck.

Leia was already there. She stepped out of the hatch to find Luke engaged in combat with several guards. Swinging his lightsaber, Luke warded off laserbolts and fought fiercely. He caught sight of Leia and said, "Get the gun! Point it at the deck!"

Leia turned to the large laser cannon. Following Luke's instructions, she stepped over the removed tarp and climbed up onto the weapon's turret platform. As she began to swivel the cannon around, Luke raised his lightsaber to fend off another attacker and repeated, "Point it at the deck!"

A guard fired at Luke and the blast hit the back of his mechanical hand. His hand was sensory wired, and Luke groaned at the sudden stab of pain. Maintaining his grip on the lightsaber, Luke pushed the pain from his mind and lashed out to dispose of the guard who'd shot him.

Across the deck, R2-D2 beeped wildly, urging C-3PO to head for a gap between the railings on the barge's starboard side, which overlooked a sandy dune. His vision still impaired from his encounter with Salacious Crumb, the golden droid said, "Artoo, where are we going? I couldn't possibly jump . . ."

R2-D2 butted C-3PO, sending him over the edge to land headfirst in the sand below. Without hesitation, R2-D2 boldly stepped off and landed beside his friend.

Luke ran along the empty deck toward Leia and the laser cannon, which was now pointed at the deck. Luke grabbed hold of a rigging rope from one of the barge's masts, then looked to Leia and said, "Come on!"

Leia ran to Luke. He tightened his grip on the rope and wrapped an arm around Leia's waist, then kicked the trigger of the laser cannon. The cannon fired into the deck as Luke and Leia swung out from the barge. Sweeping over the sand pit, they landed on the skiff beside Han, who was treating Chewbacca's wounded leg.

Lando was at the skiff's controls. Luke said, "Let's go! And don't forget the droids."

"We're on our way," Lando said with a winning smile.

A loud explosion rocked the sail barge, as Lando guided the skiff around to the barge's starboard side, where they saw R2-D2's periscope and C-3PO's legs sticking out of the sand. Lando hastily deployed two large electromagnets from the bottom of the skiff and hoisted both droids up from the dune just before a greater explosion tore through the barge.

A chain of explosions followed. As the skiff sped off across the desert, heading for the *Millennium Falcon* and Luke's X-wing starfighter, Jabba's sail barge settled into the sand and disappeared in one final conflagration.

CHAPTER 5

Imperial Star Destroyers were among the ships in the blockade orbiting Tatooine. The blockade had been in place since Darth Vader had failed to capture Luke Skywalker at Bespin. It hadn't been easy for Luke's X-wing and the *Millennium Falcon* to avoid the blockade when they'd traveled to Tatooine to rescue Han Solo, but getting off had been relatively simple, thanks to R2-D2.

While on Jabba's barge, the astromech droid had penetrated the Hutt's data system, and alerted the goons who'd remained in Jabba's palace that the Imperials were coming for them with death warrants. The Imperial ships could hardly ignore the flotilla of smuggler ships, corsair gunboats, and slave transports that lifted off from the Hutt's compound en masse; and in the battle that followed, they failed to notice the single X-wing starfighter and Corellian freighter that rose away from Tatooine by a more discreet route.

Luke was piloting his X-wing and R2-D2 was plugged into the astromech socket behind the cockpit. Han was once again behind the controls of the *Falcon*, which he'd won from Lando Calrissian in a game of sabacc some years back. After leaving Tatooine behind, the two ships veered off in different directions across space.

"Meet you back at the fleet," Luke said into his cockpit's comlink.

"Hurry," Leia answered from the *Falcon*. "The Alliance should be assembled by now."

"I will," Luke said.

Then Han broke in: "Hey, Luke, thanks. Thanks for comin' after me. Now I owe you one."

Luke smiled, then angled his ship for a distant star. Behind him, R2-D2 beeped, and Luke glanced at one of his scopes to read the droid's message. Luke replied, "That's right, Artoo. We're going to the Dagobah system. I have a promise to keep . . . to an old friend."

R2-D2 had previously accompanied Luke to Dagobah, so the droid knew Luke was referring to the Jedi Master Yoda. The artificial skin on the back of Luke's right hand had been blasted away by the hit he'd taken on Jabba's sail barge. He pulled a black leather glove over his damaged hand and thought, *Why did Ben tell me Darth Vader killed my father? Does Yoda know the truth? If he does, why didn't he tell me?*

Or . . . is it possible that Ben did *tell me the truth, and that Vader was trying to deceive me?*

Filled with uncertainty, Luke plotted the course to the Dagobah system, then made the jump into hyperspace.

In a great display of the Empire's might, a parade of thousands of TIE fighters traveled in orbit of the Death Star to mark the arrival of Emperor Palpatine. Like Darth Vader, the Emperor traveled in a *Lambda*-class shuttle. Vader stood in a large docking bay and watched the three-winged spacecraft approach his position.

He was not alone. The docking bay was filled nearly to capacity with Imperial troops in tight formation. Commander Jerjerrod, the beleaguered officer in charge of the Death Star's construction, stood near Vader and tried not to tremble. Glancing at the black-helmeted dark lord of the Sith, Jerjerrod wondered if Darth Vader had ever been anxious about anything in his entire life, then dismissed the thought as ridiculous.

In fact, Vader was feeling uneasy. Not about the Emperor's arrival, but about finding Luke Skywalker. *Luke defeated me at the first Death Star. He evaded me on Hoth, and escaped at Bespin. I cannot lose him again. The longer I remain on this space station, the more he exceeds my reach.*

The shuttle entered the docking bay and landed on its gleaming black deck. The landing ramp descended and Vader watched six Royal Guards disembark; handpicked for their fighting prowess and loyalty to the Emperor, all wore blood red helmets and robes, and carried two-meter-long pikes. After the Royal Guards took their positions at the base of the landing ramp, the Emperor himself emerged. Darth Vader and Commander Jerjerrod genuflected.

Hunched and walking with a gnarled cane, Emperor Palpatine's ghastly, withered features were barely visible under the hood of his heavy black cloak. He was followed down the landing ramp by several Imperial dignitaries. Stopping before Vader's kneeling form, the Emperor said, "Rise, my friend."

Vader rose to walk alongside the Emperor, who moved slowly past the long rows of troops.

"The Death Star will be completed on schedule," Vader reported.

"You have done well, Lord Vader," the Emperor replied, his voice a decrepit rasp. "And now I sense you wish to continue your search for young Skywalker."

"Yes, my Master."

"Patience, my friend. In time, he will seek you out. And when he does, you must bring him before *me*. He has grown *strong*. Only together can we turn him to the dark side of the Force."

For a thousand years, the Sith had maintained their order by never having more than two Sith Lords: a Master and a single apprentice. The few attempts to expand their number beyond two had always led to the Sith Lords conspiring to kill each other. Vader did not question why the Emperor dared to challenge the long tradition. He said, "As you wish."

The Emperor leered and said, "Everything is proceeding as I have foreseen." Then he cackled to himself, and the evil sound echoed across the docking bay.

Luke's arrival on Dagobah went much smoother than it had on his first visit, when his inexperience with navigating the swamp world's dense mists and towering trees had led to a crash landing. Now, his X-wing rested on a muddy knoll, just a short distance from Yoda's small cottage.

R2-D2 stood beside the starfighter and beeped disconsolately to himself; he didn't like to complain, but he found nothing appealing about Dagobah's climate, terrain, or wildlife. The tightly clustered trees were so thick with foliage that sunlight rarely reached the rainforest's floor, and it sounded like there were creatures lurking everywhere. R2-D2 looked to Yoda's house, a mud-packed structure that was partially framed by the roots of a massive tree.

The droid saw warm golden light in the oddly shaped windows, and wondered how long he and Luke would stay this time.

Inside the low-ceilinged structure, Luke sat and watched Yoda move to warm himself beside the flaming scraps of deadwood in the fireplace. Luke couldn't help but notice that the aged Jedi Master moved more slowly and carefully, and was more dependent on the twisted gimer stick he used to steady himself. It was hard for Luke to imagine Yoda using the stick to playfully whack R2-D2 as he had in the past. *He's aged so much since I last saw him.*

Yoda turned his wrinkled green head to gaze at Luke's concerned expression. "Hmm. That face you make? Look I so old to young eyes?"

"No . . . of course not," Luke said, offering a feeble smile.

"I do, yes, I do!" Yoda said. "Sick have I become. Old and weak." Pointing a crooked finger at his guest, he added, "When nine hundred years old you reach, look as good you will not. Hmm?" He chuckled to himself at this, then hobbled slowly across the room, each movement a struggle, and climbed onto his small bed. "Soon will I rest. Yes, forever sleep. Earned it, I have." He was so weak, he could barely manage to pull his blanket up over himself.

Luke moved beside the bed to help cover the aged Jedi. He said, "Master Yoda, you can't die."

"Strong am I with the Force . . . but not that strong! Twilight is upon me, and soon night must fall. That is the way of things . . . the way of the Force."

"But I need your help. I've come back to complete the training."

"No more training do you require. Already know you that which you need," Yoda sighed and settled back against his pillow.

Luke looked away. "Then I *am* a Jedi."

"Ohhh," Yoda said, then shook his head. "Not yet. One thing remains: Vader. You must confront Vader. Then, only then, a Jedi will you be. And confront him you will."

Luke was silent for a moment, trying to build up the courage to ask the question that had plagued him since his duel with Darth Vader on Cloud City. *I have to ask. I must know the truth!*

"Master Yoda . . . is Darth Vader my father?"

Yoda's eyes were full of weariness. A sad smile creased his face, then he turned painfully on his side, so he was facing away from Luke. "Mmm . . . rest I need," he muttered. "Yes . . . rest."

Luke looked at the back of Yoda's head. *Why won't he tell me? Why?*

"Yoda, I must know," he insisted.

Yoda sighed and finally said, "Your father he is. Told you, did he?"

"Yes."

Yoda's brow furrowed and he frowned with concern. "Unexpected this is," he said, "and unfortunate . . ."

"Unfortunate that I know the truth?"

"No," Yoda said. Gathering his strength, he turned over again so he could look at Luke. "Unfortunate that you rushed to face him . . . that incomplete was your training. That not ready for the burden were you."

"I'm sorry," Luke said.

"Remember, a Jedi's strength flows from the Force. But beware. Anger, fear, aggression. The dark side are they. Once you start down the dark path, forever will it dominate your destiny." Yoda's breathing had become strained, his voice a faint gasping whisper. "Luke . . . Luke . . ."

Luke moved closer to Yoda. In the nearby fireplace, the burning wood crackled.

Yoda said, "Do not . . . do not underestimate the powers of the Emperor or suffer your father's fate, you will. Luke, when gone am I . . . the last of the Jedi will you be. Luke, the Force runs strong in your family. Pass on what you have learned, Luke . . ." Yoda closed his eyes. With great effort, he spoke his last words: "There is . . . another . . . Sky . . . walker."

Luke was stunned. *Another Skywalker?! But who? And where?*

Yoda caught his breath, then his facial muscles relaxed and all his breath left him. Luke stared at Yoda's body. He simply could not believe that the Jedi Master was gone. *Come back. Without your help, I'll fail. Don't go.*

To Luke's amazement, Yoda's body then began to fade . . . until it had completely disappeared, leaving an empty space between the bed and blankets. From outside the mud-packed house came the sound of distant thunder. The blankets slowly collapsed upon the bed.

Luke was stunned. He'd already lost so many friends and loved ones that he'd wondered if the loss of one more would even hurt. Now he had his answer: The pain was tremendous. And all that was left of Yoda were his few belongings and Luke's memories.

Luke looked away from the empty bed, then looked back at it. He wasn't sure what to do. Ducking under the low ceiling, he moved away from the bed and headed for the door, leaving the fire burning in the fireplace.

Emerging from Yoda's home, Luke wandered back to his X-wing. He'd never felt so alone and apart from others, so lost and far away.

Luke and R2-D2 prepared to leave Dagobah. R2-D2 was under the X-wing, using his extendable torch to make a minor repair to the ship's lower starboard thrust engine. Luke looked to the windows of

Yoda's house just as the firelight flickered and died. The windows went dark.

The droid beeped to Luke, but he remained silent, thinking. *Perhaps Yoda and Ben were right when they warned me not to try rescuing my friends on Cloud City. I didn't rescue anyone. The only useful thing I did was travel to Bespin with Artoo; if he hadn't wound up fixing the* Millennium Falcon's *hyperdrive, everyone on board might have been captured by Vader.*

Good ol' Artoo.

Luke knelt beside the astromech to inspect his work. Reaching up to touch the X-wing's repaired engine, Luke realized he was still wearing the black glove that concealed his damaged mechanical hand.

Yoda and Ben were also right about Darth Vader. I wasn't ready to confront him then. But without Yoda, how will I truly know I'm ready?

Luke lowered his hand. "I can't do it, Artoo," he said, shaking his head. He rose to stand beside the droid. "I can't go on alone."

Unexpectedly, from a nearby grove of trees, came a familiar voice: "Yoda will always be with you."

Luke turned. "Obi-Wan!"

And there he was: Obi-Wan Kenobi. Old Ben. More precisely, a shimmering semi-transparent apparition of Ben. He moved out from behind some nearby trees to stand facing Luke.

Approaching Ben's spirit, Luke asked, "Why didn't you tell me? You told me Vader betrayed and murdered my father."

"Your father was seduced by the dark side of the Force," Ben answered. "He ceased to be Anakin Skywalker and became Darth Vader. When that happened, the good man who was your father was destroyed. So what I told was true . . . from a certain point of view."

"A certain point of view!" Luke repeated derisively.

"Luke, you're going to find that many of the truths we cling to depend greatly on our own point of view." Ben's spirit eased himself down to sit upon the length of a fallen tree. "Anakin was a good friend."

Luke realized Ben really did think of Anakin Skywalker and Darth Vader as two separate people. Listening, he sat beside Ben, who continued, "When I first knew him, your father was already a great pilot. But I was amazed how strongly the Force was with him. I took it upon myself to train him as a Jedi. I thought that I could instruct him just as well as Yoda. I was wrong."

"There is still good in him," Luke said, not just hopefully, but as if he knew it to be true.

Ben believed just the opposite: that Anakin was dead, and Vader was beyond salvation. "He's more machine now than man," he said. "Twisted and evil."

Luke shook his head. "I can't do it, Ben."

Ben's gaze flicked to Luke. "You cannot escape your destiny. You must face Darth Vader again."

"I can't kill my own father."

Ben looked away. "Then the Emperor has already won," he said with a sigh. "You were our only hope."

Maybe not, Luke thought. He said, "Yoda spoke of another."

Ben returned his gaze to Luke, studying him, trying to decide whether the young man was ready for another revelation, or if it were best for everyone if Luke remained ignorant. Ben made a decision, and said, "The other he spoke of is your twin sister."

Bewildered, Luke said, "But I have no sister."

"To protect you both from the Emperor, you were hidden from your father when you were born. The Emperor knew, as I did, if Anakin were to have any offspring, they would be a threat to him. That is the reason why your sister remains safely anonymous."

Incredibly, Luke was suddenly aware of his sister's identity. "Leia! Leia's my sister."

"Your insight serves you well," Ben said. "Bury your feelings deep down, Luke. They do you credit. But they could be made to serve the Emperor."

Luke nodded, agreeing with Ben. *Yes . . . I must bury my feelings. If the Emperor learned about Leia, he'd want her, too.*

But what about my father? What would he do if he knew Leia were his daughter?

Luke looked into the distance, as if he might catch some glimpse of what the future held. But all he saw was a heavy mist flowing over the swamp and past the trees. He glanced back to the figure that had been sitting beside him, but Ben was gone.

The planet Sullust was a volcanic world in the Outer Rim Territories. It had a highly toxic atmosphere, but beneath its rocky surface lived millions of humanoid Sullustans. They had jowled faces with wide, black-orbed eyes and large ears, and their technologically advanced subterranean cities were highly regarded for their beauty. Sullust was also home to SoroSuub, a prominent corporation that manufactured star-ships, weapons, and droids. Because an influential SoroSuub executive remained grateful to the Alliance for rescuing him from Imperial captivity, the Rebel fleet had been allowed to rendezvous in the Sullust system.

The vast Rebel fleet included several small Corellian battleships, many single-pilot starfighters, a few Gallofree Yards Medium transports, and a Nebulon-B frigate that had been converted for medical duty. The blimp-shaped Mon Calamari Star Cruisers were the largest and most unusual-looking ships, their fluid exteriors covered by bulging protuberances that gave the vessels an organic quality, as if they'd been grown, not built.

One of the Mon Cal cruisers, the 1,200-meter-long *Home One*, had been originally designed as a peaceful exploration ship; refitted with recessed weapons batteries and shield generators, it was now the personal flagship for Admiral Ackbar. Like other Mon Calamari, Ackbar was an amphibian with salmon-colored skin, large, bulbous yellow-orange eyes, and webbed hands and feet.

Ackbar stood with his Mon Calamari officers in a holographic ampitheater that had been transformed into a briefing room. Staggered rows of white plastoid seats encircled a central console unit that resembled a wheel lying on the floor; the console housed a retracted holographic projector. Ackbar watched the military leaders and a few dozen pilots file into the ampitheater and take their seats.

Princess Leia, Han Solo, Chewbacca, and C-3PO were present, as was the X-wing pilot Wedge Antilles. Among the other pilots were several aliens, including a Sullustan named Nien Nunb. Thanks to Chewbacca, C-3PO's right eye was repaired and the golden droid could again see clearly; he thought Leia looked splendid in her Alliance-issue uniform.

As Chewbacca took a seat, Han spotted Lando,

who was wearing a floor-length dress cape with an impeccably tailored Alliance uniform. Glancing at the rank plaque on Lando's tunic, Han said, "Well, look at you, a general, huh?"

Lando grinned. "Someone must have told them about my little maneuver at the Battle of Taanab."

Han knew all about Lando's skirmish with the notorious Norulac space pirates in the Taanab system. Han said sarcastically, "Well, don't look at me, pal. I just said you were a fair pilot. I didn't know they were lookin' for somebody to lead this crazy attack."

"I'm surprised they didn't ask you to do it."

"Well, who says they didn't?" Han asked. "But I ain't crazy. You're the respectable one, remember?" Han took a seat beside Chewbacca. Lando smiled broadly.

As Leia sat down beside Han, a human woman in a white gown entered the room. She had auburn hair and pale blue-green eyes, and wore a gold medallion around her neck. As a young Senator from the planet Chandrila, she had been one of the founders of the Alliance to Restore the Republic. She was now the leader of the Rebellion. Her name was Mon Mothma.

An electronic chime sounded, signaling the audience for their attention. The room fell silent as Mon Mothma stepped beside the ampitheater's central console unit. "The Emperor has made a critical error," she announced, "and the time for our attack has come."

The ampitheater's lights dimmed and Mon Mothma looked to the middle of the console unit, where a holographic projector extended up. Above the projector, a light-generated three-dimensional image of a rotating green world appeared; the green hologram was orbited by a second hologram, a relatively smaller sphere that was an incomplete structure, colored red for visual clarity. From either personal experience or familiarity with the Battle at Yavin, everyone in the room recognized the smaller hologram as an unfinished Imperial Death Star.

"The data brought to us by the Bothan spies pinpoints the exact location of the Emperor's new battle station," Mon Mothma said. "We also know that the weapon systems of this Death Star are not yet operational. With the Imperial fleet spread throughout the galaxy in a vain effort to engage us, it is relatively unprotected. But most important of all, we've learned that the Emperor himself is personally overseeing the final stages of the construction of this Death Star." Mon Mothma swallowed hard. "Many Bothans died to bring us this information. Admiral Ackbar, please."

Admiral Ackbar stepped up beside the central console and gestured to the holograms. "You can see here the Death Star orbiting the forest moon of

Endor," Ackbar said in his gravelly voice. "Although the weapon systems on this Death Star are not yet operational, the Death Star does have a strong defense mechanism. It is protected by an energy shield, which is generated from the nearby forest moon of Endor."

From the "surface" of the green moon's hologram, a yellow stream of light — representing the energy shield — appeared to project and wrap around the Death Star. Ackbar continued, "The shield must be deactivated if any attack is to be attempted."

Every pilot in the room knew Ackbar's statement as a given fact. Planetary shields were so powerful that any starship unlucky enough to career into one were either severely damaged or instantly vaporized.

The hologram of the forest moon and energy shield vanished, and the Death Star's hologram rapidly magnified to fill the space above the central console. The enlarged image was a three-dimensional cross-section that displayed an internal route to the center of the incomplete space station. Ackbar said, "Once the shield is down, our cruisers will create a perimeter, while the fighters fly into the superstructure and attempt to knock out the main reactor. General Calrissian has volunteered to lead the fighter attack."

Surprised, Han turned to Lando with renewed respect and wished him luck. Then added, "You're gonna need it."

Admiral Ackbar stepped back and said, "General Madine."

A brown-bearded, middle-aged human, General Crix Madine had been a highly decorated Imperial officer before he'd defected to the Alliance. Madine stepped forward and announced, "We have stolen a small Imperial shuttle. Disguised as a cargo ship and using a secret Imperial code, a strike team will land on the moon and deactivate the shield generator."

Hearing this, the assembled group exchanged nervous glances and mumbled among themselves. C-3PO said, "Sounds dangerous."

Leia leaned closer to Han and said, "I wonder who they found to pull that off."

Scanning the ampitheater, Madine located Han's seated figure and said, "General Solo, is your strike team assembled?"

Leia, startled, turned to look at Han. Then her surprise changed to admiration.

"Uh, my team's ready," Han said, squirming under the attention that was suddenly given to him. "I don't have a command crew for the shuttle."

Beside Han, Chewbacca raised his hairy paw and barked, volunteering.

"Well, it's gonna be rough, pal," Han said. "I didn't want to speak for you."

Chewbacca growled cheerfully, conveying to everyone that the choice was his.

Han smiled. "That's one."

"Uh, General," Leia said, "count me in."

"I'm with you, too!" Luke volunteered as he entered the room from the rear. He'd just arrived from Dagobah with R2-D2, who wobbled over to talk with C-3PO. Making his way down to the ampitheater's floor, Luke arrived before Leia, who embraced him warmly. Then, sensing a change in him, she pulled away and looked into his eyes.

"What is it?" she asked.

Luke thought, *I still can't believe she's my sister.* But he couldn't tell her now. He hesitated, then said, "Ask me again sometime."

Han, Chewbacca, and Lando crowded around Luke as the assembly broke up.

"Luke," Han said, extending his hand.

Luke took it. "Hi, Han . . . Chewie." *It feels so good to be among friends again.*

R2-D2 beeped a singsong observation to C-3PO.

C-3PO shuddered and replied, "'Exciting' is hardly the word *I* would choose."

An Imperial shuttle, the *Tydirium* was twenty meters long and had a trihedral foil design: The tall dorsal stabilizer remained stationary but the two lower wings extended during flight and folded upward for landing. Before it had been transported to the Sullust System, the *Tydirium* had been captured by the Alliance with the help of "Ace" Azzameen at an orbital outpost at Zhar. Now, looking very out of place, the Imperial shuttle rested beside the *Millennium Falcon* and several single-pilot starfighters in the main docking bay of Admiral Ackbar's Mon Cal cruiser.

Han and Lando stood between the *Falcon* and the *Tydirium*. As the Rebel strike team loaded weapons and supplies onto the shuttle, Han gestured to the *Falcon* and said, "Look: I *want* you to take her. I mean it. Take her. You need all the help you can get. She's the fastest ship in the fleet."

"All right, old buddy," Lando said. "You know, I know what she means to you. I'll take good care of her. She — she won't get a scratch. All right?"

"Right," Han said. He turned for the shuttle, then stopped and looked back to Lando. "I got your promise. Not a scratch."

"Look, would you get going, you pirate." Lando exchanged salutes with Han, then added, "Good luck."

"You, too," Han said, and headed up the shuttle's ramp.

Inside, he saw Leia briefing the twelve SpecForces Rebel commandos seated in the shuttle's aft area. The commandos wore combat uniforms of full forest-camouflage fatigues, and their unit leader was Major Bren Derlin. Han had worked with Derlin and his SpecForces soldiers on Hoth and knew they had what it took to get the difficult job done. Like the commandos, Leia wore a camouflage poncho.

There were three seats on each side of the *Tydirium*'s cockpit. C-3PO sat in the rear portside seat and R2-D2 stood close by. In front of C-3PO, Luke — also wearing a camouflage poncho — was adjusting switches on a control panel. At fore starboard, Chewbacca was in the co-pilot's seat.

Han moved past the droids and Luke and stepped down to the pilot's seat. Beside him, Chewbacca was having a hard time figuring out all the Imperial controls.

"You got her warmed?" Han asked Luke.

"Yeah, she's comin' up," Luke replied with confidence.

Chewbacca growled a complaint about the controls.

Han answered, "I don't think the Empire had Wookiees in mind when they designed her, Chewie." As the shuttle warmed up, Han looked out the window to the *Millennium Falcon*, which was just across the docking bay . . . but somehow seemed impossibly out of reach.

Han felt a chill run up his spine.

Leia entered the cockpit and placed a hand on his shoulder. He flinched and glanced at her.

"Hey," Leia said, "are you awake?"

"Yeah," Han said sadly, returning his gaze to the *Falcon*. "I just got a funny feeling. Like I'm not gonna see her again."

Speaking softly, Leia said, "Come on, General, let's move."

Han snapped back to life. "Right. Chewie."

Chewbacca roared, eager to get going. Leia took the seat behind Chewbacca.

Han said. "Let's see what this piece of junk can do. Ready, everybody?"

"All set," Luke said.

At the back of the cockpit, R2-D2 beeped.

C-3PO said, "Here we go again."

The *Tydirium* glided out of the docking bay and into space. Moving away from the Mon Cal cruiser, the shuttle's lower wings dropped to their extended position. Han steered the shuttle past the surrounding ships, then said, "All right, hang on." He threw a switch, and the *Tydirium* launched into hyperspace, on course for the Endor system.

In orbit of Endor's forest moon, the Death Star's construction continued. A formation of Imperial TIE fighters patrolled the space station's north pole, sweeping past a highly shielded tower that rose one hundred stories above the surface. The tower was topped by a control post that had been converted into a throne room and private observation chamber for Emperor Palpatine.

The Emperor's throne was a large, contoured chair with control panels in the arms; the chair rested on an elevated platform below a tall, circular window with radiating panes. A stairway extended down from the platform to the turbolifts and observation gallery. Except for the brightly colored instrument lights that ringed a pair of duty posts near the stairway, everything was black and dark gray, cold and metallic.

Standing beside his throne, Palpatine gazed out the window and surveyed the half-completed Death Star and Endor's moon. Behind him, members of the Imperial council watched silently as Darth Vader exited the turbolift on the other side of the chamber. Vader crossed a short bridge that extended over the tower's vast elevator shaft, then ascended the stairs to the upper platform.

Vader had been informed that a fleet of Rebel ships had assembled in the Sullust system, and suspected the Emperor wished to do something about it. Ignoring the Imperial dignitaries, Vader arrived before the Emperor and said, "What is thy bidding, my Master?"

Turning away from the window to face Vader, the Emperor replied, "Send the fleet to the far side of Endor. There it will stay until called for."

Vader said, "What of the reports of the Rebel fleet massing near Sullust?"

"It is of no concern," the Emperor assured him. "Soon the Rebellion will be crushed and young Skywalker will be one of us! Your work here is finished, my friend. Go out to the command ship and await my orders."

Vader bowed deeply and said, "Yes, my Master."

The shuttle *Tydirium* dropped out of hyperspace and into the Endor system. The sight of a *Super*-class Star Destroyer, two *Imperial*-class Star Destroyers, and the half-finished Death Star would have been enough for most pilots to turn and run, but Han Solo's hands remained steady on the controls as he guided the shuttle toward the immense space station.

Han said, "If they don't go for this, we're gonna have to get outta here pretty quick, Chewie."

Sitting beside Han, Chewbacca growled in agreement.

From the shuttle's comlink came the voice of an Imperial controller: "We have you on our screen now. Please identify."

Han said, "Shuttle *Tydirium* requesting deactivation of the deflector shield."

The controller answered, "Shuttle *Tydirium*, transmit the clearance code for shield passage."

"Transmission commencing," Han said, and sent the code.

Leia and Luke were still seated behind Chewbacca and Han. In a hushed voice, Leia said, "Now we find out if that code is worth the price we paid."

"It'll work. It'll work," Han said reassuringly.

Chewbacca whined nervously. As they listened to the sound of the high-speed transmission from the shuttle's comm console, Luke stared at the Super Star Destroyer that was alongside the Death Star, orbiting Endor's moon.

"Vader's on that ship," Luke said.

"Now don't get jittery, Luke," Han told him. "There are a lot of command ships. Keep your distance, though, Chewie, but don't look like you're trying to keep your distance."

Wondering how he should accomplish this tactic, Chewbacca barked a question to Han.

"I don't know," Han replied. "Fly casual."

Luke is on that ship, Darth Vader thought to himself. He was standing before the wide viewport on the *Executor*'s main bridge as the shuttle glided by.

Vader turned from the viewport. He strode up the elevated command walkway that extended above the lower-level crew pits and moved toward Admiral Piett, the *Executor*'s commander. Wearing a gray uniform and cap, Piett had been looking over a black-uniformed controller's tracking screen when he noticed Vader's approach.

"Where is that shuttle going?" Vader asked.

Piett leaned over the controller's shoulder and spoke into the computer console's comlink: "Shuttle *Tydirium*, what is your cargo and destination?"

"Parts and technical crew for the forest moon," answered the filtered voice of the *Tydirium*'s pilot.

Piett looked to Vader, waiting for his reaction. Vader said, "Do they have code clearance?"

"It's an older code, sir," Piett said, "but it checks out. I was about to clear them."

Vader looked upward. *My son is so close. So very, very close.*

In the *Tydirium*'s cockpit, Luke was suddenly filled with trepidation. Although Vader had not communicated with him telepathically, as he had before Luke's escape at Bespin, Luke sensed that Vader was aware of his proximity. "I'm endangering the mission," Luke said. "I shouldn't have come."

"It's your imagination, kid," Han said. Glancing back, he saw that Leia appeared nervous, too. "Come on," Han continued. "Let's keep a little optimism here."

Chewbacca was still doing his best to "fly casual," but he let out an anxious growl.

*   *   *

On the *Executor's* bridge, Piett was starting to wonder about Vader's interest in the shuttle. "Shall I hold them?" he asked.

"No," Vader answered firmly. "Leave them to me. I will deal with them myself."

"As you wish, my lord," Piett said. To the controller, he commanded, "Carry on."

As Han Solo waited for a response from the *Executor*, he started to feel as uneasy as everyone else in the cockpit. There was practically no chance for the *Tydirium* to escape the area; all the Imperials had to do was aim a tractor beam at the stolen shuttle and the mission to Endor was over. Han gulped and said, "They're not goin' for it, Chewie."

Then the Imperial controller's voice spoke from the comm: "Shuttle *Tydirium*, deactivation of the shield will commence immediately. Follow your present course."

In the *Tydirium's* cockpit, there was a collective sigh of relief from everyone but Luke, who remained tense. Chewbacca barked.

"Okay!" Han said, glancing back at his friends. "I told you it was gonna work. No problem." He steered the shuttle away from the *Executor*, past the Death Star, and down to the forest moon of Endor.

The moon's unspoiled surface was covered with woodlands, savannas, and mountains. The *Tydirium* traveled over an ancient forest, where trees rose a thousand meters into the sky. Intending to avoid unnecessary contact with Imperial troops, Han landed the shuttle in a clearing several kilometers from their target: the moon-based energy shield generator protecting the orbital Death Star.

The Rebels disembarked. Luke, Leia, and the commandos wore helmets that matched their camouflage outfits. Han opted against a helmet and insisted on staying in his own clothes but did select a forest-camouflage duster, a long-sleeved coat that concealed most of his form. Everyone carried blasters except for the droids and Luke, who maintained that a lightsaber was the only weapon that a Jedi needed.

Long shafts of sunlight stretched from the towering treetops to the forest floor, but the wide-trunked trees grew so close together that it was often difficult to get a clear view in any direction. Moving cautiously, Han led his friends and the twelve SpecForces commandos down a hill, away from the shuttle.

They soon arrived at an adjacent hill, and Han saw something ahead. He raised a hand, signaling the rest of the group to stop. All the soldiers dropped to a crouch, instantly blending in with the surrounding dense foliage. At the rear of the procession, C-3PO looked to R2-D2 and said, "Oh, I told you it was dangerous here."

Han, Leia, Luke, and Chewbacca peered over a

fallen moss-covered tree. Not far below their position, two white-armored Imperial scout troopers were on patrol, moving on foot. Unlike stormtroopers, the scouts were trained to an unusual degree of independence for Imperial personnel and wore lightweight body armor. Their distinctive helmets had enhanced macrobinocular viewplates and boosted comlink systems for long-range communication.

Luke noticed a pair of three-meter-long speeder bikes parked near the scout troopers. Repulsorlift vehicles with front-mounted, sharp-edged directional steering vanes, the speeder bikes hung suspended in the air just above the ground. Although the bikes were primarily used for reconnaissance, each was equipped with a ventral blaster cannon.

Leia asked, "Should we try and go around?"

"It'll take time," Luke said.

"This whole party'll be for nothing if they see us," Han pointed out. "Chewie and I will take care of this. You stay here."

Remembering Han's inclination to shoot first and ask questions later, Luke glared at his friend and stressed, "*Quietly*. There might be more of them out there."

Apparently surprised by Luke's concern, Han grinned confidently and said, "Hey . . . it's *me*."

Blaster in hand, Han started off through the bushes

with Chewbacca. Leia and Luke exchanged nervous glances, then smiled despite themselves.

Chewbacca and Han made their way down to the area below, silently positioning themselves behind two large trees near the pair of scout troopers. As one of the scouts picked up a black bag of supplies, Han stepped out from his hiding place and moved toward the scout's back. Everything seemed to be going fine until Han accidentally stepped on a dry twig. *Snap!*

The scout whirled and lashed out with his free arm, knocking Han off his feet. Han fired his blaster, sending a single laserbolt skyward before he fell back against the ground. The scout turned to his companion and shouted, "Go for help! Go!"

Luke and Leia saw the second scout run for his speeder bike. "Great!" Luke said sarcastically. "Come on." He and Leia jumped up from behind the fallen tree and ran down the hill.

Han rose fast, seized the scout who'd struck him, and threw him hard against the nearest tree. The other scout jumped onto his speeder bike and took off. Chewbacca stepped out from the trees, raised his Wookiee bowcaster, and squeezed off two shots after the scout. The first laserbolt whizzed past the speeder bike, but the second hit its mark and the speeder bike crashed into a tree; the scout went sailing over the bike's handgrip controls and hit the ground with bone-crunching impact.

Han was still fighting the first scout when Leia and Luke arrived near Chewbacca. Then Leia sighted another pair of scout troopers and shouted, "Over there! Two more of them!"

Luke followed Leia's gaze. The two scouts were already mounted on their speeder bikes — they looked back at Luke and Leia before racing off at high speed.

"I see them," Luke said, but Leia was already running for the remaining speeder bike, the one that belonged to the scout that was keeping Han occupied. "Wait, Leia!" Luke shouted. Running after her, he jumped onto the back of the bike just as Leia gripped and twisted the accelerator. Leia felt Luke's arms tighten around her waist as they launched forward into the forest.

Han turned in time to see Leia and Luke speeding off. "Hey, wait!" he called out. His white-armored opponent lunged for him. "Ahhh!" Han bellowed as he grabbed the scout's wrist and forearm and flipped him to the ground, finally knocking him out.

Luke and Leia hurtled after the two fleeing scouts. Leaning forward so Leia could hear him over the whine of the speeder's engine, Luke said, "Quick! Jam their comlink. Center switch!"

Leia pressed the switch, then accelerated. Branches

and leaves whipped past them as they followed the two scouts through the dense woodland. The scouts maneuvered over a fallen tree leaning against a cluster of other trees. Luke ducked as Leia successfully gained on the scouts by steering through the gap between the fallen tree and the ground.

"Move closer!" Luke said.

Leia gunned the engine. The two scouts veered recklessly through the woods, but Leia stayed with them. When one of the scouts fell behind, Luke saw an opportunity and said, "Get alongside that one!"

Leia accelerated again, then swung hard to the left until her directional vanes scraped against the scout's speeder bike. A cluster of trees forced Leia to break away from the scout, but while both speeders were still traveling at parallel trajectories, Luke leaped to the back of the scout's bike.

Landing behind the scout, Luke grabbed the scout's neck and twisted hard. The violent action flipped the scout right off the speeder and into a thick tree trunk. As the scout's body fell limp to the base of the tree, Luke reached for the bike's handgrips and quickly gained control.

Leia was slightly ahead of Luke, but he caught up with her. The remaining scout was straight in front of them. Luke shouted, "Get him!" But as they chased the scout around a wide group of trees, they drew the attention of two more bike-mounted scout troopers who were stationed in the forest.

The two scouts zoomed after Luke and Leia. One of the scouts fired twice, and a laserbolt glanced off the back of Luke's speeder. Luke looked back, then shouted to Leia, "Keep on that one!" He tilted his helmeted head toward the single bike in front of them. "I'll take these two!"

Luke stomped on his braking pedals and his speeder bike rapidly decelerated. Not anticipating his maneuver, Luke's two pursuers were startled as they flew by him on either side and suddenly found themselves in front of their prey. Luke launched forward, deployed his speeder bike's blaster cannon, and squeezed off a rapid burst of laserbolts at one of the scout troopers.

His aim was good. A shot connected, and the scout trooper's speeder bike went out of control and straight into a tree. The explosion was incredible. The other scout looked back to see the explosion, then faced forward and shifted into turbo drive, going even faster. Luke kept on his tail.

Far ahead of Luke, Leia was still chasing the single scout who'd evaded Han and Chewbacca. As the woods grew thicker up ahead, Leia decided to try a different tactic and aimed her bike skyward. Rising above the ground, she traveled fast under the forest canopy until she was almost directly above her quarry. Looking down, she saw the scout glance back behind him, trying to find her but failing.

Leia adjusted her bike's belly-mounted blaster cannon and fired. The scout's bike took a hit but kept on going. Leia descended from above and moved alongside him.

The scout reached to his right leg and drew a black compact blaster from his holster. Before Leia could react, he fired and scored a direct hit on her bike.

I've lost control! Leia dived off her bike just a split second before it slammed into a tree and exploded, spraying metal and plastoid everywhere. Her body tumbled to the ground.

Hearing the explosion, the scout glanced back with satisfaction to see the blast. But when he turned to face forward, he saw he was on a collision course for a giant, uprooted tree. He stomped on his brakes to no avail, then disappeared in a conflagration.

Lying on the ground where she'd landed, Leia heard the explosion. She lifted her dazed head once, then passed out.

Luke was unaware of Leia's condition and whereabouts as he chased the remaining scout through the trees. Luke moved in close, but the scout responded by slamming his bike into Luke's.

A fallen tree formed a bridge across their path. The scout zipped under the tree and Luke went over, then crashed his bike down on the scout's. The scout kept going. Both Luke and the scout looked ahead to see a wide trunk looming directly in Luke's path. Luke banked with all his might, leaning almost horizontally over the scout's bike to just barely make it past the trunk. He straightened out quickly, but his sudden maneuver caused his bike's steering vanes to lock onto the scout's. Then Luke saw another tree in his path.

Reacting instinctively, Luke dived off his bike and rolled to the ground. Freed from his weight, his bike came apart from the scout's, then lifted into the oncoming tree and exploded. Luke rose fast and saw the scout sweep out and away from the crash site and circle back through the forest.

He's coming back for me! Luke ignited his lightsaber just as the scout opened fire with his blaster cannon. Swinging his weapon, Luke deflected the fired laserbolts.

The scout kept shooting and aimed his bike straight for Luke. Luke batted away more laserbolts. When the scout's bike was almost on top of him, he stepped aside and swung at the bike's steering vanes, slicing them off. The scout's shattered bike hurtled forward, then began pitching and rolling as it slammed directly into a tree. In a fiery explosion, the last scout was gone.

Luke pulled off his helmet and tried to catch his

breath. He wondered about Leia, but thought, *If she were in any danger, I'm sure I would have sensed it.*

He was less certain about how far he was from where he'd left the Rebel strike team. Fortunately, he had a good enough sense of direction to know how to find his way back.

Luke deactivated his lightsaber and started running through the woods.

Slumped against the trunk of an immense tree, Han and Chewbacca were worried about Leia and Luke. The twelve SpecForces commandos were positioned around the area, watching for any sign of the princess or Luke. C-3PO stood beside R2-D2, whose extendable scanner antenna rotated back and forth above his domed head. Detecting movement nearby, R2-D2 beeped.

"Oh, General Solo," C-3PO said, "somebody's coming."

Han, Chewbacca, and the other soldiers raised their weapons and darted for cover. C-3PO and R2-D2 hid by a tree. Hearing approaching footsteps, C-3PO leaned out from behind the tree and said, "Oh!"

A forest-camouflaged form ran into the clearing. It was Luke.

"Luke!" Han said, stepping out from his hiding place. "Where's Leia?"

Panting hard from his run, Luke was suddenly concerned and alarmed. "What?" he asked. "She didn't come back?"

"I thought she was with you," Han replied.

"We got separated." Luke exchanged a silent, grim look with Han, then said, "Hey, we better go look for her."

Han nodded, then signaled to a Rebel officer. "Take the squad ahead. We'll meet at the shield generator at oh three hundred."

"Come on, Artoo," Luke said. "We'll need your scanners."

As Luke, Han, Chewbacca, and the droids moved off in one direction and the commandos proceeded in another, C-3PO said, "Don't worry, Master Luke. We know what to do." Then he glanced back at R2-D2 and added, "And you said it was pretty here. Ugh!"

A small, fur-covered figure had been traveling through the woods, using his stone-tipped spear as a walking stick, when he'd heard the sound of speeder bikes traveling at high speed. A native of Endor's forest moon, he was aware of the presence of white-armored invaders on his world, but he had still been surprised when his large black eyes had sighted a bright flash of light in the distance: A speeder bike had crashed and exploded against a tree. That explosion had been followed by another, and then the sound of speeder bikes was gone.

The native didn't know the origin of the white-armored invaders, but he knew they weren't friendly. Because of what they'd been doing on his world — cutting down trees, erecting large metal structures, racing around on noisy machines — he neither liked nor welcomed them.

Now, adjusting his brown leather cowl, he listened and watched the forest. Except for the cries of some alarmed birds, he heard nothing and saw no movement around the area of the explosions. After waiting to make sure no other invaders were coming, he tightened his grip on his spear and moved quickly through the bushes and past the trees, making his way toward the crash sites. If the explosions had started any fires, he would put them out. If there were any survivors, he would deal with them, too.

The furry creature was an Ewok, and his name was Wicket.

Fortunately, the crashed speeder bikes had not left any flaming wreckage. Wicket found a lifeless white-armored form near the shattered remains of one bike, but the prone figure near the other crash site was different. For one thing, this particular invader wasn't wearing white armor, but was clad in garments that had been colored to blend in with the forest; also, watching the camouflage poncho's subtle rise and fall, Wicket could see the invader was breathing.

Wicket guessed the unconscious outsider had fallen or jumped from the speeder bike immediately before it crashed. Stepping closer, he saw she wore a helmet that revealed a human face. Wicket had encountered humans before, and the face reminded him of an adult woman whose family's star cruiser crash-landed on Endor. Then he remembered another woman, an evil shape-shifting witch, and shuddered at the memory.

Wicket assumed the human before him was a woman, but didn't assume she was friendly. Approaching her body cautiously, he extended his spear and prodded her side. When no reaction came, he prodded again.

Feeling the spear's jab, Princess Leia sat bolt upright and said, "Cut it out!"

Wicket jumped back but kept his spear held high.

Leia felt disoriented, but seeing the furry creature before her, it took all of her diplomatic skills to resist laughing. He was barely one meter tall, and despite his fierce behavior, he looked almost ridiculously adorable. Wondering how long she'd been unconscious, Leia stood up slowly and stretched. *No broken bones, thank goodness.*

The creature chittered at her.

"I'm not gonna hurt you," Leia said. She looked around at the charred remains of her speeder bike, then sighed and sat down on a fallen log. "Well, looks like I'm stuck here. Trouble is, I don't know where here is." She looked to the furry creature. "Maybe you can help me." She patted the log beside her. "Come on, sit down."

Wicket growled at her.

"I promise I won't hurt you," Leia continued gently. "Now come here." She patted the log again, and again the creature growled. "All right. You want something to eat?" She removed a ration bar from a pocket and held it out to him. She broke off a small piece and popped it into her own mouth, just to show him it wasn't poisonous.

Wicket cocked his head, looking at the bar, then took a cautious step forward onto the log. He chattered to her in his squeaky Ewok language.

"That's right," Leia said. "Come on. Hmmm?"

Sniffing the proffered food curiously, Wicket moved closer and took it from Leia's hand. Then he plopped himself down beside her and began nibbling at the bar. But when Leia reached up to remove her helmet, Wicket became startled. He jumped back and again raised his spear at her.

Leia held the helmet out to him and said, "Look, it's a hat. It's not gonna hurt you. Look." She showed him the helmet was empty. Reassured, he lowered his spear and took the helmet from her to examine it. Leia went on, "You're a jittery little thing, aren't you?"

Suddenly, Wicket turned away from Leia, dropping her helmet so he could grasp his spear with both paws. His ears perked up and he began to sniff the air. He looked around warily, and whispered an Ewokese warning to Leia.

"What is it?" Leia asked. Scanning the surrounding trees, she saw nothing.

Without warning, a laserbolt zinged out of the foliage and exploded on the log next to Leia. She and Wicket rolled backward off the log to hide behind it. Leia drew her blaster pistol and held it ready, peeking over the log as another laserbolt shot out from the forest and struck near her head.

Leia ducked down as Wicket threw himself into the small gap between the log and the ground. Leia thought, *Those shots were too precise to have been misses. Someone's trying to draw me out or scare me off.* She eased herself up again, risking another glance in the direction of the mysterious shooter, who remained completely concealed by trees.

"Freeze!" said a voice from just behind Leia, causing her to jump with surprise. She turned to see an Imperial scout trooper had snuck up on her. The scout had his blaster aimed at her head, and he reached out with his other hand to take her weapon.

"Come on, get up!" the scout ordered.

Leia rose and saw a second scout — the shooter — emerge from the dense foliage. Addressing the shooter, the scout beside her said, "Go get your ride and take her back to base."

"Yes, sir."

Still beneath the log, Wicket had seen enough to know that the woman was no friend of the white-armored invaders. Gripping his spear, the brave Ewok swung hard at the right leg of the scout beside Leia. *Whack!*

"What the —" exclaimed the scout, glancing down at Wicket.

Seizing the opportunity to take advantage of the distracted scout, Leia grabbed a fallen branch and swung at his head, knocking him out instantly. Then she dived for her blaster, came up with it fast, and aimed at the other scout, who'd just jumped onto his speeder bike. The bike took off, and Leia fired away at it.

The escaping scout's bike was hit, and he collided with the parked bike that belonged to his already-subdued companion. He was thrown head over heels through the air as both bikes exploded.

Wicket poked his fuzzy head up from behind the log and regarded Leia with new respect, muttering praise.

From her earlier run-in with scout troopers, Leia knew more could be close by. Holstering her blaster, she hurried over to her small ally and motioned for him to follow her away from the area.

"Come on," Leia said. "Let's get out of here."

But as they moved into the foliage, Wicket shrieked and tugged at Leia's arm. Figuring that her newfound friend knew his way around the forest better than she did, Leia decided to follow him. Both of them forgot about Leia's helmet, which remained on the ground where Wicket had dropped it.

*   *   *

On the Death Star, two Royal Guards stood sentry on either side of the turbolift in the Emperor's throne room. Neither guard so much as flinched when the turbolift door slid open and Darth Vader entered.

Vader crossed the bridge and ascended the stairway to the upper platform where the Emperor sat in his large chair, his back to the door. Gazing out the tall circular window, the Emperor chided, "I told you to remain on the command ship."

Vader said, "A small Rebel force has penetrated the shield and landed on Endor."

"Yes, I know," the Emperor replied in an almost bored tone as he slowly rotated his chair to face Vader.

Vader hesitated, wondering how much the Emperor really did know. Then he said, "My son is with them."

This did surprise the Emperor, but he tried not to show it.

"Are you sure?" he asked.

"I have *felt* him, my Master."

"Strange that I have not," the Emperor said testily. Leaning forward in his chair, he said, "I wonder if your feelings on this matter are clear, Lord Vader."

"They are clear, my Master."

"Then you must go to the Sanctuary Moon and wait for him."

Vader was skeptical. "He will come to me?"

"I have foreseen it," the Emperor said as he eased back into his chair. "His compassion for you will be his undoing. He will come to you, and then you will bring him before me."

"As you wish," Vader said, adding a deep bow. Then he turned and strode out of the throne room.

Luke reached down with his black-gloved right hand and picked up Leia's helmet from where it had been abandoned on the forest floor. *Oh, no*, he thought. *This doesn't look good.*

"Luke!" Han called out. "Luke!"

Carrying Leia's helmet, Luke ran to rejoin the search party. He found Han, Chewbacca, C-3PO, and R2-D2 beside the charred wreckage of a speeder bike in the grass.

"Oh, Master Luke," C-3PO said with dismay.

"There's two more wrecked speeders back there," Luke reported. "And I found this." He held out Leia's helmet, then tossed it to Han.

R2-D2 beeped.

C-3PO translated, "I'm afraid that Artoo's sensors can find no trace of Princess Leia."

Everyone looked to Han. Devastated, he said, "I hope she's all right."

Chewbacca sniffed at the air and growled. Then he walked off, pushing his way through the foliage.

"What, Chewie?" Han said.

Chewbacca barked but kept moving.

"*What*, Chewie?" Han repeated.

The group followed the Wookiee until he arrived at a break in the dense undergrowth. A tall wooden stake had been planted in the ground, and a dead animal hung from it.

Everyone moved up around Chewbacca. Looking at the carcass, Han said, "Hey, I don't get it."

Chewbacca eyed the carcass and let out a hungry groan.

"Nah," Han said. "It's just a dead animal, Chewie."

Unable to resist, Chewbacca reached for the carcass.

Sensing danger, Luke jumped forward and said, "Chewie, wa-wait! Don't!"

Too late. Chewbacca had already pulled the animal from the stake, triggering the trap. A strong branch sprang and lifted above them, rapidly hauling up the net that had been concealed under the grass and leaves beneath their feet. The net wrapped tightly around the entire group, forcing them together as it lifted them high above the clearing.

R2-D2 was lying practically sideways at the bottom of the net, and let out a wild series of beeps and whistles. Chewbacca howled his regret.

"Nice work," Han said, his face pressed up against the side of the net. "Great, Chewie! Great! Always thinking with your stomach."

"Will you take it easy," Luke said. His right arm poked through the net, but the rest of his body was twisted up against the others. "Let's just figure out a way to get out of this thing." He tried to free his arm, but was unsuccessful. "Han, can you reach my lightsaber?"

"Yeah, sure." Han stretched forward, reaching out to Luke.

Hoping to help, R2-D2 opened a panel on his cylindrical body, extended a compact circular saw, and activated its rotating blade. Exhibiting a skill most often attributed to surgeons using trephines, the astromech began rapidly cutting through the net.

"Artoo," C-3PO said, "I'm not sure that's such a good idea. It's a very long dro-o-p!" C-3PO's last word was punctuated by the net tearing open, instantly releasing all the figures to tumble to the clearing below.

That hurt, Luke thought, pushing himself to sit up on the ground. He looked around. Han and Chewbacca appeared to be a bit stunned but were otherwise fine, and R2-D2 had somehow landed on his feet. *Where's Threepio?* Before he could sight the golden droid, he saw movement within some nearby ferns and bushes. Then short, fur-covered creatures emerged, pushing their way through the foliage to surround the fallen group.

The creatures were armed with primitive weapons: stone-tipped spears and knives, heavy wooden clubs, bows and arrows. They appeared to be hunters or warriors. Most had dark pelts, but one had light and dark gray-striped fur; he was further distinguished by an ornate headdress that had been made from the skull of a large animal, and a necklace of long, sharp teeth.

Two of the hunters moved up on either side of R2-D2 and brushed their paws against his exterior. R2-D2 beeped nervously.

Thinking the creatures were harmless, Han grinned at them. Evidently, this was an error; the hunter wearing the skull headdress — apparently the leader — stepped forward and jabbed the tip of his long spear at the air in front of Han's face.

"Wait . . ." Han said. "Hey!" He raised his hand and swatted at the spear. "Point that thing someplace else."

Han's antagonist turned to one of his furry companions and they had a quick, chittering discussion. A moment later, the stripe-furred creature angled his spear back at Han.

"Hey!" Han said again angrily, grabbing at the spear with one hand as he drew his blaster with the other.

"Han, don't," Luke cautioned. "It'll be all right." Luke sensed the creatures were merely trying to protect their territory and he didn't want to harm them. As a gesture of good faith, he removed his lightsaber from its belt clip and handed it over to one of the hunters.

Han's blaster was taken from him. Chewbacca was not so ready to relinquish his own weapon and growled in protest.

Luke said, "Chewie, give 'em your crossbow." The Wookiee growled again but complied.

"Oh, my head," C-3PO said as he sat up from a nearby bed of ferns. Then he saw all the weapon-wielding creatures and added, "Oh, my goodness!"

At the sight of the golden droid, the hunters gasped. Then they muttered to each other and lowered their weapons. Unexpectedly, they began to chant and bow down before C-3PO.

Chewbacca let out a puzzled bark. Han and Luke regarded the bowing creatures with wonder.

C-3PO turned his head from side to side, listening to the natives' language. Then he said, "Treetoe doggra. Ee soyoto ambuna nocka."

A few of the creatures responded in their own language. The others continued to bow and chant.

Looking to C-3PO, Luke asked, "Do you understand anything they're saying?"

"Oh, yes, Master Luke! Remember that I am fluent in over six million forms of communica —"

"What are you telling them?" Han interrupted.

"Hello, I think . . ." C-3PO said. "I could be mistaken. These creatures seem to call themselves 'Ewoks.' They're using a very primitive dialect. But I do believe they think I am some sort of god."

Chewbacca and R2-D2 found this extremely amusing. Han and Luke exchanged glances, then Han said sarcastically, "Well, why don't you use your divine influence and get us out of this?"

"I beg your pardon, General Solo," C-3PO said, "but that just wouldn't be proper."

Getting angry again, Han asked, "Proper?!"

"It's against my programming to impersonate a deity," C-3PO explained.

Moving threateningly toward the protocol droid, Han said, "Why, you . . ."

Several spears were suddenly thrust close to Han as the Ewoks moved to protect their newfound god. Han held up his hands placatingly and said, "My mistake. He's an old friend of mine."

Unfortunately, the Ewoks didn't think much of C-3PO's friends.

CHAPTER 9

A procession wound through the ever-darkening forest. Their prisoners — Han, Luke, Chewbacca, and R2-D2 — had been tied to long poles, each of which was dutifully carried on the shoulders of several Ewoks. Behind the bound captives, the remaining diminutive forest warriors carried a makeshift litter, on which C-3PO was seated like a king upon a throne made of sturdy branches and vines.

The procession moved along a shaky, narrow, wooden walkway that traveled high up to the giant trees. Soon, they reached the end of the walkway, which dropped off into nothingness. Across the abyss, a village of huts — made out of mud and sticks — and more rickety walkways wrapped around the trees. The lead Ewok took hold of a long vine and swung across to the village square. A rope bridge was extended, allowing the other Ewoks to carry C-3PO and the prisoners on to the village.

The procession wound its way into the village square. The Ewoks' tribal leader was the gray-furred Chief Chirpa, and he stepped out to greet the returning hunters. At the sight of the newcomers, mother Ewoks gathered up their babies and scurried into their huts.

The Ewoks carried C-3PO up to the largest hut and placed his wooden throne so he had a wide view of the square. Still bound to the poles, Luke, Chewbacca, and R2-D2 were propped up against a tree while Han was lifted onto a spit. Han said, "I have a really bad feeling about this."

Chewbacca growled his concern.

All activity stopped as a tan-striped Ewok came out of the big hut. He was Logray, the tribal shaman and medicine man, and he wore the half skull of a great forest bird on his head. While Chief Chirpa examined Luke's lightsaber with great curiosity, Logray surveyed the captives, then went to stand beside C-3PO. Logray addressed the assembly and gestured at the prisoners.

"What did he say?" Han asked.

"I'm rather embarrassed, General Solo," C-3PO said, "but it appears you are to be the main course at a banquet in my honor."

As one group of Ewoks began beating on drums, another started placing firewood under Han's suspended body. Understandably, Han looked increasingly uncomfortable. It was at this moment that Leia and Wicket emerged from the large hut. Leia wore an animal-skin dress that the Ewoks had made for her, and her long hair was down. Seeing her friends in their present state, she was temporarily speechless.

Luke saw her first and was surprised by her appearance. "Leia?"

Han twisted his neck to follow Luke's gaze. "Leia!"

Leia moved toward them, but the Ewok warriors raised their spears and blocked her path. "Oh!" Leia said.

"Your Royal Highness," C-3PO said from his throne, happy to be reunited with the princess.

Leia looked at the Ewoks and sighed. Gesturing to the captives, she said, "But these are my friends. Threepio, tell them they must be set free."

C-3PO remained seated as he quickly conversed with Chirpa and Logray. The two Ewoks listened, then shook their heads negatively. Logray gestured toward the prisoners and barked some orders. Hearing Logray's command, more Ewoks joined in to pile wood under Han.

"Somehow," Han said, "I got the feeling that didn't help us very much."

Luke suddenly realized he might be able to use the Ewoks' superstitious nature against them. He said, "Threepio, tell them if they don't do as you wish, you'll become angry and use your magic."

Baffled, C-3PO protested, "But Master Luke, what magic? I couldn't possibly —"

"Just tell them," Luke said.

All the Ewoks stopped what they were doing and turned to C-3PO as he said, "Horomee ana fu, toron togosh! Toron Togosh! Terro way. Qee t'woos twotoe ai. U wee di dozja. Boom!"

Many Ewoks jumped at the last word, but Logray stepped forward and challenged C-3PO, calling his bluff. The drumming resumed.

Luke closed his eyes and concentrated.

"You see, Master Luke," C-3PO said. "They didn't believe me. Just as I said they wouldn't."

Han saw some Ewoks carrying small torches toward him. He said, "Hey, wait —!" then stopped talking so he could puff his cheeks and start blowing at the flames in a desperate effort to put them out.

The golden droid didn't immediately realize Luke was using the Force to levitate his throne. Rising higher over the deck, C-3PO's arms started waving and he cried, "What-wha-what's happening! Oh, dear! Oh!"

The Ewoks fell back in terror from the floating throne. Then C-3PO began to spin as though he were on a revolving stool. In a state of total panic, he shouted, "Put me down! He-e-elp. Somebody help! Master Luke! Artoo! Somebody, somebody, help! Master Luke, Artoo, Artoo, quickly! Do something, somebody! Oh! Ohhh!"

Logray yelled orders to the cowering Ewoks. They rushed up and released the bound prisoners. One Ewok used a small stone ax to cut the restraints that secured R2-D2, and the astromech pitched forward and crashed to the wooden deck. The Ewoks helped him up, but R2-D2 was fighting mad. He beeped angrily at Teebo, the nearest Ewok, the same gray-striped leader of the group who'd captured the droid and his friends. R2-D2 opened a panel and zapped Teebo with an electrical charge. Teebo hollered and jumped away. R2-D2 gave him another zap.

Freed from his bonds, Luke continued to use the Force to slowly return C-3PO's throne to the deck. As the droid descended and gently landed, he said, "Oh, oh, oh, oh! Thank goodness."

Luke joined Leia, Chewbacca, and a very relieved Han beside Chief Chirpa's hut. Luke looked to the golden droid and said, "Thanks, Threepio."

Still shaken, C-3PO admitted, "I . . . never knew I had it in me."

Night fell on the forest moon, and the entire Ewok tribe tried to squeeze into Chief Chirpa's hut to listen to C-3PO's fireside story. The hut had a spacious interior, but some of the Ewoks had to stand outside and lean in through the windows in order to hear.

Illuminated by the glowing fire at the center of the hut, C-3PO was in the midst of a long, animated tale. Chief Chirpa sat on his small wooden throne next to Logray and the village elders. Leia and Han sat together near Chewbacca and R2-D2. Luke stood near an open doorway at the back of the room. As the droid spoke, Wicket came up beside Han and snuggled against his leg.

Although C-3PO had always maintained that he wasn't much of a storyteller, he was very entertaining as he presented a short history of the Galactic Civil War. He pointed several times to the Rebels in the room, and made pantomime movements accompanied by his own audio mimickry of starship engines and explosions. After he described Obi-Wan Kenobi's duel with Darth Vader and imitated the sounds of lightsabers clashing, R2-D2 began beeping excitedly.

"Yes, Artoo," C-3PO said. "I was just coming to that." He resumed his story, and the Ewoks were completely captivated by his account of the Battle of Hoth, Han Solo's ordeal on Cloud City, and their recent escape from Jabba's palace.

When C-3PO was done, Chief Chirpa, Logray, and the elders conferred, then nodded in agreement. Chirpa stood and made a brief pronouncement.

Watching the Ewoks, Han leaned closer to Leia and asked, "What's going on?"

"I don't know," Leia replied.

The Ewok elders talked with C-3PO, who then turned to Leia and Han and exclaimed, "Wonderful! We are now a part of the tribe."

"Just what I always wanted," Han said as more Ewoks swarmed over him with hugs. Other Ewoks began banging rhythmically on their drums, and Chief Chirpa's hut was filled with happy, screeching cheers.

Luke's lightsaber had been returned to him, and as he watched his friends celebrate, he was suddenly overcome by a feeling of dread. *It seems so safe here, but it won't last . . . not so long as the Emperor reigns.* He turned for the doorway and stepped out into the night. He didn't notice that Leia had seen his exit.

Chewbacca was being mobbed by young Ewoks, who were endlessly amazed by the Wookiee's height. The Wookiee barked to Han.

Han said, "Well, short help is better than no help at all, Chewie." Then Han found himself receiving another embrace from Wicket. Han grinned and said, "Thank you."

Han broke away from Wicket and moved up behind C-3PO, who was engaged in conversation with Chief Chirpa. Turning to Han, C-3PO translated, "He says the scouts are going to show us the quickest way to the shield generator."

"Good," Han said. "How far is it?" C-3PO looked

at Han blankly, so Han gestured to Chirpa and said, "*Ask* him."

C-3PO turned back to Chirpa and said, "Grau neeka —"

The golden droid stopped talking because Han was tapping his shoulder. He turned back to Han, who added, "We need some fresh supplies, too."

Returning his attention to Chirpa, C-3PO rephrased his question: "Chee oto pah —"

But Han tapped his shoulder again.

"And try to get our weapons back."

C-3PO turned back again to Chirpa, this time beginning, "Umma freeda —"

C-3PO felt Han grip his upper arm, forcing him to turn around again. Han said impatiently, "And hurry up, will ya? I haven't got all day."

Han walked off. C-3PO's head jerked back and forth, not knowing which way to turn. If he didn't know better, he would have sworn Han Solo was trying to confuse him.

Leia followed Luke outside. He was leaning against a rail on the torch-illuminated wooden walkway that extended from Chirpa's hut. Leia stepped up beside him and said, "Luke, what's wrong?"

Luke turned and looked at Leia for a long moment. "Leia . . . do you remember your mother? Your real mother?"

"Just a little bit," Leia said. "She died when I was very young."

"What do you remember?"

"Just . . . images, really. Feelings."

"Tell me."

Leia was surprised by Luke's curiosity, but responded, "She was very beautiful. Kind but . . . sad. Why are you asking me this?"

"I have no memory of my mother," Luke said sadly. "I never knew her."

"Luke, tell me. What's troubling you?"

Luke hesitated, then said, "Vader is here . . . now, on this moon."

"How do you know?" Leia asked with alarm.

"I felt his presence," Luke answered, lowering his gaze to stare at a plank on the walkway. "He's come for me. He can feel when I'm near. That's why I have to go." He looked at Leia and continued, "As long as I stay, I'm endangering the group and our mission here. I have to face him."

"Why?" For a moment, she wondered if Luke was seeking revenge after his last duel with Vader. She was hardly prepared for what he said next.

"He's my father."

"Your father?" Leia gasped, her face contorting in astonishment. The thought of Luke being related to Vader was horrific.

"There's more," Luke said. "It won't be easy for you to hear it, but you must. If I don't make it back, you're the only hope for the Alliance."

Disturbed by Luke's words, Leia moved slightly away from him. "Luke, don't talk that way. You have a power I . . . I don't understand and could never have."

"You're wrong, Leia. You have that power, too. In time you'll learn to use it as I have." Again, he looked away from her. He continued, "The Force is strong in my family. My father has it . . . I have it . . ." Then he looked to Leia as he added, ". . . and my sister has it."

Leia stared into Luke's eyes. What she saw there frightened her, but she didn't draw away. And she began to understand.

"Yes," Luke said. "It's you, Leia."

"I know. Somehow . . . I've always known."

"Then you know why I have to face him."

"No! Luke, run away, far away. If he can feel your presence, then leave this place. I wish I could go with you."

"No, you don't," Luke said. "You've always been strong."

"But why must you confront him?"

"Because . . . there is good in him. I've felt it. He won't turn me over to the Emperor. I can save him. I can turn him back to the good side. I have to try."

Leia was overwhelmed by conflicting emotions. Part of her wanted to believe Luke could save their father, and that their father was truly worth saving. Yet she also knew that Vader was responsible for countless atrocities. He'd even supervised her torture on the first Death Star, and cut off Luke's hand, and yet . . . *And yet he's our father. And Luke believes there's good in him.*

Luke and Leia held each other close. He kissed her cheek, then slowly let her go and moved off along the walkway. Han stepped out of the hut just in time to see Luke vanish into the darkness.

Han walked up toward Leia, then realized she was trembling. He stopped short and said, "Hey, what's goin' on?"

"Nothing," Leia replied. "I — just want to be alone for a little while."

"Nothing?" Han said, not buying it. "Come on, tell me. What's goin' on?"

Leia looked at him, struggling to control herself. "I . . . I can't tell you."

"Could you tell Luke?" Han fumed. "Is that who you could tell?"

"I — " Leia choked on her words.

Exasperated, Han said, "Ahhh . . ." He turned, storming off toward the hut. Then he stopped, suddenly realizing things were not what he'd thought they were. He turned to walk slowly back to Leia. He kept a short distance from her, and said, "I'm sorry."

Leia looked to Han and said, "Hold me."

And he did.

High in the pre-dawn sky of Endor's forest moon, the unfinished Death Star was clearly visible against the fading stars. Darth Vader's shuttle left the massive satellite and traveled down to the Imperial outpost that had been constructed on the moon. The outpost's largest structure was an energy shield generator: rising nearly 150 meters into the sky, it was a four-sided pyramid-shaped tower that supported a wide focus dish; the dish's central emitter antenna was directed to project a powerful deflector shield around the Death Star.

Near the shield generator, an elevated landing platform rested on two columnar turbolift housings and rose above an area that had been cleared of trees. As Vader's shuttle touched down on the floodlight-illuminated platform, a four-legged All Terrain Armored Transport walker lurched toward a gantry that extended below the platform and between the support columns.

Vader disembarked, proceeding to the platform's turbolift. Two stormtroopers accompanied him on his descent to the gantry level, where he emerged from the lift to find the AT-AT had docked with the platform. The AT-AT's hatch slid up to reveal an Imperial commander, three stormtroopers — and Luke Skywalker.

Luke's wrists were secured by binders. He gazed at Vader with complete calm.

The gray-uniformed commander stepped toward Vader and said, "This is a Rebel that surrendered to us. Although he denies it, I believe there may be more of them, and I request permission to conduct a further search of the area. He was armed only with this."

The commander handed Luke's lightsaber over to Vader. Vader said, "Good work, Commander. Leave us. Conduct your search and bring his companions to me."

"Yes, my lord." The commander signaled to the three stormtroopers, and he returned with them to the AT-AT.

Vader and Luke walked slowly toward the turbolift. Vader said, "The Emperor has been expecting you."

"I know, father."

Vader glanced at Luke and said, "So you have accepted the truth."

"I've accepted the truth that you were once Anakin Skywalker, my father."

Vader stopped to face Luke and said menacingly, "That name no longer has any meaning for me."

"It is the name of your true self," Luke replied. "You've only forgotten. I know there is good in you. The Emperor hasn't driven it from you fully." Looking away from Vader, Luke rested his arms on the gantry's railing and gazed at the surrounding forest. "That was why you couldn't destroy me," he continued. "That's why you won't bring me to your Emperor now."

Vader seemed to ponder Luke's words, then said, "I see you have constructed a new lightsaber." He ignited the brilliant green blade of Luke's weapon, and Luke — still facing away — stiffened as he heard its deadly hum.

Vader examined the lightsaber, admiring its craftsmanship. "Your skills are complete," he said. Turning his back to look away from Luke, he added, "Indeed, you are powerful, as the Emperor has foreseen."

Taking a cautious step forward, Luke pleaded. "Come with me."

"Obi-Wan once thought as you do," said the black-armored Sith Lord. He turned to face Luke. "You don't know the power of the dark side. I must obey my Master."

Luke shook his head. "I will not turn," he said boldly, "and you'll be forced to kill me."

Less certain of the future, Vader said, "If that is your destiny —"

"Search your feelings, father," Luke interrupted. "You can't do this. I feel the conflict within you. Let go of your hate."

If only I could, Vader thought. *If only I could.*

He said, "It is too late for me, son." Then he signaled to the two stormtroopers who'd been waiting by the turbolift. The troopers stepped up behind Luke as Vader said, "The Emperor will show you the true nature of the Force. He is your Master now."

Vader and Luke stared at each other, until Luke broke the silence and said, "Then my father is truly dead."

The younger Skywalker walked directly into the turbolift, with the two stormtroopers sticking close beside him. Inside the lift, he turned to face his father, who remained on the gantry, looking at him. Then the lift door slid shut, leaving Vader alone on the gantry.

Vader stepped to the railing and tried to collect his thoughts. *I must obey my Master. I must deliver Luke to him. But if Luke can kill the Emperor, perhaps . . . perhaps then I will be free.*

Vader saw the sun was beginning to rise. He turned away from the railing and returned to the turbolift.

At the predesignated time of 0300, Princess Leia, Han Solo, Chewbacca, the droids, and their two Ewok guides — Wicket and a scout named Paploo — met up with Major Derlin and the other eleven Spec-Forces Rebel commandos. Shortly after dawn, the group arrived at a ridge that overlooked the Imperial shield generator and landing platform. On the landing platform, an Imperial *Lambda*-class shuttle lifted off, extended its lower wings, and flew skyward, on course for the Death Star.

Leia had changed back into her Rebel uniform and camouflage poncho. Surveying the Imperial outpost, she said, "The main entrance to the control bunker's on the far side of that landing platform. This isn't going to be easy."

"Hey, don't worry," Han said. "Chewie and me got into a lot of places more heavily guarded than this."

Wicket and Paploo chattered to each other, then spoke to C-3PO. Leia turned to the golden droid and asked, "What's he saying?"

C-3PO translated, "He says there's a secret entrance on the other side of the ridge."

Paploo knew a shortcut. The Rebels followed him.

In the Sullust system, the Rebel fleet prepared for their flight to the Death Star. Lando Calrissian was in the cockpit of the *Millennium Falcon*. His copilot was the Sullustan Nien Nunb. Behind them, two Rebel soldiers checked and adjusted the *Falcon*'s navigational and shield controls.

Lando guided the *Falcon* past the larger battle cruisers. He was followed by a group of single-pilot starfighters that included X-wings, A-wings, B-wings, and Y-wings.

"Admiral, we're in position," Lando reported into his comlink. "All fighters accounted for."

"Proceed with the countdown," Admiral Ackbar's voice answered from the comm. "All groups assume attack coordinates."

Nien Nunb checked his controls and muttered something in his native tongue. He sounded nervous.

"Don't worry," Lando said, "my friend's down there. He'll have that shield down on time." As Nien Nunb flipped some switches, Lando continued to himself, "Or this'll be the shortest offensive of all time."

From the Mon Cal cruiser, Admiral Ackbar said, "All craft, prepare to jump into hyperspace on my mark."

"All right," Lando replied. "Stand by." At Ackbar's signal, he pulled a lever and the stars suddenly appeared to streak past the cockpit window as the *Falcon* roared into hyperspace. The *Falcon* was quickly followed by the single-pilot starfighters. Then Ackbar's cruiser and the other larger vessels vanished in the same direction, until the entire Rebel armada was en route to the Endor system at faster-than-light speed.

On Endor, Paploo arrived beside some bushes along a ridge, then turned and whistled to Wicket and the Rebels. Leia, Han, and the others spread through the thick undergrowth along the ridge, looking down from their position to see the control bunker that led into the base of the energy shield generator. Outside the bunker entrance was a clearing where four Imperial scout troopers stood, with their speeder bikes parked nearby.

Chewbacca growled an observation, and Paploo chattered in Ewokese to Han.

Han said, "Back door, huh? Good idea."

Wicket and Paploo asked C-3PO to explain what the Rebels hoped to accomplish. When C-3PO finished, the two Ewoks had a quick exchange, then Paploo jumped up and scampered into the bushes.

Leia moved close beside Han. Looking at the Imperial scouts, Han observed, "It's only a few guards. This shouldn't be too much trouble."

Remembering Han's last encounter with a group of scout troopers, Leia said, "Well, it only takes one to sound the alarm."

Ever confident, Han grinned and said, "Then we'll do it real quiet-like."

C-3PO asked Wicket where Paploo had gone. Wicket told him. Startled, C-3PO exclaimed, "Oh! Oh, my. Uh, Princess Leia!"

Leia turned around and clamped her hand over C-3PO's vocabulator. When he settled down, she removed her hand. C-3PO lowered his voice and said, "I'm afraid our furry companion has gone and done something rather rash."

Chewbaca barked. Leia, Han, and the others watched in distress as Paploo emerged from the bushes below them. He was only a short distance away from the scout troopers.

"Oh, no," Leia said.

Han sighed. "There goes our surprise attack."

Paploo silently pulled his furry body up onto one of the parked speeder bikes, then began flipping switches at random. Suddenly the bike's engine fired up with a tremendous roar.

"Look!" shouted one of the scout troopers. "Over there! Stop him!" The scouts raced toward Paploo just as his speeder bike launched into the forest at incredible speed. The little Ewok clung tight to the handgrip controls and shrieked.

Three of the Imperial scouts jumped onto the remaining speeder bikes and sped away to pursue the bike thief. All the fourth scout could do was stand at his post and watch them go.

Up on the ridge, Leia, Han, and Chewbacca exchanged delighted looks. Han said, "Not bad for a little furball. There's only one left." Turning to C-3PO, he added, "You stay here. We'll take care of this."

As Han and Chewbacca moved off toward the bunker, C-3PO stepped over beside Wicket and R2-D2. The golden droid declared, "I have decided that we shall stay here."

R2-D2 beeped his concern for Paploo, but the little Ewok was actually enjoying his swift ride through the forest. At the moment, Paploo's only physical contact with the speeder bike was his paws wrapped around the controls; the rest of his body was airborne, suspended over the bike's saddle. He felt like he was flying.

Maintaining his grip on the controls, Paploo maneuvered his body so he was partially perched on the saddle. The three Imperial scouts came up fast behind him. When one of the scouts had the Ewok in his sights, he fired his bike's blaster cannon. The laserbolt struck the back of Paploo's bike. Paploo was unharmed, but his bike went into a dizzying roll.

The Ewok somehow reoriented his spinning bike, then steered into a sharp curve around a tree. Another laserbolt whizzed past him, and he decided it was time to get off.

He sighted a long vine dangling in his path. He released his bike's controls, grabbed a dangling vine, and swung up high into the trees. A moment later, the three scouts tore under him in pursuit of his still-flying, rider-less bike.

Back at the bunker, Han snuck up behind the remaining Imperial scout. Han tapped him on the shoulder, then turned and ran around the bunker, letting the scout chase him. When the scout came around the bunker's corner, he was confronted by the waiting and armed Rebel strike team. Demonstrating some wisdom, the scout surrendered immediately.

Han pressed a control switch in the bunker's doorway and the door slid open. With their weapons drawn, Han, Leia, Chewbacca, and four Rebel commandos entered the bunker's dark interior. The door slid closed behind them.

On the Death Star, in the tower high above the space station's north pole, Darth Vader and Luke — his wrists still secured by binders — arrived at the

Emperor's throne room. As before, two Royal Guards stood silently on either side of the turbolift door. Exiting the turbolift, Vader and Luke crossed the bridge over the elevator shaft, then ascended the stairway to stand before the Emperor.

"Welcome, young Skywalker," the Emperor said from his throne. "I have been expecting you."

Luke had never seen the Emperor before. The Emperor's hooded visage was disfigured: flesh sagged from his bulging forehead and around his piercing yellow eyes — even his voice sounded ravaged by the evil that flowed through his veins. Luke gazed at him defiantly and thought, *He looks like a corpse.*

The Emperor smiled, displaying rotten teeth as he glanced at the binders on Luke's wrists. He said, "You no longer need those," then made a slight gesture with his finger. The binders fell away and clattered noisily against the floor.

Luke looked down at his hands, then back at the Emperor. He thought, *It's as if he's inviting me to try and kill him with my bare hands. And he looks so weak.* But Luke had learned from Ben and Yoda that looks could be deceiving, so he remained standing where he was, at Vader's side.

The Emperor glanced at his red acolytes and commanded, "Guards, leave us." The two red-armored sentries turned and disappeared behind the turbolift.

Then the Emperor returned his gaze to Luke and said, "I'm looking forward to completing your training. In time you will call *me* Master."

"You're gravely mistaken," Luke replied. "You won't convert me as you did my father."

"Oh, no, my young Jedi," said the Emperor, rising from his throne threateningly to step closer to Luke. "You will find that it is *you* who are mistaken . . . about a great many things."

Vader said, "His lightsaber," and presented Luke's weapon to the Emperor.

Taking the lightsaber, the Emperor said, "Ah, yes, a Jedi's weapon. Much like your father's. By now you must know your father can never be turned from the dark side. So will it be with you."

"You're wrong," Luke said. "Soon I'll be dead . . . and you with me."

The Emperor laughed. "Perhaps you refer to the imminent attack of your Rebel fleet."

Luke looked up sharply. *He knows.*

"Yes," hissed the Emperor, "I assure you we are quite safe from your friends here." He turned to walk back to his throne.

"Your overconfidence is your weakness," Luke stated.

The Emperor stopped and glanced back at Luke. With a sneer, he replied, "Your faith in your friends is yours."

He's wrong, Luke hoped. *He's so wrong.*

Vader said, "It is pointless to resist, my son."

The Emperor eased back into his throne and faced Luke. "Everything that has transpired has done so according to *my* design," he said. "Your friends up there on the Sanctuary Moon are walking into a trap. As is your Rebel fleet!"

Oh, no, Luke thought. *No!*

The Emperor continued, "It was *I* who allowed the Alliance to know the location of the shield generator. It is quite safe from your pitiful little band. An entire legion of my best troops awaits them."

Luke looked from the Emperor to Vader, then to his lightsaber, which remained in the Emperor's clutches.

The Emperor leaned forward in his throne. In a tone that reeked of mock sympathy, he said, "Oh . . . I'm afraid the deflector shield will be quite operational when your friends arrive."

On Endor, inside the Imperial bunker, Han, Leia, Chewbacca, and the Rebel strike team stormed through a door and entered the main control room. There they found an Imperial officer standing beside three black-uniformed generator controllers; the startled men turned away from their computer consoles to see the armed Rebels.

"All right!" Han shouted at the controllers. "Up! Move! Come on! Quickly! Quickly! Chewie!"

Chewbacca growled and leveled his bowcaster at the controllers. Behind him, an open doorway offered a view of the turbine generator chamber that powered the energy shield that was projected at the Death Star. A blaster-wielding Imperial officer came running in from the generator chamber, but an alert Rebel commando knocked him out.

As the controllers were herded away from their consoles, Leia glanced at a viewscreen that displayed a two-dimensional graphic of the shield-protected Death Star. Checking a chronometer, she said, "Han! Hurry! The fleet will be here any moment."

Han turned to one of the Rebel commandos and said, "Charges! Come on, come on!" The commando tossed a bag of proton grenades to Han.

Outside the bunker, C-3PO, R2-D2, and Wicket were still watching from the bushes when they saw several stormtroopers and controllers suddenly emerge from the surrounding forest. The Imperial soldiers rushed to the bunker's doorway and entered.

Realizing that their allies were probably unaware of the incoming Imperial troops, C-3PO cried, "Oh, my! They'll be captured!"

Wicket chattered urgently in Ewokese, then darted away from the droids and into the forest.

"Wa-ait!" C-3PO wailed. "Wait, come back!" He clapped a hand down on top of R2-D2's dome and said, "Artoo, stay with me."

Back inside the main control room, Han was about to plant an explosive charge when an Imperial officer appeared in the doorway that overlooked the turbine generator and said, "Freeze!"

Han spun fast and threw a bag of explosives at the officer. The officer cried out as the bag hit him in the chest and carried him over the railing behind him. Before Han could make another move, an overwhelming number of stormtroopers flooded into the control room.

Han, Leia, and the others had no choice but to relinquish their weapons. Chewbacca howled in anger.

A black-uniformed Imperial commander walked up to Han and said, "You Rebel scum."

The *Millennium Falcon* dropped out of hyperspace and blasted into the Endor system. In the *Falcon*'s cockpit, Lando and Nien Nunb looked through their window to see Endor's forest moon and the unfinished Death Star, which appeared to grow larger with each passing second of their approach. Lando glanced at his sensor scopes and watched dozens of blips appear as the rest of the Imperial fleet emerged from hyperspace behind him.

Lando's comm unit designation for the mission was Gold Leader. He said into his comlink, "All wings report in."

"Red Leader standing by," Wedge Antilles answered from his X-wing starfighter.

"Gray Leader standing by," came the reply from a Y-wing.

"Green Leader standing by," said the commander of the A-wing starfighters.

Wedge said, "Lock S-foils in attack positions." Wedge's squadron included S-foil-equipped X-wings and B-wings; in response to his command, the X-wing pilots unlocked their wing-connecting assemblies to spread their double-layered wings, and the B-wings' cannon-tipped airfoils extended from their primary wings.

All the Rebel ships headed straight for the Death Star. On the Mon Cal cruiser, Admiral Ackbar watched the starfighters massing outside his viewport and said, "May the Force be with us."

In the *Falcon*'s cockpit, Nien Nunb tried to get a reading on the Death Star's energy shield but found nothing on his scopes. He pointed to the control panel and said, "Ah-teh-yairee u-hareh mu-ah-hareh."

Fortunately, Lando understood his Sullustan copilot and replied, "We've got to be able to get *some* kind of a reading on that shield, up or down."

Nien Nunb could imagine only one possibilty: The Death Star was using long-range sensor jammers to deceive the Rebel fleet. "Mu-ah-hareh mu-kay, huh?" he asked.

Lando said, "Well, how could they be jamming us if they don't know . . . we're coming." And then Lando realized the truth: *They know.* Somehow the Empire had anticipated the Rebel assault.

"Break off the attack!" Lando yelled into his comlink. "The shield is still up."

"I get no reading," Wedge answered over the comm. "Are you sure?"

"Pull up!" Lando ordered. "All craft pull up!" The *Falcon* and the fighters of Red Squad veered off desperately to avoid the invisible energy shield.

Inside Admiral Ackbar's cruiser, alarms sounded. "Take evasive action!" Ackbar commanded his crew. Turning to a comlink, he said, "Green Group, stick close to holding sector MV-Seven."

A Mon Calamari controller called out, "Admiral, we have enemy ships in sector forty-seven."

Ackbar swiveled in his seat to face the controller and said, "It's a trap."

Sure enough, the *Falcon* and the other ships had veered straight for an armada of Imperial Star Destroyers. At a glance, Lando guessed there were about twenty. He recognized the largest vessel — a *Super*-class Star Destroyer — as the same ship that had nearly captured the *Falcon* after he'd helped rescue Luke from Cloud City.

Then Lando saw the TIE fighters.

"Fighters coming in," he said into his comlink. It

was an understatement. Hundreds of TIE fighters were streaking away from the Star Destroyers and racing for the Rebel fleet. Most of the Imperial fighters were Interceptors, identifiable by their bent and elongated dagger-shaped solar collector panels. The Interceptors were the latest in Twin Ion Engine design, and were far more lethal than standard TIE fighters. In an instant, dozens of fierce dogfights ensued around the giant Mon Cal cruisers.

Lando adjusted the *Falcon*'s targeting computer so he could fire the turbolaser cannons from the cockpit. The number of speeding TIE fighters and all the crisscrossing streaks of laserfire were so overwhelming that it was almost impossible to see the stars beyond the battle zone. Nien Nunb steered after a pair of TIE fighters and Lando fired the *Falcon*'s cannons.

"There's too many of them!" a Rebel pilot shouted from his starfighter's cockpit. A moment later, the pilot's ship was struck by enemy fire and was gone.

Flying through the battle, Lando ordered, "Accelerate to attack speed! Draw their fire away from the cruisers."

"Copy, Gold Leader," Wedge answered, and instructed his X-wing squad to follow his lead. The starfighters angled off from the larger Rebel ships.

High atop the Death Star, the space battle was visible through the tall circular window behind the Emperor's throne. From his seat, the Emperor faced Luke and said, "Come, boy. See for yourself."

Luke moved toward the window. In the distance, Rebel and Imperial starfighters appeared as swirling pinpoints of light. Laserfire streaked between the fighters. There were many explosions.

The Emperor said, "From here you will witness the final destruction of the Alliance and the end of your insignificant Rebellion."

Luke's lightsaber rested on the right arm of the Emperor's throne. The Emperor extended his bony fingers to the lightsaber and said, "You want this, don't you? The hate is *swelling* in you now."

He's right, Luke thought. *I hate him for everything he is, and everything he's done.*

"Take your Jedi weapon," the Emperor continued. "Use it. I am unarmed. Strike me down with it. Give in to your *anger*."

Luke turned away from the Emperor. *I won't give in. I won't.*

The Emperor continued, "With each passing moment you make yourself more my servant."

"No!" Luke shouted as he spun to glare at the evil wretch.

"It is unavoidable," the Emperor leered. "It is your destiny. You, like your father, are now *mine*!"

CHAPTER 11

Princess Leia, Han Solo, Chewbacca, and the Rebel commandos were led out of the bunker by their Imperial captors. Outside, they found the other members of their strike team standing together with their hands clasped behind their heads. They were surrounded by more than a hundred Imperial troops. One captured commando was especially conspicuous: He had obtained a scout trooper uniform before being apprehended, and he still wore the armor, minus the helmet. Obviously, he'd failed in his effort to infiltrate the Imperial soldiers.

An 8.6-meter-tall, two-legged All Terrain Scout Transport walker loomed above the soldiers; the AT-ST's pilot was visible atop the vehicle, his upper body rising through the hatch of the command cabin. Although not as tall as four-legged AT-AT walkers, the AT-ST was still an intimidating vehicle, especially since its blaster cannons were trained on the Rebels.

Leia spotted another AT-ST lurch past the trees on the ridge from which the Rebels had first glimpsed the bunker. *It was all a trap*, Leia realized. She thought of the Bothan spies who'd died in their effort to acquire and deliver the secret data regarding the new Death Star to the Alliance. *The Bothans were pawns. Everything — the data, the stolen Imperial shuttle, the clearance code for the shield passage — was a scheme to bring the Rebel fleet to Endor.*

"All right, move it!" said a stormtrooper behind Leia. "I said move it! Go on!" As Leia's group walked over to join the other Rebels, Leia glanced at Han. From his stunned expression, she knew he was thinking the same thing: Their situation was hopeless. They were more surprised than relieved when they heard a familiar voice call out from the forest, just beyond the clearing where they stood.

"Hello!" shouted C-3PO as he stepped out from behind a tall tree's wide trunk to stand beside R2-D2. "I say, over there! Were you looking for me?" The droids moved back behind the tree.

Chewbacca howled at the droids, urging them to run. Leia thought, *The droids are up to something. But what?*

The bunker commander turned to a squad of stormtroopers and said, "Bring those two down here."

"Let's go," said the stormtrooper squad leader. The white-armored troops headed off into the forest.

As the stormtroopers approached the droids, C-3PO turned to R2-D2 and said, "Well, they're on their way. Artoo, are you sure this was a good idea?"

The stormtroopers ran up and aimed their blaster rifles at the droids. "Freeze!" said the squad leader. "Don't move!"

"We surrender," C-3PO said, raising his hands.

But just as the stormtroopers were about to seize the droids, a band of Ewoks jumped down from the surrounding bushes. The Ewoks carried clubs, stones, knives, and spears, and every one of them had been itching to fight the invaders who'd cut down so many trees on their world. Their attack was swift and ferocious, and most of the stormtrooper squad fell without knowing what had hit them.

"Ohhh!" C-3PO cried as the brave Ewoks pummeled the stormtroopers. "Stand back, Artoo."

R2-D2 looked up to see Wicket arrive with Logray, Chief Chirpa, Teebo, and a small army of Ewoks. Wicket waved to the droids and chittered.

In a nearby tree, an Ewok raised a hollowed horn to his lips and sounded a battle call. The call was heard and repeated by an Ewok in another tree. Then the Imperials and Rebels were mutually astonished when hundreds of Ewoks rose from the bushes that surrounded the bunker's perimeter.

Most of the Ewoks wielded wooden bows. The

archers took quick but careful aim, then released a flurry of stone-tipped arrows at the Imperial soldiers.

Stormtroopers screamed and dived for cover. Han grabbed the nearest stormtrooper and flung him hard into another. Chewbacca did the same. Leia saw her blaster amidst a pile of confiscated weapons and snatched it up fast. She kicked a stormtrooper aside, then raised her blaster at the AT-ST pilot who hadn't been fast enough to lower himself into his vehicle. Leia fired, disabling the pilot.

The other Rebels quickly engaged the stormtroopers in hand-to-hand combat and took back their blaster rifles. As the clearing outside the bunker became rapidly littered with white-armored bodies and fallen weapons, several stormtrooper squads returned fire at the Ewoks. Most of the furry archers went scrambling into the woods, and the squads went after them. A pair of scout troopers hopped on their speeder bikes and joined in the pursuit.

Han spotted his blaster on the ground. He picked it up, knocked yet another stormtrooper aside, then moved fast alongside Leia, heading for the bunker's open doorway. But as they neared the bunker, the door slid shut to seal off the entrance. They dived against the recessed door as Imperial laserfire tore around their position. Most of the stormtroopers had gone after the Ewoks; Han and Leia fired back at the ones who hadn't.

In the woods, the stormtroopers fired at anything that moved. But despite their superior firepower, they rarely found their targets; the forest's density made it difficult to get a clear shot at anything, and the troopers frequently lost their balance on the uneven terrain.

The Ewoks exploited the stormtroopers' disadvantages at every opportunity. Swinging from vines and leaping out from behind bushes, they knocked the troopers off their feet and sent them tumbling down hills and into sinkholes, where they were met by more Ewoks with stones, clubs, and axes.

The AT-ST walkers proved to be a greater challenge for the Ewoks. Each armor-plated walker was equipped with maneuverable blaster cannons and a concussion-grenade launcher, and the pilots and gunners did their best to keep the Ewoks running. As a group of Ewoks scurried out of the way from a cannon-firing walker, they saw two of their fellows soaring high above the forest floor in stick-framed, leather-winged gliders. Both of the daring flyers carried stones.

As one flyer swooped over the walker, he dropped a stone that merely bounced off the vehicle's upper hull. The other flying Ewok had more success when he unloaded two stones onto the heads of stormtroopers. But as one trooper collapsed to the ground, his blaster fired a stray shot that went straight up and punched a hole through the second glider's wing. The Ewok shrieked as his glider spiralled out of control and crashed near the base of a large tree.

The fallen Ewok's allies raced to pull him out of the path of an oncoming walker, then slung a vine across the ground and held tight to the vine's ends in an effort to trip the vehicle. But when one of the walker's footpads snagged the vine, the Ewoks were instead yanked off their feet and dragged across the ground. Releasing the vine, they rushed to see if their nearby comrades had readied the catapults.

Elsewhere, Wicket had hastily enlisted with a division of Ewoks who hunted with bolas. They waited in the bushes until a group of stormtroopers rushed toward their position, then stood up, swung the bolas over their furry heads, and released the stone-weighted ropes at their targets. The bolas whipped around the troopers' heads, shattering their helmets and breaking bones. Wicket gave it his best try, but wound up getting tangled in his own bola and knocked himself down. Luckily, only his ego was bruised.

Back at the bunker, Leia reached for the control panel that was set within the doorway's frame. The door wouldn't open. "The code's changed," she said. "We need Artoo!"

Han looked below the control panel, found a socket, and said, "Here's the terminal."

The stormtroopers hadn't confiscated Leia's comlink, probably because they'd assumed it wouldn't be of any further use to her. They were wrong. She pulled the device from her pocket, switched it on, and said, "Artoo, where are you? We need you at the bunker right away."

R2-D2 was still with C-3PO, watching the Ewoks fight the stormtroopers, when he received Leia's transmitted communication. The astromech beeped to the golden droid, then moved away from beside the tree where they'd been standing.

"Going?" C-3PO said with alarm. "What do you mean, you're going? But — but going where, Artoo? No, wait! Artoo!" Artoo kept moving, and C-3PO hurried after him. "Oh, this is no time for heroics. Come back!"

In the woods, the Ewoks loaded heavy stones onto primitive catapults, then fired at an AT-ST walker. The stones flew past the trees and hammered at the walker's command compartment, but barely left a dent. Then the command compartment rotated to aim its cannons and fired back. The Ewoks fled as their catapult was blasted to bits.

The battle against the Empire didn't seem to be going much better in space. The Rebel fleet was greatly outnumbered. As more starfighters were lost to TIE interceptors, all Lando could do was fire at Imperial ships and try to stay alive.

Through the *Falcon*'s cockpit window, he sighted Wedge's X-wing. "Watch yourself, Wedge!" Lando shouted into his comlink. "Three from above!"

Wedge saw the three TIE fighters on his scopes and said, "Red Three, Red Two, pull in!"

The other pilots did as ordered and went after the TIE fighters. Red Two blasted one into spacedust and said, "Got it!"

Red Three said, "Three of them coming in, twenty degrees!"

"Cut to the left!" Wedge said. "I'll take the leader!" A moment later, Wedge fired his cannons and the lead TIE fighter was gone. Another TIE fighter zoomed in on Wedge's tail. Wedge sent his X-wing into a tight bank away from a Mon Cal cruiser. His pursuer failed to execute the bank and exploded against the larger ship's hull.

Wedge saw three more TIE fighters veer past his ship. He said, "They're heading for the medical frigate."

Lando steered the *Falcon* through a complete roll as he fired at one of the three TIE fighters. The TIE fighter exploded, and Lando went after the other two. As he wrapped around the medical frigate, the soldier who was serving as his navigator said from behind, "Pressure steady."

More laserfire spat out from the *Falcon*'s cannons, and two more TIE fighters exploded. But as Lando started to loop back to the medical frigate, he noticed the Star Destroyers had continued to maintain their distance from the battle. He said, "Only the fighters are attacking. I wonder what those Star Destroyers are waiting for."

On the main bridge of the Super Star Destroyer *Executor*, Admiral Piett and the Imperial Fleet Commander stood before the bridge's wide viewport and watched the battle that raged near the Death Star. Another officer approached them from the walkway that bisected the bridge and said, "We're in attack position now, sir."

"Hold here," Piett ordered.

"We're not going to attack?" asked the Fleet Commander, surprised.

"I have my orders from the Emperor himself," Piett stated with pride. "He has something special planned. We only need to keep them from escaping."

On the Death Star, the Emperor, Darth Vader, and a mortified Luke continued to watch the warring starships in the distance. From his throne, the Emperor said, "As you can see, my young apprentice, your friends have *failed*. Now witness the firepower of this fully armed and operational battle station." The Emperor pressed a button on his throne's armrest and said into his comlink, "Fire at will, Commander."

Luke, in shock, glanced at the Emperor, then returned his gaze to the Rebel fleet.

In the Death Star control room, buttons were pressed and switches were thrown. A black-helmeted Imperial gunner reached overhead and pulled a lever. Commander Jerjerrod gave the command: "Fire!"

The giant laserdish on the completed half of the Death Star began to glow. Then a powerful beam shot out toward the Rebel fleet and smashed into a Mon Cal cruiser. The cruiser exploded in a blinding flash.

The power of the explosion rocked the Rebel fleet. Inside the *Millennium Falcon*'s cockpit, Lando was stunned.

"That blast came from the Death Star!" he exclaimed. "That thing's operational! *Home One*, this is Gold Leader."

"We saw it," Admiral Ackbar answered. "All craft prepare to retreat."

Lando said, "You won't get another chance at this, Admiral."

"We have no choice, General Calrissian," Ackbar replied. "Our cruisers can't repel firepower of that magnitude."

"Han will have that shield down," Lando promised. "We've got to give him more time."

*   *   *

On Endor, Leia, Han, and a small group of Rebel commandos fought desperately to maintain their position outside the bunker that led to the shield generator control station. Four stormtroopers had found cover behind a fallen tree on the ridge that overlooked the bunker, maintaining a definite tactical advantage as they fired down at the Rebels below. Han was wishing he had a grenade to lob at the troopers when he saw a band of spear-wielding Ewoks leap out from the bushes above and behind the ridge. Pouncing quickly, the Ewoks made quick work of the white-armored soldiers.

But the bunker door remained closed. Leia wondered, *Where's Artoo?*

Just then, C-3PO called out, "We're coming!"

Han and Leia saw the droids moving on the ridge, trying to make their way down to the bunker, as an enemy-fired laserbolt streaked past R2-D2's domed head. Han traced the angle of fire to spot the shooter: a stormtrooper hiding behind some nearby bushes. Han raised his blaster, fired, and struck the shooter squarely in the middle of his helmet. The trooper fell back against the ground.

"Come on! Come on!" Han shouted to the droids.

More stormtroopers fired at the bunker. C-3PO ran up beside Leia as R2-D2 scooted over next to Han. Positioning himself beside the doorway's computer terminal, R2-D2 extended his computer interface arm and plugged into the terminal socket.

C-3PO said, "Oh, Artoo, hurry!"

But before the astromech could open the door, a stormtrooper fired a laserbolt that struck directly in front of him. The droid screeched as the blast launched him backward from the terminal to the far side of the doorway, where he slammed against the door's metal frame. Han sighted R2-D2's attacker and fired his blaster; the stormtrooper fell to the ground.

C-3PO stepped beside R2-D2, then backed away as an electrical surge suddenly coursed through and over the astromech's body. Artoo screeched again, then every compartment on his body popped open to deploy his many tool-tipped appendages.

"My goodness!" C-3PO cried as smoke poured out from his friend's domed head. "Artoo, why did you have to be so brave?"

Han and Leia gaped at R2-D2's disabled form, then Han said, "Well, I suppose I could hot-wire this thing." He turned for the door's control panel.

"I'll cover you," Leia said. She began firing at the stormtroopers, allowing Han to concentrate on the door's mechanisms. Sparks flew as he broke the control panel open and fumbled with some exposed wires.

Leia had no idea what was happening with the Rebel fleet, but she knew that if she and Han failed to knock out the energy shield generator, the battle would be lost.

The Death Star fired its superlaser again, and another Mon Cal cruiser was instantly vaporized. As Wedge Antilles raced his X-wing away from the explosion, he wasn't sure if he'd heard Lando Calrissian's last message correctly, and asked him to repeat.

From the *Millennium Falcon*, Lando shouted, "Yes! I said closer! Move as close as you can and engage those Star Destroyers at point-blank range."

On the *Home One*, Admiral Ackbar heard Lando's transmission and said, "At that close range we won't last long against those Star Destroyers."

Lando replied, "We'll last longer than we will against that Death Star — and we might just take a few of them with us."

Ackbar agreed with Lando's improvised plan; *Home One* and the remaining cruisers began speeding toward the Star Destroyers. The Rebels were practically on top of the enemy ships when they opened fire on the Star Destroyers' control bridges and communication towers.

TIE fighters zoomed in to defend the Imperial warships and went after the Rebel starfighters with even greater maliciousness. An X-wing pilot blasted at a Destroyer's port-side deflector-shield generator dome and shouted, "She's gonna blow!" The dome exploded, but a moment later, TIE fighters fired at the X-wing and it blossomed into a ball of fire.

"I'm hit!" cried a Rebel pilot from his flaming Y-wing. The Y-wing spiraled away from the TIE fighters and smashed into a Star Destroyer.

On the Death Star, the Emperor was unconcerned by the way the battle had shifted to the Star Destroyers. He gazed at Luke, who remained by the circular window, and said, "Your fleet is lost. And your friends on the Endor moon will not survive. There is no escape, my young apprentice."

Luke glanced at Darth Vader. He thought, *If there's even a trace of Anakin Skywalker left, he wouldn't stand by and allow this to continue.*

But all Darth Vader did was return Luke's gaze.

The Emperor opened his yellow eyes and said, "The Alliance will die . . . as will your friends."

Luke glared at the Emperor and wished the wretched man would choke on his words.

"Good," the Emperor said, closing his yellow eyes and smiling. "I can *feel* your anger. I am defenseless."

Luke glanced at his lightsaber, still resting near the Emperor's right hand on the throne's armrest.

"Take your weapon!" the Emperor challenged. "Strike me down with all of your *hatred* and your journey toward the dark side will be complete."

Luke turned away, trying to resist the temptation to kill the Emperor. Then he thought, *But if I don't kill him, how many more innocent people will die?*

Luke moved fast, turning to face the Emperor as he used the Force to make his lightsaber fly from the throne's armrest to his waiting hand. His lightsaber blazed to life and he swung fast at the Emperor's head.

Luke's lightsaber never reached its target. Darth Vader's red-bladed lightsaber ignited a split second after Luke's, and Vader deftly blocked the attack.

Seeing the two lightsabers crossed mere centimeters in front of his horrible face, Emperor Palpatine cackled. He hadn't seen a lightsaber duel in years, and was now delighted by the prospect of watching a father and son try to kill each other.

I won't kill you, father, Luke thought. *I won't!*

Then Vader pushed Luke back away from the Emperor, and Luke was suddenly fighting for his life.

On Endor, AT-ST walkers continued to prowl the forest and fire at the scurrying Ewoks. As a walker moved past a tree-covered hillside, two Ewoks looked up at the tallest and furriest new member of their tribe: Chewbacca. The Wookiee reached for a long vine that dangled from the treetops, then barked to his short allies.

The two Ewoks threw their arms and legs around him and clung tight as he seized the vine. Chewbacca howled a battle cry as he leaped away from the hill, carrying the Ewoks with him. They swung over the forest floor and landed with a loud thud on top of the nearest Imperial walker.

Inside the walker's cockpit, the pilot and gunner heard the noise above their helmeted heads. A moment later, the gunner sighted an upside-down Ewok hanging in front of the pilot's viewport. The gunner pointed and said, "Look!"

The walker's pilot looked to the viewport. The Ewok chuckled, then slid out of view. The pilot said to the gunner, "Get him off of there!"

The gunner stood and pushed up the roof-mounted entry hatch. When the hatch was fully opened, Chewbacca reached down and hauled the gunner straight out of the cockpit. The gunner screamed as he was hurled from the top of the vehicle.

Before the walker's pilot realized what had happened, the two Ewoks leaped down into the cockpit and clubbed him. Shoving the pilot's body into the cramped compartment behind the seats, the Ewoks reached for the steering controls.

Chewbacca was nearly thrown from the walker's roof as the vehicle lurched forward, but he bent down and quickly eased himself through the hatch. The Ewoks made room for him as he settled into the pilot's seat.

Through the viewports, Chewbacca saw another walker nearby; it was firing at a group of fleeing Ewoks. Chewbacca and his companions decided to put a stop to it.

The Wookiee guided his walker through the woods, then fired the blaster cannons at the other walker. The enemy walker's command cabin exploded, spraying metal in all directions. When the Ewoks on the ground looked back at the vehicle, all that remained was its two legs and a shattered drive engine. The Ewoks cheered.

Without breaking his walker's stride, Chewbacca aimed his cannons at the Imperial ground troops and fired. Laserbolts tore through the forest, and the stormtroopers ran to escape the barrage.

The explosions drew the attention of the remaining two scout troopers. As they flew in tandem formation past the trees on their speeder bikes, an Ewok tossed a looped vine into the path of the scout at the rear. The other end of the long, heavy vine had been anchored to the base of a tree; when the thrown loop lassoed the bike's steering vanes, the snagged bike began whipping around the tree at high speed. The bike carried its rider on a rapid clockwise trip until the vine was completely wrapped around the tree's trunk and the bike crashed and exploded.

The last scout trooper was also done in by a well-placed vine, which the Ewoks had stretched a short distance above the ground between two trees. Striking the vine, the scout was knocked from his saddle while his bike hurtled forward and collided with another tree.

The Ewoks continued to fight with cunning innovation, using the forest's natural resources against the Imperial invaders. When they saw two Imperial walkers moving swiftly through the woods, they simultaneously released two vine-suspended logs from the treetops; the massive logs swung like twin hammers, smashing into both sides of the first walker's command cabin. As the second walker moved past the bottom of a hill, Ewoks stationed at the top of the hill unleashed stacked timber; the walker was unable to maintain its balance against the avalanche of rolling logs. Both walkers exploded.

With most of their walkers destroyed, the Imperial ground troops were fast becoming overwhelmed by their adversaries. No matter where they ran, the Ewoks were waiting for them with stones and arrows.

Back at the bunker, R2-D2 was still out of commission and C-3PO cringed in the doorway. Leia continued to fire at stormtroopers, keeping them at bay while Han worked on hot-wiring the door.

Han said, "I think I got it. I got it!" The wires sparked and a connection was made, but instead of opening the access to the bunker, a second blast door slid into place in front of the first.

As Han frowned and turned back to the wires again, Leia exchanged shots with stormtroopers in the bushes. Suddenly, a laserbolt struck her left shoulder. Leia cried out in pain and fell against the doorway.

Han didn't even try to find Leia's shooter. Trying to protect her, he grabbed her and eased her down so she was sitting with her back against the base of the door's control panel. C-3PO stepped near them and said, "Oh, Princess Leia, are you all right?"

Han crouched to face Leia and checked her wounded arm. He said, "Let's see."

"It's not bad," Leia said, slightly breathless.

"Freeze!" said one of two stormtroopers, who'd appeared suddenly behind Han. Both troopers had their blaster rifles aimed at Han's back. Han didn't move, and kept his eyes on Leia.

"Oh, dear," C-3PO said.

"Don't move!" commanded the stormtrooper.

Han didn't budge. Leia shifted only slightly, just enough so Han could see that her right hand still grasped her blaster pistol. Han realized his own body blocked the stormtroopers' view of Leia's blaster. Then he returned his gaze to Leia. Speaking just loud enough so only she could hear, he said, "I love you."

"I know," she replied.

"Hands up!" said one of the stormtroopers. "Stand up!"

Han raised his hands and stood up slowly, then turned. Leia's blaster spat twice, and each shot pierced the stormtroopers' armor-plated chests. They collapsed beside the bunker.

As Han turned toward Leia, he saw an AT-ST

walker approaching. The walker came to a stop with its cannons aimed at Han. Han raised his hands and said to Leia, "Stay back."

Han bravely faced the walker, and was astonished when the hatch opened at the vehicle's roof and Chewbacca stuck his head out. The Wookiee barked triumphantly to Han.

"Chewie!" Han said, lowering his hands and grinning from ear to ear. Then he gestured toward Leia and said, "Get down here! She's wounded!" But before Chewbacca could move, Han said, "No, wait . . ." Then he turned to Leia and said, "I got an idea."

CHAPTER **13**

On the Death Star, Luke and Darth Vader were engaged in a duel that was even more vicious than their battle on Cloud City. Luke had grown stronger since their last encounter, and his skill with his lightsaber had improved greatly. As they swung at each other in the Emperor's throne room, Luke sensed the advantage had shifted to him.

Luke drove Vader back to the stairway that descended to the turbolifts, then kicked out with his left leg, knocking Vader from the upper platform. Vader groaned as he flipped over backward and landed on the metal floor below.

From his throne, the Emperor watched the fight with glee. "Good," he said. "Use your aggressive feelings, boy! Let the hate flow through you."

Standing at the top of the stairway, Luke watched Vader rise on the lower platform. Vader said, "Obi-Wan has taught you well."

Luke deactivated his lightsaber.

"I will not fight you, father," he said.

Vader kept his lightsaber activated as he slowly ascended the stairs. His movement was slightly stiff and robotic, as if he were moving on damaged legs without feeling any pain. Luke wondered if Ben was right about Vader, that he was more machine than man. Then he thought, *No! Darth Vader may be a mechanical monster, but not my father. Not Anakin!*

When Vader was almost beside Luke, he said, "You are unwise to lower your defenses." He brought his lightsaber up fast, but Luke ignited his own lightsaber in time and blocked the attack. Vader swung again and again, and Luke parried each blow. Then their blades met and they maintained the contact, keeping their lightsabers braced against each other. Over the humming of the lightsabers, Luke heard Vader's labored breathing and realized, *He's getting tired.*

Vader broke the contact and swung hard at Luke, but Luke evaded the red blur of his opponent's weapon and jumped backward, landing in a duty post that was encircled by eight illuminated control consoles. As Vader brought his lightsaber up between two console pedestals, Luke deactivated his own lightsaber and leaped high toward the ceiling, executing a reverse flip that delivered him to a catwalk that stretched above the throne room. Landing on his feet, Luke looked down from the catwalk to see Vader, still standing beside the duty post, breathing hard.

Luke said, "Your thoughts betray you, father. I feel the good in you . . . the conflict."

"There is no conflict," Vader said.

Luke moved across the catwalk so he was positioned above the stairway. Gazing down at Vader, he said, "You couldn't bring yourself to kill me before, and I don't believe you'll destroy me now."

"You underestimate the power of the dark side," Vader answered from below. "If you will not fight, then you will meet your destiny." His right arm moved fast, and he hurled his still-activated lightsaber up at Luke.

Luke ducked the lightsaber, but its blade cut through the supports that held the catwalk. Luke felt the catwalk drop, and sparks showered around him as the metal supports tore from the ceiling and he tumbled to the floor below. Uninjured, he rolled under the Emperor's elevated platform and ducked into a dark alcove.

Vader's lightsaber had deactivated after it had sliced through the catwalk supports. As the Dark Lord of the Sith descended the stairs, he extended his hand and his lightsaber traveled through the air to return to his grip. Behind him, the Emperor rose from his seat, laughed, and said, "Good. Good."

Vader activated his lightsaber and went hunting for his son.

Outside, Lando Calrissian's plan was working: the Death Star had not fired at the Rebel fleet since the Rebels had brought the battle into the midst of the Star Destroyers. However, the Star Destroyers were openly firing at the Rebel cruisers and starfighters, and Lando knew the Alliance's fate now depended on whether his allies on Endor could knock out the Death Star's energy shield.

From the *Millennium Falcon*'s cockpit, Lando sighted TIE fighters angling toward a Rebel cruiser. He said into his comlink, "Watch out. Squad at point oh-six."

Gray Leader said, "I'm on it, Gold Leader."

Red Two swooped in to lend a hand, and the TIE fighters were decimated. From his X-wing, Wedge Antilles exclaimed, "Good shot, Red Two."

"Now . . . come on, Han, old buddy," Lando said to himself. "Don't let me down."

On Endor, in the same control room within the bunker where the Rebel strike team had been apprehended, the control room commander, his second commander, a security officer, and three seated controllers believed they were winning the battle. When a transmission from an AT-ST walker was received, all six men turned to see the image of the walker's pilot on the room's main viewscreen.

"It's over, Commander," the helmeted pilot announced. Holding his comlink over his mouth, he continued, "The Rebels have been routed. They're fleeing into the woods. We need reinforcements to continue the pursuit."

The officers and controllers looked away from the viewscreen to the control room commander. He could see from their excited expressions that his men were eager to go after the Rebels. They could see that he was looking forward to it, too. "Send three squads to help," said the commander. "Open the back door."

"Sir," said the second commander, and carried out the order.

They had no idea that the helmeted pilot on their viewscreen had been Han Solo.

The bunker door opened and the Imperial troops rushed out. They were surprised to find themselves suddenly surrounded by armed Rebels and Ewoks. Most of the Ewoks carried spears and bows and arrows, but some brandished blaster rifles they'd confiscated from fallen stormtroopers.

The Imperial soldiers turned to face the open door behind them. Han and Chewbacca stood at either side. Han grinned at the duped troops, then he and Chewbacca entered the bunker with several Rebel commandos. The commandos carried the explosive charges they'd retrieved from the stormtroopers.

Arriving in the control room, the Rebels quickly planted high-powered proton grenades onto the control panels and beside the turbine generator. Chewbacca growled, urging everyone to hurry.

Han turned to a Rebel commando and said, "Throw me another charge." Han caught the grenade, twisted its arming mechanism, and used the device's magnetic plate to secure it to the ceiling. When the last charge was in place, the Rebels left the control room and ran as fast as they could for the bunker's exit.

Darth Vader stalked the low-ceilinged area below the elevated platform in the Emperor's throne room. Holding his lightsaber ready, he searched for his son in the semi-darkness and said, "You cannot hide forever, Luke."

From the shadows, Luke answered, "I will not fight you."

"Give yourself to the dark side," Vader urged. "It is the only way you can save your friends."

Luke closed his eyes. *I'm sorry, Leia and Han. I'd do anything to save you, but I must resist the dark side.* Suddenly, Luke felt a dull ache in his head, and sensed that Vader was using the Force to probe his mind.

"Yes, your thoughts betray you," Vader spoke, confirming Luke's suspicion. "Your feelings for them are strong. Especially for . . ."

Luke tried to block his thoughts — and failed.

"*Sister!*" Vader said. "So . . . you have a twin sister. Your feelings have now betrayed her, too. Obi-Wan was wise to hide her from me. Now his failure is complete. If you will not turn to the dark side, then perhaps she will."

"*No!*" Luke screamed in anger as he ignited his lightsaber and rushed at Vader. Sparks flew as they traded blows in the cramped area, and Luke felt the hatred within him build with each passing second. *You'll never take Leia, and you'll never take me!*

He kept swinging, forcing Vader to retreat from under the platform until they arrived at the short bridge that overlooked the elevator shaft. Vader fell back against the bridge's railing, then was knocked to his knees. As he raised his lightsaber to block another onslaught, Luke slashed through Vader's right hand, severing it at the wrist. Metal and electronic parts flew from Vader's shattered stump, and his lightsaber clattered uselessly away, rolling over the edge of the bridge and into the apparently bottomless shaft below.

Luke angled his lightsaber at Vader's throat, then held the blade there, watching Vader's struggling form.

On the stairway behind Luke, the Emperor was unable to contain himself. "Good! Your hate has made you powerful. Now, fulfill your destiny and take your father's place at *my* side!"

Luke knew what the Emperor expected. *He wants me to kill Vader. He wants me to kill my own father.* Luke looked at his father's mechanical hand, then to his own black-gloved right hand. *Am I becoming like my father? Is that my destiny after all?*

Then Luke made the decision for which he had spent a lifetime preparing. He deactivated his lightsaber, turned to the Emperor, and said "Never!" Luke flung his lightsaber aside and stood there unarmed.

The Emperor scowled.

"I'll never turn to the dark side," Luke vowed. "You've failed, Your Highness. I am a Jedi, like my father before me."

With immeasurable displeasure, the Emperor said, "So be it . . . *Jedi.*"

Han Solo ran out of the Imperial bunker shouting, "Move! Move! Move!" Chewbacca and the other Rebels ran away and dived for cover. A moment later, the bunker exploded, followed by the turbine generator and the reactor core. The generator tower was suddenly consumed by a series of explosions, and the enormous dish-shaped shield projector array came crashing down to the ground.

The destruction of the moon-based Imperial outpost was immediately acknowledged by the space cruiser *New Home*'s Mon Calmari crew. Admiral Ackbar announced, "The shield is down! Commence attack on the Death Star's main reactor."

From the *Millennium Falcon*, Lando Calrissian responded, "We're on our way. Red Group, Gold Group, all fighters follow me." Lando looked to Nien Nunb and laughed. "Told you they'd do it!" Nunb laughed, too.

Wedge Antilles' X-wing, two A-wings, another X-wing, and a single Y-wing starfighter swung away from the Rebel fleet. The starfighters followed the *Falcon*, which flew straight and fast for the unfinished superstructure of the Death Star.

In the Emperor's throne room, Darth Vader remained lying against the railing on the bridge above the elevator shaft. Vader had known Emperor Palpatine long enough to know what would happen next. He watched the Emperor descend to the bottom of the stairs and face Luke.

The Emperor said, "If you will not be turned, you will be *destroyed*." Then he raised his arms and extended his gnarled fingers toward Luke. Blinding bolts of blue lightning shot from the Emperor's hands, and Luke was suddenly enveloped by crackling bands of energy. He tried to deflect the lightning but was so overwhelmed that his knees buckled. He collapsed onto some canisters near the bridge's railing.

As the Emperor continued to strike Luke with energized bolts, Vader struggled to his feet. Badly wounded, he moved slowly to stand beside his Master.

Sneering at Luke, the Emperor said, "Young *fool* . . . only now, at the end, do you understand."

More blue lightning coursed over and through Luke. He fought to remain conscious and clutched at a canister to keep from falling into the adjacent shaft.

"Your feeble skills are no match for the power of the dark side," the Emperor leered. "You have paid the price of your lack of vision." He released another bombardment of power at Luke, who writhed on the floor in unbearable pain.

Using the last of his strength, Luke lifted his arm, and reached out toward Vader. "Father, please," Luke groaned. "Help me."

Vader could see that Luke was on the verge of death. He looked to the Emperor, then back to Luke, who had curled into a fetal position on the floor.

"Now, young Skywalker . . ." the Emperor snarled, "you will die."

Luke had not imagined pain beyond what he had already suffered, but then he was hit by a wave of power that was even more staggering. His harsh screams echoed across the throne room.

Beside the Emperor, Darth Vader continued to stand and watch. He looked to the Emperor again, then back to Luke.

And then, in a moment, something changed. Perhaps he remembered something heard in his youth a long time ago: an ancient prophecy of the Chosen One who would bring balance to the Force. Perhaps the vague outlines of someone named Shmi and a Jedi named Qui-Gon struggled to the surface of his consciousness. The most powerful, the most repressed thought of all could have emerged from the darkness:

Padmé . . . and her undying love for someone he once knew well. And despite all the terrible, unspeakable things he'd done in his life, he suddenly realized he could not stand by and allow the Emperor to kill their son. And in that moment, he was no longer Darth Vader.

He was Anakin Skywalker.

He grabbed the Emperor from behind. The impossibly wretched Sith Lord gaped and squirmed in his embrace, continuing to release blue lightning, but the bolts veered away from Luke and arced back to strike the Sith Lords.

Dazed, Luke looked up to see the lightning travel through Vader and the Emperor. A burst of high-energy photons made Vader's own damaged skull briefly visible through his armored helmet. Somehow, despite his severed hand, Vader had managed to lift the Emperor high over his head. With one final burst of his once-venerated strength, Darth Vader hurled the Emperor into the elevator shaft, then collapsed at the shaft's edge.

Emperor Palpatine screamed as his body plunged down the seemingly bottomless shaft. When he was almost beyond sight, his body exploded, releasing dark energy and creating a rush of air up through the throne room.

From where he lay, Luke could tell by the rasping rattle from Vader's helmet that his breathing apparatus was broken. Luke crawled the short distance to his father's side and pulled him away from the edge of the abyss.

The *Millennium Falcon* and the Rebel starfighters flew low over the Death Star's surface. From his X-wing's cockpit, Wedge sighted the wide exhaust port that would be their entry point through the space station's superstructure to reach the reactor core. Wedge said, "I'm going in."

Wedge's X-wing dived into the exhaust port, followed by one of the two A-wings.

Lando said, "Here goes nothing," and guided the *Falcon* into the exhaust port with the other Rebel fighters right behind him. But then three standard TIE fighters zoomed in after the Rebels — and they were quickly followed by a trio of dagger-winged TIE interceptors.

At its present stage of construction, the Death Star's superstructure resembled a series of interconnected mazelike tunnels. Wedge maintained his lead position, flying past crisscrossing girders and lift tubes at an alarming speed. Despite the fact that the *Falcon* was bulkier than the single-pilot fighters, Lando was experienced with handling the old freighter through tight areas, and followed Wedge and the A-wing pilot without difficulty.

When Wedge wrapped around a tight corner to

enter a different tunnel, all the Rebel ships made the turn. The six TIE fighters followed, but one Imperial pilot lost control and collided with a large metal pipe that ran the length of the tunnel; his fighter exploded, but the others increased speed to pursue the Rebel ships.

Lando adjusted a switch on his console, then said into his comlink, "Now lock on to the strongest power source. It should be the power generator."

"Form up," Wedge told the other fighters. "And stay alert. We could run out of space real fast."

Indeed, the tunnel appeared to be narrowing. As they continued to race for the reactor core, laserfire tore past them from behind. The X-wing at the rear of the group was hit and exploded in the tunnel.

Lando looked past the X-wing and A-wing in front of him and saw that the tunnel forked in two directions. Hoping to shake their Imperial pursuers, he said, "Split up and head back to the surface. And see if you can get a few of those TIE fighters to follow you."

"Copy, Gold Leader," answered an A-wing pilot.

At the tunnel juncture, Wedge went left and Lando followed him. The other Rebel starfighters veered to the right. Lando checked his scopes and saw there were now only two TIE interceptors behind him.

Wedge saw their route was becoming even more difficult to navigate, and he threw his X-wing into a short dive to avoid striking a low girder. Behind him, Lando attempted the same maneuver, but the *Falcon*'s oversized sensor dish smashed against the girder and broke free from the hull. Wincing at the sound of shredding metal, Lando said, "That was too close."

Nien Nunb agreed.

Beyond the Death Star, the battle between the Rebel and Imperial fleets raged on. When one Rebel commander suggested they retreat, Admiral Ackbar answered, "We've got to give those fighters more time. Concentrate all fire on that Super Star Destroyer."

Following Ackbar's order, the Rebel cruisers and remaining starfighters targeted the *Executor* and began firing. The Super Star Destroyer rapidly became battered by explosions. On the *Executor*'s bridge, Admiral Piett was standing beside an Imperial commander in front of the viewport, and they saw the damage being inflicted on their ship.

Piett was about to issue a command when a controller from the lower-level crew pit said, "Sir, we've lost our bridge deflector shield."

"Intensify the forward batteries," Piett ordered. "I don't want anything to get through." Returning his gaze to the viewport, Piett saw another explosion. Losing his composure, he shouted, "Intensify forward firepower!"

"Too late!" yelled the commander beside him, who saw an out-of-control A-wing spinning straight for the bridge.

The A-wing smashed into the *Executor*'s bridge and exploded, causing the entire ship to veer off course. Damage-control crews were unable to seize command using the auxiliary control centers, and the *Executor* was dragged into the Death Star's gravitational field. The other Star Destroyer crews watched in horror as the *Executor* plunged like an enormous knife into the Death Star and exploded.

For the first time since the battle had begun, the Death Star was rocked by explosions. Inside, Imperial troops ran in all directions, confused and desperate to escape. As one group ran past a hangar, they noticed a strange figure: a blonde young man dressed in black, who struggled to haul Darth Vader's body to the same *Lambda* shuttle that had transported them from Endor's forest moon. Not surprisingly, none of the Imperial soldiers offered to help Luke Skywalker.

Luke stumbled, too weak to support his father's heavy body any further. *Don't worry, father. I won't leave you here!* Trying not to cause more damage to his father's right arm, he dragged him across the hangar deck to the shuttle's landing ramp. He was only at the base of the ramp when he collapsed from the effort.

Vader lay prone against the ramp. From the corridor outside the hangar came the sound of more explosions. Breathing hard, Luke looked up to his father's masked visage.

"Luke," Vader gasped, "help me take this mask off."

Luke didn't have to look at the life systems computer on Vader's chestplate to know what his father was suggesting. Luke said, "But you'll die."

"Nothing can stop that now. Just for once . . . let me look on you . . . with my own eyes."

Slowly, hesitantly, Luke lifted the helmet, leaving the faceplate still secured over his father's face. Setting the helmet aside, he reached to the faceplate and carefully removed it from the black durasteel shell that wrapped around his neck. And then he saw his father's face for the first time.

His flesh was ghastly, deathly pale and brutally scarred. There were dark circles under his eyes, and from what Luke could see, it appeared his skull had been hideously damaged. Luke tried to conceal his initial shock, then found himself staring into his father's eyes. They were blue, like his own.

Anakin smiled weakly and said, "Now . . . go, my son. Leave me."

"No," Luke said, placing his hand on his father's shoulder. "You're coming with me. I'll not leave you here. I've got to save you."

Anakin smiled again. "You already have, Luke. You were right." Choking, he gasped, "You were right about me. Tell your sister . . . you were right."

Anakin slumped back against the ramp. Luke leaned over him and said, "Father . . . I won't leave you." Then Luke noticed that his father's breathing apparatus was no longer making any noise.

Anakin Skywalker was dead.

Wedge's X-wing and the *Millennium Falcon* flew out of the tunnel and entered the Death Star's reactor core. The Rebel pilots were immediately followed by the two TIE interceptors that had pursued them since they'd split off from the other starfighters.

The reactor core was an enormous circular chamber. At its center was the main reactor, a massive power transference assembly with a ceiling-mounted generator.

"There it is!" Wedge said.

"All right, Wedge," said Lando. "Go for the power regulator on the north tower."

"Copy, Gold Leader," Wedge replied. "I'm already on my way out."

Wedge angled toward the ceiling and fired proton torpedoes at the upper area of the power regulator, causing a series of small explosions. As Wedge looped around and away from the main reactor, Lando fired the *Falcon's* missiles.

The missiles scored direct hits on the main reactor. Lando winced at the brilliant light of the blast, but never lost control as he followed Wedge's escape route. Behind him, one of the two TIE interceptors was struck by the explosive release of energy and was vaporized. As the remaining TIE interceptor accelerated in pursuit of the *Falcon*, the reactor's upper assembly began to crash down from the ceiling. Just as the *Falcon* sped back into the tunnel, the entire reactor core was filled with superheated gases that rushed after the starships and into the tunnel.

Lando followed Wedge's lead through the tunnel, retracing their path through the Death Star's superstructure at an even greater speed as they tried to outrun the explosion. Behind him, the TIE interceptor also increased speed.

Admiral Ackbar and his Mon Calamari officers saw the explosions that were tearing across the Imperial space station. Ackbar said, "Move the fleet away from the Death Star."

Fire and smoke filled the Death Star hangar, and a crashing gantry nearly smashed the front of the shuttle as it lifted from the deck. Seated behind its controls, Luke deftly turned the ship so it faced out, then hit the thrusters. He'd barely cleared the hangar doorway when the entire docking bay exploded behind him. Luke breathed a sigh of relief when he realized he'd made it.

A moment later, Wedge's X-wing hurtled out of the exhaust port and headed straight for the forest moon. He saw that the Rebel fleet had already moved to a safe position, distancing itself from the impending blast.

Behind the *Falcon*, the wave of intense heat caught up with the TIE interceptor and the ship was transformed into a fireball. This encouraged Lando to fly even faster. Through the cockpit window, he saw the star-filled hole at the end of the tunnel just as the space around the *Falcon* caught fire. A mass of jet flame geysered from the exhaust port, then the *Falcon* blasted through it and away from the Death Star. Lando let out a loud victory cry as he punched the thrusters.

The Death Star exploded. The blast was so brilliant and enormous that it could be seen from the forest moon's daylit hemisphere. There, the Ewoks and the Rebel ground troops cheered at the sight.

"They did it!" C-3PO cried with excitement. He was standing on a grassy hill with R2-D2, Chewbacca, and a group of Ewoks, and none of them could have been happier.

Nearby, Han was bandaging Leia's wounded arm. They looked up at the explosion's smoky remnants across the clear blue sky. His expression betraying his concern, Han turned to Leia and said, "I'm sure Luke wasn't on that thing when it blew."

Leia looked away from the explosion and smiled. "He wasn't. I can feel it."

Hesitantly, Han said, "You love him, don't you?"

Leia was puzzled by Han's question, but answered, "Yes."

"All right," Han said, putting on a brave face. "I understand. Fine. When he comes back, I won't get in the way."

Leia realized Han's misunderstanding and said, "Oh. No, it's not like that at all." She leaned closer to Han and said, "He's my *brother*."

Han was stunned by this news. Leia smiled, and they embraced.

EPILOGUE

Darkness had fallen on the forest moon when Luke carried a flaming torch to the logs he'd stacked in a clearing. He set the torch to the logs and they began to burn. On top of the pyre lay his father's armor; the image of Vader would burn away.

Standing alone, Luke watched the fire and felt the heat of its blaze. Although he had accomplished much that day, he couldn't help but feel a tremendous sense of loss. Not for Darth Vader, but for Anakin Skywalker, the father he'd barely known.

The flames rose high into the night. Fireworks exploded overhead, and then starfighters streaked across the sky. Luke realized his allies were celebrating.

And not just on Endor's moon, for news of the Rebel victory had spread quickly across the galaxy. Later, Luke would learn there had been fireworks over Cloud City, parades on Tatooine, and joyous public rallies on Naboo and Coruscant.

When the pyre had burned out, Luke went to find his friends.

High above the forest floor, a huge bonfire was the centerpiece of a wild celebration in the Ewok village square. All of the Rebels — even the droids — wound up dancing with the Ewoks, some of whom were enjoying the unusual percussive qualities of confiscated Imperial-issue helmets. Others hammered at the helmets just for fun.

Leia changed back into the clothes the Ewoks had made for her. Lando arrived and was enthusiastically greeted by Han and Chewbacca. Then Luke arrived and his friends rushed to greet and embrace him. Wedge and Nien Nunb were also warmly greeted by all.

Despite the happy reunion, Luke still felt distracted, his thoughts elsewhere. Stepping away from the others, he gazed out into the night and wondered, *Could I have done anything differently, or sooner, to have helped my father? I guess I'll never know.*

And then he saw them: two shimmering apparitions that appeared before him in the darkness. Yoda and Ben Kenobi. Then a third apparition materialized beside them — a figure whom he instinctively knew was a younger Anakin Skywalker, from the days before his Jedi father's fall, his features unscarred and . . . happy. Luke was right: He was a Jedi like his father before him. The apparitions smiled at Luke, silently telling him that the Force would be with him always.

Leia came to Luke's side and took his hand, then led him back to the others.

The celebration went on long into the night.